INSEPARABLE

SIOBHAN DAVIS

Printed by Createspace, An Amazon.com Company
Paperback edition © December 2017

ISBN-13: 978-1981192267
ISBN-10: 1981192263
Editor: Kelly Hartigan (XterraWeb) editing.xterraweb.com
Cover design by Robin Harper www.wickedbydesigncovers.com
Cover image © Ott Klmn Otto Kalman kostudio www.123rf.com
Formatting by The Deliberate Page www.deliberatepage.com

NOTE FROM THE AUTHOR

This book delves into some heavy subject matter which may cause triggers for some readers. I cannot be specific, because it would ruin the story, however, if you are concerned about a particular trigger you can query it via email to siobhan@siobhandavis.com.

PROLOGUE

Present Day – Angelina

Life is just a flow of interconnecting moments in time. A combination of well-thought-out actions and spontaneous reactions. A sequence of events and people moving in and out of your personal stratosphere.

At least, that's how I've always viewed it.

Like a squiggly line veering up and down with no apparent pattern. Plotting the highs; pinpointing the lows. Showcasing the happy times. Highlighting the mistakes and the resulting consequences. Calling into focus all the myriad of things I should've done differently if I had known.

When I was a kid, I was obsessed with the notion of time—making a beeline for the fortune teller every year when the carnival descended on the wide, open grassy field just outside town. I saved my pocket money all year round so I could have my fortune told. The idea that you could see into the future, to know what was around the corner, held an enormous fascination for me.

I wanted to make something of my life.

To dedicate myself to a profession that helped others.

To know happiness awaited me.

To receive confirmation that the two most important people in my life would always be in it. Because even the thought I could lose Ayden or Devin always sent horrific tremors of fear rushing through me.

For as long as I can remember, it had always been the three of us. Best friends to the end. The awesome-threesome. Forever infinity. It was a friendship more akin to family. A meeting of minds and hearts and promises. A connection so deep that we swore nothing or no one would ever come between us. We committed ourselves in a secret bond when we were twelve, and the commitment was imprinted on my heart in the same way it was inked on my skin.

I could never have predicted what was to come.

That I'd be the one to destroy everything.

No fortune teller *ever* told me that.

For years, I've thought of nothing but the what-ifs and obsessed over so many questions.

What if a fortune teller had told me what would come to pass?

Would things have been different?

What would I change?

Would I have had the strength to stay away from my two best friends? To forge a completely different path in life? To deny something that was intrinsically a part of myself? Could I slice my heart apart knowing it was the right thing to do?

For years these questions have plagued me.

But I'm too afraid to confront the truth, even though it's front and center. Even though I carry it with me like a thundercloud, hovering and threatening but never opening up, never letting the storm loose.

Some truths are far too painful to acknowledge out loud.

As if to speak the words would confirm what I already know about myself.

That I'm weak, selfish, and not at all the person I thought I was.

Perhaps that's why we don't have that cognitive ability—to see the future, to know what lies ahead. I've thought of it often. If it's evolution. If at some time in the future humans will be able to sense the path of their destiny. To alter their fate. To assume full control over every aspect of their life with conscious decision.

For now, all I've got is that squiggly line and a huge helping of regret.

What good comes from continually looking back? From locking myself in the haunted mansion of my past? Meandering with the ghosts of guilt and shame? For a girl who spent her happy youth so focused on the future, it's a very sorry state of affairs. But I'm stuck in this washing machine that is my so-called life. The faster it churns, the more I lose myself. So, I try to stop time. To stand still. To numb myself to my reality. To blank out feeling and emotion. To close myself off. To never allow another human to imprint on my heart or to see into the black, murky depths of my soul.

The honest truth is, if I'd had a crystal ball—if I'd known what was going to happen—I still wouldn't have changed a thing.

Because I would've missed those high points. Those happy memories that are the only thing keeping me alive right now.

If that's what you can call my current existence.

And that makes me the most selfish, conceited liar on the planet.

PART I

Senior Year of High School

CHAPTER ONE

Angelina

Tap. Tap. Tap.

I emit a high-pitched shriek, almost jumping out of my skin. Blood rushes to my head as I spin around in my bedroom. Devin has his face pressed into the glass of the French doors, peering in. His nose is all smushed up, and he's wearing his trademark shit-eating grin. Dropping my book bag on the floor beside my bed, I walk over, flinging the doors open with gusto. "Dev, what the hell? Are you trying to give me a coronary?"

He saunters into my room, flopping down on the bed like he owns it, his customary grin still planted firmly on his lips. "Hey, baby doll. Come sit." He pats the bed, stretching out his long, sculptured torso before propping up on his side.

I perch on the edge of the mattress, slapping his leg. "Don't call me that. I'm not one of your conquests."

"I was thinking more along the lines of a faithful pet." He smirks, attempting to smother his laughter as he watches the scowl appear on my face.

"Don't push your luck, asshole."

"Ange." He pats the bed alongside him again. "Come here." He looks at me through hooded lashes, and his green eyes smolder in that intense way of his. Strands of his black hair fall over his forehead as his gaze bores a hole deep inside me.

Devin defines drop-dead gorgeous. With his sinful good looks, ripped body, and dark brooding intensity, it's no wonder every girl in town hangs off his every word.

Lost under the magnetism of his penetrating focus, I forget how to breathe. "Come. Here," he mouths this time, failing to hide his knowing smirk.

Yeah. Dev's well aware of the effect he has on the female population, myself included.

I sigh but give up fighting the inevitable. Toeing off my shoes, I crawl up the bed, dropping down beside him. He reaches out, twirling strands of my long, dark hair around his finger. His eyes hold mine as his fingers weave in and out of my hair, and I zone out, like I've been drugged. Clamping my lips shut, I stifle the blissful moan building at the back of my throat. His hands feel *so good* in my hair. My blood pressure soars, butterflies go crazy in the pit of my stomach, and a familiar ache throbs between my legs.

I shouldn't have these feelings for Devin, but I've been harboring them for years, and I'm sure I'm going to spontaneously combust one of these days. Pent-up frustration and potent longing are my constant companions. An incessant reminder of all that is denied to me.

He's oblivious, of course.

I'm in an exclusive ten percent club—that minuscule pool of girls in senior class who have yet to sample the Devin experience.

Although I know all about it.

The girls at school can't keep their legs or their mouths shut.

I've heard all the stories these last couple of years, and I wish I could wash my ears out and scrub my brain free of the heartbreaking knowledge. Devin is gaining quite the rep around town. And not just for his man-whore ways.

"What are you doing home on a Saturday night anyway?" I ask, while he continues threading his fingers through my hair. I'm pleased that I manage to sound semi-coherent, and it's good to know he hasn't nuked all my brain cells.

Devin is hardly ever at home anymore. Especially not on a weekend night. There are copious parties to attend and numerous willing girls to fuck. Getting laid and drunk appears to take precedence over our friendship these days, and I've had to sit back and watch it happen with a heavy heart. Most times, I only see him at school, and then it's sporadic and fleeting. Occasionally, he'll drop into the diner where I work, but those visits are becoming few and far between. It's the been the same these past few months, ever since we started our final year, and it hurts. Way more than I've let on to anyone.

I miss my best friend, and I hate that a rift has formed in our seemingly unbreakable bond. Worse is I don't understand how this has happened or why.

My other best friend and neighbor, Ayden, has been more vocal and less concerned about rocking the boat. His impatience with Devin is growing by the day, and the cracks are splintering in our friendship. I never thought I'd see the day when we were anything but joined at the hip.

Things are changing, and I don't like it.

"I wanted to see you more than I wanted to go out," he admits, startling me with his honesty.

The romantic, nostalgic, girly-girl part of my brain is ready to throw a party, but the more logical, guarded side of my brain kicks in, cautioning me to chill the fuck out. I narrow my eyes as I scrutinize his face. "Are you high or drunk right now?"

He frowns, and his hand stalls in my hair. "Of course not."

I snort. "You say that like it's outside the realm of possibility you'd be either of those things."

He removes his hand from my hair, and I feel bereft. "We both know who I am, Ange, but I'm surprised you think I'd turn up here like that. Not with you. Never with you."

"Is that supposed to make me feel special?" I blurt.

"You *are* special, and you know it." He leans in, kissing the top of my head, and his chest brushes against mine, sending a flurry of fiery tingles whipping through me. Heat from his body washes over me, and I close my eyes, praying for self-control. The urge to touch him is almost overpowering. It's one of the reasons why I haven't pushed him as much as Ayden. If we were to start spending more time together, I don't know that I could contain my feelings. As it is, I don't know how much longer I can continue to hide them.

I've spent years crushing on Devin, and I'm close to my breaking point. A sharp, stabbing pain pierces me straight through the heart.

I shouldn't feel this way about one of my best friends, but I can't help it. I've been in love with him for so long, even if he doesn't have a clue.

He doesn't look at me like that.

Neither of my besties do, and that's the way it should be.

I'm the one stuck with faulty internal wiring. We have grown up as close as three kids can be. He should be like a brother to me. In a lot of ways, he is.

But, God, he's so much more.

"How'd you get on my balcony anyway?" I ask, the thought suddenly occurring to me.

He drops his head onto my pillow, chuckling. "How do you think?"

My mouth falls open, and I slap him across the chest. "Devin Robert Morgan, you did *not* climb the tree?!" He sends me a devilish wink, and I slap his chest again. "You idiot! You're not a kid anymore, and you're lucky you made it in one piece." Devin is well over six-foot tall and while he doesn't have Ayden's football player's body, he has a toned, muscular physique that has all the girls drooling.

Yours truly included.

"Chill. Old Man Willow can handle my awesomeness."

My bedroom is at the back of our house, and I have my own private balcony. An old oak tree holds court directly outside my room, its spindly branches like giant fingers stretching toward our house. When we were younger, the boys used to climb the tree in the dead of night and jump over onto my balcony. Mom never knew, and thus began a weekly tradition that spanned years.

Every Friday night, Devin and Ayden climbed that tree to my room. And every Friday night, we sat up until the early hours, whispering, laughing, and watching the stars. We went through a *Lord of the Rings* phase one year, and Devin likened the tree in my yard to the willow tree in Tolkien's legendary tale, and, henceforth it became known by the same name.

Our Friday night tradition ceased when the boys stretched up and out and became too big to climb it. It also coincided with the time of Devin's transformation—when he morphed into one of the town's most notorious bad boys.

"You know my mom works the night shift in the hospital almost every Saturday night. You could've just used the front door."

"And where's the fun in that?" he quips, smirking, and I roll my eyes.

"Wanna hang out on the balcony? For old time's sake?"

I examine his face, noting a vulnerability I haven't seen in a long time. My chest tightens in awareness. Something brought him here tonight. Something forced him to seek out my company.

Not that I'm in any way complaining. The last thing I'd ever do is deny him anything. Even if his actions unconsciously continue to hurt me.

"Sure. That'd be fun. I'll get some snacks. Can you grab a couple blankets from my closet?"

"You're the boss."

I arch a brow, and he chuckles. "Glad you know the lay of the land." I grin, before throwing caution to the wind. "We should call Ayden." I know he's visiting his grandma in the nursing home—he always goes with his mom the last Saturday of every month—but he'll be back soon.

"No." Devin's reply is swift and laced with determination.

"Don't tell me you two aren't speaking again?" It's a familiar pattern these last few months, since something went down between them during summer break, and I hate it. Hate all the tension and discord. All the fighting.

"That's not it. I just…" He trails off, looking down at his feet. "I just want to be alone with you." He lifts his head, and I'm surprised to see such raw, naked emotion glistening in his eyes. I feel his pain as acutely as if it's my own. It's like I've been punched in the gut. "I need you, Ange," he whispers.

I step toward him without thinking, planting my hand on his rock-hard chest. His heart beats steadily under my palm through the thin material of his shirt. "I'm always here for you. Always. You never have to doubt that."

He cups my face, peering deep into my eyes. "You're way too good to me. You should hate me."

My brow furrows. "Why on earth would I hate you?" Devin is trampling all over my heart, but he doesn't know that, and it's not like he's doing it on purpose. He can screw whomever he likes, and it's none of my business. Doesn't matter that every girl, every kiss and every caress I'm witness to, adds another scar to my heart. Outwardly, there is no reason why he should feel like this, so I don't understand what's going on in his head.

"Because this … this divide between us is all my fault."

I skim my hand up his arm, and he flinches slightly. Heat seeps from his skin through my fingertips, igniting my blood and fueling my desire. I gulp, trying to put a leash on my lust. "It's all our faults, and it's not too late to fix it." I peer into his eyes and start drowning. We stare at one another, and an electrical current charges the air. My chest heaves up and down, and his gaze flits to my mouth. His heart thuds more powerfully under my touch. Butterflies swarm my gut as I grapple with the situation. His eyes darken, and his pupils dilate as he continues to stare at my mouth. I don't know what's going on, but the tides are changing. Fate is swirling—I sense it, feel it, as if it's corporeal.

Is this just me or is he feeling something too?

He jerks back suddenly, and the connection is broken. Heat floods my cheeks, and I shake my head of all errant thoughts. Thinking such thoughts will only earn me a world of trouble, and I could do without that this year. "I'll get the snacks," I mumble, exiting the room as quickly as my feet will carry me.

CHAPTER TWO

Devin pops the can on his soda, tipping it into his mouth. I pull the blanket up under my chin in a feeble attempt to ward off the incoming nighttime chill. We are seated on adjoining bean bags out on the balcony, sharing a blanket. A bucket of popcorn and a bag of chips rest between us. Overhead, a smattering of tiny stars twinkles in the night time sky. There is something almost reverential about nightfall that has always drawn me in. No matter how shitty the day has been, I can sit out here on my balcony looking up at the stars and everything feels right with the world again. Perhaps that's why I'm such a demon in the mornings. It goes against my natural predisposition.

Getting to share this tonight with Devin is the icing on the cake. The only thing that could make it perfect is Ayden, but I'm not willing to go into battle a second time tonight on his behalf. A sorrowful pang hits me in the chest.

"Do you ever wish you could go back in time?" he asks without looking at me. "To return to when we were kids and we thought we were invincible?"

I tap a finger off my chin as I think about my reply. "Yes and no." He twists his head to face me, the unspoken question lingering at the back of his eyes. "You know I've always been more invested in the future," I start explaining, and he nods.

"Because you have a set goal. You've always known what you want to do. It's one of the things I admire about you." A light flush stains my cheeks, and he chuckles. "Still can't take a compliment, I see." I shove his shoulder, and he laughs. Then his expression turns serious. "I envy you on that, you know. Your purpose and your determination. Your ability to make plans."

"You can have that too, Dev. It's not too late."

The look in his eyes speaks volumes. He doesn't want to talk about this. It's the same old story every time college comes up in conversation. Ayden and I already have early acceptances to the University of Iowa, but Devin has no concrete plans in place yet. He's smart. Abnormally so for someone who regularly skips class, but he always hands in his assignments on time and his steady 4.0 GPA is impressive. He has plenty of options if he chose to exercise them. "I want you to attend UI with us. It won't be the same if you're not there."

He looks away, and I sigh. There's no point continuing this conversation—it'll only be one-sided, the way it always is when the subject of college and the future crops up. Silence engulfs us for a bit and then I clear my throat, returning to the original topic. "But sometimes I do wish I could go back." His head snaps around. "Everything was much simpler when we were kids." Hormones and confused feelings weren't a factor back then. Basic physiology didn't matter. Ayden and Devin were my best friends, and it didn't matter that they had penises and I had a vagina.

Nothing mattered except the connection we shared.

Then we grew up, and everything turned to shit.

"Damn straight," he concurs. "They were the best years of my life."

Damn it. Now he has me all melancholy, and I don't often go there. I watch his throat work overtime as he drains the rest of his drink in one go. "Thirsty?" I chuckle.

"Yep," he says, popping the P. He snatches a handful of chips and starts munching.

"Did you have dinner?" I ask, most likely already knowing the answer. He shakes his head, reaching for the bag again. I push to my feet. "I made lasagna and there's tons left. I'll heat you up some." I always cook extra for Devin and his younger brother Lucas. Ever since their mom took off the summer we turned eleven, parenting has been significantly lacking in the Morgan household. It's only gotten worse the last year since Cameron, Devin's older brother, joined the marines. He's been deployed overseas ever since and doesn't make it home that often. Devin has assumed more of a parental role with Lucas, but it's hard on him. Between school—when he makes it there—fight nights at the boxing club, and his part-time job at the local gas station, he's not home a lot, and family dinners aren't a staple in the Morgan house. Their father works long hours at a nearby factory, and he spends most nights drowning his sorrows in one of the local bars. Even when he's home, he keeps himself scarce. I can't remember the last time I was in Devin's house or the last time I saw his father. It's been that long. But Mom was insistent after Mrs. Morgan left and especially after social services paid a few visits. She forbade me from going over there, making it known Devin and his brothers were welcome in our house anytime, but I wasn't to step foot in his. As I've grown older and heard the rumors about his dad's womanizing, drinking, and fighting, her request makes complete sense. But, as a kid, I sulked a lot over that one rule.

The Morgan boys stayed over quite regularly those first few years after their mother left, but I never really thought much about it. Mom stepped in again after Cameron left, letting Devin and Lucas know they are always welcome to join us for dinner. If they don't stop over, I usually refrigerate the leftovers in case they turn up later.

Case in point.

He leans back, looking at me upside down. "You don't have to do that."

"Shush, asshole. You know the score, and you should've said something before."

"I don't want to be a burden." He spins around on the beanbag, pinning me with an earnest look.

"Since when?" I joke, trying to lighten the mood. Things are rather strange tonight.

"Since ever." His tone is sullen, his face impassive.

I crouch down in front of him. "What's wrong, Devin? I know something is up. You can talk to me. I won't judge."

His Adam's apple bobs in his throat. "Can't a guy hang with his best friend without the third degree?" he snaps, and I lurch back as if slapped. A bitter taste floods my mouth. "Shit!" He jumps up as I straighten my spine, quickly disguising the hurt from my face.

I'm a master at hiding my true feelings from Devin, so it's a cakewalk. Doesn't mean the rebuke hurts any less. I've seen others bear the brunt of Devin's temper in the past, but it's rarely ever me. The only time we've ever snapped at one another is in the middle of a heated argument.

"I'm sorry, Ange. That was uncalled for, and I didn't mean it." He gulps again, averting his eyes. His hands land on my shoulders. "What you think of me matters so much. More than you could ever realize."

"What does that mean exactly?"

He runs the tip of one finger across my cheek in a move that's decidedly tender. "Your skin is so smooth," he whispers.

My heart flutters wildly in my chest, and that same intense dark look shimmers in his eyes. He leans forward, and my heart starts somersaulting. Gently, he presses his forehead to mine, closing his eyes as he wraps his arms around me. He emits a musky, woodsy scent that is fresh and inviting, all male, and pure Devin. The warmth of his body heats every part of me, and I close my eyes, savoring every thrilling second.

Devin is usually very hands-off. The polar opposite of Ayden who is hugely touchy-feely, thanks to growing up in a very loving environment surrounded by three younger sisters. "It's why I do what I do. Why it has to be this way," he rasps.

"You know I don't have a clue what you're talking about."

"I'm counting on it."

"Weirdo." Throwing back his head, he laughs. "Seriously, Dev. You're acting even more weird than normal tonight."

He feigns hurt. "The lady doth wound me."

I hold onto his forearms as I peer up at him. "I'm worried about you."

"Don't." He presses a kiss to my forehead. "I don't want you worrying about me." He removes his hands from my waist, and I want to cry out in protest.

"Then stop all the drinking and fighting and screwing around." The words pop out of my mouth unbidden, but I'm not sorry I said it. Too often I've bitten my tongue around him, for fear of pushing him away, but I can't stand back and watch him push that self-destruct button anymore. "You're throwing your life away."

A muscle ticks in his jaw. "Don't go there. Not tonight. Please. I just can't hear it tonight."

I scan his face, and that earlier vulnerability is back. I don't know what's happened to turn him all melancholy and defenseless, but I'm not going to press him right now. For the first time in ages, it's like the old Devin is in the house, and I'm not going to push the issue and ruin things.

"Okay." I nod, giving him a gentle shove. He plops back down onto the beanbag. "Make yourself comfortable and I'll bring you up a plate."

I trudge down the stairs with a frown. Devin has always kept a part of himself hidden away. From an early age, both Ayden and I realized that, and we learned to accept it, but, now I wonder if we should've been more insistent when we were younger. Forced him to share, because whatever the hell his demons are, they are eating him alive.

I'm watching the microwave circle round and round while my thoughts wander. The click of the door wrenches me out of my head, and I whip around as Ayden strolls into the kitchen. "Perfect timing." He grins, leaning in to kiss my cheek. "Enough in that for two?"

"Didn't you eat either?" I shake my head as the microwave pings.

"I did, but what can I say? I'm a growing boy." He smirks, patting his flat stomach while leaning back against the counter. The movement causes his shirt to stretch across his impressive shoulders. Where Devin is lean with defined muscles in all the right places, Ayden is a chiseled rock-hard specimen of the perfect man. Years of football training have honed his body into a solid block of muscle. From broad shoulders to a tapered waist with an eight-pack and huge muscular thighs, there isn't an ounce of fat anywhere on his body.

How he manages to eat like a horse and still look like a modern-day blond, spikey-haired Greek God is beyond me. "Like what you see, Lina?" he teases, grabbing an apple from the bowl and sinking his teeth into the soft flesh. His blue eyes blaze with mirth.

"In your dreams, loser." I nudge him in the ribs. "And you'd better stay on my good side if you're looking to be fed."

He straightens up, saluting me. "Yes, ma'am."

I snort while carefully removing the hot plate from the microwave and placing it on the countertop. "Man, you *are* such a loser." I cut another piece of lasagna and place it in the microwave. "Heads up, De—" I'm interrupted before I can finish my sentence when Devin strolls into the kitchen, talking over me.

"Are you trying to …" He stops talking the instant he spots Ayden.

Ayden's playful persona is shelved, and he folds his arms sternly across his chest. "What are you doing here?" His tone is clipped.

"Same thing you are, no doubt." Devin returns Ayden's hostile glare.

"No chicks lined up tonight?" Ayden asks in a derogatory tone. Tension cuts through the air, and my shoulder muscles stiffen while I add salad to Devin's plate. I silently count to ten in my head. "Surprised you remember how to get here."

Devin sends Ayden a filthy look, and that same unspoken truth flits between them. "Funny," Devin drawls, fisting his hands at his sides. "Considering I live right next door. And I'd hardly forget where my favorite girl lives." He plonks himself onto a stool, continuing to shoot daggers in Ayd's direction as I slide the steaming plate in front of him.

"That's a fucking joke," Ayden retorts, cracking his knuckles. "You barely give her the time of day anymore unless you want something."

Devin's mouth twists into a snarl, and he looks ready to swing for him. "Really? Screw you, asshole. Saintly Ayden who barely looks sideways at any other girl. Want to tell us what that's all about?"

"I don't have to explain anything to you, jerkoff. Why are you even bothering? Have you finally run out of girls to bone and Lina's a last resort?"

Everything locks up inside me at the insult, and I'm glad I have my back to them so they can't see how devastated I am by Ayden's comment. The microwave pings and I reach for it as if on autopilot. My whole body is shaking internally and there's a lump the size of a bus wedged in my throat.

The stool screeches as Devin stands up. "Don't you fucking dare disrespect Ange like that," he yells. "Take that back or you and I are done. Completely."

Ayden rushes to my side, taking my hands in his. "Lina, I didn't mean any disrespect to you. You know how I feel about you. How important you are." I can't keep the hurt off my face this time, and he curses, squeezing my hands tighter. "This isn't about you at all. This is between me and him."

I shove his hands away. Anger is a low burn in my veins. "That is bullshit and you know it. You are both shutting me out again and I'm sick of it. We can't even be in the same room without you two bickering about stuff I know nothing about!" My gaze bounces between them. "Was it a conscious decision to keep me in the dark?"

Devin sits back down. "If you needed to know, we'd tell you, baby doll, I promise."

"Do not fucking call her that! She is not one of your whores," Ayden roars, and I just want this night to be over.

"Stop." I rub a tense spot between my brows. "Please, just stop it. For the first time in forever, we are all together on a Saturday night. I'm begging you to call a truce. Even if it's only for tonight. Let's forget all this crap and just hang out like we used to."

My plea falls on deaf ears—scrap that, make it arrogant, pigheaded, idiotic ears. The guys continue to face off, and this is easily the singular most awful moment of my life. My two best friends have been at odds for the last three months, and I can't bear it. I can't bear to lose our awesome-threesome. To see everything fall apart because they are too stubborn or too stupid to talk things out. I want to scream in frustration. Either that or bash their obstinate heads together.

Can't they see they are ruining everything?

Devin lowers his chin and starts wolfing his food. Ayden continues glowering at the back of his head, and I lose my cool. Yanking Ayden's lasagna from the microwave, I slap it onto a plate and shove it in his chest. "Okay, fine. Have it your way. You are both complete and utter assholes. Finish your food and get the hell out of my house."

Then I storm out of the kitchen without a backward glance.

CHAPTER THREE

"You didn't need to do it!" I hiss, kicking the bark in frustration as I haul ass up the tree. "I'm capable of punching Adam all by myself you know!"

Devin chuckles, swatting my butt as I pull myself up into the treehouse. "I know that, Ange, but you need to at least **pretend** you're a girl. You can't go around punching all the guys."

"Says who?" I demand petulantly, sitting down on one of the beanbags and crossing my legs. "And last time I checked I **am** a girl." I roll my eyes.

"We were doing you a favor," Ayden cuts in, sitting down beside me. He pulls the blanket out from behind him, draping it across my shoulders. "You'll get in trouble in school, and your mom would be pissed."

"You're both in trouble now, and I don't like that. I don't want you getting into trouble on my account."

"Suck it up, princess," Devin says, handing me a can of soda from our secret stash. I growl at him. He knows I hate it when he calls me that. "We're always going to protect you, so you might as well get used to it."

"And Adam can't put his hand up your skirt and expect us not to punch him," Ayden supplies, justifying their behavior.

My anger fades at their words. If there's one thing I've always counted on, it's my two best friends jumping to my defense. But I wonder if things will be the same when we're older. Things are already changing. Like the way I can't stop blushing when Devin stares at me in that intense way of his, and I'm not the only one who's noticed how cute he is. A lot of the girls at school are checking *out both my best friends, and I don't like it. They're mine, and no one else can have them.*

"You won't always be there to save me," I say in a quiet voice.

"Who says we won't?" Ayden asks. "We'll always be best friends."

"We should make a pact," Devin suggests, and my eyes light up.

"Yes! A blood pact, like in the movies!" I rub my hands in glee.

Devin's eyes gleam mischievously as he raises his hand to high-five me.

"No way, guys. No blood. We're not vampires." Ayden folds his arms sternly, and Devin and I burst out laughing.

"I'm not suggesting we drink each other's blood, Ayd." Shaking my head, I tear a page out of my school journal and start writing.

"Whatcha doing?" Dev asks, removing a pocket knife from his book bag.

"Writing out the pact," I say, sending them both a "duh" look. "We'll all sign it and seal it with our blood."

"Nuh-uh," Ayden says, shaking his head. "I'm not cutting myself."

"Pussy," Devin proclaims, smirking.

"Am not," Ayden protests.

"Are too," I say, holding out my finger to Devin. "I'm not afraid. Do it." He holds my wrist, and my skin tingles from his touch. We stare at one another, and for a split second, time seems to stand still. I feel a brief, sharp sting as he makes a small incision in the skin at the top of my finger, but I don't react. His eyes don't leave mine as he makes a cut in his own finger, and we smile at one another.

"Oh, all right," Ayden huffs, holding out his hand, trying not to grimace as Devin makes the cut.

We sign the piece of paper and press our bloody fingers to the page, repeating the words together.

The awesome-threesome will never die. Best friends for infinity. No matter what, we will always be there for each other.

∞ ∞ ∞

I turn over in the bed, feeling a multitude of congested emotions in the aftermath of my dream. It's quite prophetic that that memory should return to me now. I remember that day as clearly as if it was yesterday. I remember how happy I was that night, believing our bond would last for eternity. God, I was so naïve. I sigh, curling into a ball as knots twist and turn in my gut. I could continue to wallow in the past or get my head out of my ass and go do something. The latter wins out, and I yank the covers off and hop up with determination.

After I've showered, dressed, and eaten, I head out to my balcony with my book bag, aiming to go over my study notes again for the math test tomorrow.

The sun is high in the sky, and even though the air is warmer than last night, I've always been a cold creature, so I bring the blanket out with me. Sinking into the beanbag, I fix the plaid blanket around me, trying to ignore Devin's scent which seems to have embedded itself into every fiber of the material. I remove my book, pad, and pen and settle into studying.

An hour later, I toss my books aside with a sigh. It's no use. I can't focus my brain. My mind is still too preoccupied with the two boys in my life. I think about Devin's insinuation last night—the implication that Ayden is hiding romantic feelings for me. It's true he hasn't been with many girls, and he hasn't had a steady girlfriend since tenth grade, but I don't believe it's for the reasons Devin suggested. Ayden has his heart set on college football and then NFL. As our school's star quarterback, with an impressive record on the field, he has a good chance at making it.

Ayden and I are a lot alike in many ways.

From an early age, both of us have known what we wanted to do with our lives, and we are both stubbornly determined and focused on those goals. For as long as I can remember, Ayden has lived and breathed football. Although he doesn't talk about it to me much anymore, his dedication is clear for everyone to see. For years, he's spent every weekend practicing with his dad, going to all the local games, and attending all the Hawkeye games in Kinnick Stadium. His dad, Carl, had had a promising football career until it came to a devastating end when he broke his leg at nineteen. I know he's so proud of Ayden and rooting for his only son to have the sports career that was denied him.

My phone vibrates in my pocket and I fish it out, smiling as Mariah's face pops up on the screen. "Hey, chica."

"Hey, yourself. You want to meet at Mona's?" Mona's is the most popular diner in town. I work at The Good Eats Diner, across the road, which is popular with an older crowd.

"Sounds good. Meet you there in twenty?"

I leave a note on the counter for Mom, in case she wakes up early and wonders where I am. Then I grab my purse, keys, and my jean jacket and hightail it out of the house. My old VW Golf chugs to life, and I offer up thanks. If it wasn't for Devin and his mad mechanical skills, old Betsy would be in a metal grave right now. Dev has brought her back from the brink so many times. Mom offered to buy me a new car last month, but I turned her down. I don't want her spending her money, and I'm rather fond of my battered little car. Call me sentimental, but Ayden and Devin helped me choose it when I turned sixteen and got my driver's license, and letting it go feels like a betrayal of our friendship. Which is ridiculous, especially considering our relationship is all but in the toilet right now.

I park in front of the diner and jump out, waving at Mariah through the glass. She's nabbed our favorite spot in the middle of the diner beside the window. I love people-watching, and it offers the perfect position to observe without being obvious.

"I ordered your usual," Mariah says as I slide into the booth across from her.

"Cool. Thanks. So, how did last night go? I want all the details." Mariah went with her boyfriend, Cody, to one of the senior parties last night. I sometimes go with them, on nights when I'm not working, but I wasn't feeling it last night. I hadn't been in the mood to watch Devin slobbering all over the latest groupie. And if I'd known he wasn't going, I still would have stayed home in the hope that he'd come over.

I'm pathetically predictable.

"It was kind of boring until Devin showed up."

I shake my head, harrumphing. "Yeah, that figures." I should've known he'd go partying once I booted him out. As that old saying goes, a leopard doesn't change its spots.

She leans over the table with her mouth open to speak as Jennifer brings our coffee. "If it isn't my two favorite gals." Her wide smile is genuine.

"Hi, Jenn. Thanks." I smile at the kind, older waitress. She's worked at Mona's for as long as we've been coming here, and she was super generous with her time and her advice when I started waitressing myself.

"Any time, sweetie. Food won't be long." She affectionately ruffles the top of my head.

Mariah waits until Jennifer is out of earshot. "What don't I know?"

Mariah is the only one who knows about my crush on Devin. I don't have many female friends—growing up a tomboy and having two boys for best friends pretty much put paid to any lasting female friendships when I was a kid. Once I became a teen, things changed, and, suddenly I had a whole bunch of new girlfriends. Until I figured out most of them were using me to get to Ayden and Devin. I've been overly cautious since then. Apart from a couple of girls I'm friendly with in school, Mariah is my only real girlfriend. We've been close since we were fourteen, and I trust her with my life.

"Dev dropped by last night." I proceed to give her the lowdown on everything that happened.

Jennifer returns with our pancakes and bacon just as I've finished filling Mariah in.

"Well," Mariah says, carefully cutting up her bacon. "That explains a lot."

"What did he do?" I know he did something, or some*one*, more to the point. I add an extra layer of steel over my heart in preparation.

"He seemed sober when he arrived, but he lost no time getting absolutely wasted. Like, I've never seen the dude so out of it. He was falling all over the place and mouthing off to anyone who dared cross paths with him." She shakes her head, slowly chewing her food. "I hate to say it, Ange, because I know how much you care for him, but he's a train wreck waiting to happen."

I put my fork down. "I'm worried about him. He was acting weird last night. Something is going on with him, but, of course, he refuses to tell me anything. When we were kids, I was their equal, but now, both Ayden and Devin seem to think I need to be protected from stuff, and it irritates the crap out of me." I yank a piece of bacon with my teeth, chewing ferociously.

"That means they care."

"I know, but it's still annoying. They can care without keeping secrets." She pins me with a knowing look. "It's not the same," I protest. "My secret is secret for a reason." Her face is frustratingly neutral as she waits me out. "My secret would kill our friendship stone dead. The dynamics have already changed, and the admission that I"—I look around, making sure no one is in ear shot, and lower my voice—"am in love with Dev would be the final nail in the coffin."

"Maybe, or maybe not. Perhaps, if Devin knew how you felt about him, he would stop all the sleeping around and drinking. Maybe he would be a better person for you."

"He should want to be a better person for himself. You should never change for anyone else."

Mariah beams. "Spoken like a true wannabe psychologist."

I grin back at her. "Damn straight, girlfriend."

Her expression softens. "Becky was all over him again last night."

I grit my teeth, pushing my half-eaten plate away. "I don't have a violent streak, but she makes me wish I did. That girl pushes all my buttons."

"You and half the school." Mariah shoots me a sympathetic look. "He pushed her away again. Devin is a lot of things, but he's a loyal friend."

"I know, but it grates on my nerves that she keeps trying with him. And I know the reason she persists is to wind me up." For the last two years, Becky Carmichael has been a major pain in my butt. Besides my friendship with the guys, I don't know what I've done to earn her attention and her wrath. She goes out of her way to try to make my life miserable. Most of the time, I refuse to let her bitchiness get to me, but sometimes it's hard to rise above it. I thought once you stood up to bullies they eventually backed down. Not Becky; it seems to spur her on.

"She's a loser, and everyone knows it. You only have to put up with her for eight more months. How bad can it be?"

∞ ∞ ∞

Mom is in the kitchen, yawning over a steaming mug of coffee, when I return home. "You're up early," I remark, bounding into the room and kissing her enthusiastically on the cheek. She smells like vanilla and strawberries, and it's wonderfully comforting.

"By some miracle, the hospital was quiet last night, so I got to leave a few hours early."

"You still look tired. You should go back to bed." Dark shadows linger under her eyes, and she looks paler than usual. Mom has that delicate, porcelain-type skin. Perfectly flawless but it can leave her looking a little washed out at times.

"I want to spend some time with you. We see so little of one another these days." There's no word of a lie in that statement. Since ownership of the hospital changed six months ago, Mom works the night shifts now—three days on, two days off—so we are like passing ships in the night. She is usually sleeping during the day while I'm at school, and then I have study or work on the evenings she is off. It sucks, but as a single-parent family, it's a necessity. Thank God, she had the foresight to negotiate a college fund for me in the divorce settlement or she'd probably be working herself into an early grave.

"I'm up for that. What would you like to do?"

"I thought we could take the boat out on the lake? If we wrap up nice and warm, it won't be too cold."

"Sounds lovely, if you're sure you're up to it? I don't mind lazing about here if you're tired."

She smiles, mussing up my hair. "I'm never too tired for you, kiddo."

I wrap my arms around her. "I love you, Mom."

"I love you too, sweetheart. So, so much." Her lips press the top of my head, and I sigh contentedly.

Although I had periods, when I was younger, when I really missed having a dad in my life, I've long since gotten over that. Mainly because Mom is amazing, and we have a great relationship. It helped that she told me the truth when I was old enough to handle it. Now, I'm glad I don't know my father or his stuck-up wealthy family who have made no effort to keep in touch either. I have zero plans to ever set eyes on the rich financier or his family.

Ayden's dad, Carl, has been like a surrogate dad to me over the years. And Mom is the most awesome mother on the planet, so, between the two of them, I don't really feel like I've missed out on anything. Family comes in all shapes and sizes these days. Mine works, and I wouldn't change it for the world.

∞ ∞ ∞

An hour later, we are both freezing our asses off on Clear Lake. There are no other idiots out here today, so the water is placid, the surroundings eerily quiet except for the gentle hum of the boat's engine and the odd bird chirruping overhead. A twinge of grief hits me in the chest, like it does every time we take Grandpa's boat out. It's been three years since he passed, and I still miss him so much. Watching Mom grieve her last parent was tough to bear witness to. Because of her unsocial working hours, Mom doesn't have a lot of friends either. She had no one to lean on, and while she tried her best to shield it, she couldn't disguise the utter torment she was going through. I'll never forget how helpless I felt. And how much it strengthened my resolve in relation to my planned psychologist career. I want to be able to help people deal with their issues. To know I'm giving something back.

Mom looks sad, and I know her mind has gone there too. Little wisps of her blonde hair escape her hat, blowing across her unlined face, but she doesn't even notice. Time to drag both of us out of our despondent state. "What was it you said about it not being too cold?" I ask, my teeth chattering. "It's almost Baltic out here."

"It'll toughen you up," she retorts with a gleam in her eye.

"Or I'll get frostbite," I moan.

Mom laughs. "Always so dramatic."

"I'm a teenager. We're supposed to be dramatic." I playfully stick my tongue out at her.

"Speaking of drama, did something happen between you and Ayden?"

I pull my woolly hat down over my ears, frowning. "Why do you assume that?"

"Because he came over earlier, and he had a bunch of lilies for you."

We share a knowing smile. Turning up bearing lilies is Ayden's signature way of apologizing. I give Mom a censured version of what went down last night. While we are close, and I tell her most everything, there are some things I keep close to my chest.

Like my unrequited love for Devin.

And how Ayden sometimes sleeps in my bed.

I get freaked out in the house alone at night, so Ayden keeps me company on occasion. I know Mom would read more into that than there is. Plus, I don't want her feeling guilty. She *has* to work, and I'm almost eighteen years old—old enough not to get spooked by the thought of things going bump in the night.

"So, that's why Ayden's groveling," I finish explaining.

"Have you heard from Devin?"

I nod. "He sent me a text." A one-word text at five a.m. "Sorry."

She moors the boat to a nearby buoy and comes to sit down beside me. She wets her lips, opening and closing her mouth as if she's struggling to speak. I wait for her to compose herself. "I know how much those two boys have meant to you, honey. How much they still mean to you, but I think you need to consider the possibility that things might never be the same. People grow up. Move on in their lives. Friendships aren't always what they used to be."

"Not ours." My words resonate with confidence I only partly feel. I can't lie to myself. I am worried about what will become of us, but I'm afraid to verbalize it. Like it will make it real if I say the words out loud.

I trace a finger over the small infinity tattoo on the inside of my left wrist. Ayden and Devin have one too. It was Dev's idea—naturally—and he found a tattoo place that didn't give a rat's ass about age of consent. We snuck off one day, took the bus to Minneapolis, and got inked up. It's not the traditional infinity symbol. Dev designed his own and gave a sheet with the drawing to the tattoo artist to replicate. I smile as I trace the intricate, successive loops with the tip of my finger. Each line is delicate and fine, but they are all interwoven, and together they stand out. It symbolized us, Devin had explained. Interconnecting and stronger as a unit, just like our friendship. The memory replays in vivid Technicolor in my mind.

Ayden's lower lip is trembling, and Devin and I trade knowing looks. "Just hang in a little longer," I tell Ayd. "And think of how awesome it's going to look." My eyes move to the tattoo artist, bent over my wrist, inking my skin with focused precision. Ayden winces, and I wish I could reach over and hug him. Devin and I have barely flinched, but Ayden's tense and jumpy, and I know he's not enjoying the experience. He's only doing this because we coaxed him into it, like we have done so many times with so many things, and I love him for his devotion to our friendship, even if we constantly push him out of his comfort zone.

A massive lump builds at the base of my throat, and I'm struggling to swallow over it.

Mom looks down at my wrist and then peers into my damp eyes. Her arm goes around my back, and she pulls me into her side. A sob rips from the very innermost part of me. I should know better than to try to fool her. She can always see straight through to my soul.

The day we got the tattoos was one of the few times when I can honestly say Mom was really disappointed in me. Not that I got the tattoo, per se, but that I did it without speaking to her first. While I was quietly confident she would have let me make the decision myself, at fifteen, I was too afraid she'd say no. I didn't want to let my best friends down, and I wanted a permanent mark of our friendship. A reminder of what we meant to one another.

What I failed to understand then was there is no such thing as permanent. Everything can change in a heartbeat. The only thing that is guaranteed is in the moment. Perhaps that's why I'm always trying to confirm what's around the corner. Why I'm so fixated on the future and knowing what lies in store for me. Because I'm scared everything is transitory.

"I didn't mean to upset you, honey. But you need to prepare yourself. Life doesn't always work out the way you expect it to."

CHAPTER FOUR

Ayden is sitting on our porch as Mom parks her station wagon in the driveway. He is holding a bunch of lilies, and staring at me through the window of the car. "That boy is so in love with you," she says, and there's a wistful quality to her tone.

"No, he isn't," I protest, shaking my head. "You're my mom. You're supposed to think every boy's in love with me." I watch him watching me, looking for any signs that he's head over heels in love, and I just don't see it. He doesn't look at me the way I imagine I look at Devin when I'm mooning over him.

Her subtle laughter lingers in the air. "You are beautiful, inside and out. No boy is immune to your charms."

I roll my eyes, reaching for the door handle as I watch Ayden straighten up. "You're definitely sleep-deprived, or crazy, or maybe a bit of both." I shoot her a goofy grin. "Hardly any of the boys look my way in school, and I haven't been asked out on a date in almost six months. Trust me, boys are definitely immune to my charms."

The boy is, anyway. I don't think Devin's even noticed I've got a vagina and boobs. I'm firmly relegated to the friend zone.

"And you know why that is," Mom continues, refusing to let this go.

"Hmm. Let me think." I tap a finger off my chin as Ayden descends the steps toward the car. "Because Ayden and Devin scare them all off?" It's not like I haven't considered that before.

Mom chuckles again. "Well, there's definitely that, but I was going to say your beauty and your spirit frightens them. Boys are too afraid to approach you."

I bark out a laugh. "Oh my God, Mom! You are crazy! I always suspected it, but now I know for sure."

"What's so funny?" Ayden asks, opening my door. "Hi, Natalie." He smiles at my mom. For years both Ayden and Devin called Mom Mrs. Ward. It was only when I turned thirteen and she clued me in on the details of her wretched history with my abusive father that I realized how much it must've hurt to hear them calling her that day after day. That night, when the boys had climbed to my balcony, I asked them to call her Natalie and never to utter the words "Mrs. Ward" ever again. To this day, neither of them has forgotten.

"Trust me, you don't want to know," I murmur, fighting a blush. If she says anything to embarrass me in front of Ayden, I'll never live it down.

"Angelina seems to think the reason no boys ask her out on dates is because you and Devin are cockblocking, but I happen to believe it's because they are too intimidated by my daughter."

"Mom!" I shriek, my cheeks turning ten different shades of red. "Language!" I splutter, as if our roles are reversed. She throws back her head, laughing at my obvious embarrassment. I risk a glance at Ayden, and he's clearly fighting a laugh. "Don't you dare, and if you ever repeat this conversation I'll tell everyone it was you who flashed Mrs. Peterson when you were twelve." The suspicion had naturally fallen on Devin, because that was more his MO. No one would've believed Ayden capable of such a thing, but you should never underestimate the power of peer pressure. I snicker to myself.

Mom collapses in a fit of laughter, and I shake my head. *Is sleep deprivation a real illness? Like it reduces your brain cells to mush or something?* "I, just, there are no words, Mom. Seriously, you are killing me here. And how'd you even know that word. That's wrong. So wrong. I need to go inside and scrub out my ears."

She lightly punches my arm. "Hey, missy. I'm not that old, I'll have you know."

My gaze softens. "I know, Mom. How could I ever forget when you're frequently mistaken for my sister?" True fact. It's happened a bunch of times when we've been out. Mom had me when she was nineteen, and she barely looks a day over thirty. Even though I'm dark to her blonde, we have the same blue eyes, same heart-shaped face, and, although, I'm taller than her by a few inches, we have the same slender build with curves in all the right places. You could say I hit the gene pool lottery, not that I care much about that stuff. It drives Mariah crazy that I'm so blasé, and though I don't do any sports or physical exercise—my ballet classes don't count, according to her—and eat like a pig, I still manage to maintain the same weight. Good genes, like I said. Mom is petite and slim, and she has a healthy appetite too.

"I didn't realize I was interrupting comedy hour," Ayden says, teasing. "I can come back."

I climb out of the car, sliding underneath his impressive frame. "No way. I want my lilies."

"Who says these are for you?" There's a glint in his eye I haven't seen in a long while.

"Idiot." I elbow him in the ribs. "Who else are they for?"

Ayden rounds the front of the car, thrusting the flowers out in front of Mom. I can't stop the grin from spreading over my mouth. "Natalie. These are for you."

Mom maneuvers around him, laughing. "Nice try, Ayden, but I'm not getting in the middle of your lover's spat."

"Mom!" I shriek, throwing my hands into the air. "Enough already!"

She is still laughing as she skips up the steps and into the house.

"Sit with me?" Ayden asks, holding his arm out. I loop mine in his and let him lead me up onto the porch. We sit down on the bench, and he carefully lays the flowers atop the small wicker table.

I swing my legs back and forth, waiting for him to start.

"I'm really sorry, Lina."

I glance at him, and there's no doubting the sincerity in his expression. I sigh. "I know you are. I hate that you two aren't getting along. That I'm caught in the middle."

As if on cue, the rumbling sound of Devin's truck pricks my eardrums as it rounds the bend onto our street. Ayden tenses beside me. We watch in silence as Dev swings the truck into his driveway, kills the engine, and climbs out. He looks over at my house, immediately noticing us sitting on the porch. His face locks down, and he looks away. Shoving his hands in his pockets, he strides into his house, violently slamming the door behind him.

"Awesome." I rest my head back, closing my eyes.

"It's not your fault." The bench groans as Ayden swivels around to face me.

"It doesn't matter whose fault it is. I just want it fixed. I want to go back to the way things were."

Ayden brushes a few strands of loose hair back off my forehead, and my eyes fly open at the unexpected contact. "I don't know if that's ever going to be possible," he admits, and there's a tornado of sadness in his gaze.

I sit up a little straighter, twisting around. Our knees brush. "Why won't you tell me?"

"It's better you don't know."

"It's not fair," I huff, jutting out my lip. "What happened to our awe-some-threesome pact? And not keeping secrets?"

He takes my hands in his, looking down. "We were kids then, Lina. We're not anymore. You can't expect things to stay the same." He lifts his chin, and I can't bear the pitiful look on his face.

"I knew things would change, but I thought we'd always be friends." My heart aches. This all sounds so final. *Was I naïve to believe we'd be friends forever? Am I the only one who felt like that? Did either of them even mean it when they were promising we would always be in each other's lives?*

"Me too." His words go some way toward comforting me. Pulling me in to his chest, he wraps his burly arms around me. "I'll always be your friend, Lina. I'll always be here for you."

I place my hands on his shoulders as I peer into his eyes. "Promise?"

He presses his lips to my forehead. "I promise."

∞ ∞ ∞

"Night, Mom," I say, yawning as I wander into the living room in my sleep shorts and tank top.

She rises from the couch, enveloping me in her warm embrace. "Goodnight, sweetheart. I'll see you tomorrow evening. We'll have dinner together before I leave for the hospital."

"Great. I'll see you then." I kiss her on the cheek. "Love you."

"Love you too, sweetie." She kisses the top of my head, and I walk to the stairs, yawning again.

I'm tucked up in bed, reading, when a loud oomph sounds from outside. My heart starts hammering in my chest, and butterflies are running rampant in my gut as adrenaline courses through my body. "Ange," Devin whisper-yells. "Let me in."

I hop out of bed like there's a rocket up my ass, racing to the double doors and flinging them open with a dramatic flourish. Devin saunters into the room with that cocky swagger of his, sending me a saucy wink, and accelerating my blood pressure with that one casual look. He drops onto the edge of my bed. Rolling up the left side of his jeans, he rubs a raised red mark on his shin.

"What happened?" I sink to my knees in front of him.

"Whacked it off the tree as I was jumping over."

I roll my eyes. "Don't expect any sympathy from me. I told you not to do that."

He looks at me through hooded lashes, slowly perusing my body, his eyes lingering in that uber-intensive way of his, and it's as if he's stripped me bare. He continues staring at me, and I've lost the ability to breathe. I gulp, and he lowers his voice an octave as he speaks. "It's not your sympathy I'm after."

My cheeks flood with heat, and he chuckles. Flirtatious Devin is a beast I can't tame or one-up, so I don't even try. In desperate need of distraction, I scurry to my bedside table, rummaging through the drawer like I can't find what I need. Anything to deflect from my reddening cheeks. He says nothing, just watching me acting like a crazy person. When I'm confident my cheeks are less embarrassing, I snatch the tube of arnica cream up and turn to face him. "Here, this will stop it bruising."

His lips twitch, and I know he wants to tease me further, but, for whatever reason, he stays quiet while I massage the ointment into his skin. He tenses slightly at my touch, and I try not to feel hurt by that.

When I'm done, I screw the cap back on and toss it on top of my bedside table. Air flees his mouth in a loud gush as I flop down beside him. "Hey."

"Hey." He smiles, and it's like being trapped in a laser beam of hypnotic hotness. His sea-green eyes twinkle mischievously, and his long lashes appear even longer, blacker, and thicker. Strands of his inky-black hair brush the edge of his forehead, and I long to run my fingers through it. His strong jaw is peppered with stubble, and I imagine the feel of it against my fingertips. His gorgeous mouth is slightly parted, and I long to run my tongue across his lips.

His face is perfection. I could stare at him all day long and never grow tired of it.

"I'm sorry about last night, Ange."

I snap out of it, blinking the haze away. "I know. It's okay." I can never stay mad at either of them for long.

"No, it's not." He reaches out, taking hold of one of my hands. Little fiery shivers zip up and down my arm as he starts tracing small circles on my palm. My mouth is dry and butterflies are dancing a jig in my chest. "You're too easy on us, Ange. You forgive too quickly."

"You say that like it's a bad thing." My voice comes out breathless and I hope he doesn't notice.

"It's okay to get mad, you know. You can tell me you hate me, and it won't send me away."

What the hell? This again? I barely even notice when he laces his fingers through mine, too busy trying to work out what's going on in that confusing, beautiful head of his. "Devin, I couldn't hate you if I tried. And hate consumes too much energy. Hating *anyone* is a waste of time."

He lifts our conjoined hands, bringing it to his mouth. I almost fall off the bed when he brushes his lips across my fingers. Heat floods my cheeks and pools down low. "You have the purest heart, Ange. You're good, through and through. I don't know how you haven't kicked me to the curb by now."

"Stop it. Why are you saying this? Do you want me to hate you? Is that it?"

He pulls our linked hands to his chest, right over the spot where his heart beats—steady and sturdy, vibrating under the tips of my fingers. His response startles me. "Sometimes I do." Waves of hurt lash me, and instinctively I try to wrench my hand away, but he holds on to it, placing it flat over his heart. "But not for the reasons you think, and don't worry, I'm far too selfish to ever let you go." He scoots over beside me, until there is barely any space between us. All the air seems to get sucked out of the room. He continues to hold my hand over his chest, and, with his other hand, he cups my face. "I want you to know something, but I don't want you to react. I just want you to take these words and hold them close to your heart, because, if anything should happen to me, I would hate for you to not know this."

"Dev—"

He leans in and kisses me. It's quick, no more than a fleeting brush of his lips against mine, but, gosh, it's everything. My lips are on fire, and it's spreading, heating every single part of me. I don't know what it means. If it means anything at all. Devin doles out kisses as freely as God doles out forgiveness.

"Shush, Ange." He brushes his thumb over my lower lip, and I dread to think what emotions are showing on my face right now. "No reaction, remember." I can only nod, fighting another blush. "You're the most important person in my world. For all time. Even when you think you aren't, know that you are. Even when I can't show you or say all I want to say, know that you are. Even if I leave, I'm still with you, in here." He places his hand on top of my chest, where my heart is beating so erratically it threatens to escape my ribcage. "Like you're in here." He pats my hand, the one still being held protectively against his chest. "You'll always be in here," he whispers.

"Why are you saying this?" I whisper back, startled to find tears welling in my eyes. This feels too much like a goodbye. "Are you ... going somewhere?"

He stares deep into my eyes. "I don't know. Things are fucked up right now. I don't know what's going to happen."

He averts his eyes, and a lonely tear rolls down my face. "You're scaring me. If you're in trouble, I want to help."

He lifts his chin, and his eyes are filled with so much pain. I gasp. Without thinking, I slide my arms around his waist and rest my head on his chest. The words are lying on the tip of my tongue. I want to tell him I love him. That I'll help make it better, but I can't lay all that on him when he's obviously already dealing with so much.

"The best way you can help is by staying away."

I jerk back at that. "What?" I frown. "What are you saying? I don't understand."

He presses his forehead to mine. "I can't drag you into my shit. I won't do that. Not to you."

Our eyes connect, and we stare at one another. My heart is pounding in my chest. I want to tell him to drag me into his shit. Hell, he can drag me anywhere, and I'll willingly go. I'll do anything to be with him.

His mouth is so close. Right there for the taking. With so much emotion lying between us, it would take nothing to close that gap. But I'm confused. My head is spinning in a million different directions, and I don't know what's transpiring between us. He clasps the back of my head, winding his fingers into my hair, and I almost forget how to breathe. His gaze flicks to my mouth, and my lips part automatically. The air is charged with anticipation. His eyes lower to my snug tank, where my nipples are already pebbled and straining against the material. I'm too afraid to look down. To discover if he's as turned-on as me.

His eyes return to my lips, and flares of confusion spark in his gaze. We don't move, and the only sound in the room is our joint heavy breathing. I've just decided to pull my bravery hat on when he pulls back, moving away so fast it's as if someone is pulling a string, yanking him farther and farther from my grasp. It seems kinda prophetic. He stands up suddenly, swiping a hand across the back of his head and sending me a sheepish smile. "I've got to go."

Shaking the fog from my brain, I hop up. "Wait!"

He halts at the double doors, turning around with his palm raised to stop me in my tracks. "Don't forget what I said, beautiful."

I thrill at the endearment.

When it comes to him, I'm so easy to please.

"Promise me, Ange. Promise me you'll never forget."

"I won't, Dev. I won't ever forget."

CHAPTER FIVE

Devin's words are still playing on a continuous loop in my mind the next morning as I get ready for school. I put some bread in the toaster, and fill the coffee pot with water. Touching my lips, I smile to myself at the memory of Devin's fleeting kiss. It takes me back in time.

"What's taking Ayden so long?" I moan, shivering under the blanket in the treehouse. My fingers shake as I flip my cards over, and I scowl at the pathetic hand I've been dealt.

"Practice must've run over," Devin says, shrugging, doing his best to maintain a strict poker face as he glances at his cards.

"I think I'm going to go inside. I'm freezing." I fold my cards over.

"I don't want to go home yet." Devin opens his arms. "Come here. I'll warm you up." My cheeks turn fire-engine red, and a big grin slips over his mouth. "Come on, baby doll. Whatcha waiting for?"

Recently, he's graduated from calling me princess to calling me baby doll. I'm not sure I like it any better, but I'm afraid if I tell him to stop, he won't call me anything but my name, and I like that he has a special name for me. It makes me feel important.

I crawl over to his side, butterflies running rampant in my chest. Slipping under his arm, I instantly feel warm. He tightens his arm around me, and I snuggle in closer to his chest, closing my eyes, and savoring the touch of him against me. He pulls the blanket up under our chins. "Better?" he whispers, and I nod. I'm not looking at him until my cheeks have calmed down.

Some nights, I dream about this. About him holding me and kissing me and being his.

"I heard something today, but I'm not sure I should tell you."

I blink my eyes open at that. "We don't keep secrets, so spit it out."

"That douche Adam is going to ask you out."

"Really?" I'm surprised because all the douche does is tease me mercilessly.

Dev frowns. "You're not going to say yes, are you?"

I shrug. "I don't know. Maybe." *Absolutely not, but I'm curious to see how Devin reacts.*

His frown deepens. "Why would you go out with him? I thought you didn't like him."

I chew on my lip. "I don't, not really, but some of the other girls are teasing me because I've never kissed a boy, so maybe I should go out with Adam, get it over and done with, and then they'll back off."

Devin stiffens underneath me. "That's a stupid reason to go out with him, and I'm not letting you. I don't trust him not to hurt you."

"It's not up to you."

Silence descends, and it's not the comfortable type.

"What if I kissed you?" he whispers, and my cheeks heat again.

"What?" I sit up a bit straighter, looking into his eyes.

"Just so you can get it over with and you won't have to date the douche then."

My face drops, along with my heart. "Thanks, but I don't want to force you to do something you don't want to do."

He frowns, and his eyes drop to my mouth. "Who says I don't want to kiss you?"

My brows climb to my hairline. "You do?"

His lips curve into a cheeky smile. "It's not like it'd be a chore. You're hot, Ange, and you're my best friend. And your first kiss should be with someone who cares about you, and someone you care about, and we care about each other, right?"

I frown, nodding, confused over whether this is a pity offer or not. I want to kiss him, but only if he wants to kiss me. I don't want charity. Before I can raise more objections, he tilts my chin up with his finger. "Let's stop talking, and just do this." His eyes probe mine for permission. The butterflies in my chest are going crazy, and my heart's beating so, so fast. My mouth feels dry as I nod.

He keeps his eyes locked on mine as he lowers his head and kisses me. I close my eyes, wanting to fully absorb the rush of sensation sweeping over me. My *lips move shyly against his, and he wraps his arms around my back, holding me close as he continues kissing me. Fireworks are exploding inside me, and I love the feel of his lips caressing mine. I don't want him to stop.*

"What the hell?" Ayden asks in a gruff tone, startling us, and we break apart. My cheeks are roaring red as I cast a quick glance at Devin. His eyes bore into mine, as if he can see straight through to my soul, and he isn't disguising the look of adoration on his face. My heart soars as I turn to face the music.

∞ ∞ ∞

"Penny for them?" Ayden asks, catapulting me out of the past. He's lounging against the doorframe to the kitchen and watching me with an amused grin. I jump at the same time the toast pops in the toaster.

"Oh my God. Don't creep up on me like that. My heart almost gave out."

"You need to be more observant, Lina." He strides toward me, tugging on the ends of my ponytail. "I could've been a mass murderer, and you'd still be there staring off dreamily into space."

My cheeks flare up at his words, and he sends me a strange look. "What were you daydreaming about anyway?"

"Nothing important." The lie flies out of my mouth. Admitting to Ayden that I was reliving the moment of my first kiss with Devin would not go down well, considering the current situation. And the fact he wasn't pleased with the discovery his first time around. "Want some?" I hold up a piece of toast as a peace offering–slash–diversion tactic.

Mariah always says if you want to distract a man, offer them food or sex, and since the latter is off the table, food it is.

And Ayden is like a lamb to the slaughter. "Hell yeah." His belly rumbles, as if on cue.

"Didn't you eat?"

"Of course, I did." He snatches a piece of toast, slathering it in raspberry jelly. "But I'm always hungry. You know that." He yanks on my ponytail again, and I nudge him aside with my hip.

"You must cost your mom a fortune in groceries."

"I do, but she loves me." He wiggles his brows, taking a massive bite of toast.

"Doesn't everyone," I tease, but it's the truth. Ayden can do no wrong in most people's eyes. He's an all-round good guy who works hard at school and football and doesn't cause his parents any trouble. He's like the anti-stereotypical jock. He's popular, and every kid in school knows his name, but he doesn't party hard, and he hasn't screwed his way through the cheerleading squad like most of his teammates. He keeps his head down and his nose clean.

He shrugs nonchalantly.

"And so modest, too!" I singsong as I skip out of the kitchen and up to the bathroom.

Ten minutes later, I'm tucked up in my coat in the toasty cab of Ayden's brand spanking new Jeep. His parents surprised him with it a couple months back when he got confirmation of his football scholarship to UI, and now he insists on driving me everywhere, when he can.

See what I mean? All-round nice guy.

It's also the reason why most of the senior class thinks we're dating. That and the fact he hasn't hooked up with anyone since summer break.

"Great," I groan, as Ayden pulls into a vacant parking space at school and I spot Becky Carmichael holding court outside the entrance. "My week is off to a stellar start." He follows my gaze out the window.

"Ignore her."

"I try, but she makes it so difficult sometimes. She loves testing my patience to the limit."

"She's just jealous."

I splutter. "As if!"

Becky is head of the cheerleading squad, and she's got a trophy case full of awards from all the beauty pageants she won as a kid. She is always immaculately dressed, sporting the latest trends, and primped to within an inch of her life. I figure she must be up at the crack of dawn each day to look so perfectly groomed. Me? I roll out of bed at the last possible moment, having hit that snooze button at least five times. My beauty routine consists of brushing my teeth and quickly dragging a comb through my hair. Skinny jeans, shirts, blouses, and my well-worn Converse is my usual attire.

"Why do you always put yourself down?" he asks. "I hate that."

"I'm not putting myself down. I'm just rejecting your assumption that Becky's jealous of me. There isn't anything I have that she is jealous of. Well, besides being besties with you and Devin, but I know it's more than that."

"You are like a breath of fresh air, Lina. Don't ever change." He kisses me on the forehead, and we both climb out of the Jeep at the same time. We walk together, his arm around my shoulders as usual. Becky scowls as we pass, but I pretend not to notice. It drives her bat-shit crazy when I act like she doesn't exist, and it's the most effective weapon in my arsenal.

Ayden waits with me while I extract what I need from my locker, and then he walks me to class. It's the same routine every day. "Have a good one, babe." He presses a kiss to my cheek.

"You too." I curl my fingers around the door handle.

"Oh, and Lina?" I glance over my shoulder at him. "She's jealous of you because you are effortlessly beautiful and the sweetest, nicest girl on the planet. No matter how hard she tries, she can't live up to that."

My mouth hangs open as he blows me a kiss and saunters off, grinning and whistling under his breath.

The morning snails by and it feels like forever until lunchtime rolls around. Mariah waves from her seat as I enter the cafeteria. I load my plate with pasta and chicken, grab a bread roll, some fruit, and juice, and head in her direction. I plop down beside her, across from Gabrielle and Madisyn. They all stare at my tray, and I grin. "What? I'm hungry. And I'm not on shift or at ballet practice today."

"You're so lucky. I think I've put on five pounds just looking at your plate," Madisyn says, sighing enviously as she tucks strands of her dark blonde hair behind her ears. Madisyn is gorgeous with generous curves in all the right places. Guys practically salivate behind her back, but she suffers from major self-esteem issues. She hates that she's taller, broader, and curvier than the average girl, and she's constantly on some diet or other.

"Aren't you worried it's all going to catch up with you when you're older and you'll blow up like Mrs. White?" Gabi asks, picking at her chicken salad. Mrs. White won the Miss USA title when she was nineteen, and she returned home a bona-fide celebrity. Then she got pregnant, married the guy, popped out a few more kids, and her weight ballooned. She became a virtual pariah overnight, which is damn ridiculous. All because she stacked on the pounds, and who the hell's business is it but hers anyway? I can't stand narrowminded prejudicial people, and this town seems to have more than its fair share of bigots. Every time I'm reminded of that story, it strengthens my resolve to leave small-town living in the dust. I like the idea of being a small fish in a very big pond and having more privacy. Although, Mason City isn't a total hick town, and it's not like everyone knows who I am, it's still far too nosy for my liking. The idea of big city living appeals to me. Hugely.

"Nope," I answer truthfully. "Why waste time worrying over something that might never happen?"

Madisyn and Mariah grin, and Gabrielle just rolls her eyes. I stab my pasta with my fork, shoveling it in my mouth and moaning purely for show. Gabi throws a piece of tomato at me, and I angle my head, catching it in my mouth.

"Now that's skill," Ayden says, plopping down beside me with a grin.

Gabrielle sits up straighter in her chair, thrusting her chest out. She has the biggest crush on Ayden, but it isn't reciprocated. Not that she lets it get to her too much. If Madisyn lacks self-confidence, Gabi has it in spades. It's funny watching their interactions though. Ayden doesn't quite know what to make of her, and half the time I think he's genuinely scared of her.

"What's up, loser?" I nudge him in the ribs. "Why are you deeming to grace us with your presence?" Ayden usually sits with the football team, although he has been known to make exceptions for me on occasions.

"I don't need an excuse to sit with my best girl." He winks at me, before wolfing his pasta, which is about triple the size of mine.

"Oh, there's Devin," Madisyn pipes up, waving in his direction. Mariah is the only one of my friends who knows the deal with the guys. In school, both Ayden and Devin have been at pains to hide their growing animosity.

But I guess that's evolving.

Devin takes one look at Ayden and does a U-turn, heading to one of the bigger tables where a few guys he hangs with are sitting with some of the cheerleaders, Becky included. I watch as he sits down beside Will, across from my archnemesis. Becky leans across the table, batting her eyelashes and pouting prettily at Devin. He says something to her, and her entire face lights up.

Mariah subtly kicks my leg under the table, and I whirl around. Ayden is watching me with a wary look on his face. I only pick at the rest of my lunch, miserable at the thought of Becky flirting with Devin across the way.

"Want to come back to my place?" Mariah asks at the end of the school day as we walk outside. My eyes quickly scan the parking lot, cursing when I fail to spot Devin's truck. "We can study for the calculus test together."

"Sure, but could we go to my house? I want to see Mom before she leaves for work." I shift my heavy book bag from one shoulder to the other. "And I want to drop by the gas station to talk to Devin before his shift starts if that's okay?"

"No sweat. I'm cool with that."

I drop my bag on the back seat of Mariah's car and send a quick text to Ayden. He waves at us as we drive by.

I turn up the radio, and we both sing along to our hearts' content. Mariah taps a beat off the steering wheel, and we grin goofishly at one another.

My good mood evaporates the second she swings the car into the gas station where Devin works. Devin is leaning back against the side of his truck, and Becky Carmichael is pressed up against him, her hands tracing circles on his chest.

A nasty taste floods my mouth, and a bout of jealousy swiftly kicks me in my lady parts. Disappointment, anger, and hurt race through me, and I'm hopping out of the car, striding toward them, before I've consciously processed the movement.

CHAPTER SIX

My fists are clenched in rigid knots at my side as I quicken my pace. Devin notices me first, and he removes Becky's hands from his chest and slides sideways. "Hey, Ange." His smile is guarded, because he knows me too well. He understands I'm about three seconds away from personal nuclear detonation.

Becky purses her lips and sends me a smug smile. I want to pummel her into next week. The thought should shock me, but it doesn't. She has pushed me to breaking point, and I'll do whatever it takes to keep her away from Devin. Even the thought of him and her hooking up makes my skin crawl and my heart rip into smithereens. "Mason City's very own Virgin Mary, in the flesh," she drawls, returning to Devin's side. "You're interrupting. Now run along and do whatever it is girls like *you* do."

I plant my hands on my hips and glare at her. "Girls like *me?*"

"Sweet but boring. Haven't you figured it out yet, *Ange?*" She enunciates Devin's nickname for me in a derogatory tone. "Guys don't want sweet and boring. They want girls who put out and know how to have a good time. Why do you think no one asks you out? They know it's a waste of their time." Her words poke new holes in my tender heart. "So, shoo, run along now and play Barbies or whatever you and Mary Sue over there have lined up."

Devin slings his arm over my shoulder, hoisting me into his side. Turning the full extent of his wrath on Becky, he narrows his eyes and glares at her. The smile drops off her face, and she visibly shrinks. "If anyone's leaving, it's your skanky ass." His voice is low and menacing, and emotion clogs my throat. "If I ever hear you speaking to Ange like that again, I won't be responsible for my actions. No one speaks to her like that. No one!" he snarls, and she jerks back as if he's slapped her. "Get the fuck out of my face, and stay the hell away from me. I'm not interested, and I never will be."

Pushing her discomfort aside, she plants her game face on, smiling seductively at him. "Come on now, Dev, don't be like that. She knows I'm just kidding."

"No, you weren't," I grit out. "And you heard him, get lost."

"You'll come crawling to me, Devin, begging for it, and I'll remind you of this conversation." She backs up with a smug look on her face. There isn't much I admire about Becky, but her supreme self-confidence is something else.

"I hope you have an endless supply of patience," Dev retorts. "Because hell will freeze before that day comes."

She blows him a kiss, and I growl under my breath. "Oh, I can be patient for you. One hundred percent. You're worth it." Her mouth pulls into a sneer as she sends me one final contemptuous look. "Later, gorgeous." She blows him another kiss before jumping in her car and tearing off with a squeal of tires, leaving a cloud of smoke trailing in her wake.

"I hate her." The words fly out of my mouth, fueled by the anger still pumping through my veins.

"I thought you didn't waste any energy on hate?" He spins me around, loosely wrapping his arms around my waist.

"I've changed my mind."

He kisses the end of my nose. "Don't change for anyone, least of all her."

"Why did she have her hands all over you?"

"She caught me off guard is all."

I harrumph, mumbling under my breath. *Who lets people manhandle them without knowing?* Devin smiles. "Don't tell me you're actually jealous of Becky Carmichael because that would be a travesty."

"I'm not jealous," I lie. "I'm sick of her taunts and her pranks and her constant attempts to annoy me. I just want her to leave me the hell alone."

His smile fades. "She's still tormenting you? I'll put a stop to it."

"No, you won't. That'll only make things worse. I can fight my own battles." More so, I want him nowhere near that manipulative bitch. I might despise her, but I can't deny she's stunning and she knows how to have guys eating out of her hand. And contrary to popular opinion, I'm not naïve. Devin is a red-blooded male who likes sex. Becky is gorgeous and sexy and experienced in all the ways I'm not. Yes, she's a bitch and everyone knows it, but she has no shortage of guys drooling over her. I don't want Devin falling prey to her charms. The other girls are bad enough, but it he hooked up with Becky, I don't think I could ever forgive him.

"You know what she said was bull, right?" He searches my eyes. I shrug, and he grips my chin. "Hey, she's full of shit. Guys don't ask you out because they know Ayden and I will kick their ass if they don't treat you with respect, and most of them are too afraid you'll reject them."

I laugh. "Come on, Dev, don't be ridiculous." It's a version of what Mom said, but I didn't believe her either.

His lips curve up, and his eyes twinkle as he blinds me with a dazzling smile. I kinda zone out of it. "You're fucking gorgeous, Ange, although I'm not surprised you don't realize it. And you are the least boring person I know. Becky is mean and spiteful and jealous. That's why she picks on you so much. She hears the way the guys talk with reverence about you, and it annoys the crap out of her, but don't let her get to you, and don't let her change you. She's not worth it. You're one of a kind, and you shouldn't ever change because you're absolutely perfect exactly the way you are."

∞ ∞ ∞

I left the gas station high on his words. I wanted to kiss him so badly in that moment, but I had to remind myself he was just being a good friend. Any anger I'd felt over the scene I encountered when we'd pulled up flittered away. I floated on a cloud for the rest of the week, and the week after, buoyed up by Devin's defense. Becky steered clear of me too, which was a plus, although she and her minions didn't miss any chance to shoot daggers my direction whenever we crossed paths. But nothing could deflect my good mood. Not even the fact I haven't spoken to Devin since that day, apart from brief passing words in the corridor at school.

Lucas eats dinner with us every night now. Mom mentioned how Devin had dropped by explaining he had taken on more shifts at the gas station and he was worried about Lucas being by himself so much.

I love having Lucas around. He looks so much like Devin did at fourteen. He has the same lustrous inky-black hair and the same piercing green eyes, but he lacks that intensity that is pure Devin. Lucas has a more relaxed, softer expression, and he's less brooding than his older brother. On nights when I'm at home, he tends to eat dinner and finish his homework here, and then we watch some TV before he returns to his house. I like having him here, especially on nights when Ayden has late practice. Otherwise, I'd be climbing the walls by myself. I know Mom needs her job at the hospital, and that it pays well, but the house is so empty and lonely when it's just me here.

It's Friday night, and the diner is dead as a doornail, so Lucille let me off early. Mariah is at the movies with Cody so I'm at a loose end. I was going to invite Devin to come over and watch a movie with me, but his truck is missing from the driveway, so I guess he's still at work or off partying somewhere. Ayden is celebrating with the football team, after their earlier victory. I caught the first half of the game before I had to leave for my shift, and they were hammering the opposition, so I'm not surprised they came out on top. He'd texted me after with the score, begging me to come join the party, but I'm not in the mood.

Lucas is sitting on his porch when I get out of my car. "Hey." I wave to him, and he waves back, smiling. I lean over the fence. "You wanna watch a movie with me?" His eyes light up momentarily, but then he casts a nervous glance over his shoulder. "It's okay if you already have plans," I assure him.

"No, no, that's not it." He stands up, brushing bits of debris off the back of his jeans. "It's just …" He kneads the back of his neck, and his forehead crinkles. "Dad's home."

I arch a brow. Mr. Morgan being home before midnight on a Friday night is *not* a regular occurrence. Maybe Lucas just wants to hang with his dad. "No sweat. I'll leave the door unlocked for you. Come over or don't. It's totally your call."

He chews on the corner of his lip. "I want to, but Devin wouldn't like Dad knowing I'm in your house." He jumps over the steps, landing steadily on the lawn. "I just won't tell him. He probably won't miss me anyway."

I say nothing until we're both in the house. "Why wouldn't Dev want your dad to know you're here?"

Lucas scrunches up his nose, shrugging. "You'll have to ask him."

Strange.

I make popcorn and grab some cookies and sodas and head into the living room. "You want to watch the next episode of *Gossip Girl*, or did you have a movie in mind?" Lucas asks, as I place the food on the coffee table.

When the series first aired, five years ago, I was too young and too much of a tomboy to care, even if everyone was raving about it. Now that it's coming to an end, there's renewed interest in it, so I decided it was time to check it out. Lucas was a willing partner in crime, and we were both hooked from episode one, and now it's our shared guilty pleasure. I'm addicted, so it takes zero persuasion to convince me. "Nope, that's good. I'm in need of a Dan fix." No surprises I'm swooning over intense, misunderstood outsider Dan instead of golden boy Nate.

We settle on the couch, beside one another, and I toe off my shoes, tucking my feet underneath me. We're both riveted, and apart from the occasional gasp or expletive, we don't say a word until it's over.

"I think you have a little drool there," Lucas teases, pretending to wipe the corner of my mouth.

"Very funny. And don't think I didn't notice you swooning over Serena."

"She's hot. I'd do her." He winks, and I laugh. Chip off the old block. He twists around on the couch so he's facing me, and there's a mischievous glint in his eye. "If you could do anyone in the whole world, you have your choice of dudes, who would you pick?"

Your brother. The thought forms instantly, but it's not like I can admit that. "Penn Badgley, duh!" I reply, stating the obvious choice. I *have* just spent the last forty-five minutes ogling the fictional character he portrays.

"Liar." Lucas's lips twitch.

I shove him playfully. "No, I'm not." *Yes, I am.*

He leans in, and his voice turns low. "I know who you'd really pick, but you're too afraid to say it out loud." My skin feels hot and my cheeks are burning. He leans in even closer, and his face is only a hairsbreadth from mine. "You can tell me. I won't tell him." Crap! *He knows? Have I been that obvious?* He twirls a lock of my hair around his finger. "I'll tell you my secret crush if you tell me yours."

If he knows, does that mean everyone else does too? I'm completely flustered, and he's making me feel uncomfortable. "Stop it, Luc."

"What the hell, Luc?" A voice bellows from behind us, making us both jump. Devin stalks in front of the couch, folding his arms, and faux-glaring at his brother. "You better not be hitting on my girl."

My girl?

Lucas grins.

"Ange." Dev's voice softens as he speaks to me while keeping his gaze on his little brother. "Did this punk cross a line?"

"What?" I hop up. Even though it's clear Dev is teasing, I don't want the brothers falling out on my account. "No, of course not. It's nothing like that. We were just goofing around."

Luc stands up, slapping his brother on the back. "Dude, come on. I know she's yours. I'd never dishonor the bro code. I was just messing with her."

My body overheats at his words and the fact Devin doesn't dispute them.

"Cool, but I'll knock you on your ass if you ever upset her. You hear me?"

"Jeez." Lucas straightens his wrinkled shirt. "What's up your ass today?"

"You. Now scoot. Dad's gone out. I'm going to keep Ange company for a while, but I'll be home straight after."

Lucas slaps him on the back. "It's cool, man. Take your time." He gives me a quick hug. "Sorry for being a jerk."

I hug him back. "We're good. Forget about it." *God, please forget about it.*

Lucas leaves an eerie silence in his wake. The TV plays in the background as Devin and I stare wordlessly at one another. Neither one of us moves a muscle, and electricity sizzles in the air. Bruising shadows paint the space under his eyes, and his complexion is paler than usual. Considering I've barely seen his truck outside the house in two weeks, and there are no obvious injuries to his face or body, it's clear he's been at work most every night. He looks exhausted, but that doesn't impede the hungry look in his eyes. My insides are tied into knots, and a familiar ache pools in my core. His gaze bounces between my lips and my eyes, and the smoldering look he's giving me infuses me with courage.

I clear my throat. "Lucas said he knows I'm yours. What exactly does that mean?" I'm pleased my voice rings out loud and confident.

I hold his gaze as he moves ever so slowly toward me. He stops directly in front of me, and I look up at him. His hair is styled in a faux hawk today, and he looks hotter than ever. A layer of light stubble coats his jawline, and I give in to the urge to touch him. My fingers trace lightly over his five o'clock shadow. Closing his eyes, he emits a strangled moan that turns my limbs to Jell-O. Reaching up, he places his hand over mine. His eyes open, and he stares deep into my eyes. I stop breathing at the blatant look of desire on his face.

Ohmigawd.

Ohmigawd.

He curls his free hand around the back of my neck, his fingers twisting in my hair. "I'm not strong enough tonight," he whispers. "Not when I need you. And I need you so bad, Ange. I can't deny this any longer, even though I should."

My heart is literally in my mouth, which has suddenly turned dry. "What are you saying?" I whisper back.

His hand flexes on my neck, and he releases his other hand from my face, gripping my waist and pulling me in flush to his body. We're pressed up against one another, and there is only a minuscule gap between our faces. My pulse throbs wildly, and my heart is slamming around my ribcage in hopeful excitement. A shiver whips up my spine.

"You're so fucking beautiful, Ange. Inside and out." His fingers dip under the hem of my shirt, and the feel of his warm hand on my skin causes my knees to buckle. He strengthens his hold, and his eyes flare black as he stares at me. The heat from his body seeps into mine, and the throbbing between my legs is almost painful. If he pulls away this time, I might have to knee him in the nuts.

"I've waited a long time to do this," he admits, "and I can't wait a second longer."

Then his lips crash onto mine, and I'm drowning in Devin's kisses.

CHAPTER SEVEN

He's devouring my mouth like he needs me to breathe. I'm kissing him back with the same intensity, clawing at his shirt until my fingers find bare skin. His tongue invades my mouth, exploring without apology, and our tongues start a frantic dance. My hands wander up his back, discovering strong, hard muscles, and I pull him in tighter to me. Inside, I'm mentally fist pumping the air. I've wanted this for so long, and now that I'm in Devin's arms and he's kissing me like he can't get enough of me, it's everything I'd hoped it would be and more.

Angling my head, he deepens the kiss, moaning my name under his breath. My core is aching in a way it's never ached before, and I rub against him greedily. When he rocks his hips against mine, the most powerful need rockets through me. I whimper, grinding my pelvis against him so he's left in no doubt how badly I want him. He's rock-hard in his jeans, and that only accelerates my arousal.

His lips move to my neck, suctioning on, and I shiver all over. "Devin." My plea is desperate, but I couldn't care less.

"Want to take this upstairs?" he rasps.

"God, yes." My voice is breathy and thick with desire.

"Wrap your legs around me, baby," he instructs. I jump up, doing as I'm told, and his strong arms hold me up as his mouth continues to worship my neck. He starts walking toward the stairs, and I close my eyes, reveling in the sensations he's evoking in me. I've made out with other guys before, and done plenty of stuff, but none of those guys made me feel even a tenth of what I'm feeling right now.

Devin lifts his mouth from my neck, and I cry out in protest. He chuckles while walking us up the stairs. "I don't want to drop you, beautiful." He pecks me briefly on the lips as he mounts the last few steps, and I inspect his flushed, darkened expression with a certain amount of pride, wondering if I have the same sexy, dazed look on my face.

He brings me into my room, laying me down gently on my bed. Removing his shoes, he climbs over me, keeping himself propped up on his elbows as he stares down at me. I want to freeze frame this moment. To bottle the look on his face for all eternity. *He wants me.* It's written all over his face, and even if he was to try to deny it with words, he can't deny the expression on his face. It's there in black and white. *Devin wants me too.* I mentally scream with excitement.

Pushing strands of my hair back off my face, he kisses me sweetly, so at odds with the way he was ravaging me downstairs. If he changes his mind now, I *am* going to kick him in the nuts. "Ange?" he whispers, brushing his lips across my cheek. "Are you sure you want to do this with me?"

He's that vulnerable little boy again, and I'm the one holding his heart in the palm of my hand.

I cup his face. "I've never been more sure of anything. I've been saving myself for you." True fact. I could've had sex a bunch of times by now, but I want my first time to be with someone I love. Specifically, Devin.

A look of shock mixes with pleasure on his face. "You're a virgin?"

"Why do you look so surprised?" My hands creep under his shirt, and he shivers at my touch.

"You've dated, and I know some of those guys."

"Yes, and I've done plenty of other stuff, but I never went any further. I want my first time to be with you, Devin. It was always meant to be you."

He rests his head on my shoulder, and his breathing is labored. "I'm not worthy of you."

"Bull." I gently push his shoulders, and he lifts his head up. "Surely that's my decision to make? And I made it years ago, when I promised myself that I'd only give my virginity to you. Don't back out. I know you want this as much as me, and if you leave me like this, I'll—"

He cuts me off with a passionate kiss. "I'm not backing out. I'm too fucking selfish to do the right thing."

My hands wander up his spine as he presses me into the bed, kissing the shit out of me. My body is on fire, and I want to feel him naked against me. Gently, I push him off, sitting up quickly and whipping my shirt up and over my head. A welcome cool breeze coasts over my warm skin. Devin sits up, stripping his own shirt off but never taking his eyes off me. His fingers caress the skin at my neck in light, soft, featherlike touches that have me shivering all over. His hand moves lower, across my clavicle, and down lower still. I suck in a breath as the edge of one finger brushes across the swell of my breasts. My nipples harden under the thin cotton material of my bra. "You're so gorgeous, Ange. So beautiful," he whispers, before ducking his head and drawing my breast into his mouth through my bra.

I gasp as a shot of lust darts straight to my core. Devin eases me back down on the bed, lavishing equal attention on my breasts; one hand cups and teases one breast while his mouth goes to town on the other. He skillfully alternates, while I writhe and moan underneath him, on the verge of falling apart already, and he hasn't even touched me down there. I grind my hips against his, and he nudges my legs apart, positioning himself exactly where I want him. I moan out loud. "Dev, please."

He chuckles, lifting his head up to look me in the face. "Trust me, baby. I want to worship every inch of you and make sure you're ready."

"I'm ready." The words fly out of my mouth, and he chuckles again.

"I'm going to take good care of you, Ange." His expression turns serious. "Do you trust me?"

I nod profusely. "I trust you."

He unclips my bra in a lightning-fast move. "Good, because I will always look after you. Always."

Discarding my bra, he continues to worship my bare breasts before moving down my body, nipping, licking, kissing, and sucking as he goes. Sweat drips down my spine, and the covers feel damp underneath me, but all I care about is the flurry of sensations he's awoken in me. My hips have a rhythm of their own, my hands a mind of their own, as I grip his ass and pull him against me. He smiles knowingly as he pops the button on my jeans, dragging the denim down my legs and tossing the jeans on the floor. Kneeling over me, he draws a slow, lazy trail from my head to my toes. "Damn, you are so fucking unbelievably gorgeous. Even better than I imagined." He takes my ankle, holding it up, pressing a light kiss on the back of my calf.

"You've imagined me naked?" My voice comes out breathless and needy.

"So many times."

His words thrill me silly.

His mouth continues a journey up my leg. When he reaches my inner thigh, he places my leg back on the bed and pushes my thighs apart. My core is throbbing through the flimsy material of my panties. "I need to feel you, taste you." His eyes burn hot as he asks the silent question. I nod my acquiescence, and he pushes my panties aside, sliding his finger inside me. I'm so wet it's almost embarrassing. His finger moves slowly in and out, and I arch my back and close my eyes. "Eyes on me, beautiful." I blink them open, attempting to focus on his face. "I want to see your every expression." He adds another finger, and I gasp. He pumps his fingers into me faster and harder, and a crescendo of sensation is building deep in my core.

"Oh my God, Devin!" I rock my hips up, riding his fingers with unashamed abandon. "Don't stop."

In one swift move, Devin rips my panties away, and then his mouth is on me while his fingers continue to work me hard. I shatter in a fireball of colorful emotion, my body bucking wildly on the bed and the strangest sounds trailing from my mouth.

When I come down from my orgasmic high, I push the matted strands of my hair out of my eyes and grin at him. He looks conflicted, and my smile fades. Nervous he's going to back out, I sit up and lean in, kissing his swollen lips. "That was incredible."

I palm the bulge in his jeans, and he groans, his eyes rolling back in his head as I stroke one finger up and down the length of his straining cock. Opening his jeans, I twist around, pushing him down flat on the bed. "And it's my turn to look after you now."

His eyes smolder with longing, and I make quick work of his jeans and boxers, throwing them on top of my pile of discarded clothing on the floor. I stare in awe at his gorgeous, naked body, my gaze latching onto his long, thick erection and wandering up the toned planes of his abs and his smooth chest. He locks his hands behind his head, smirking at my obvious ogling. My eyes discover the dark purple bruise along the side of his ribcage, just under his armpit. The fact I didn't notice it until now is testament to his considerable hotness and his skillful mouth and fingers. I frown. "Were you fighting again?" Carefully, I trace my fingers over the bruise.

Every trace of desire leaves his face, and a mask of indifference repaints his features. He locks up instantly, swatting my hand away and sitting up. Swinging his legs around, he plants them on the floor, lowering his head into his hands. I curse my stupid, stupid mouth, crawling over and wrapping my arms around his shoulders from behind. "It doesn't matter, forget I said anything."

His body is stiff as a board underneath me. I plant kisses along his neck, over his jawline, and up to his cheek. "Dev, please. I want you to make love to me."

Silently, he lifts me off him and stands up. He rakes a hand through his hair, averting his eyes. "I want that too but not like this."

"What?" I pull the covers up, wrapping them around my body, feeling suddenly vulnerable. "I'm sorry I ruined the mood. Please forget I said it and come back to bed." He reaches for his jeans and pulls them on. Tears prick my eyes. "I don't want you to leave."

He sits down on the corner of the bed, winding his hand around my neck. "I want you, Ange, but I want to make it special, because you deserve that. I don't want your first time to be like this."

"Why not?" Honestly, I don't know what his objection is.

"You need to be sure you want to give this to me."

"I am sure, Devin. I've been sure basically my whole life."

His eyes pop wide, and he leans in, kissing me sweetly. I wrap my arms around his neck, and the sheet drifts down my body. I press into him, trying to deepen the kiss and put things back on the right path, but he breaks the kiss and removes my wrists carefully. "You deserve better than me," he whispers.

"No." My voice radiates with conviction. "Don't tell me what I want or what I deserve." Another thought occurs to me, a hideously horrific one. "If you don't want this with me, just say it, Dev. If this was a mistake, I need to hear those words." My mind frantically scans over the last half hour, wondering if I've somehow coerced him into this, but he wanted this as much as I did. I saw it in his eyes.

"Of course, I want you. I'm about to fucking explode in my pants. This is not about me not wanting you."

My eyes flit to his straining erection and that goes some way toward reassuring me. "I don't understand."

He kisses me softly, before rising. Bending down, he grabs his shirt and pulls it on. Tears well in my eyes again, and I curse myself for saying anything about the bruise. That flicked some switch in him, and now he's leaving. He kneels in front of me, taking my hands. "Don't cry, Ange." His thumb brushes across my cheek, gathering moisture, and a pained look appears on his face. "I want you to be sure, and I want to make it special. Your first time should be magical."

"With you, it would be." I choke over a sob, and I hate that I'm so pathetic.

He presses a kiss to my forehead. "Think about it, and if it's still what you want, we'll make some plans."

"I don't need to think about it." Or make stupid plans. This was spontaneous, and it felt so right. I've spent years thinking about this night, but in all my dreams it never ended with him leaving just as we were getting started. My heart aches.

"Then do it for me. I need to be worthy of you."

I don't understand. I really don't, but Dev is a stubborn ass once he's made his mind up on something. There is nothing I can say that will change his mind, and I'm not going to beg. I still have some modicum of self-respect.

He stands up, cupping my face, staring at me tenderly. "I care about you so much, Ange. Too much to let you make a mistake." He kisses me one last time. "We'll talk tomorrow or Sunday. Sleep tight, beautiful."

And with those parting words, he walks away, leaving the shattered pieces of my heart in tatters on the floor.

CHAPTER EIGHT

We don't talk about it the next day or Sunday or at any stage over the next two weeks, because Devin is avoiding me. He only returns to his house late at night, and during school—when he shows—he shuns me like I'm contaminated. Hurt and my stupid pride stops me from confronting him. Ayden knows something's wrong, but he doesn't pry. Mariah is furious with Devin, and she wastes no opportunity to glare at him in passing, although she's glad he didn't go through with it. Her view is I should only give him my virginity if we're officially together, and if he's not ready to make a commitment, then I shouldn't sleep with him.

Her reasoning is sound, and if it was any other guy, I wouldn't need convincing, but this is Devin we're talking about. Everything is always different when it comes to him.

It's obvious he regrets it, and for a guy who hardly ever turns a girl down, his rejection stabs deep, poking at hidden sores and festering wounds, leaving my self-confidence in shreds.

I've gone over the events of that night a thousand times in my head, and, at no stage, did he give me any inclination he wasn't into it as much as I was.

My comment about his bruised ribs changed the atmosphere, and ruined the moment, and I'd like to know why.

Dev trains hard at the local boxing club, and it's not uncommon for him to have a black eye or be covered in bruises and cuts from fight nights.

And he's gotten mixed up in plenty of fights outside the boxing ring, too, always quick and eager to lash out with his fists. So, I don't understand what it was about that bruise that triggered his mood swing. Or why he's felt the need to ignore me ever since.

Yanking myself out of my depressive inner monologue, I slick some pink lip gloss over my lips and survey my reflection in the mirror. I don't usually wear this much makeup, but I need an additional confidence boost as I'm determined to have it out with Devin, and I want to look my absolute best. My cheeks are painted in a fine coat of wispy pink blush, and my eyes look wider and bluer under the frame of thick mascara and sultry brown eye shadow. My hair is freshly washed and falling in soft waves down my back. My gaze stares back at me, glinting with righteous indignation.

Today, Dev will have no choice but to speak to me, and I'm not leaving without some answers. I've gone beyond hurt and shame and ventured into a new phase: I'm just plain ol' mad. Even if he doesn't want to have sex with me, he doesn't get to treat me like this. I'm one of his oldest friends, and he spouts crap about respect all the time. It's about time he started practicing what he preaches. He can man up and own his actions. I'm done being treated like a piece of worthless garbage.

Ayden's parents always invite Mom, me, Devin, and his brothers to their house for Thanksgiving dinner. It's become our annual tradition, and I know Devin will be there, because he won't let Lucas down.

Taking one last look in the mirror, I tug my black lacy peplum top down a little, flashing more cleavage. My skinny, dark-pink jeans are close-fitting and sculpted to my ass. Grabbing the soft cashmere cardigan, I slip my feet into my high-heeled black boots. Bending over, I shake my head and loosen my hair. Satisfied, I head downstairs to grab the pumpkin pie from the kitchen.

"Honey!" Mom exclaims when I step into the kitchen. "You look gorgeous. Trying out a new look?"

I shrug casually. "It's Thanksgiving. I thought I should make more of an effort."

Her wise eyes miss nothing. "Uh-huh." She smiles.

"What?" My voice is gruff. "I'll change if it's that big of a deal."

Her hands land on my shoulders. "Sweetheart. Stop. You look beautiful, and there's no need to change. I'm just wondering if there's any ulterior motive? Like any boy you might be trying to impress?" Her lips fight a twitch.

Goddamn it, that woman misses nothing. "Nope," I lie. "Can't a girl just look nice without there being an ulterior motive?"

She kisses my cheek. "Of course. Come on." She lifts the dish with the potatoes. "We don't want to be late."

I take the pumpkin pie and follow her out of the house.

Ayden opens the door to us, and the look on his face is priceless. His jaw slackens, and his eyes almost bug out of his head as he drags his gaze over me. "Wow, Lina. You look stunning."

Jeez, I really need to do more with my appearance if a bit of makeup, a fitted top, and some heels has everyone noticing. "Thanks. You look nice too." And he does. His blue, white, and red checkered shirt is open over a plain white top that fits his broad shoulders and muscular chest perfectly, as if it was spray painted on his body. He's wearing low-hanging dark-navy jeans, and red and neon Air Max. His blond hair is still a little damp from the shower but spiked up in his usual style. Ayden is a seriously good-looking guy and a sweetheart to boot. *Why couldn't I fall in love with him?*

"Ayden," Mrs. Carter says in a chastising tone of voice, "are you going to let our guests in or leave them standing out there in the cold?" She takes the pie from my hands, ushering us inside with a welcoming smile.

"Chill, Mom. It's not my fault the sight of Lina looking so utterly gorgeous eradicated all logical thought." He winks, offering me his arm which I gratefully accept. Mom beams at me, sharing a knowing look with Mrs. Carter as we move through the house.

Sounds of laughter greet my ears as we step into the living room. Lucas is laughing with Mr. Carter over by the window, and he lifts his hand in a wave. I smile at him, returning his wave. My heart starts pounding in my chest at the sight of Devin, sitting on the couch with Ayden's youngest sister on his lap, reading her a story. Ayden's other two sisters are seated on the couch across from them, hanging off Devin's every word. Ellie is twelve and Mia is thirteen now, and both are at the age where they are properly noticing boys for the first time. Mia has been crushing on Devin for a little while. Not that I'm in any position to criticize her for that. I feel like pulling her aside and telling her not to waste her energy.

Devin obviously knows we've arrived, but he hasn't looked up from the book to acknowledge me and that ticks me off.

"Hi, Dev." I practically shout the words.

Ever so slowly, he looks up. Shock is splayed all over his face as he stares at me. A flash of something blazes in his eyes before he composes himself, clearing his throat. "Hey, Ange."

I offer him a strained smile. Kayla jumps off his lap, running at me. "Lina!" She throws her arms around my legs, and I almost lose my balance, but Ayden is there to steady me.

"Careful, munchkin." He ruffles her hair. "Don't knock Lina over."

I bend down, pulling her in for a hug. "Hi, Kayla. I made your favorite pie."

She squeals with delight. "Did you put fairy magic in it like always?"

Out of the corner of my eye, I spy Mia throwing her eyes to the ceiling. She forgets she was as fascinated with fairies at age seven as Kayla is. I kiss the top of Kayla's nose. "Come on? You really need to ask me that?"

She giggles, and I whisper in her ear. "I only put fairy magic in your slice so it's your job to make sure I cut the pie."

She holds out her hand. "Deal." We shake on it, and the feel of her small, soft hand in mine helps erase some of my anger. I remember when Mrs. Carter brought Kayla home and how enamored all three of us were with her. As we got older, I regularly babysat with Ayden, and she feels as much my sister as his. I hate that I don't have much time for her anymore.

I straighten up, and she tugs on my hand, attempting to drag me back to the couch—back to Devin and her book. Oh, hell to the no. As much as I need to speak to Devin, I'm not doing it with an audience, and I most definitely am not going to sit by his side and pretend that everything is perfect. Extracting my hand from hers, I kiss the top of her hair. "You go back to your book. I need to help our moms in the kitchen."

Her little face drops, and I feel like the biggest bitch on the planet, but self-preservation wins out. Ayden trails me into the kitchen with a puzzled look on his face. "Can I help?" I ask his mom.

"Relax, enjoy yourself," Mrs. Carter says, shooing me away with her hands. "We have this under control."

I shuffle awkwardly on my feet, not wanting to go back into the living room. "Want to hang out on the back porch?" Ayden asks, and I gratefully nod.

The crisp fall weather blasts me in the face as soon as we step outside. I shiver, and Ayden tucks me in under his arm, pulling us both down on the love seat. He drags a thick blanket over us, and I snuggle into him, enjoying the familiar feel and smell of him. He toys with my hair as we sit in silence, both staring out at the manicured lawn. "Did he say something to you?" he asks after a bit.

"No."

"So what is it? And don't tell me it's nothing. I know when my two best friends are avoiding each other."

I want to tell him, but I'm not sure how he'll react. If what Dev has alluded to is true—that Ayden has romantic feelings for me—then the news that I've been intimate with Dev won't go down well. And I don't want him to feel like he has to pick sides. Whatever beef I have with Devin is mine alone. Besides, it's not like I'm the only one hiding stuff. Devin and Ayden are still frosty with one another, and I've no clue why. "It's nothing you need to worry about, and I'm going to talk to him about it later."

"Let's do it now," Devin says from behind, startling me. He's lounging against the doorframe, watching us, with his arms crossed and his expression guarded.

"So you're talking to me now?"

He pushes off the door and saunters toward me. "I was never not talking to you."

"Oh, puh-lease. Don't feed me that bull. You've been avoiding me for weeks."

Ignoring me, he eyeballs Ayden. "Can you leave us? I need to speak to Ange in private."

"That's up to Lina." Ayden glares at Devin.

I chew on the inside of my cheek. This will hurt Ayden but not as much as letting him stay will. "It's okay. I need to talk to Dev on my own."

He kisses my cheek. "Fine." Standing up, he sends an icy look in Dev's direction. "But if you hurt her anymore than you already have, I'll kick your ass until you're inhaling blood."

"I have no intention of hurting her, but if I do, you have my permission. I'd welcome the ass kicking."

Ayden begrudgingly concedes, walking off with one final look over his shoulder.

"Why have you been avoiding me?" I blurt. Might as well rip the Band-Aid off in one go. I try to prepare myself for the oncoming onslaught, but it's a futile exercise where Dev and my heart are concerned.

He sits down beside me, staring out into the backyard. "I don't want to upset you, and I've been putting off this conversation because I know it's probably not what you want to hear."

My heart sinks, and pain explodes in my stomach. "You regret it?" I whisper, not looking at him.

"I'd rather regret the things I haven't done over the things I have," he says, cryptically, while I try to work out the hidden meaning.

"So you don't regret what we did but regret not having sex?"

He laughs, but the sound is biting, strained. He turns to face me, pain radiating from his eyes. "Regret and you are all too synonymous in my mind."

"Don't let me down gently or anything," I mutter, feeling more and more dejected with every word coming out of his mouth.

He laces his fingers in mine. "I could live a million lifetimes and never be good enough for you."

Not this again. "That's what this is about?" He nods. "You're being ridiculous, and we're only talking about having sex, not my entire life." Honestly, I never thought I'd see the day where Devin made such a deal out of something he freely offers around.

"You don't get it." He shakes his head.

"So, enlighten me then?" My tone bristles with barely disguised frustration and simmering anger.

"It could never be just sex with us. You were willing to give me something I don't deserve. Something I can't take. Something that belongs to someone else."

"And, like I said, that choice is not yours to make. It's mine, and I want it to be you."

He removes his hand from mine, stroking his stubbly jaw. "It's not going to happen, Ange."

"So that's it?" I twist around, demanding he look me straight in the eye. "You'll happily fuck any slut who opens her legs for you, but I'm here practically begging and you're saying no?"

Naked emotion splays across his face. Reaching out, he cups my face between his calloused hands. "None of those girls mean anything to me, but you, you're … you're everything."

"Then treat me like it!"

"Christ!" He drops his hands from my face and stands up. "What the hell do you think I'm trying to do? This would be so much easier if I didn't care about you so fucking much."

I snort at the irony. "How the hell do I know?" I hop up, rage doing a number on me. "You won't ever give me a straight answer, and you issue mixed signals all the time."

"Well, let me make this clear for you then," he grits out, his own anger surfacing. "You and I will never be anything more than friends. I don't regret what happened between us even though it shouldn't have happened, but we will never do anything like that again, and we sure as hell won't be having sex. Does that spell it out for you?"

"Loud and clear." I'm glad my anger is holding the tears at bay, although I'm sure they'll emerge at some point. I stomp toward the door, spinning around on my heel at the last minute, determined to have the final word.

"I guess I should thank you. You've done me a massive favor. I am not going to waste a single second more thinking about you, and, as for being friends, friends don't treat other friends like this." My eyes fall to the tattoo on my wrist. "The friend who went with me to get this"—I circle the infinity symbol—"would never have treated me so horribly, but I guess you wouldn't know that because you're no longer the same person. You're no longer someone I can call a friend."

CHAPTER NINE

My words were thrown out in the heat of the moment, and I wanted to instantly take them back, but I'm too upset to do the right thing. For once, I want to let him stew. Not that he seems in any way concerned. He sits around the dinner table laughing and joking as if he hasn't got a care in the world. I guess I'm a lot less skilled in the acting department, because I can't disguise my anger or my hurt, and I'm sullen and withdrawn, barely speaking and only picking at the gorgeous dinner Ayden's mom has prepared. When Kayla drags me up by the hand to cut her slice of pumpkin pie, her sweet good nature and infectious laughter finally pulls me out of my head.

As I serve up dessert, I decide to pull my big girl pants on and hold my head up high. Show Devin I can ride above his rejection and that I'm not going to curl up into a ball and die just because he doesn't reciprocate my feelings. I slide my chair closer to Ayden's and give him my full attention. At least I have one friend I can continue to count on. "Do you want me to kick his ass?" he whispers, in between mouthfuls of pie.

"Don't bother," I whisper back. "It's not worth it."

"Are you ever going to tell me what he did?"

"Are you?"

We stare at one another, neither backing down, both trying to work out what the other knows, and it's creating tension where tension shouldn't exist. That's the problem with secrets—they drive a stake right through the heart of relationships, invoking all kinds of imaginary inventions, all manner of protective protestations.

"Maybe the psychic will reveal all," he whispers, and I know his teasing tone is an attempt to lighten the mood.

"You're still okay to come with?"

He purses his lips, cocking his head to the side. "You know I'd never let you down. I said I'd go and I'm going." One of America's most renowned psychics is holding an event in Minneapolis just after Christmas, and I've had tickets for months—I'm a sucker whenever any of these shows roll close to town. Mom indulges my strange hobby, and I've lost count of the amount of times she's taken me to the fortune teller at the annual carnival and how often she's driven me to these psychic events, but I already told you she was awesome, right?

"Ahem." A loud throat clearing pulls us out of our whispered conversation. My cheeks flush as I notice every pair of eyes fixated on us. Mr. Carter smiles. "We can leave if you'd like some privacy?" he jokes.

Mom's face is radiant as her gaze bounces between us, and I know she thinks she's figured this out. Little does she realize the grumpy-faced guy sitting on her left is the real object of my romantic and sexual obsession. Devin glares at Ayden, and Ayden returns it and then some.

Mrs. Carter nudges her husband in the ribs. "Carl, leave them alone." She rises in her seat, collecting plates.

Ayden stands up. "Sit down, Mom. You cooked, we'll clean." I rise and start stacking the dirty dinner plates, carrying them into the kitchen.

Lucas and the girls help clear the table, and then it's just Ayden and me in the kitchen. I'm rinsing while he loads the dishwasher.

"Don't you make a great team," Devin snarls, stepping into the kitchen with two empty wine glasses.

"Cut this shit out, man." Ayden sends him a filthy look. "And grow the fuck up."

Devin opens the refrigerator, almost yanking the door off its hinges. "Me, grow up? That's fucking rich."

Ayden folds his arms across his chest. "Did you deliberately set out to alienate your two closest friends or did this fuck-up happen by chance?"

Devin pours white wine from the bottle into the two glasses. "Did you deliberately set out to piss me off?"

"What the hell are you talking about?" Ayden shakes his head.

Devin recorks the wine, placing it back in the refrigerator. He turns toward us, jabbing a finger in the air between us. "You two acting all lovey-dovey at the table."

"We weren't acting all lovey-dovey," I protest, leaning my butt against the sink. "We were just talking."

His lips curl into a sneer. "Sure you were." He lifts the two glasses. "I've always believed you were different than other girls, but maybe I was wrong. When you don't get what you want from me, you run straight to him and try to rub my nose in it."

My anger flares up again. How dare he insinuate I'm using Ayden to make him jealous or that I could simply substitute one for the other. How dare he dismiss my feelings for him so flippantly. Before I can utter a word in my defense, my remaining best friend cuts in.

"You are way out of line, dude." Ayden shakes his head again. "I'm her friend. I'm trying to be yours too, but your head is so far up your ass you can't see it."

"Whatever. It's not like I care."

And with those awesome parting words he leaves the kitchen to bring the moms their wine.

Ayden sighs in exasperation. "I don't know what the hell to do with him."

"That makes two of us." I look down at the floor, not wanting to verbalize this but needing to at the same time. "I think you were right."

"I usually am." I hear the slight smirk in his tone. "But about what this time?"

My hair hangs around my face like drapes as I look up at him. "About our friendship." I trace the edge of my tattoo. "Nothing is permanent, and everything changes even when you don't want it to."

$$\infty \; \infty \; \infty$$

"I want to go to the party," I proclaim a few hours later. The oldies are in the sitting room still drinking wine and chatting. Ayden's sisters are in their bedrooms, and Devin and Lucas left after dinner. Ayden and I have been sitting in the den, casually scrolling through the TV channels. We've both been in a funk since the kitchen showdown with Devin.

"He'll probably be there."

"I know." He's the main reason I want to attend. Now that my initial anger has faded, guilt is doing a number on me. I didn't mean for him to think I was flirting with Ayden on purpose, and now that I've had time to think over what he said, I'm not feeling as hurt as I was before. Don't get me wrong; I still don't understand it, and the hurt won't fade anytime soon, but I do believe him when he said he cares about me. I can't compel Devin to act a certain way, and if he wants to deny the attraction between us, I can't make him change his mind.

If it means losing him as a friend, then I'll willingly endure the heartache to keep him in my life. I'll find a way of mending things with him, and repairing my punctured heart, starting with an explanation. "I need to fix things with him."

Ayden opens and closes his mouth in quick succession. He drums his fingers off his knee and then exhales noisily. "Okay. Let's go. I could do with getting out of here."

In the bathroom, I slick some more lip gloss on my lips, dab some powder on my shiny nose, and run my fingers through my hair, while Ayden goes to update our parents.

I run to my house to grab my coat and scarf while Ayden starts up the Jeep. I blow circles in the frigid air as I walk briskly to his car. "Brrr." Rubbing my gloved hands together, I plonk my butt on the passenger seat. "It's freezing out."

"I know. The windshield is already frosting over. I think it might snow."

He drives slowly and carefully on the icy roads. Cars line both sides of the street outside Zach's house, and the *thump, thump* of music greets my ears as we climb out of the Jeep. I strip off my cardigan, smoothing my top down, exposing more cleavage than normal. Ayden cusses under his breath. "Jesus, Lina. I can't let you go in there like that. They'll eat you alive."

I waggle my brows, dumping my cardigan on the seat and shucking into my coat before I get frostbite. "They can try."

Ayden rolls his eyes, taking my hand and leading me toward the house. Zach is one of Ayden's football buddies, and his parents always go out of town on Thanksgiving, giving him and his older brother free rein to throw parties. Although this is my first time attending, I've heard tales from previous years—Zach's Thanksgiving parties are legendary.

A few people from school are outside smoking, and they all tip their head at Ayden as he holds my elbow and ushers me into the house. I'm hit by a wall of heat, smoke, and pungent smells as we step inside. I unbutton my coat and remove the scarf from my neck, fanning my face with my hands. A few of Ayden's teammates high-five him as we pass. "This way," he says, steering me toward the back of the house.

"Ange!" Mariah screams my name across the kitchen, enthusiastically waving her hands in the air. A grin graces my lips as I cross to her. "You made it." She grabs me into a hug.

"Hey, man." Cody greets Ayden with a slap on the back, handing him a beer.

"Nah, I'm good. I'm driving." He grabs a soda out of the ice bucket instead, popping the lid.

I shuck out of my coat, folding it in a pile and placing it on the windowsill. "I'll take it." I have my greedy hand out before Cody can whip the beer away.

Ayden frowns a little but wisely says nothing. We chat as we sip our drinks, watching a few idiots out in the back garden trying, unsuccessfully, to light a bonfire. I surreptitiously scan the kitchen, but there's no sign of Devin. Maybe he didn't come after all.

After a bit, Mariah links her arm through mine. "Let's dance."

She drags me out to the main living room, pushing her way into the middle of the thrusting crowd. I've a nice buzz from the beer, my limbs are already loose, and I never need much persuasion to dance anyway. We dance for a few songs, and then I need the bathroom. "I'll come with," Mariah hollers in my ear, and we shove our way through the crowd. The downstairs bathroom is locked, and there's already a line, so we traipse upstairs, standing behind a few girls already waiting. I dab a hand across my damp brow and lift the hem of my top, flapping it up and down in a desperate attempt to cool off.

"Girl, you're on fire tonight." Mariah smiles, knocking my elbow. "Did you see all the dudes checking you out on the dance floor?"

"Nope." Truth. I get lost in the music and the sway of my body when I dance, and everything else fades into the background.

"You're so clueless." She rolls her eyes. "What am I going to do with you?"

"Get the fuck out!" a familiar male voice roars from somewhere behind me, and my head whips around.

"Sorry!" Two girls squeal, clamping hands over their mouths, as they quickly close one of the bedroom doors. They start giggling. "She's such a lucky bitch," the dark-haired girl says, and while I don't know her name, I recognize her from the cheerleading squad.

The blonde bobs her head, agreeing. "Becky played it perfectly. She knew he'd come around."

An icy chill creeps up my spine as her words register, and I'm no longer hot. Bile rises in my throat, and I take a step forward.

"Don't." Mariah's warning is soft and low.

"I need to see this for myself." With blood thrumming in my ears, and my heart jackknifing in my chest, I walk toward the bedroom. The two girls convulse with laughter as they pass me, sending amused looks in my direction.

My palms are sweaty as my hand curls around the door handle. Mariah tugs on my elbow, beseeching me with her eyes. "You won't ever be able to un-see what you're about to see."

"I know."

But I'm still doing this.

I gulp over the acidic taste in my mouth. Adrenaline courses through my veins, and butterflies have taken up residence in my stomach. My limbs are almost visibly trembling as I open the door.

I make no sound, even though I'm dying inside. Devin is nude, flat on his back, on the large bed, and a naked blonde is on top of him, riding him energetically like she's on a bucking bronco. I'm rooted to the spot, unable to tear my eyes away even though I already want to erase the image from my mind. Devin grabs her hips, grunting as he urges her to move faster, completely oblivious to my presence.

Nothing new there.

Nausea swims up my throat, and I think I might be sick. Becky turns around, still bouncing up and down on him, grinning manically when she sees me. "Here for some tips, Mary?" She winks, reaching behind her and cupping Devin as she continues to ride him.

His eyes blink open, and he notices us for the first time. "What the fuck?" His words are slurred, his gaze unfocused.

A tear trickles down my cheek as unrestrained heartache plugs every empty space inside me. "How could you do this?"

"Not everything revolves around you, Ange," he snarls, lifting Becky off him and depositing her on the bed beside him. She starts mouthing off, but he glares at her and she clams up, tugging the covers up under her arms. I want to avert my eyes, not to look at the sight of the love of my life naked beside my archenemy, but it's like my eyes are superglued to his. I can't look anywhere but at him. He wraps a hand around his erection, stroking up and down. "Liking what you see, Ange?" He winks, and my mouth floods with bile.

"You make me sick."

He snorts, continuing to stroke himself as his gaze lands on my chest. "Showing a lot of skin there, baby doll." He slurs his words. "Was that for my benefit or *Ayden's*?" He spits the word out like it physically hurts him to say it.

"Screw you, asshole."

He laughs again, and my hands clench into fists at my side. Sounds of voices behind me draw my attention to the growing crowd. Devin notices too, finally dragging a sheet over himself. He sits up straighter in the bed. "Now, now. Don't be so flippant, not when we both know how much you want that. You're just pissed because I turned you down."

Becky bursts out laughing, and a few titters erupt from the crowd at my back. My cheeks inflame.

Mariah tugs on my elbow. "We're leaving," she whispers furiously, glowering at Devin.

"What happened to you?" I shake my head. "I don't even know you at all."

His face contorts, and he sneers at me. "Know me as in the biblical sense?" He smirks. "No…you're right. You don't know me in that way, and you never will. Girls like you don't know how to please guys like me. Unlike"—he frowns, pausing for a second as he drunkenly stares at Becky—"uh, Becky here." She shoots him a withering look as he slings his arm around her neck, smacking a loud kiss off her cheek. "Becky knows how to fuck like a porn star, and I don't get any of the grief. You, on the other hand, are all about feelings and hearts and love and shit. Kill me fucking now. Couldn't you just be happy with the orgasm I gave you?

Nah, you had to whine and moan and beg for more." The crowd erupts in laughter, and more tears slide silently down my face.

It's that exact moment when my heart ruptures in my chest. I can almost physically feel it. The splintering and cracking, the breaking apart of my heart and my soul. The death of something vital inside me.

Strong arms wrap around my waist, and I'm lifted from behind. "Let's not do this here," Ayden says calmly, tucking me under his arm. He levels a vicious look at Devin. "We're done. And if you ever go near Lina again, I will personally beat you to within an inch of your life."

"Fuck you, douche." Devin flips Ayden the bird as Becky nestles into his side, cooing and smiling like the cat that got the cream.

Ayden shields me protectively as we make our way out of the house. He settles me in the car first, buckling my belt, and staring at me with wide-eyed concern. I'm rocking back and forth in the seat when he cranks up the engine.

The sobs start in earnest the second he pulls away from Zach's house, and once the dam is breached, there's no stopping it.

CHAPTER TEN

I'm still sobbing when we arrive back home. The lights are out in both our houses, so Ayden parks in my driveway and carries me to the front door. My face is buried in his neck as I cry.

"I know you're upset, Lina, but you're gonna wake your mom, and I know you don't want that," he whispers.

I sniffle, swiping at the hot tears coursing down my cheeks. Wrapping my arms around his neck, I cling to him as I attempt to stifle my cries. We enter the house and he closes the door carefully while keeping one arm underneath me, holding me up. Silently, we go to my room, and he places me on the bed, stroking my face with immense tenderness. "Do you want me to stay or go?"

"Stay," I sniffle. "Please." I turn my back to him, yanking my clothes off and tossing them on the ground. I scrape my hair back off my face and tie it into a messy ponytail before sliding under the covers in my undies. I don't even have the energy to pull on my pajamas, let alone wash my face free of makeup. Ayden has stripped down to his boxer briefs, and he climbs in beside me.

We face one another, on our sides, and he reaches out, twining our hands. "He's an asshole, Lina, but I know he cares about you. That wasn't him speaking tonight. He was wasted."

"Don't make excuses for him."

"I'm not. It doesn't excuse his behavior, and I'm not saying it for his benefit. I'm saying it for yours because I've never seen you look so distraught, and I know how much he means to you. I … I know you love him." His face contorts unpleasantly.

"I don't want to love him if that counts for anything." Truth. In this moment, I would give anything to have my heart belong to *anyone* but Devin.

"In his own way, he loves you too."

I wrench my hands from his, massaging my temples. "Stop. I don't want to hear it. You don't treat the people you love like that, no matter how messed up you are."

Ayden sighs. "I will never forgive him for what he did tonight, never, but he doesn't know how to love, Lina. That's not what he's grown up with. Your mom would burn the world down to protect you, and my parents have sacrificed so much for me and my sisters, but Devin has no experience of that."

"I know that, but he had us. We loved him, but I guess we weren't enough."

His tongue darts out, wetting his lips. "I need to know exactly what he did. I heard the tail end of what he said to you tonight, and I've had my suspicions about what happened between you two recently, but I'd really rather hear it from you."

I tell him, holding nothing back, even though I know it might hurt him to hear it, but I refuse to keep secrets from him any longer. I've already lost one of my best friends, and I don't want to risk losing the other by not being completely truthful. He listens without interruption, rubbing soothing circles on the backs of my hands while I talk.

"I'm going to fucking kill him," he seethes when I finally finish speaking.

"I don't want you to. I just want to forget. To put it all behind me and move on."

"I meant what I said earlier. I'm done with him. If he wants to push that self-destruct button, he's on his own."

"I don't want you to pick sides."

"The lines are already drawn, Lina, and this day has been sneaking up on us for some time. I can't be around him. I can't watch while he ruins his fucking life and tries to ruin yours. Enough is enough. We need to cut him loose."

I know Ayden is right, and after the way he humiliated me tonight, there is no way I can be friends with Devin anymore, but the thought alone almost kills me. Caustic pain is ripping my insides to shreds, and sobs rumble from my chest again. Ayden doesn't hesitate, pulling me into his warm, strong arms and cradling me to him. I circle my arms around his waist, and snuggle in closer. His scent and his body heat soothes the frayed edges of my broken heart. After a bit, I look up at him. "Thank you for always being there for me. For always being my friend." I cup his face. "I love you, Ayden."

"I love you too, Lina." He kisses the top of my head. "I've always loved you, and I'll continue to love you for as long as you'll let me."

Resting my head on his chest, I close my eyes, grateful to not be alone.

A soft thud, followed by less-than-subtle cursing, wakes me a few hours later. A blanket of dread washes over me as my eyes dart to the double doors. Ayden sits bolt upright in the bed, rubbing his eyes. I glance nervously at my bedroom door, terrified Mom is going to come barging in and freak out at the sight of Ayden in my bed and Devin with his drunken face smashed against the glass doors. Ayden snarls the instant the shadowy form on my balcony starts hammering on the glass.

"Quick, make him go away before my mom wakes."

Ayden flings the covers off and stalks across the floor in his boxers. He yanks the doors open and Devin stumbles, almost falling into the room. I get up, grabbing Ayden's checkered shirt off the floor and slipping my arms through it. Ayden is holding Devin upright by the shoulders, glaring at him. The smell of whiskey slaps me in the face, and my stomach twists sourly.

"Get out of here," Ayden whispers. "She doesn't want to see you."

Devin looks over Ayden's shoulder, attempting to eyeball me, but his eyes are rolling in his head. He's still completely wasted, and I shudder to think how he got home. "Ange, I'm so sorry." His words are slurred, and it'd be funny if it wasn't so heartbreaking.

"I don't want your apologies. I want you to leave." I fold my arms over my chest, looking off to the side. If I look at him all drunk, vulnerable, and apologetic, I may cave, and I can't cave.

Not this time.

"I didn't mean it. I was drunk and high."

I snort. "You didn't mean it, so, what, that makes it okay?"

He pushes Ayden's hands away, staggering a little on his feet. Gripping the side of the door, he leans against it, and it pains me to see him in such a state. "It's not okay. I know that. But I'll fix it. I'll make it up to you."

"I don't see how. It's not like you can un-fuck my enemy." All the hurt and pain pours out of me. "It would've been bad enough seeing you like that with any girl, but Becky Carmichael? Seriously? You expect me to believe you didn't mean it when you fucked her? Don't make things worse by lying. This was totally premeditated to inflict the worst pain imaginable." I push my face in his, anger turning the whites of my eyes red. "Well, mission accomplished, Devin. You have totally shattered my heart. I hope you're proud."

"Please, Ange. I didn't know it was her. I swear."

"What, your dick just happened to impale Becky by accident? Don't insult my intelligence."

He reaches for me, pain etched across his face. "I can't lose you. Not you, Ange."

"Too late. You should've thought about that before you rejected me and publicly humiliated me with that slut."

He drops to his knees, clutching my bare legs. "I'll tell everyone I was drunk and that I didn't mean it, and I'll have nothing more to do with Becky. Please, Ange. Please forgive me. I'm begging. I'll do anything." He trails his mouth along my legs, causing goose bumps to raise along my flesh.

I can feel my resolve wavering, but I don't want it too. I've always forgiven Devin way too easily, but I can't do it this time. This time he has gone too far. "Stop, Dev. Just stop. I want you to leave."

He looks up at me with bloodshot glassy eyes. "Please, Ange. Don't shut me out. I need you."

I beseech Ayden with my eyes. I can't fold, and I'm too afraid that I'm going to. I need his strength to help me do the right thing. "That's enough," Ayden says, cutting in. He grabs Devin by the shoulders, yanking him off me. Devin drops to his butt, pulling his knees up to his chest. Ayden wraps his arm around my waist from behind, and the movement pushes the open shirt wider, exposing my undies. I clutch onto his forearms, and the feel of his skin under my fingertips and his body pressed against mine reinforces my determination.

Devin's eyes narrow and his nostrils flare as his gaze jumps from Ayden to me and back again. He staggers to his feet, sneering as he straightens up.

He glares at me, his eyes trailing up and down my body, noticing Ayden's shirt and our joint state of undress. "You fucked him?"

"What? No! I…"

He stalks toward me, and Ayden pulls me tighter to his body. "You gave *him* your virginity?"

My cheeks flare up. "Screw you! Whether I did or didn't is none of your business. I said get the hell out and I meant it."

"I bet you're loving this." Dev glowers at Ayden.

"There isn't any part of this I'm loving, and I don't want to beat your ass, but I will if you don't leave. You've done enough damage. Just go."

Dev throws his leather jacket on the floor, flexing his fists. "Make me." He moves into a fighting stance.

Ayden steps in front of me, gently nudging me back. "Stay out of this." He cricks his neck, and his hands ball into fists.

I jump in between them, slamming a hand into each of their chests. "Stop. No fighting."

"It's too late for that," Dev says. "Step aside, Ange. This is between me and Ayd now."

"The hell I will." I cross my arms and glare at him. Superfast—especially in his inebriated state—he lifts me up, throwing me over his shoulder and dumping me on the bed. Then Ayden charges him, and they go down, wrestling on the floor. They throw punches at one another, and I wince as flesh impacts flesh, bone crunches, and blood starts flying. I sit cross-legged on the bed, in a sort of daze. When we were kids, Ayden and Devin were always play fighting, and as I watch them throw savage anger-driven punches at one another, I wonder how the hell we got to this place, hating how far we've fallen. Still, I can't make my body move to put a stop to this, so I sit there, morbidly fascinated as they beat the living crap out of one another.

They roll around the floor, crashing into my bedside table, knocking the contents over. Still, they don't stop, lashing out with their fists, grunting and groaning as they release months of pent-up frustration.

Ayden is heavier and broader than Devin, but Dev is the one skilled with his fists, and it doesn't take much for him to gain the upper hand. He sits on top of Ayden, holding him down with his thighs as he rains blows on his face. Ayden's head flips from side to side with each successive punch, and he raises his arm to try to shove Devin off. Devin presses down on his arm, slamming it to the floor, repeatedly smashing his fist into the bone. Ayden lets out an almighty roar as a ripping, creaking sound reverberates around the room. That breaks me out of my daze, and I jump up at the same time Mom comes running into the room.

"Jesus Christ! Boys! Stop it!" She grabs Devin by the shoulders and hauls him off Ayden.

I race to Ayden as he rolls on his side, clutching his arm and wailing. "Oh my God, Ayd. Are you okay?"

"Ambulance," he moans, cradling his arm to his chest. "My arm."

I kiss his cheek, smoothing hair back off his bloody, bruised face, before I hop up and grab my purse, rummaging for my cell. I punch the buttons with trembling fingers.

Mom holds Devin back, glancing at Ayden with a horror-struck look. "What did you do?" she whispers, shock layering her tone.

Devin shucks out of her embrace, dropping to his knees beside Ayden. I talk to the operator, watching as tears spill down his cheeks.

"I'm sorry, Ayden. I'm so sorry."

I end the call and stomp to Devin's side. "I want you out of my house. Right now. That's his throwing arm and I think you've just broken it." Mom is crouched by Ayden's side, gently examining his arm with a worried expression.

The look of remorse on Devin's face is genuine, but I'm too mad to care. "You ruin everything, Devin, and I can't do this anymore." I yank him up by his shirt. "Get out of my house, and get out of my life."

He opens his mouth to offer more empty apologies and false promises, no doubt, but I shake my head. "There is nothing left to be said. I don't want to see you anymore. From now on, you are dead to me."

CHAPTER ELEVEN

Devin

I'm standing in our decrepit bathroom, under the dim light, naked from the waist up, washing the blood from my skin, and wondering how I've sunk so low. That night in Ange's bedroom replays in my mind, like it has fifty thousand other times since it happened.

I didn't want it to happen. Didn't mean for it to happen.

Not like that.

I fucking freaked. Lost my control and gave into my all-consuming need for her, but it wasn't the right time. I wasn't supposed to make my move until I was worthy of her, until it was safe to declare my feelings, but, damn, the way she looked at me that night—like she wanted to eat me alive—blasted every logical thought straight out of my head.

No one has ever looked at me like that—with a combination of lust, love, and adoration—and it was like being struck by a bolt of lightning, a blast of pure goodness straight through my darkened heart. I've always suspected she returned my feelings, but I didn't know for sure, not until recently, because she's usually so cagey around me, purposely hiding her true feelings for fear of messing up what the three of us have, I guess. But she lost the battle that night, and the love and longing in her eyes tore down my barricade, and I was helpless to resist.

One taste. One touch. I told myself it was okay to be selfish one time and then I'd try my best to explain it without ruining the promise of forever. Thank God, she mentioned the bruise. It was the reminder I needed. If she hadn't, I would have taken her, and it would've been so much harder to walk away.

I want to tell her how much she means to me—how I love her dangerously, compulsively, addictively, more than it feels normal to love another person. I want to promise her I'll be hers when the time is right, because she deserves the entire world and I'm not able to give that to her yet.

But I fucked up again. Because I should've talked to her the very next day, instead of chickening out of it, going to extremes to avoid her. Fact is, I was shitting myself. Terrified I was too weak to resist and not strong enough to do what needed to be done. I thought there'd be time, but there wasn't. There isn't.

I'm all out of time, and I've no one to blame but myself.

I destroyed everything tonight, and I'll be lucky if she ever speaks to me again. Not only that, but I've isolated Ayden too. He'll never forgive me if I've ruined his football career, and I won't be able to live with myself if I've taken his future.

I grip the edge of the sink and look away from the mirror, sickened at the sight of myself. A tornado of emotion is choking me from the inside out. I slump to the floor, burying my head in my hands. *What the fuck have I done?*

I know Ayden won't ever forgive me for the way I treated Ange. Hell, I'll never forgive myself.

She wasn't supposed to be there. She hardly ever goes to parties, and Ayd's not overly fond of them either. This is totally not their scene. *Why the fuck were they there?* I lie on my side, dragging my hands through my hair. Shit, shit, shit. *What the hell am I going to do?*

I shouldn't have gone partying last night. Not when my emotions were brewing in a whirlwind of my own making. Watching Ayden and Ange whisper sweet nothings to one another across the table, during Thanksgiving dinner, when *everyone* was watching, broke something inside me. I don't know if she did it on purpose to hurt me back, or if she genuinely loves him too, or if I simply pushed her into his arms with my rejection, but the futility and helplessness needed an outlet, and I found myself in my truck, driving to Zach's without making any conscious decision to go there.

I lost all semblance of reality after my tenth beer and my third joint. When Becky approached me, I honestly had no idea who she was. My vision was hazy, my brain whacked, and I could hardly stand up straight. All I knew was I needed to lose myself in a warm body. To fuck the recklessness out of my mind. If I'd known who she was, I never would've gone there. Not in a million years. She's tried to get her claws in me for years, and I've grown adept at rejecting her advances. I've always known I was a challenge she wanted to conquer purely to mess with Ange's head.

Tonight, I fucked up spectacularly, and I'm terrified there's no coming back from it. Although I've spent years purposely staying away from Ange, I don't know if I can do it anymore. I'm tired of fighting my feelings for her, even if I know it has to be like this.

Maybe, in some warped way, what happened tonight was for the best.

Where I fail, I think she'll succeed. I saw the look on her face when she told me I was dead to her. If I'm not strong enough to stay away, I think she's strong enough to keep me at arm's length.

That should make me happy because it'll ensure she's safe.

But it feels like I've died. Like the only part of myself that was good, the part that existed purely for her, has flittered away like dust in the wind, and now all I'm left with is ugliness and an empty void in the place where my heart should be.

It's nothing less than I deserve. I hate myself for what I did tonight, and it'll be a cold day in hell before I find any peace, let alone forgiveness.

I cringe as I recall the shit that came out of my mouth. And we had an audience. It's bad enough that Becky heard me spewing all that crap, but half our senior class did too. I dishonored Ange, and I'll never be able to take that back. All because I was pissed and hurting and drunk and confused. I lashed out at the one person who has always been my savior. My guardian angel. My greatest defender. My staunchest supporter.

The girl I have loved from the time I understood what that word meant.

I have hurt her beyond comprehension, and the devastated look in her eyes will stay with me forever. I might as well have reached inside and torn her heart clear from her chest. A sharp ache slays me on the inside, and I curl into a ball as a tear slips out of my eye.

Why did I do it?

I try to imagine what it'd be like to walk in on some blockhead fucking Ange senseless, and whatever semblance of control I have left explodes as rage and jealousy pummel my insides. I've no Goddamned right to feel like this, and if it's even a glimpse of what she's feeling right now, then I know there's no coming back from this.

I've ruined us.

I always knew this was coming.

That the time would come when she had to pick one of us, because I know Ayden's in love with her too. Not that he's ever admitted it to me, but I know that's why he's been so secretive lately.

I'd been a cocky jerk. Believing it would be me. But tonight, I've sealed my fate. She'll run straight into his arms, and I'll have sent her there.

I've lost my two best friends and the love of my life, and I can't blame anyone but myself.

I deserve the world of pain coming my way. I deserve to rot in a cesspit of unhappiness for the rest of my life for ruining the most perfect girl to ever grace the planet.

I deserve to lose her love and respect. To lose their friendship.

I deserve it all.

Dad is right.

I am a useless piece of shit and I'll amount to nothing.

I'm garbage, and they're better off without me anyway.

Ayden

I always thought my feelings would be the sword to come between us. Never in a million years did I think Devin would be the one to destroy our bond. That his inability to keep it in his pants would end our story in such a sordid way. Devin's desire to plant his seed in every vagina within a ten-mile radius has ripped our friendship apart. I thought we were stronger than that, but we're not.

I will never forgive him.

Never.

All he had to do was stay away from her. He promised me he would. But he couldn't even do that much for her, for me.

Who does that? What kind of friend could do that to another friend?

My arm throbs, and I cradle it to my chest, still struggling to accept the fact Devin did this to me. I know I got a few good punches in too, but I would never have let it get so far. I would have stopped myself. I saw the look in his eyes as he lashed out, and the desire to inflict pain was written all over his face. In that moment, he hated me, truly hated me, and I doubt he could have stopped himself even if he wanted to.

That thought sticks in my gut.

My feelings when it comes to Devin right now are a clusterfuck of epic proportions.

But I know what I need to do.

I need to stay away from him. Lina needs to stay away from him. We'll cut him loose, and he can bury himself in pussy and booze to his heart's content.

He's written the end of our story, and there's no happy epilogue. He's made his choice, and he'll have to deal with the consequences because he's out of our lives.

I'm going to erase him as if he never existed.

CHAPTER TWELVE

Angelina

I hold Ayden's hand in the ambulance on the way to the hospital. We don't talk, but no words are necessary. When they take him away to x-ray his arm, I pace the hallways, praying it's not broken.

Ayden's parents are inconsolable and too upset to look for answers right now, which I'm grateful for because I don't know how to explain it to them. But Mom isn't so easily deflected. "We're going on a coffee run," she says to the Carters. "We'll bring you back some." Gently taking my arm, she steers me down the corridor to the elevator. She doesn't say a word until we're seated in the small coffee station downstairs, nursing steaming-hot coffee. I take a sip, grimacing at the bitter taste. This stuff would put hairs on your chest.

"I know you're upset about Ayden, but I need to know what that fight was about and why both those boys were in your room in the middle of the night."

"Please, Mom." My tone is pleading. "It's six a.m. and I'm exhausted. Can't we do this later?"

She smiles over my head, waving at two nurses who pass by. "The Carters will need answers, and I don't want to lie to them." Stretching across the table, she takes my hand. "You can tell me anything, honey. You know that. You have nothing to fear from telling the truth."

I sigh, rubbing my tired face. "You know I tell you most things, Mom, but I haven't told you everything."

"Sometimes moms just know." I arch a brow, and she squeezes my hand, smiling softly. "If this is about you loving Devin, I already know. I've always known."

Tears threaten to surface again. "It doesn't matter, because he doesn't love me back and he's humiliated me in front of most of our class, and now he might have ruined Ayden's football career, and I don't think I even know him anymore. Devin's ruined everything, and I feel so sick." A sob travels up my throat, and I force myself to take deep breaths, to calm down. I don't want to lose it in the cafeteria of Mom's workplace and embarrass her or myself.

She gets up, moving around the table, and sits down beside me. "Tell me what happened, sweetheart. It'll help to talk about it."

It flows out of me like a river, and Mom pats my arm as I fill her in, leaving nothing out. I rest my head on her shoulder when I'm finished, thoroughly emotionally and physically drained.

She kisses my forehead. "I'm sorry that happened to you, sweetheart, and I'm sure Devin feels terrible too."

"Good. He deserves it."

She brushes hair back out of my face. "I know you don't really mean that, but I understand, and your feelings are completely normal. I'm angry that he's hurt you, and hurt Ayden, but that boy has been hurting for years. It doesn't excuse his actions, and although I've tried to help where I can, it's no substitute for a loving home. I'm sure he didn't mean to deliberately hurt either of you. You and Ayden mean the world to him."

"Not anymore."

"You'll figure this out."

I sniffle. "I already have, Mom. I can't be his friend. Not after this. He's the one who told me I'm always too quick to forgive, and he's right. I can't forgive him this."

"You might feel differently in time."

I twist around, staring at her in confusion. "Mom, I just told you he rejected me, screwed my archnemesis, and then drunkenly embarrassed me in front of everyone, yet you sound like a fully paid-up member of his fan club. What gives?"

She cups my face gently. "I hate that he's done that to you, and I'll bet he hates himself for it too, but it doesn't change who he is. Devin is a good kid struggling in a shitty world. He's lost but he'll find his way back to you. And you have a massive heart and the capacity to handle this. You'll forgive him."

I shake my head, anger resurfacing. "Mom, didn't you hear what I said? He doesn't want me. He doesn't love me! He'd rather screw that skank bag than call me his friend."

"Sweetheart, that boy has been in love with you as long as you've been in love with him. If he's pushing you away, he's doing it to protect you, and I can't hate Devin for caring about my little girl that much, no matter how poorly he went about it."

Devin's words from a few weeks ago drift through my mind, but I dismiss them, too angry and hurt to believe he meant it. I frown, scratching the back of my head. "You're nuts. Like seriously, I'm kinda freaking out because this is not normal, Mom."

She chuckles. "I consider that a good thing."

I roll my eyes. "But you're always sending Ayden and me googly eyes. I really don't get it."

"Ayden will be your friend for life, honey, and I love how well he takes care of you."

"But that day when he was on the porch with the lilies, and we were in the car, you said—"

"That Ayden loves you too? I know he does, but love comes in many guises, and you can love more than one person at a time."

"I feel like I've stepped into some warped alternate realm or like some alien being has invaded my mom's body because this conversation is so surreal."

She chuckles again. "You're young, honey, and I know you feel things intensely, but emotions change, priorities shift, and people wander in and out of your life. I know it probably feels like the end of the world, but everything will right itself. I still remember how terrified I was when I finally plucked up the courage to confront your father about his abuse, and the day the divorce was granted was the best and the worst day of my life. I was so scared that I wouldn't be able to take care of you by myself, but time is a great healer, and when you reach your lowest point, you find inner strength you never realized you had. The best piece of advice I can give you is not to make any rash decisions. Let things settle before deciding what to do. Right now, you're hurting, and understandably so, but things might look different in a few days or a few weeks. Don't cut Devin out of your life until you're sure it's what you want to do, but if it is, then I'll support your decision. I care about both those boys, and Lucas too, but you're my daughter, and you'll always come first."

As we walk back to the ward, I'm mulling over Mom's words of wisdom, thinking how lucky I am to have won the mother jackpot. Everything else may be turning to crap in my life, but she's the one true constant I can always rely upon.

And that thought temporarily papers over the fissures in my heart.

CHAPTER THIRTEEN

Ayden's arm is broken, and he's in a cast from his hand to just above his elbow. The doctor suggested he take a few days off school, but he's way too stubborn to succumb to expert medical advice, so, when he turns up at my door bright and early on Monday morning, I can't say I'm surprised. A familiar smile lights up his face. "Why are you so cheery?" I ask in a puzzled tone, shoveling another spoonful of cereal in my mouth.

"Your gorgeous face always puts a smile on mine."

His lips twitch, and I stick my tongue out at him, but his words help thaw out my frozen heart. "You don't have to do this for me," I tell him, walking to the sink to rinse out my bowl.

"I'm not leaving you to face the fallout on your own." I expect he'd cross his arms and attempt to stare me out of it if he was capable of the maneuver.

I put my bowl and spoon in the dishwasher, closing it with my hip. "I won't be alone. The girls have my back." Yesterday, Mariah, Madisyn, and Gabrielle all rallied around, dropping by to assure me they'll support me in dealing with all the crap coming my way. Mariah is fit to kill Devin, but we've agreed that the best course of action is to ignore him and Becky. Easier said than done though.

With his good arm, Ayden grabs my waist, pulling me to him as I attempt to pass. He presses a kiss to the top of my head. "And I'm glad they are there for you, but I want to be too."

Tears sting my eyes, and I inwardly curse. The last thing I want to do today is turn all teary-eyed and give Becky and her minions more ammunition. "You should be resting."

"I can rest after school. I'm going to have tons of free time on my hands now I can't train."

"What did Coach say?" I saw his car parked outside the Carters yesterday, and it doesn't require much brainpower to figure out the topic of conversation.

He shrugs. "Not a lot he can say. Obviously, he's upset and concerned, but the season's just about over, and it's, hopefully, only a temporary setback." He slouches against the counter, smiling at me.

I frown a little, eyeing him curiously. "You're taking this remarkably well."

He shrugs again. "Stressing out about it isn't going to change anything. Anyway, Dad's doing enough of that for the both of us."

I cringe, recalling his dad's angry tirade the morning we returned from the hospital. Words like "good for nothing" and "chip off the old block" were bandied about. "Does he still want to press charges against him?" I can't even say Devin's name out loud without it causing enormous pain. Mom said to give it time, that it won't hurt as much, but, so far, the pain hasn't eased at all.

"Mom talked him down, but he's banned Devin from the house. Not that it matters, because I want nothing to do with him anyway."

I nod over the painful lump in my throat, not wanting to get into it again. "Let's get out of here. Might as well get this over and done with."

Heated words are exchanged when Ayden tries to take my book bag as we leave the house. "You're freaking injured, and I can carry my own bag."

"I've still got one good arm," he protests, raising his uninjured arm in demonstration. "And I'm not an invalid."

I roll my eyes as I throw my bag in the Jeep, rounding the driver side. "I know you aren't, but it's time you let me look after you, and don't even attempt to argue with me because we both know you need to do what you're told and not jeopardize your recovery."

I swing myself up into the Jeep, adjusting the seat for my shorter legs. I run my hands over the steering wheel in awe, my temporary panic over the impending shit-storm in school forgotten in the excitement of getting to drive Ayden's Jeep around for weeks.

"I like looking after you," he huffs, buckling himself in. "And I hate not being able to drive my own Jeep or do other stuff for myself."

I lean over, patting his knee. "Poor baby." He pouts, and I laugh as I turn the key and crank the engine. "Just sit back, relax, and enjoy being treated like royalty."

He flips me the bird, and I roar laughing as I ease the Jeep out of the drive.

Anxiety returns with gusto the nearer we get to school, and I'm on the verge of a full-blown panic attack by the time I swing the Jeep into a vacant space in the school parking lot. My knee taps up and down, and my heart's beating ferociously in my chest.

"Relax, Lina." Ayden pivots in his seat, placing his hand on my knee, stalling the jerky motion. "It will be fine. Just remember, you're not at fault. You haven't done anything wrong."

I draw in a brave breath as I jump out of the truck. Ayden slides awkwardly out his side, slinging his bag over his good shoulder. When I round his side, he takes my hand in his, and we head into the building together. The sneaky looks, hushed whispers, and sly finger-pointing starts instantly, but I keep my chin up, doing my best to ignore it. Ayden's grasp on my fingers strengthens, and a muscle clenches in his jaw as we walk toward my locker. We round the corner, and I slam to a halt. Devin is sitting on the ground in front of my locker, with his knees bent. A small crowd has gathered in front of him, whispering and giggling as they wait for the show to commence.

Well, they can wait. I'm not going to give them anything else to gossip over.

"I can't believe his nerve," Ayden mumbles under his breath.

"Just ignore him. That's what I'm planning on doing," I whisper back.

The crowd grows quiet as we approach, drawing Devin's attention. He looks up and climbs to his feet. I open my locker without looking at him or the gossipmongers.

"Can I talk to you both in private?" Dev implores in a hushed tone.

I ignore him, pulling books haphazardly out of my locker and stuffing them in my bag. Ayden's good arm rests on my lower back, offering reassurance. He silently fumes, glaring at Devin.

"Please," Dev says.

His voice cracks a little, and damn, if it isn't hard to react to that, but I harden my heart in protection. "There is nothing you have to say I want to hear," I reply without looking at him. I slam my locker shut with more force than necessary, whirling around into Ayden's waiting embrace.

"And we don't need to put on another show. God knows they're still gossiping over the last one," Ayden growls under his breath.

"Well, when can we talk?" Dev persists.

Ayden looks to me for guidance, and I know he'll follow my lead. Encased in his protective arms, I risk a quick glance at Devin over my shoulder. He looks like death warmed up. His pale skin is bruised in several places, his lip is cut, and he looks like he hasn't slept or shaved in days. "I don't want to talk to you," I whisper. "Just leave me alone."

A grief-stricken look washes over his face. "Please, Ange. I know I fucked up, but please give me a chance to explain."

I shake my head as tears start to well in my eyes. "I can't. It hurts too much." Ayden tightens his hold on me, and I'm careful not to press into his injured arm as I snuggle in closer.

Devin hangs his head, his thick, dark hair falling in sleek waves over his forehead. "I'm so sorry."

"It's too little too late," Ayden adds. "If we ever meant anything to you, you'll stay away. It's what we both want."

The crowd is straining to hear our conversation, and judging by the unhappy frowns and confused scowls, I'd say we've disappointed them. News of Ayden and Devin's fight in my bedroom has spread like wildfire—according to Mariah—so no doubt everyone was hoping for round two to kick off this morning. Maybe now they'll leave us alone. Find something more salacious to gossip over.

"What about what I want?" Devin asks.

Ayden harrumphs. "Do you think either one of us is willing to put your needs over our own? You've left us no choice but to do this, and it's best for everyone." Ayden steers me away from Devin. "Just stay out of our way and we'll stay out of yours."

Except, as the days pass by, it's almost impossible. Where once I'd hardly see Devin in school, now he's everywhere. We pass each other in the corridor pretending we don't notice one another. He always seems to be at his locker, across the way, whenever I'm at mine. We arrive and leave the cafeteria within seconds of each other, as if we've planned it.

Where once I spent hours holed up in my bedroom, with my nose pressed to the window, hoping for a glimpse of him, now I can't avoid him. When I come out of my house each morning, he's climbing into his truck. When I get home after school, ballet, or work, he's arriving home at the same time. Turns out, ignoring your neighbor when you desperately want and need the space is a virtual impossibility.

And it's not that he's staging it. I know him well enough to know he wouldn't do that. While it's obvious by the covert glances he sends my way that he's hurting, and missing me as much as I miss him, he's respecting my wishes, *our* wishes, and steering clear.

The inevitable confrontation with Becky never materialized, but I'm not naïve enough to think she's letting it go. No, Becky is a strategist and she's taking her time, planning it meticulously to swoop in and strike at the most opportune moment. The longer she goes without acknowledging me, the more on edge I feel, and I hate that she's getting to me. Even the sight of her sours my stomach, and I can't get the vision of her naked rocking on top of Devin out of my head.

During week two of my post-Devin new life, Lucas decides to begin a none-too-subtle pro-Devin campaign. While I know he means well, his intervention is both unwelcome and in vain. "I've never seen him like this. Like I think he's clinically depressed," Lucas says as we're cleaning the kitchen after dinner on Wednesday night. Mom has already departed for her shift at the hospital.

"I don't want to talk about it."

"Come on, Ange. I know you don't mean that. I know you love him."

I glare at him, putting all my hurt, anger, and frustration behind it, even though it's unfair to take it out on the wrong Morgan brother. "I don't want anything to do with your brother, and that includes discussing him. Please, drop it."

"You haven't denied it. Go on, just admit it. You still love him."

His lips curve up, and except for the fact he's fourteen and clueless, I'd probably swing for him. Instead, I lose it, throwing my hands into the air. "What the hell do you want me to say, Lucas? Did I love him? Yes," I hiss, blood flowing angrily through my veins. "I loved him, and he rejected me and humiliated me and threw our entire history in my face, and it fucking killed me. You have no idea how much he hurt me, and not just for Becky. Imagine you had to watch the boy you love screw his way around town while barely giving you the time of day. Imagine you had to watch while he got into fights, got high and drunk, barely even knowing his own name. Imagine how many nights you stayed up sick with worry in case he drove his truck into a ditch. Then imagine you go to school and have to listen to every skank relay in minute detail what he's like in bed knowing you'll never get to experience it because he just doesn't think of you like that! That's what I've had to endure, and I can't take it anymore."

A strangled sob erupts from the very core of my soul, and I double over, clutching my stomach as hot tears slide down my cheeks. Damn Lucas for dragging all this to the surface again. I'm so sick of feeling like this, and I want it to stop.

He takes a step toward me, compassion and sorrow etched across his face. I hold up a hand to stall him. "I think you should go now, Lucas. I need to be alone."

"I'm sorry, Ange. I really am. He's an idiot, but if it's any consolation, he's miserable too."

"It isn't, and I meant what I said. I don't want to talk about your brother, and if you can't abide by my wishes, then we'll have to stop hanging out."

He nods his head sadly. "I hear you loud and clear. I won't bring him up again."

And, mercifully, he doesn't.

CHAPTER FOURTEEN

It's week three post-Devin, and the pain is still like a constant, knotty, twisty ache in my chest. My appetite has all but vanished, and I've actually lost weight. Madisyn is disgusted at how effortlessly I've shed the pounds, but I can't summon the energy to banter with her about it. Ayden and I spend practically every spare minute together. His dad is still frothing at the mouth over his arm and Devin, so he's avoiding his house like the plague and he spends most nights at mine. Mom gave me a stern talking to before leaving for work this evening. She has somehow found out he's sleeping in my bed most nights she's away, and she made it abundantly clear it's not to continue.

"Was she pissed?" Ayden asks, while we are sprawled on the couch watching *Gossip Girl*—I've converted him to the dark side as well. He keeps his injured arm propped on the arm of the couch as I snuggle into his other side.

"Mom doesn't get pissed, and she rarely raises her voice. You know that—she's the epitome of cool, calm, and collected." And I know it's because of the abuse she was subjected to while married to my dad. She doesn't ever want to lose control and lash out with her tongue or her fists, because then, in her mind, she's no better than him. "She just doesn't think it's a good idea with my emotions all over the place. I think she thinks we're going to screw each other's brains out and regret it or something."

Ayden stiffens imperceptibly underneath me, and I worry that I've just offended him.

"Anyone home?" Mariah calls out, staging an unplanned timely intervention.

"In here," I shout back and she comes bounding into the living room.

"Am I interrupting?" she asks with a saucy grin on her face.

"Don't be silly." I lift my head off Ayden's chest, pulling myself into a more respectable upright position. "We were just watching TV."

"Cody's out in the truck," she tells Ayden. "They're going over to Zach's to watch the game if you want to join them? He can drive you back and pick me up at the same time."

Ayden swings his muscular legs around, planting them on the floor. "I know when I'm not wanted," he grins, pushing to his feet.

I help him into his jacket, draping one side over his injured arm. Wrapping my arms around his neck, I kiss his cheek. "Have fun."

He messes up my hair. "With those guys? Hardly." He caresses my cheek. "Try to stay out of trouble."

I give him a gentle push, following him out to the door. "Idiot. Go! I'll see you later."

I grab a couple of sodas on my way through the kitchen, tossing one to Mariah as I throw myself back down on the couch.

"You two seem cozy." She toes off her shoes, bringing her feet up underneath her.

I shrug. "We've always been like that. You know Ayden's the touchy-feely type."

"Not according to Cassie. She said they barely even got to second base."

"They didn't date for that long, and Ayden's a gentleman so that doesn't surprise me."

"You know what I think?" Her warm hazel eyes glimmer with excitement.

I groan. "I don't think I want to know."

"He's in love with you, and he's just waiting for you to give him a signal, and then he'll make his move."

My mouth pulls in a grimace. "I don't see it. I mean, we've slept in the same bed at least three or four nights a week for the last few weeks, and he hasn't acted in any way inappropriately." His obvious daily morning stiffy doesn't count.

She rolls her eyes. "How are you this clueless? I'm seriously getting worried about you. Duh!" She slaps her palm into her forehead. "He's hardly going to move in for the kill when you're still all upset over Devin. Give the guy some credit."

I twist around on my side so I'm facing her. "Do you really think he's in love with me?"

She puts her soda down on the coffee table, pinning me with an earnest look. "Yes, I do. He worships you, Ange. He'd do anything for you, and he's been jumping to your defense constantly in school."

I flop down on my back, sighing. "I wish he wouldn't do that. I can fight my own battles." And I've been putting out plenty of fires on my lonesome, although the cutting remarks and titters seem to be dying down.

"I know that, and he knows that, but Ayden loves you, and he wants to protect you, and it's so romantic," she swoons with a dreamy look on her face. "But the million-dollar question is do you love him?"

Her question drives several emotions to the surface as I contemplate how to reply. Of course, I love Ayden. That's never been in any doubt, but do I love, *love*, him? *Is Mom right? Can you love more than one person at the same time? And have I been in love with him, too, but just didn't know it? Did my fixation with Devin obscure my true feelings for Ayden?* All I know with certainty is that I brighten up when he arrives, and he's the one person who is guaranteed to bring a smile to my face on even the darkest of days. I've come to rely on the warmth of his arms and the safety of his embrace and the tender way he cares for me. He is loyal and protective, and he never lets me down. Yes, my heart doesn't spike to coronary-inducing proportions when he touches me or looks at me adoringly like it does with Devin, but that doesn't mean I don't love him.

"I—"

"Ange." Devin cuts me off before I can finish my sentence, and I jump up, startled, my heart beating ninety miles an hour.

Mariah spits her soda all over the carpet. "Holy fuck, Devin. Don't creep up on people like that!" she splutters, hastily wiping her wet mouth. Devin is standing awkwardly in the doorframe, holding a hand-wrapped package in his hand. "I'll get a towel to clean the floor." She hastily brushes past him, shooting me a "what the hell" look as she goes.

I stand up, facing him, my heart skipping. "Why are you here, and how long were you standing there?"

His tongue darts out, moistening his lips, and I hate how my eyes involuntarily follow the movement. "I have something for you, and, eh, not long." He scratches the back of his head, quickly averting his eyes.

Liar. He heard what Mariah asked me, and he interrupted before I could respond. "I don't want anything from you, and you need to leave."

He takes a step toward me, his eyes radiating pain. A fresh bruise darkens the skin on his cheek, and a blanket of sadness envelops me. I don't know if he had an official fight or if he got into it with some douche. I know nothing about his life now, and that thought upsets me so much. I hate that it's come to this but not enough to let him back in. That's only asking for trouble, and I'm in a world of pain as it is.

"I miss you so much, Ange. I can't bear this. Please, please give me another chance. I'm begging you. I'll do whatever you want me to do, but please don't shut me out."

His green eyes glisten with so much emotion, and although he looks tired and strained, he still looks unbelievably beautiful, and the urge to touch him hasn't dissipated in the slightest. My hands twitch involuntarily at my side. Pressure weighs on my chest like a ton of bricks. He may as well have a hand around my heart, squeezing it to nothing. "I miss you too, but it doesn't change anything."

It can't.

I can't continue to allow him to hurt me.

He hands me the package. It's wrapped in pale pink wrapping with tiny little hearts on it. I look from the package to him. "What is it?"

"It's a present for you." Before I can protest, he has placed it in my hands, curling my fingers around the edges. Blissful tremors zip up and down my arms from his touch, confirming what I already know.

I'm still attracted to him, still in love with him—I think I always will be.

I open my mouth to speak, but he covers my mouth with his fingers. "Don't say it. Just open the present and think about it, and if you still feel the same way, I'll keep my distance. I promise."

I nod, hating how tears are bubbling under the surface, just waiting for an opportunity to let loose. In an ultra-smooth movement, he reels me into his arms, resting his chin on my head. He sighs, and I close my eyes, tears trickling down my face. *Why does it feel so natural to be in his arms like this? Like his body was sculpted to fit perfectly against mine? Like his arms were carved to hold me in the exact right way?*

An image of Becky riding his cock surges to the forefront of my mind and I pull out of his embrace, confused, upset, and horrified all at once. "Why, Devin? Why her? Of all the girls, why did it have to be her?" I sob, and Mariah comes rushing into the room.

"You need to leave." Her tone is ice-cold. "Right now, or I'm calling Ayden."

His mouth pulls into a severe line. "I'm leaving." His eyes pin me in place, and they burn fiercely. "I don't know, and I wish I could undo it, but I can't, so all I can promise is to make it up to you. Open the present and, when you're ready, call me and we can talk." He turns around, and walks away, stopping abruptly in the doorframe. I'm clinging to Mariah's arm, tears streaming down my face. He looks over his shoulder, and his expression softens. "I know you probably don't believe this, but I hate that I've hurt you, and I'd give anything for a do-over." His chest visibly inflates, and tears pool in his eyes. He stares at me in that magnetic way of his, and the air changes, simmering with dark intensity. I lose the ability to breathe as our gazes remain locked on one another. Mariah and I are both momentarily frozen in place while we wait for him to speak. "Never forget, Ange." His voice is soft, reverential, sincere. "You promised."

Then he walks out, taking another piece of my heart with him.

CHAPTER FIFTEEN

"Good God," Mariah exclaims, holding a hand to her chest as I stand rooted to the spot. "That was crazy intense, and so freaking hot, and he wasn't even speaking to me. I need a drink."

"Excellent idea," I hear myself saying, watching in a daze as she crosses to Mom's liquor cabinet and swipes a bottle of vodka. I'm tempted to guzzle straight from the bottle, but waking up lovesick, heartbroken, and hungover holds zero appeal.

She pours two shots, handing one to me. I knock it back, relishing the burn as it coats the lining of my throat. "I think he means that," she admits. "And he's been telling everyone in school he was wasted at the party and he didn't mean a word of what he said to you, that he cares about you."

I just shrug, because actions speak louder than words, and Ayden was right; it is too little too late.

"And he beat Brandon to within an inch of his life for badmouthing you at Mona's the other night."

Guess I know how he got that bruise now. I should feel something hearing that, but I'm still numb. Numb over everything that's happened. And numb over Devin's words. I remember what he said. How I promised never to forget that we are in each other's hearts. But I don't want to be reminded of it now. Not when I'm broken, and we're apart, and there's no likely development that changes either of those scenarios.

"I see it every time I close my eyes at night," I admit, staring off into space. My voice is devoid of any emotion. "Her riding him. I don't think I'll be able to forget."

Mariah sighs, leaning her head on my shoulder. "I'm sorry, Ange. I should've stopped you from going into that room."

"You tried, and I wouldn't listen, and you were right. I can't un-see it. I can't forget it. And I can't forgive him."

We're both silent as Mariah pours two more shots, and we drain them in one go. "I don't know if this makes any difference, but Cody knows Becky's older brother, and he said she's practically spewing blood because Devin's ignoring her and rejecting her advances."

That should make me happy, but it only reinforces my view that she's planning something. Becky is not the type to give up until she gets what she wants, and she wants Devin. She has this figured out, and, whatever is going down, I doubt it's anything I'll benefit from.

∞ ∞ ∞

I don't know how long I sit on my bed staring at the pretty pink wrapping while I rotate Devin's package over and over in my hands. Ayden stayed for a few minutes after Mariah left, and I told him about Devin showing up and giving me the present. A funny expression came over his face, but he wouldn't elaborate when I questioned him, and he went home just after that.

The house feels desolate without him, although it suits my mood perfectly.

I toss the package on the bed and take a steaming-hot shower, trying to empty my mind of all thoughts of boys, but it's a pretty futile exercise.

When I'm in my pajamas and snuggled up under the covers, I run my finger under the edge of the pink paper, slowly peeling it back. My heart is jackhammering in my chest, and I'm almost too afraid to look. I remove the wrapping and stare at the black rectangular object in my hand. When I flip it over, I gasp, and my stomach is tied in knots.

It's a framed drawing of me sitting under Old Man Willow. I'm wearing jean shorts and a white tank top with my purple hoodie knotted at my waist. My Converse are neatly placed at my side, and there's a soda can and a half-eaten apple on a plate in front of me. I'm engrossed in a book, and there's the biggest smile on my face. My hair is brushed to one side, resting on my left shoulder, with strands falling softly across my forehead. The detail in the drawing is exquisite, and Devin hasn't missed a single thing. The edge of the infinity tattoo on my wrist is visible, and he's even colored the bright blue nail polish I was wearing. The tiny smattering of freckles across my nose seem more pronounced under the rays of sunlight washing over me. The likeness is incredible, and I'd challenge anyone to look at this and not instantly recognize it as me. He's even drawn the right tones in my hair and the faint blush on my cheeks.

I don't know when he drew me like this, only that it was one day this past summer, most likely early July because my Converse still look shiny and new.

I had no idea he was watching me, let alone sketching me. He's so talented, and it's a damn shame he isn't planning on doing anything with it.

A messy ball of emotion lodges in my throat, and tears spill out of my eyes unbidden. Squinting through damp, blurry eyes, I read the inscription at the bottom, sobbing openly as the familiar words imprint indelibly on my heart.

"You're the most important person in my world, Ange. For all time. Even when you think you aren't, know that you are. Even when I can't show you or say all I want to say, know that you are. Even if I leave, I'm still with you. I'm a part of you, just like you're a part of me, and you'll always be in my heart. Never forget. You promised."

He's signed off in his messy scrawl, adding the infinity symbol beside it.

I clutch it to my chest, sobbing profusely, as I lie down on the bed, my heart physically paining me. Turmoil and confusion are like my two new best friends, but they offer no words of wisdom. No solid advice. I want Devin. I want him so badly. *Miss him like crazy, but how can I give in after what he's done?*

After hours of torment, I finally succumb to sleep, and the darkness is a welcome relief.

Lucille calls first thing the next morning to ask if I want to work an extra shift at the diner. Two of her full-time waitresses have come down with some bug, and she's desperate. I readily agree, knowing it will be busy—all Saturdays are—and I need respite from my muddled head.

The day flies by, and before I know it, darkness has descended, casting eerie shadows on the sidewalk outside. I'm absolutely shattered as I head outside at the end of the night, yawning and fighting to put one foot in front of the other.

"You look exhausted, babe," Ayden says, lounging against the side of his Jeep as he waits for me.

"Hey, Ange," Joshua Higgins says, nudging his head in my direction.

"Hi, Josh. He roped you in as designated driver?" I guess, watching him flick the keys back and forth between his fingers.

Josh grins. "Yep. I've been driving his majesty around town all day."

I bark out a laugh as Ayden removes my bag from my shoulder, tossing it in the back seat. I lean into Josh, pretending to whisper conspiratorially. "I think he's secretly enjoying being so helpless and all his bitching and moaning is just an act."

"I think you could be right," Josh says with a wink, jumping into the driver seat and powering up the engine.

"You're both hilarious," Ayden deadpans. "Now get your cute butt in the back seat and let's go home."

"Yes, sir, bossman." I salute him, laughing as I haul ass into the Jeep.

"Careful, Lina, or I'll have to summon the tickle monster." Ayden climbs awkwardly in beside me, and Josh floors it the instant he shuts the door.

I grip the headrest in front to keep myself upright, alarm registering as Josh speeds up the road. "You wouldn't dare," I tell him.

"Wanna bet?" Ayden's clear blue eyes glisten with mirth.

"Are you challenging me?"

His grin turns wicked. "What if I am?"

"As much as I'm game, you're injured, so it's not happening."

"Chicken shit." He does a one-armed impression of a chicken while making repeated "bwok, bwok" sounds, and he looks ridiculous.

Josh is howling with laughter in the front seat, and my lips are fighting a smile. I plant my game face on, purely for show. "Oh, it's on, mister. It's on like Donkey Kong." I lunge for him the same time his good arm darts out, reaching for me, and I duck down, shrieking. Clamping my arms in to my body, I try to straighten up which is actually hard to do with your arms glued to your side. Ayden's fingers creep along my waist, aiming for my armpit, and I scream, losing control of my arms as he tickles the crap out of me. I'm wriggling and writhing on the seat, trying to slip out of his reach while attempting to tickle him back, but he's too strong, even one-armed, and I know defeat when I see it. "Okay! You win!" I screech, my body contorting like I'm possessed. "You're the master tickle monster."

He laughs, pulling me into his side, and kissing my temple. "You're such a glutton for punishment. How many times did we tickle the shit out of you as kids?"

My mind inevitably goes there, and my laughter shrivels up and dies. Once they discovered how ticklish I was, Ayden and Devin used to gang up on me on a regular basis. I was fighting a losing battle every time, and I never once got the upper hand. They used to tickle me to death, and I'd huff and puff and pretend to be mad, but secretly I loved it. One time, I even peed my pants they were tickling me that hard, and they almost pissed theirs in return when they saw what they'd done to me.

Devin called me pissy pants for a whole year after that. I try to laugh at the once funny memory, but it comes out as more of a strangled, anguished sound. Ayden has gone quiet too, and I know he's reminiscing as well. I snuggle up beside him, leaning my head on his shoulder, hoping his close-ness and his warmth can eradicate the omnipresent pain. "What was the gift?" he asks, his fingers toying idly with my hair.

I catch Josh watching us in the mirror, and I don't want to say any-thing in front of him. It's not that I can't trust him—although he's on the football team, he's not an arrogant douche like most of the players—I'm just not comfortable discussing it in public. Devin's gift was hugely per-sonal and so very special, and I don't want to share that with anyone. Not even Ayden. "I'll tell you when we get home," I say, deflecting.

Back at the house, Mom is still up, waiting for me to come in. "You look tired, honey." She draws me into a bear hug.

"I am." I yawn. "It's been a long day."

"Why don't you two go into the living room, and I'll fix us some hot chocolate?" she suggests, and I duly comply.

I sit on the couch, flexing my neck from side to side, trying to loosen the tense kink. The atmosphere is undeniably strained.

"You don't want to tell me," Ayden astutely supplies, leaning back in the recliner as he studies me carefully.

"He gave me a picture. A drawing of me from last summer, and he wrote some stuff on it." That's about as much as I'm prepared to relinquish. As much as I love Ayden, and as much as the three of us were close, this is something intimate between Devin and me, and although we're not even on speaking terms, it doesn't seem right to show anyone else. He drew that picture, wrote those words, for my eyes only.

His Adam's apple jumps in his throat. "Oh."

The only sound in the room is the muted noise from the TV, playing absently in the background.

"Have you changed your mind?" he asks. "Are you going to let him back in?"

I chew on my bottom lip as I contemplate how to reply. Mom is humming a song in the kitchen, her soft, lyrical voice reaching us from here. "I don't honestly know."

He stands up. "I miss him too, you know." His earnest eyes pin mine in place. "But he's not going to change." He bends down, kissing my cheek. "I'm calling it a night. I'll see you tomorrow."

"Thanks, Natalie," I hear him tell Mom, "but I'll take a rain check. I need to get home."

"What was all that about?" she asks, handing me a mug of steamy chocolaty goodness.

"What do you think?"

She pats my arm. "Things will right themselves. You'll see."

I wish I shared her optimism.

Ayden gives me a wide berth the next day, and I wish I knew what he was thinking. I spend all day considering my options, and by nightfall I know I've reached a point where I'm at least ready to listen to what Devin has to say. I peek out the window, but his truck isn't there. I set up camp by the window for the remainder of the night, but Devin doesn't return before midnight, so I head to bed, vowing to talk to him in school the next day.

Jack Frost paid a visit overnight, and the roads are slippery and icy as I drive us at a snail's pace toward school. Ayden is quiet this morning, and I hate that I might be the cause of it. We sit in the toasty car after I've parked and killed the engine, glancing at one another like we're strangers. "This is ridiculous," I supply, after a few minutes of unpleasant silence. "Just say what's on your mind."

"He'll only hurt you again."

"You seem sure about that, how come?"

He sighs, pulling his hat off and running his fingers through his gorgeous blond hair. "Because he's in a dark place, Lina, and he can't help dragging others down with him."

I twist around to face him. "Then we can't abandon him. He needs us more than ever."

An agonized look contorts his handsome face. Leaning forward, he stares out the window, lost in thought, drumming his fingers against the glove box. I wait patiently for him to process whatever is going through his mind. When he finally turns to face me, a look of steely determination has replaced the previous torment. "Can you just be his friend? Can you honestly forget what he's done and just be there for him when the shit hits the fan? Because it will."

I toy with the hem on my shirt. "I can try."

"God, Lina." Ayden palms my face. "You're the best person I know. A far better person than I am." Pain and self-loathing flares momentarily in his eyes before he disguises it. "I know you'd still do that for him even though he's hurt you."

I curl my hand around his face. "I'd do that for you too. In a heartbeat."

He presses his forehead to mine. "I know you would, babe."

A loud thud jolts us apart when someone slams their hand down on the hood of the Jeep. Brandon and Travis sneer at us through the windshield, making vulgar gestures with their hands.

"Fucking asshats!" Ayden hisses, scrambling out of the Jeep.

I hop out my side, racing around to his side before he does something he regrets. "If you have something to say, jerkoffs, just say it," he demands.

"We always knew you three were close, but we didn't know you swapped her around. How does one go about getting on the roster?" Brandon rakes his gaze up and down my body. "I'm in the mood for some fresh pussy."

"Fuck you, asshole." Ayden flexes his one good fist, veins straining in his neck.

Josh and a couple of Ayden's other football buddies materialize on the sidewalk. "If you have something to say to Carter, you can say it to all of us," Josh coolly states.

"Fucking douches," Brandon murmurs, taking a step back. "Who died and said you were in charge? Lighten up, jerks. None of you know how to take a joke. As if I'd want to go anywhere near her prissy ass." He sneers at me, and I plant a bored expression on my face.

Ayden growls, taking a step forward. I put myself in front of him. "Don't. He's not worth it." I twist around. "Get lost, asshole."

"Suck my dick." He flips me the finger before sauntering off in the direct of the front entrance.

"Thanks, man." Ayden nods at Josh.

"Anytime. He's just pissed because …" Josh trails off with one sharp look from Ayden.

"Because Dev gave him that black eye for spouting shit about me," I finish for him. "Can we go?" I implore Ayden with my eyes. "I'm freezing my ass off out here."

"Here, take this." He yanks the hat off his head, putting it on me. Hair covers my face, blocking my view, before Ayden brushes it aside, tucking it neatly under the edge of the hat. Josh and the guys look on in amusement, and my cheeks heat up.

"Come on." I pull on his arm, and he smirks, tucking me in to his side as we walk.

"I cannot wait to graduate and not have to see half these people ever again," I admit, stepping into the building. I whip the hat off, running my fingers through my hair, trying to tame my tangled locks. "I am sick of all this bullshit, and these people annoy the fuck out of me." It's as if every single person was waiting for me to arrive and has decided to watch my every move. More than three weeks have passed since the party, and I thought the interest levels had waned, but I guess that was wishful thinking. At least Christmas break is just around the corner, and I will have a welcome reprieve from being the center of attention.

As we round the next corridor, Ayden yanks hard on my shoulders, swinging me back around. I look up at him, scowling. "What the hell? I think you just dislocated my shoulder."

Ayden takes my hand and starts pulling me back the way we came. I struggle with him, attempting to remove my hand and halt our retreat. "Ayd, stop. My locker's the other way."

"Let's ditch today. We can go ice skating."

"You have a broken arm." I pin him with a "duh" look. "And you never ditch." I don't bother mentioning how clumsy he is on the ice because that doesn't need to be articulated. I yank my hand from his, coming to a complete stop. "Wait up."

"Or we can grab a movie or drive out to Des Moines and go shopping."

"You hate shopping." My eyes narrow to slits, and everything goes on high alert inside me. "What's back there? What don't you want me to see?"

He makes a grab for my arm, but I sidestep him, slowly backing up, conscious that we have an audience, and that people are whispering in hushed voices. "Leave it, Lina," he pleads. "Let's just go."

I consider it for a split second, before spinning around and racing down the corridor. I won't shy away from this. Ayden curses, and I hear the pounding of his footsteps following me. The crowd parts, almost collectively wiping their hands in glee. All they're missing are buckets of popcorn and sodas. I don't know what I'm about to discover, but I know it involves Devin and that it's nothing good.

When I round the corner, I blink in rapid fire succession, sure my eyes are playing tricks on me. But it's no trickery. Becky is flattened against Devin's locker, and his arms cage her in as he leans in to kiss her. She grabs his waist, pulling his body flush to hers as their lips lock. I slow my pace and come to a complete standstill. It's as if the whole school has come out to witness this. Groups of students line the corridors watching my reaction with baited breath.

Becky is making a meal out of this, moaning at the top of her voice and grinding her hips against Devin's. She tilts her head, granting him access to her neck, and her triumphant eyes meet mine. Bit by bit, my heart starts shutting down, one wounded piece at a time, and a hard, thick, impenetrable, layer seals it tight, locking every emotion inside with it.

Ayden laces his fingers in mine, and I look up at him, noting the compassion, anger and pain radiating from his eyes. I wet my dry lips. "You still up for ditching?"

"Hell yeah." His smile is tinged in sadness.

"Let's go." I take one last look in Devin and Becky's direction. Devin's pained eyes meet mine, completely at odds with his body language. His arm is wrapped around Becky's shoulder now, and she's snuggling into his chest, gloating and preening for her adoring crowd.

Well, she's welcome to him.

I'm done.

Keeping a firm hold on Ayden's arm, I turn us around and walk out of school without uttering a word.

CHAPTER SIXTEEN

Ayden and I spend the day shopping, watching movies, and eating a ton of junk food. He keeps an endless stream of chatter up, and I participate in the conversation but it's half-hearted. Nightfall has descended by the time I park the Jeep in Ayden's drive.

I give him a massive hug, and he envelops me in his arms. "Thanks for today. You're the best."

"Anything for my favorite girl." He smooths hair off my forehead. "You want me to stay?"

Yes. No. I don't know. "Better not. Mom's still on the warpath."

"Will you be all right?"

"I'm fine."

"Call me if you need me, no matter what time. You need me, I'm there."

I lean up on my tiptoes and kiss his cheek. "You mean the world to me, you know that, right?"

"Ditto, sweetheart." He tweaks my nose, and then we part ways.

Mom has already left for the hospital, so I ping her a quick text to let her know I'm home. I texted her earlier, so she knew to expect a call from the school, and she sends me back a brief message letting me know she fixed everything with Principal Wells.

My mom is the coolest mom on the planet.

After taking a long, hot soak in the tub, I pin my wet hair into a messy bun on top of my head and wander to my bedroom to get stuck into homework. A loud rap on the French doors surprises me a couple hours later. I don't look up. I don't need to. I know who it is and I can't believe he has the nerve to show up here. Red-hot rage replaces the blood coursing through my veins as I hop up and stalk to the doors.

"Go away!" I hiss, opening the doors a tiny fraction. "I don't ever want to see you again."

"Ange, please." He throws out his hand, pushing the door open wider and forcing his way inside. "You need to let me explain."

"I don't need to let you do anything, and I won't listen to any more of your lies!" I shout, and he flinches. "I fucking hate you, Devin. I hate you more than I hate any other living thing."

His fingers wind around my wrist. "Ange, I know you don't mean that."

I jab my finger in his chest, nostrils flaring, veins pumped full of angry adrenaline. "Then I guess you know nothing, because I mean every word that comes out of my mouth. You disgust me. You make me sick, and, quite frankly, Becky is welcome to you. You two deserve each other."

"It's not what it seems."

I snort with laughter, yanking my wrist out of his grasp. "I don't want to hear it, Devin. I'm done with this. With you. I want you to get out and stay out."

He reaches for me again, and I lurch back, stumbling over my feet and falling flat on my ass.

"Please, baby doll. Please let me explain."

I lose control of my tenuous emotions, climbing to my feet with my fists clenched. "I told you I don't want to fucking hear it!" I screech, shoving him hard. He falls back, a look of shock splayed across his face. "I saw everything I needed to today." My head whips around, and I'm racing across the room in a flash. Grabbing the picture he drew of me, I stomp toward him, shoving it in his chest. "And you can take this. I don't want it." I cast a glance around my bedroom, mentally picking out the things that belong to him. I dart around the room, picking up his sweaters, shirts, books, DVDs, CDs, and other stuff that belongs to him. His worn boxing gloves and the trophy he won at the Iowa High School State Boxing Tournament are added to my pile. His face is a mask of calm as he silently watches me dashing around the room like a madwoman. I return to his side thrusting my bundle into his arms.

"If I find anything else, I'll box it up and leave it on your porch."

"I don't want this stuff. I gave it to you."

He tries to hand it back to me, but I step aside. "I don't want it. I want no reminder of you here. I'm going to remove every trace of your existence until you are nothing but a figment of my rotten imagination."

Troubled eyes meet mine. "Don't do this. I'm begging you. I need you to remember what I said. I—"

"Do I look like I give a flying fuck?!" I holler, incensed beyond the point of rage. I shove him again, and the urge to hit something, hit *him*, is almost overwhelming. I've never been prone to violence, but I guess there's a first time for everything. "Get out. Get out or I'm calling the cops. And don't ever come back here again," I threaten, vowing to get a lock on those doors, or to barricade them altogether.

"Fine. Have it your way, but I'm not taking this stuff." He dumps it all on top of my dresser. "I understand you're mad, but you'll thank me when you calm down." He opens the doors and steps out onto the balcony. A switch flips inside me at his words and his irritatingly cool demeanor. How dare he show up here acting like he hasn't done anything wrong. Like he hasn't ripped my heart to shreds, and left my self-confidence and my reputation in tatters on the floor.

I lose all sense of reason.

A primitive roar escapes my mouth, and I snatch the items up, throwing them over the balcony at him as he scrambles down the tree. He looks up at me like I've lost my mind.

Perhaps I have.

One by one, I fling items at him, aiming for his head as rage does a complete number on me. "I hate you!" I scream, throwing a bunch of CDs. They clatter to the ground, breaking apart. The items of his clothing are next. He's on the ground now, with his hands in his pockets, looking up at me with the saddest expression on his face. I throw the trophy at his head, but my aim is off, and it bounces on the ground to his left. "Stay the fuck away from me, Devin!"

I pick up the last item, hurling the framed picture at his head with all the strength I can muster. This time my aim is bang on. He ducks down, barely avoiding impact. The glass frame shatters into a million tiny shards at his feet. "And you can take your empty words and shove them where the sun doesn't shine!" I yell.

I slam the double doors shut, as a warm arm slides around my waist from behind. "Shush, Lina. It's okay. I've got you."

I collapse against Ayden's chest, crying hysterically as I watch Devin bend down, picking up his belongings off the ground. He retrieves the drawing from behind the broken glass, carefully rolling it up and tucking it under his arm. He casts one last look in our direction, and I yank the curtains across the doors, plunging us into darkness.

The sobs pick up in earnest, and Ayden carries me to the bed where he holds me all night long, uttering soothing words until my exhausted brain finally succumbs to sleep.

The next day at school is officially the worst day of my life. Everywhere I turn, people are pointing the finger and gossiping about me. News that Becky and Devin are exclusive and official spreads like wildfire throughout the halls. At lunchtime, she sits beside him, fawning all over him, and it's enough to slaughter my appetite. Ayden sits loyally by my side, attempting to draw me out of my melancholy mood. Mariah wants to personally castrate Devin, and she spends the whole lunch period sending threatening looks at Becky and Devin while I attempt to pretend like my heart isn't smashed to pieces.

I'm in the smaller, less popular bathroom at the far side of the building just before the last class of the day, washing my hands in the sink, when Becky and her cronies swan in. The door snicks shut as they line up around me. Becky tilts her head to the side, her eyes scrutinizing me with thinly concealed disgust.

"What do you want?" I bark, keeping my head up and my shoulders back. I wipe my wet hands down the front of my jeans.

"I want to set the new ground rules."

My mouth pulls into an amused grimace. "This should be good." I fold my arms over my chest. "Let's hear 'em."

She steps forward, putting her face in mine. Her features are twisted with malice as she glares smugly at me. Funny how a person can look aesthetically pretty when they're completely ugly on the inside. She prods a bony finger in my chest. "First, let's get one thing straight. I'm in control around here. You don't get to call the shots, and you don't get to stand there and mock me."

"Screw you."

She shoves me, hard, and I fall back against the counter. I straighten up, ignoring the surge of adrenaline flooding my veins. "I told you I always get what I want, and Devin is mine. All mine. You are not to come anywhere near him. You are no longer friends with him. He is invisible to you."

I snort out a laugh. "Wow, never thought the day would come where I'd agree with anything that came out of your mouth, but I have absolutely zero issue with anything you have said. I'm done with the loser. You're welcome to him."

Shoving past her, I walk toward the door, ignoring the blood rushing to my ears. I'm yanked back by my hair and slammed against the wall. A stinging pain slides across my cheek as she pushes me into the wall, digging her knee into my lower back. "I wasn't done talking, and you will leave when I tell you to leave."

I wriggle out of her hold, my cheek scraping across the coarse stone in the process. I jerk away from her. "Get the fuck out of my way. I'll leave when I want to leave."

Her fist thrusts out, and she punches me in the gut, winding me. I double over, clutching my stomach in disbelief. I know Becky's a bully, but I've never known her to be physically abusive. "You're fucking pathetic, and it's laughable that you thought he'd have any interest in you. I won't warn you again, Mary. Stay the hell away from Devin, or you'll suffer the consequences."

Over the next few days, Becky and her minions wage a subtle campaign of terror. Despite the fact I ignore Devin, and I've had no contact with him, those bitches follow me everywhere around school, and they've even taken up residence at the diner, taunting me with excessive demands during every shift. Ayden is enraged, especially after what went down in the bathroom. We fought relentlessly over it. He wants to intervene, but I refuse to allow his involvement—that wouldn't be in any way helpful. I need to deal with this, and I need to be clever about it. The last thing I want is to get hauled in front of Principal Wells. My record is impeccable thus far, and stuff like that matters to me. I want to leave high school with a clean sheet and my head held high, so, for now, I try to steer clear of the bitches and avoid confrontation.

Christmas comes and goes, and I'm glad when it's over. The effort involved in pretending to be happy is draining. A few days before we're due to return to school, I accompany Ayden to the hospital to get his cast off.

"Freedom!" he yells, fist pumping the air as we step out into the parking lot. I giggle when he picks me up, swinging me around. "This calls for a celebration."

"What do you have in mind?"

"A few of the guys are grabbing dinner and a movie later if you are up for it?"

"Sure." I shrug. "Count me in."

I laugh myself silly when we get in the Jeep and Ayden lavishes kisses on the steering wheel. "Dude, you are so weird."

He powers up the engine, almost purring with satisfaction. "You hear that, baby. You hear that beautiful sound."

I roll my eyes, and he leans over the console, smacking a kiss on my lips. My eyes pop wide in surprise. "Today's a good day, Lina." He winks, easing the Jeep out of the space and into the line of traffic exiting the hospital. His blond hair has grown longer over the winter, curling around his ears and the top of his neck. He looks at me and smiles, his gorgeous blue eyes brimming with happiness. Leaning back in his seat, he sighs contentedly. "I'm hitting the open road with a beautiful girl by my side and there's no school, no practice, we're free as birds, baby."

His enthusiasm is infectious, and I find myself laughing along with him.

Later, we drive to the movie theater and meet up with Josh, Cody, two of the other guys, and their girlfriends. Conversation flows freely in the adjoining diner as we eat, and, for the first time in ages, I feel relaxed and more like myself. Ayden keeps his arm around me as he banters with his teammates while I chat with Mariah and Gabi—who has just started dating Josh—across the table.

The jovial mood lasts right up until we set foot in the movie theater and the first people I see are Devin and Becky. My initial instinct is to turn on my heel and run, but screw them, they're not driving me out of here or ruining my night. Ayden stiffens beside me, taking my hand and keeping me close to his side. "Ignore them."

Ayden is a protective force behind me as we stand in line to buy our tickets, his arms circling my waist and his head resting atop my chin. I avoid looking over at Becky and Devin but I'm acutely aware of their presence. Everyone is, and tension is palpable in the air.

We grab popcorn and soda and head toward the doors. "You go with the others," Ayden says, nudging me forward. "I need to use the restroom." He pecks my cheek, and walks away. I follow Mariah and the others, claiming the last two seats in the row, right by the aisle, for Ayden and myself. The lights dim, and I pull my knees into my chest as the screen sparks to life.

All the tiny hairs on the back of my neck lift, and my heart starts thudding in my chest, for no apparent reason, but I know better. I've always been in sync with Devin, and I don't need to look up to confirm he's in close proximity. Out of the corner of my eye, I spot the form hovering in the aisle, his penetrating eyes boring a hole in the side of my skull. I ignore him, hoping he'll go away, but he stays rooted to the spot, his hands in the front pockets of his jeans, just staring at me. Every head in our row turns to look at him, but he doesn't seem to care, standing rigidly still and willing me to turn around and look up at him. I've no clue where Becky is, but I'm guessing she's not in the vicinity.

Mariah subtly elbows me in the ribs, and my eyes flit to hers. "I know," I mouth.

He's still there, and I wonder what he hopes to achieve. After a couple minutes, unable to withstand it any longer, I look up at him. It's the first time we've looked each other in the eye in weeks. His gaze roams my face as he stares at me with lethal quietness. I regard him flippantly, refusing to betray any hint of emotion, and it's like some form of silent standoff. A simmering charge ignites the space between us, and the air is laden with unspoken words. His eyes drill into mine, as if he's trying to implant his thoughts in my head. I don't know why he's even bothering or why it matters at this stage.

He's chosen his side, and we've chosen ours.

Leaning his hands on the edge of Ayden's chair, he lowers his head, closing some of the gap between us. It's almost as if he's challenging me to speak. Well, hell will freeze before I'm the first to break. I can be stubborn as fuck when I want to be.

He's claiming the attention of random moviegoers now, and several curious faces are trained in our direction. Then Ayden is there, looming like an all-powerful protector behind him. "Your girlfriend's on the way back from the bathroom, so I suggest you get your ass out of here before she notices. Lina has put up with enough of Becky's bullshit."

"What?" Devin turns to face Ayden.

"Don't pretend like you don't know. You two are practically joined at the hip." True fact, but Becky never antagonizes me when Dev is around. She only does it when there are minimal witnesses and she knows she can get away with it.

"Ayd!" I hiss. "Drop it, and sit down." The opening credits roll. "The movie's about to start."

Devin glances at me with a frown before walking away, plonking into a seat three rows in front of us. Becky swans in a minute later, tossing her blonde hair over her shoulder and skipping into her seat. She wastes no time draping herself around Devin, but he pushes her off and I spot the tell-tale glint of anger in his eyes as he whispers furiously in her ear. Her head whips around, her eyes narrowing as they lock on mine. I rest my head on Ayden's shoulder, and focus on the screen, doing my best to ignore the couple in front of us, but my treacherous eyes have other ideas, and despite my best efforts, my gaze keeps returning to them.

Devin sits upright in the chair staring at the screen while Becky nuzzles into his side. She takes his arm, wrapping it around her shoulder only for him to remove it almost straightaway. Then she's whispering with an ugly, angry expression on her face, and I can almost see the steam billowing out of her ears. This goes on for about the next twenty minutes, and it would be almost comical if I could find anything about this entire clusterfuck that's funny. Five minutes later, after another angry tirade from Becky, Devin stands up and stalks out of the place. Becky flees after him, sending me a murderous glare on her way out.

"There must be trouble in paradise if that display was any indication," Mariah says in a low voice as we make our way out to the parking lot after the movie has ended.

"I don't care, and I don't want to talk about it." My tone is harsher than I mean it to be. "Sorry, M." I loop my arm through hers. "I know you mean well, but I'm determined to put all that behind me. I'm fed up with feeling depressed and upset and tonight was fun for the most part, and it's reminded me that life is for living, and I'm done acting like a lovesick harpy. Devin is a closed book, a non-entity in my life, and that's how I prefer it. Life's less complicated that way."

She squeezes my arm. "I understand, and I'm glad you are moving on. I hate seeing you so sad, and tonight, in the diner, is the first time I've seen you smile and laugh in weeks."

"I'm sorry I've been such a Debbie Downer, and I promise that's the last you've seen of it."

"I just want you to be happy."

"Me too."

"What about you and Ayden?"

"What about us?"

"You never answered me that day, and he's good for you. You two are so cute together. I think you should give it a shot, and then we can go on double dates all the time."

"Who's going on double dates?" Ayden asks from behind as we pull up in front of his Jeep.

"The four of us." Mariah is quick to reply, wiggling her brows mischievously.

"I'm down with that plan," Ayden says, grinning at me. "Tonight was fun."

"It was," I agree, neither one of us prepared to mention the temporary blip in our otherwise awesome night.

"You should've gotten tickets to the psychic show tomorrow night," Ayden says, opening the passenger door for me. "Then you could've come with Lina and me."

"That psychic shit is all fake hocus-pocus," Cody says, helping Mariah into the back seat.

Ayd grins at me. "Careful what you say around Lina. She's very touchy when it comes to this particular subject."

"Fact." I twist around in my seat, shooting Cody a warning look. "I'm a true believer."

"You're too smart to fall for that bullshit," Cody replies. "It's all fake. It's well known they have scouts in the crowd and they've done their homework. They find stuff out and make it seem like someone from the other side is sharing the intel, when it's all complete and utter bullshit."

"You're such a cynic, Cody."

He shrugs, buckling his belt as I do the same. Ayden revs the engine, driving out of the parking lot.

"I'll admit I'm naturally cynical," Cody confirms, "but a healthy dose of cynicism does no harm. Being too trusting is a flaw. Trust has to be earned, and that's not going to happen at a mass event where everyone has paid twenty bucks a ticket."

I cannot argue with his logic, even though I'll never admit that out loud, certainly not less than twenty-four hours before Ayden and I attend the event. But the truth is, for years I've loved going to see fortune tellers and psychics because several of them have reinforced my future life choices, and I've needed that reassurance that life is going to pan out as I've planned it.

But now I'm questioning everything.

Especially the future.

And I'm realizing how naïve I've been and that maybe it's time to grow up. Time to understand that I can't control every single facet of my life. I can only control those aspects that I can directly influence.

Yes, I think it's time I wised up. Faced facts.

No one can predict the future, because the choices you make, and the choices others make that impact you, can set you on a completely different path at any time, without any prior notice. *And if that's the case, then what's the point in knowing what lies ahead?*

Because that version of the future can always change.

CHAPTER SEVENTEEN

"I expected you to be more excited," Ayden says the next night, when we're on our way to the show.

I look over at him. "I am, but maybe Cody had a point last night. Maybe it's time I stopped worrying what the future holds and just be in the moment, ya know?"

"Being in the moment is good, but there's nothing wrong in having an interest in the paranormal. Millions of people the world over are fascinated with it, and you've always gotten a kick out of that stuff."

"I think I've been too fixated with trying to control my future, when it's not something that can be controlled."

"True. Your future will be what *you* make it." He parks, cutting the engine, and his brow furrows. He looks off into space. "Do you think you can change the course of your life?"

I nod, slipping my arms into my jacket. "I do, there are always choices, and the world's our oyster, right?"

We get out and walk toward the arena. Ayden pulls the zipper up on my jacket, removing his scarf and wrapping it around my neck. I kiss the inside of his wrist, smiling up at him. "What?" he asks, taking my hand, a look of confusion on his face.

"You're always looking after me." I look at him, *really look* at him, and it's almost like I'm seeing him, *properly seeing him*, for the first time. Ayden is unfailing in his support, loyalty, and protection of me, and I think I've taken that too much for granted. Mariah's words from last night have been circling round my brain all day, and I wonder if the boy I should be with has been right under my nose all this time. Whether I obsessed over the wrong boy next door. "And I want you to know I appreciate it, and"—my cheeks heat—"it's nice. It's nice to know I can always count on you."

He reels me into his arms. "You can. You can count on me for life."

∞ ∞ ∞

The auditorium is massive, but we have excellent seats, right in front of the stage. The show starts promptly at eight, and, despite my earlier protests to the contrary, I get sucked in almost instantly, fascinated by the apparent accuracy of the medium's readings and the joyful, emotional response of the members of the audience. The energy is crackling and the buzz is electric as he roams the aisles, gesturing at various people, validating information to shocked gasps of amazement. "This is what they do folks. Your loved ones want you to have no doubt that the message is coming from them."

When he halts at the end of our row, I almost stop breathing. "I've got a man here," he says, looking between me and Ayden. "I feel like he's here for you." He points at Ayden. "He's older, and he's pointing at his heart. He died of a massive coronary. I feel like he could be your grandfather, that's what he's telling me. His name was Don or—"

"Ron," Adyen says. "My grandfather's name was Ron."

He points at the signet ring on Ayden's left hand. "He's telling me that was his ring."

Ayden nods, gulping, his eyes wide and dazed. My heart is racing. Never, in all our years of coming to shows, has anyone ever turned up for one of us.

The medium chuckles. "Okay, he's showing me, like, this kinda funny story now, about a kid that burned his ass on the fire. He had to stand up naked in the center of the crowded living room while a woman with red hair put cream on his butt. Does that make sense to you?"

Ayden nods, his lips twitching. "That happened my dad when he was a kid. Grandpa used to love telling that story."

The medium's expression turns more serious. "Your grandpa's telling me you're troubled. You're afraid to take the right path, and he's worried about you." Ayden's face pales, and he goes really still. "Ron says it's okay to be yourself and to make your own choices in life. Go for it. The people who love you will understand." The medium's eyes fall to me, and he smiles, before moving on to the next person.

"Are you okay?" I whisper to Ayden who still looks like he's seen a ghost. I allow myself a little inner chuckle at that thought, cause he kinda has just seen a ghost. "That was pretty cool."

He nods absently, still staring, with stark, wide, dazed eyes, off into space.

The rest of the show flies by, and before I know it, we are back in the Jeep and on our way home.

"Wanna grab some food?" Ayden asks a little while later, and it's the first words he's spoken since we left.

"I could eat," I acknowledge, my tummy rumbling in agreement.

Ayden pulls into a diner just off the highway, on the outskirts of town. The place is lit up like the fourth of July, and it's empty with the exception of an older couple sitting in a rear booth. We plonk our butts in a booth and order burgers and milkshakes. I stretch my hand across the table, lacing my fingers in Ayden's. "Are you still freaked out?"

"A little," he admits, propping his elbows on the table. "Grandpa died six years ago, but it feels as if it was only yesterday, and it was a shock."

"You believe it?"

He considers my question for a long time. I slurp on my Oreo shake, waiting for him to reply. Slowly, he looks me in the eyes, and nods. "He knew too much for it not to be true."

Inside, I'm a giddy mass of excitement. You'd swear someone had come through for me, but, after my melancholy last night and today, it seems like validation, that I haven't wasted years believing in a load of nonsense. I take another slurp of my drink. I think of what the psychic said. "Is something troubling you? Because you know you can talk to me about anything."

He digs his fingernails into his thigh. "I know that, and I would if it was anything serious."

My eyes scan his face, and I know he's lying, but I'm not going to push if he isn't ready to tell me. "Okay, well I'm here if you ever need to talk."

Things return to normal after that, and whatever tension I imagined seems to have disappeared.

Back at the house, Ayden helps me out of the Jeep, his hands lingering on my waist. His cheeks are flushed and red from the cold, and he's gone all quiet on me again. We walk hand in hand to my front door. "Thanks for taking me tonight." I peck him on the cheek. "It was mucho interesting."

"You can say that again." He grins, stepping away. "I'll see you tomorrow, Lina."

"Night, Ayd."

I've only put one foot through the door, when his hands land on my waist and I'm spun around. I haven't even a second to catch my breath before his mouth descends on mine and his fingers wind through my hair. His lips are soft but cold as they mold against mine, his kiss tender yet urgent. My arms encircle his neck, and he pulls me closer, holding me firmly in place as he angles his head and deepens the kiss.

Oh. My. God. Ayden's kissing me.

And I'm kissing him back.

And it feels … good.

My hold on his neck intensifies, and I kiss him harder, parting my lips and letting his tongue enter my mouth. Ayden moans, and his kiss turns greedy as his lips worship mine. Our bodies are pressed together, and we're kissing frantically, like we won't ever get to do it again. He fists my hair in his hands, groaning as his tongue ravishes my mouth. I'm hot underneath my coat and sweater, and there are too many layers between us. I want to run my fingers over his skin, to feel his heart thudding under my hand.

He breaks the kiss, abruptly, keeping a firm hold on me as he presses his forehead to mine. "Lina, Lina." His voice is dripping with desire, and our joint rampant breathing is the only sound in the still night air.

I peer into his eyes, and he cups my face. "Kissing you is every bit as amazing as I hoped it would be." My cheeks flare up, and he chuckles. "Say something."

"Um, wow?!" Not the most intelligent response, but his kisses have turned my brain to mush.

His smile turns hopeful. "Does that mean you don't regret it?"

My voice is breathless when I speak. "I don't regret it." I shake my head. "I don't regret it at all. In fact, I want to do it again." This time I kiss him, and it's softer and sweeter than our last kiss, but it still warms me on the inside.

He pulls away first again. "If we're going to do this, I think we should take it a step at a time, to be sure we're both in it for the right reasons."

"What does *this* mean to you?" I don't want any crossed wires.

He kisses the tip of my nose. "I want you to be my girlfriend. Half the school thinks you already are anyway. What do you say?"

I don't stop to think about it. I just want to *feel*. To allow my emotions to decide without logic or concern or any other number of obstacles stopping me from taking a chance. Ayd is my best friend, and I trust him not to hurt me. I trust him with my life, and, right now, I want this with him. I like the way he makes me feel—safe, protected, loved, cared for. "I want that too."

"Yeah?" His expression is hopeful again. "You're sure you're ready?"

I know what that's code for—you're sure you're over him? "Yes, I'm ready. I want you as my boyfriend." And it's only half a lie. I don't know if I'll ever be over Devin, but I can't spend the rest of my life pining for someone who doesn't want me. While I still don't understand it, Devin is *hers* now. He'll never be mine, and it's time I faced up to that fact and moved on with my life.

Besides, I don't want to be with someone who doesn't know his own mind—who says one thing and does another, who hurts the people he professes to love.

I want to be with someone who sees me as their everything.

Someone who respects me and treats me right.

Mom has taught me that. My whole life she's told me to never accept being treated any less than what I deserve. When she found herself trapped in an abusive marriage after a whirlwind romance at eighteen, she tried to make the best of it at first, but after I came along, and the abuse escalated, she found the strength to walk away, to refuse to accept that treatment for herself or her daughter. I know it wasn't easy at first—she's been honest about that—but she persevered, and I'm determined to prove I'm my mother's daughter.

I think I'd lost sight of that these past few weeks, allowing my anger and hurt to conceal the truth of the situation. Devin hasn't treated me right for months, and I allowed him to treat me badly, to walk all over me like a piece of crap.

That ends right now, and the acknowledgment feels good.

Ayden cherishes me, and he makes me feel special and wanted, and although it's risky, I just know if things don't work out between us he'll always be my friend. I'm taking control of my life and forging a new direction, and it feels great. "I didn't realize it until now, but I've been waiting for you. I want this with you. Nothing would make me happier."

The biggest grin splashes across his face before he lowers his mouth to mine, kissing me again. I inwardly swoon. His kisses are hot and sweet and I'm tingly all over. I can't keep the happy smile off my face when he finally breaks apart. "I could kiss you all night long, Lina, but I meant what I said about pacing ourselves. There's no need to rush into anything."

And I appreciate that, because it's one thing to kiss Ayden and agree to be his girlfriend, but thinking about having sex with him, about giving him my virginity, is a whole other minefield I need to work through. I kiss the back of his hand. "I agree, and I'm happy to take things slow."

He leans in one final time, pecking my lips briefly. "Goodnight, babe. Sleep tight."

I watch him trek across the gap between our houses, swinging his body over the fence and into his yard. My fingers trace my swollen lips, and I can't stop smiling. I wave as he blows me a kiss before stepping inside his house.

As I turn to enter my house, my gaze lands on the person watching from the house next door. Devin is leaning against the front of his truck, staring straight at me. It's too dark to decipher his expression, and I'm glad I can't tell what mood he's in, because Devin has ruined too many precious moments recently.

And he's not ruining this special night.

I meant what I just said to myself.

Devin has treated me poorly for the last time.

He's not going to ruin this for me.

I won't let him.

CHAPTER EIGHTEEN

Ayden and I spend the whole day together Sunday, and when he kisses me goodnight at my door, I think my heart might burst with sheer happiness.

"Someone's in love," Mom croons when I step into the kitchen.

I can't keep the dreamy smile off my face as I open the refrigerator, removing the carton of juice. "He makes me really happy."

She brushes my hair aside, kissing my temple. "I'm glad to see a smile back on your face. You had me worried there for a while, kiddo."

I pour a glass of cranberry juice and turn to face my mother. "You know what you said before, about loving two people at once, do you really believe that?"

She looks quietly contemplative. "I do, although it's never happened to me, but I believe the heart has huge capacity for love, and the inner workings of a woman's heart is a beautiful, precious, complex thing. Look how easy it is to love a sibling, a parent, and a lover at the same time in different ways? Who says you can't have romantic feelings for more than one person at a time? And if you do, who is to say it's wrong? All you should worry about is being true to yourself and treating those you love right."

It always amazes me how open my mother is to the notion of love when her own experiences haven't been good.

"Is it wrong for me to be with Ayd when I think I'll always love Dev?"

"You need to follow your heart, sweetie. What is your heart telling you now?"

"That I want to give this thing with Ayden a try. I don't think I ever really considered him before, but now it feels right."

"Then that's all that matters. You are with him for the right reasons, and you know he has a good heart, and I don't have to worry about him treating you right because he already does."

I try to keep Mom's words close to my heart the next morning at school as Ayden and I walk hand in hand to my locker, reminding myself that I haven't done anything wrong. Our hand holding isn't unusual, and no one bats an eye. However, when he stops to kiss me on the lips outside the classroom door, sounds of shocked gasps and whispered words surround us, and I know I'll be subject of gossip again today.

Ignoring the slack jaws and wide eyes, I drop into my seat, removing my books from my bag. Mariah angles her chair back, sending me a toothy grin. "I'm so happy for you guys."

I smile. "Thanks."

"Perhaps you're not quite as virginal as you like to make out," Alicia, one of Becky's minions, coos, leaning on my desk, and putting her face all up in mine. "You're really a sneaky little slut, aren't you? Stringing both those boys along." She tut-tuts. "Now your cover's blown, it's going to be open season."

A few titters ring out, and she slides into a seat across from me with a smug look on her face.

"I'm not surprised you're an expert on sluts considering you're such overused merchandise. That was you blowing Michael Chavis in the chem lab the last Friday before Christmas break, wasn't it?" I tap a finger off my chin, pretending to think about it. "Or was it Nick Farmer? Oh, my bad, he was the Wednesday."

Laughter and a few catcalls echo around the room.

Alicia cocks her head to the side. "You think you're funny? You won't be laughing when Becky gets a hold of you."

"I'm quaking in my boots," I deadpan.

"You will be," she hisses, glaring at me.

∞ ∞ ∞

"If looks could kill, you'd be under ten feet of earth by now," Gabi says, pointing her spoon in my direction. "Becky is fuming, and I fucking love it. About time someone stuck it to that sanctimonious bitch."

"She's just pissed over Friday night, but she'll get over it. No doubt she'll be back to her charming self in no time."

"Heads up," Mariah says. "Here comes lover boy."

Ayden is walking toward me, his eyes like laser beams trapping me in place, looking super-hot and totally gorgeous and I don't know why I've never properly noticed before. "Hey, babe." He slips into the seat beside me, kissing me on the cheek.

"Hey." My cheeks flush as I feel ten million eyeballs glued to the back of my head.

He chuckles, leaning in to plant a quick kiss on my lips. "We'll be old news soon."

But as the week progresses, the looks and hushed whispers continue, and it grates on my nerves.

Becky finally corners me on Thursday after P.E., in the changing room, shoving me into my locker with force. "Get lost." I push her away, and her nostrils flare. Several of my classmates look over anxiously but no one says anything. Most everyone is too afraid to cross Becky to dare intervene.

"Or what? You'll rat me out to your boyfriend? Can't fight your own battles?"

"Ayden has nothing to do with this."

"If that's true, why did he threaten me?" She plants her hands on her hips, snorting out a laugh. "As if that carries any weight, but, honestly, I didn't think you could be any more pathetic, but I was wrong."

"I don't know what you're talking about." I yank my bag out of my locker.

"Sure you don't."

I roll my eyes, slinging my bag over my shoulder. "I'd have to respect you to care about what you think, and I don't, so, I don't give two shits what you believe. Now get out of my way," I push past her, setting out to hunt down my boyfriend and find out what the hell is going on.

"I waited for her outside the bathroom at the theater and I told her to lay off you," Ayden admits in the Jeep on the drive home.

I groan, propping my feet up on the dash. "You can't get involved. It'll only make things worse."

"She fucking assaulted you, Lina, and you wouldn't even report her!"

"Because I'm not a tattletale, and I need to keep my record squeaky clean. I don't want anything jeopardizing my college place and you know that. Besides, it was weeks ago, and she hasn't touched me since, and if she does, I'll be ready for her next time. You need to let me handle this, or else I just look weak."

He sighs. "I won't sit back and watch her take crap out on you, so I'm not making any promises."

I should be mad at him for treating me like a helpless idiot, but I can't be mad at him for trying to protect me. I touch his face. "Thank you for protecting me, and I do appreciate what you're trying to do, so maybe next time we can discuss it before you bitch her out?"

He leans over, kissing me quickly on the lips. "I can agree to that."

"Good, because the last thing I want is that slut coming between us."

"She won't." He swings the Jeep into his driveway. "We won't let her."

"You want to stay over tonight?" I ask, a little shyly. "Mom's working a double, so she won't find out." He looks conflicted. "Or you don't have to. It's cool." My cheeks flare bright red when I realize he might think I was asking him for sex. Since Mom found out he warmed my bed some nights, he hasn't stayed over at all, and I just miss having him sleep beside me.

"Hey." He hauls me into his lap, wrapping his strong arms around me. "I love sharing a bed with you, but your mom asked us not to do that, and I feel funny about going behind her back."

I bark out a laugh. "Oh my God, you are such a stickler for the rules." Not that that in any way surprises me. Growing up, Dev and I were the rule breakers and Ayd was the one constantly saving our asses. Not that I'm completely reckless. I'm not stupid, and I'd never deliberately flout the rules if it was something important, but Ayden is so serious about *everything*. Dev and I teased him relentlessly growing up. "We're teenagers, Ayd, we're supposed to disobey our parents, and Mom is no fool. She knows we're dating now, so she's practically expecting it, and we really shouldn't disappoint her."

His lips twitch, and he starts tickling me. "You have an answer for everything, missy."

I shriek, squirming on his lap as he continues his onslaught. His eyes zone in on my lips, and his gaze darkens with lust. His mouth is on mine in a flash, and he kisses me deeply. Snaking my arms around his neck, I kiss him back with the same need, running my fingers through his hair and crushing my body to his. I feel him underneath me, hardening and lengthening, and it skyrockets my own arousal into orbit. I grind against him, feeling him right where I need him, moaning into his mouth.

"Lina." His voice is thick with lust. "I want to stay with you tonight, but I don't think we should have sex yet."

I peer into his eyes. "You don't want that with me?"

He grips my head firmly, his eyes blazing with sincerity. "Of course, I do, but it's a big step and I want you to be sure."

I nod, relaxing at his honesty. "I know, and when I asked you to stay, I wasn't asking for that. I miss sleeping beside you."

His features soften, and my heart melts at the adoring look in his eyes. He pecks my lips briefly. "Me too, and I'm glad we're in agreement on this."

"This feels very grown up," I tell him later that night as we lie side by side in my bed.

He reels me in close, and I nuzzle against his bare chest. He's wearing pajama pants and I'm in my comfy PJs and socks and it's not in any way awkward as I thought it might be after our earlier chat. "This feels right."

I look up at him, smiling. "It does. It really does."

He kisses me softly, and I kiss him back, basking in the strength and warmth of his embrace. The kisses turn more heated, and he pulls me even closer to his body, and I can't help moaning when his erection strains, pushing into my belly. My fingers trace circles on his chest while his tongue plunders my mouth. I straddle him, grabbing tufts of his hair and rocking my hips into his, kissing him over and over, need consuming my entire body. My lips leave his mouth, trailing along his jaw, nibbling on his ear, and my teeth graze his neck as I move lower. I pepper his chest with kisses, my tongue darting out to lick his nipples, and he emits a primal groan that has my core pulsing with need.

My fingers creep to the waistband of his pajama pants, hovering there. I lift my head up, looking at him. "I know we agreed no sex, but we can do other stuff, right?"

A vein throbs wildly in his neck as he licks his lips. "If you're sure."

I don't take my eyes off him as my hand slips under his pants. "I'm sure." He makes a strangled sound when my hand wraps around him, and

I start pumping slowly, up and down, in a rhythmic motion. Still keeping my eyes on him, I tug his pants down, watching as he springs free. I kneel up, taking a moment to ogle his gorgeous body. "Ayd," I whisper. "You are too beautiful for words."

His eyes roll back in his head as I lean down, wrapping my mouth around him and taking him as deep as I can. I work him slowly at first, relishing every flick of my tongue, every taste of his smooth skin and the salty, sweaty scent of his arousal. Gripping the base of his cock, I pump up and down as my lips works faster and faster, my teeth lightly grazing his throbbing length. He starts thrusting more urgently into my mouth, and I squirm as my own need accelerates. I think I could come like this.

His breath is oozing out in exaggerated spurts, and his legs are spasming as I cup his balls and gently squeeze. He tries to pull away, but I clamp on, suctioning my mouth to the top of his cock while my hand continues stroking his length. "Lina, I'm going to …" He tries to pull out, but I stay locked on, and he spasms, crying out as his release emits in hot spurts into my mouth and down my throat. I stay with him until I've swallowed every last drop. When his body has stopped thrusting, I pull away, sitting up and eyeing him with a naughty glint in my eye.

He props up on his elbows, looking at me with a stunned expression on his face. "Holy shit, Lina. Where the fuck did you learn to do that?" I open my mouth to speak, but he holds up one palm, stalling me. "Second thoughts, I don't want to know." He opens his arms. "Come here, sexy."

I crawl up his body, snuggling into his side, draping one leg over his. He kisses me passionately, holding my face and keeping me pinned to his side. Then, our positions are reversed, and he's got me flat on my back as his lips start worshiping me everywhere. "I want this off." He tugs at my top and I sit up, slowly peeling it off. He stares at me, and my nipples harden under his attentive gaze. "You are so unbelievably gorgeous, Lina. My God." Bending his head, he gently sucks one nipple into his mouth, and my head falls back as I whimper. My entire body is tingling and awash with sensation as he lavishes attention on my breasts, his hands roaming up and down my sides until I'm hot and aching all over. He lifts his head up. "I want to taste you too. Is that okay?"

"Please." I don't even recognize my own voice, dripping with lust and urgent need. He removes my pajama pants and strips me of my panties until I'm lying bare underneath him. "So fucking beautiful," he murmurs, cupping me down there. My eyes shutter and my back arches off the bed. "Ayden, please. I'm already so close."

He slips one finger inside me, and it glides in smoothly. "Fuck." He adds another, and my strangled moan would be embarrassing if I actually cared. But all I care about right now is getting off. His lips join his fingers, and I almost buck off the bed. "Careful, baby." With one hand on my hip, he holds me in place, his tongue working overtime to match the frantic pumping of his fingers.

I shatter explosively, screaming as the orgasm rips through me, igniting every nerve ending and every cell, flooding my body with blissful sensation. As I come down from my high, I open my eyes to find him watching me, a mix of joy and concern on his face. Tears prick my eyes, and his smile drops. "Hey." He moves up the bed, curling around me from behind. "Did I hurt you?"

"God, no." I swipe away the tears. "These are happy tears. I never thought we could have this and that it'd be so good, feel so right, and I just ..." *I love you.* I think it but I can't say it. Not yet. Not now. Now when I feel so conflicted. *How can I feel like this with him when every part of me still mourns the loss of Devin?* I'm so confused, and I can't help feeling guilty for my thoughts, so I can't tell him I love him, not until he owns my full heart.

"I know, baby," he whispers, and his hot breath tickles my neck. "You don't have to say it. I feel it too."

CHAPTER NINETEEN

Another couple of weeks rolls by, and life moves on. I barely see Devin or Becky, and outside of school, ballet, work, and football practice, Ayden and I spend every spare minute with each other. My friends are already teasing me that we've become one of those couples who are constantly joined at the hip. If Mom knows Ayden is warming my bed again, she isn't saying anything. While we still haven't had sex, and we haven't discussed it again, our make-out sessions are getting very hot and heavy, and I know it's only a matter of time. And I feel ready to give that part of myself to him, so I'm thinking it might be time to reopen that particular topic of conversation.

Devin still occupies far too much of my headspace, and that little pang in my heart still aches for him, but I'm not moping any more, and I'm getting on with things, which is the way it should be. But I miss him like crazy, and I know Ayden must too, but we never talk about him—it's as if he doesn't exist.

After the bell rings on Friday, signaling the end of another school week, I join the throngs in the corridor and walk to my locker to collect my things before heading to Ayden's football practice. I know the coach from the UI Hawkeyes will be here to check up on my guy, and I'm sure he's nervous. Thank God, there was no permanent damage to his arm. I smile when I spot his tall blond head towering over everyone as he waits by my locker. He's there every day after class ends without fail. I watch him watching my every step, and his gaze smolders as he drinks me in. I don't think he'll need much convincing to take our relationship to the next level.

"Hey, sexy." He draws me into his arms, immediately meshing his mouth with mine. The kiss turns scorching hot straightaway, and we're devouring one another. Delicious tingles skip around my body, and I grab fistfuls of his hair, moaning against his mouth, forgetting about the outside world as his kiss pulls me deeper and deeper into our own little universe. Ayden is an incredible kisser, and the excitement of being able to kiss him at will hasn't faded. He grinds his pelvis into mine, and I gasp into his mouth, feeling how much he wants me. To know he desires me for all the right reasons, and he doesn't deny me anything, makes me unbelievably happy.

Everything with Ayden is just easy-breezy.

Without breaking the kiss, he moves us around the corner so we have a little more privacy. He runs his hands up my side, casually brushing the side of my breast as his mouth continues to worship mine. My fingers dig into his hips, and I hold him tighter against me as we continue to eat one another.

Without warning, he's ripped off me, and I stand there, blinking, confused, dazed, watching as Devin shoves Ayden up against the wall. "What the fuck do you think you're doing?" Dev demands, his nostrils flaring.

"What I do with *my* girlfriend is none of your business." Ayden pushes him off.

"You were practically dry humping her in front of everyone. Show some respect."

Ayden throws back his head, fake laughing. "Oh my God, this is priceless. You think you can lecture me on respect? What a fucking joke."

A heated flush travels up my chest as I notice the growing crowd of gossip-hungry bystanders. I step toward the boys. "We're not getting into this in front of everyone again."

"Back up, Ange," Devin says, his eyes darting to my swollen mouth. "This is between Ayden and me." Emotion burns red-hot in his eyes as he stares at me. Ayden growls, and Devin whips his head around, shoving Ayden again. His eyes narrow to slits as he puts his face all up in Ayden's. "You think I don't know what you're doing?" He glares at his former best friend. "You planned this all along. That's why you told me to do it. You wanted her all to yourself, and I'm the fool because I didn't see it." Devin slams his fist into the locker right by Ayden's head, and I jump.

"Stop talking crap," Ayden snaps. "If you want to blame someone, point the finger at yourself. Your inability to keep your dick in your pants is the reason you lost her, and trying to pin this on me is pathetic. I love her and I'm taking care of her, and that includes keeping her away from you and that skank you call a girlfriend."

"Fuck you, man. She was mine, and you knew it, but you took her anyway."

"Not my fault you didn't stake your claim when you had the chance."

"You know why I didn't! You're a fucking asshole." Devin thrusts his fist into Ayden's face, and I scream. Ayden charges Devin, pushing him across the corridor as people scurry out of his path, slamming his back into the wall of lockers. The metal rattles and shakes as they trade blows, punching and swinging and knocking the shit out of one another.

Mariah sidles up to me, hooking her arm in mine. Cody sends me an apologetic look. "Do something," I beg him. "Please."

Devin's head jerks back and blood sprays from his mouth. Ayden punches him full force in the stomach, and Devin tumbles to the ground. Ayden jumps on top of him, landing blow after blow, and I watch in horrified shock as Cody and Josh try to haul him off.

A loud, shrill whistle erupts in the corridor, and the crowd disperses, leaving room for Coach Arnold and Principal Wells to make their way through.

"Go home," the principal shouts, flapping her hands about as she gestures to the nosy bystanders. "The final bell has rung, and there's nothing to see here."

Coach drags Ayden up by the scruff of his neck, shaking his head in disappointment. Blood seeps out of his nose, and the top of his shirt is torn and bloody. Cody helps Devin to his feet, and I gasp. His nose has doubled in size, and blood gushes out of it, dripping over the cut in his lip and the bruising along his jawline. His cheekbones are swollen, and one eye is half-closed and puffy. He looks worse than he does after an official fight, and I can't believe Ayden did that to him. He's like he lost all control.

"In my office. Now." The principal is furious as she stomps in the direction of her office.

Coach has a firm grip on Ayden's elbow as he steers him after the principal. "Can you take Lina home," Ayd calls out to Cody, deliberately not looking at me.

"Sure, man."

Devin rips a strip off the end of his shirt, shoving it into his nostrils in an attempt to stop the bleeding, and then he hobbles down the corridor after the others, completely ignoring me too. Mariah tugs on my arm. "Come on, let's go."

I shuck her arm off. "I'm not leaving without Ayd."

Cody crosses his arms. "Ange, you heard him. He wants you to go home."

I plant my hands on my hips. "I don't care. He doesn't make decisions for me. I'm staying and that's that."

I stalk off, dropping into a seat outside the principal's office to wait it out.

Shouts and the sound of arguing trickle from the room, and I know the guys are in deep shit for this. Principal Wells has a strict no-violence policy, and there will be hell to pay for sure.

About ten minutes later, the sounds of approaching footsteps prompt me to straighten up in my seat. My eyes pop wide as Mr. Morgan appears in my line of sight. He's wearing dirty khaki work pants and a white shirt that's smeared with grease. His handsome face is drawn in a hard grimace, and his fists are clenched at his sides. He stops in front of the door, glancing down at me. Recognition dawns on his face. "It's Angelina, right?"

"Yes, sir."

An amused smile curves up the corners of his mouth. "I haven't seen you in years." His green eyes, so similar to Devin's, roam up and down my body, and I squirm in my seat as my palms grow sweaty. "Look at you." His eyes narrow and darken, and he pins me in place with a look that sends chills creeping up my spine. "All grown up." His gaze darts to my chest, and, instinctively, I bring my bag against my body, hugging it to my chest.

The door swings open, and the principal looks from Devin's dad to me, frowning. "Mr. Morgan. Were you planning on joining us?"

Racing footsteps approach. "Stop looking at her!" Devin yells at his dad.

Mr. Morgan slants a venomous look at his son. "Shut your mouth. You're in no position to make demands."

"If everyone can just calm down," the principal says, stepping aside. "Please come in, Mr. Morgan. We're just waiting on Mr. and Mrs. Carter to arrive."

"Won't that be fun," Devin's dad drawls, turning to look at me one final time. Without invitation, he takes my hand, bringing it to his mouth and planting a sloppy kiss on my skin. I shudder, my mouth turns dry, and my stomach lurches unpleasantly. "What a pleasure it was to meet you again. I look forward to our next encounter." The grin he gives me is predatory in the extreme, and a rush of unease settles over me.

Devin yanks his father into the room by the elbow, shooting me a panicked look. "I'm sorry," he mouths.

The principal eyes me with concern. "It's time you went home, Ms. Ward."

"I'm waiting for Ayden, and he's my ride."

"Mr. Carter won't be finished for some time. I strongly suggest you make alternative arrangements."

I risk a peek into the room, and my eyes lock on Ayden's. He's hunched over in his seat, looking like he has the weight of the world on his shoulders. "I'm waiting for my boyfriend."

Mr. Morgan leans back in his chair, crossing his feet at the ankles and sneering at Devin. Devin stares straight ahead as if he's looking at nothing.

The clickety-click of heels tapping off the tiled floor alerts us to the arrival of the Carters. "Honey," Mrs. Carter says, placing her hand on my shoulder. "You should go home."

I have a sudden urge to bare my teeth and snarl. *What's up with everyone thinking they know what's best for me?* Biting back my frustration, I smile at Ayden's mom. "I'm waiting for Ayd."

Finally, everyone leaves me alone, and the door shuts as the meeting resumes. Coach storms out a short while later, shaking his head and looking at his watch. He doesn't say a word to me as he runs down the corridor. Fifteen minutes later, the door opens and Ayden steps out. I stand up, and he takes my hand. "Let's get out of here." He hurries me along the corridor before the others make an appearance.

We don't speak for ages, not until we're coasting on the highway, going the opposite direction to home. "Where are we going?"

"I don't know, but I just need to drive around for a while till I cool down."

"What happened?"

"We've both been suspended for a week."

"Shit."

"Dad is fuming, and Coach is pissed at me too especially because he had to ban me from practice tonight." He slams the steering wheel in frustration, accidentally pressing the horn. "Fuccckkk!"

I put my hand on his knee. "I'm sorry."

"Screw Devin. This is all his fault."

I bite my tongue, rubbing his knee in what I hope is a soothing gesture.

Ayden swings the car into the hard shoulder, drawing it to a stop. He leans over, capturing my lips with his, kissing me until I can scarcely breathe. He puts his forehead to mine. "Actually, can we just go to your place and chill out on the couch? You're all I need, and all I want, right now."

"Of course, babe." I trace my fingers along the coarse bristle on his jaw. "Whatever you want."

After an hour at home, making out like demons on the couch, it's obvious that Ayden is still full of pent-up energy. I prop up on my elbows, hovering over him while he fondles my ass through my jeans. "We could go upstairs?" I suggest, my eyes boring into his. His hands stall on my butt, and then he jumps up, taking my hand without uttering a word.

Pulling me down on the bed beside him, he kisses me firmly, draping his leg over mine. I palm the bulge in his jeans, stroking him through the denim. Without talking, we shed our clothes, kissing and touching until we're both naked and panting. Ayden kisses his way down my body, more urgently than normal, nudging my thighs apart as he buries his head between my legs. I wriggle around, gasping when his tongue dips inside me. He works me fast, and I fall over the ledge quickly. Panting, I sit up, shoving him down on the bed. I straddle him, rubbing myself over his erection.

"Lina, babe, I've only got so much self-control," he says, grabbing my hips and lifting me off.

I prop up on an elbow, brushing my hair back off my face as I stare earnestly at him. "I'm ready. I want you to make love to me."

He grabs my face. "Are you sure? If this is about wh—"

"This is about you and me and me wanting you to be the one to take my virginity. I want you to be my first, Ayden. Please don't make me beg."

His expression softens. "You know I'd never do that."

"Then I want to do this. Now. With you."

He stares at me silently for a couple minutes. Reaching over the edge of the bed, he grabs his jeans and pulls out a condom. My heart is pounding so hard, and the nervous flutter in my chest expands as I watch him rolling it on. Gently, he moves over me, holding himself up as he peers deep into my eyes. "We can stop at any time."

I place my hand on his bare chest. "I trust you."

His brow puckers, and he gulps, holding himself perfectly still over me, not moving a muscle. I tense up. He has a faraway look in his eyes that confuses me. "Ayd? Are you okay?"

He refocuses on me, smiling as he leans down, kissing me softly. "I'm fine. Don't worry. I've got you."

"Are you sure *you* want to do this?" I ask, heart pounding in my chest.

He kisses me more passionately. "I'm sure. Stop worrying."

"Okay." I nod, offering him a watery smile. He positions himself between my legs, and heat floods my body. He kisses me again. "It's probably going to hurt a little, but I'll go slow."

I capture his lips in a hot kiss, and ever so slowly, he starts inching inside me. Everything tenses up. "Relax, babe, loosen your limbs." He presses his mouth to that sensitive area on my neck and I widen my legs, sinking deeper into the bed. He pushes in a little more and a searing pain rips through me.

I wince, and he stops. "Don't stop. I'm okay," I assure him.

He continues worshiping my mouth and my neck, trailing his wet mouth down my body, teasing my nipples with his tongue, as he slowly fills me up. Once he's all in, he stays in place, continuing to kiss me all over until he doesn't feel so foreign inside me anymore. "You can move," I whisper, my cheeks heating. "I won't break."

"Tell me if it hurts." Very gently, he starts moving, and it stings but not as much as when he first moved inside me. I buck my hips up, and he increases the pace a little, and the sting fades a little, transforming to a more pleasant sensation. "Is this okay?"

"It doesn't hurt any more. Go faster."

His grin turns wicked, and he pulls my legs up around his waist. "Wrap them nice and tight, and hold on." His thrusts become quicker, more urgent, and my body responds, arching against him as all manner of unbelievable sensations surge through me. I'm peppering his face and chest with kisses, clawing at his back and his ass, imploring him to move faster. He chuckles before his expression turns dark and he devours my mouth, riding me hard, and I can't get enough. I grind against him and things are building inside me again. His entire body trembles, shaking and pulsing as he finds his release, and then I'm there with him.

We lie sated in each other's arms without speaking for a couple minutes as the magnitude of what we've just done sinks in.

He angles his body, lying on his side, and tilts my chin up. "Lina, are you okay?"

I peck his lips, snuggling into him as I smile. "I'm perfect."

"No regrets?"

I shake my head, smiling again. "Not a single one. I'm glad we did it." I lace my fingers in his, planting a soft kiss to the underside of his jaw. "I'm glad I did it with you."

CHAPTER TWENTY

The next week drags. School feels empty without Ayden, and his parents have grounded him so I can't even drop by in the evenings. I take some extra shifts at the diner, purely to pass the time. Having so much free time isn't good for me—because my mind wanders to places I wish it wouldn't. I don't regret sleeping with Ayden, but it's brought certain feelings to the surface again, and I know I shouldn't be thinking about Devin, but it's not that simple to cut someone from your life, especially when they've occupied such a huge part of it.

My heart is gloomy again, and I wonder if things will ever become uncomplicated.

Ayden is released from his penance the following Saturday, and we head to the movies with all the gang.

Things return to normal on Monday, but I'm uncharacteristically mute in the Jeep on the drive to school, although Ayd doesn't appear to notice.

The week is busy with senior portraits, and I've signed up for two advanced placement courses to gain some additional credits for college, so I don't actually see much of Ayden. On Friday night, he travels with his family to visit relatives, and I won't see him until tomorrow night.

Lucas stays after dinner, for the first time in ages. He's stretched out on the couch while I'm snuggled under a blanket on the leather recliner. We binge watch *Gossip Girl*, munching on popcorn. "You know," I say during the commercial break, "you don't have to rush off after dinner every night. I miss having you around."

He snorts. "Sure you do. I don't think Ayden would appreciate me cramping his style."

"He's not here all the time."

He shrugs. "It'd feel disloyal to Devin."

"That isn't anything to do with you."

He twists around on his stomach, resting his head on his hands. "He's my brother. I've got to have his back. Besides, I'm pissed with Ayden for what he's done."

I sigh, tucking my hair behind my ears. "Ayden hasn't done anything. This is all on Devin."

"But is it?"

I frown. "What aren't you saying?"

"Just that you might not have all the facts."

I sit a little more upright. "Like what? It's pretty black and white to me, and he's been with Becky these last seven weeks." Not that I'm counting or anything.

He cranks out a laugh. "Please don't tell me you're buying into that. He hates her."

My eyebrows climb up to my hairline. "Eh, yeah, I don't think so." I'm recalling her loud and very vocal recount in the library of Devin fucking her under the bleachers after school on Wednesday. Unless she's got him under some hypnotic spell, I'd say Devin likes her enough. Guess there's no accounting for taste.

I put my popcorn down, feeling a sudden bout of nausea swim up my throat. I shouldn't care. I've got Ayden, and Devin's made his own bed.

But, unfortunately, I do.

"I don't know what's going on, because he still treats me like I'm a little kid, so he doesn't confide in me, but I'd bet a hundred bucks that she's forcing him into this."

"Can we change the subject? The last thing I want to do is spend my Friday night talking about those two."

"I know he still cares about you. Like, a lot."

I childishly block my ears. "Stop, Luc. Please, I'm begging you."

Reluctantly, he nods, redirecting his attention to the TV.

Later, when I'm tucked up in bed, just before I fall asleep, I think back to Devin's words from the day of the fight. "She was mine, but you took her anyway," he'd told Ayden.

She. Was. Mine.

I hate the little well of hope that churns inside me at those words.

And I hate the part of myself that's still craving that.

Massive guilt comes crashing down on me, and I turn over in the bed, squeezing my eyes shut and willing my heart and my head to just get with the program. *I'm happy with Ayden, and Devin has already proven unworthy of me, so why can't I evict that stupid notion from my mind?*

I'm woken from sleep sometime in the early hours of the morning to the sound of raised voices outside. Screams and shouts have me flipping the covers off and racing to my balcony to investigate. Brisk chills accost me the second I open the French doors, and I snatch my robe from the top of my dresser, tying it securely around my waist. The shouts are coming from the front of the house, and I can't see from here, so I run back into the house, toeing my sneakers on at the front door, and tiptoe outside.

The lights on Devin's truck are fully on, bathing his house in luminous light. The driver side door is open, hanging off the hinges and trailing the ground. I gasp as I spot the massive dent in the side of the truck. The rear fender is mangled and hanging loose. Flooded with nervous adrenaline, I hop over the fence between our houses and race toward the Morgans' front door. A massive thud is followed by the sound of wood splintering from the rear of the property, so I run around the side of the house toward the backyard. A door slams shut at the back of the house, and all the windows rattle.

I almost trip over the body on the ground. "Oh my God!"

A low moan rings out as the person curls into a fetal position. I drop down on my knees, clamping a hand over my mouth as my eyes widen. "Oh my God! Devin! Are you okay?" Gingerly, I touch his face, panicking when warm liquid trickles between my fingers.

"Ange?" His speech is garbled, and judging by the pungent smell of whiskey in the air, I'm going to hazard a guess that he's totally smashed. He reaches out a hand, circling my wrist. "Ange?"

"It's me. Can you stand? Where does it hurt?"

"Everywhere," he whispers. "I hurt everywhere."

"We need to get him out of here," a voice says from behind, and I almost jump out of my skin. Lucas's hand clamps over my mouth, muffling my scream.

"Holy fuck, Luc. You scared the shit out of me."

He slides his arm under Devin, pulling him up. Devin cusses, cradling his ribs as he wraps his arm around his brother's shoulders. I prop him up on the other side, and together, we manage to get him into my house.

I flick the lights on in the kitchen and pull out a chair. I burst out crying when the true extent of Devin's injuries is revealed. His face is covered with blood, his hair matted with the stuff. He's wearing an open gray button-down shirt with a plain white T-shirt underneath, and both are spattered with blood. One sleeve is ripped. He winces as Lucas lowers him into the chair. Drying my eyes, I dash to the sink, filling a bowl with warm water. "Can you get the first aid kit from the bathroom upstairs, please," I ask Luc over my shoulder.

He nods, sprinting upstairs.

I pull a chair out in front of Devin and sit down, examining his face to see how bad the damage is. "I need to clear away the blood, Dev. This might sting."

Luc returns to the kitchen, handing the medical box to me. I remove some cotton pads, dip them in the water, and then gently dab at his face. He grips the arms of the chair, but he makes no sound as I slowly and carefully wipe the blood and grime from his face. Bile floods my mouth. "I think you might need stitches," I admit, eyeing the large gash at his temple. The rest of his face is like a colorful patchwork quilt of contusions and cuts.

"No hospital," he slurs, his eyes struggling to focus on mine. Lucas starts pacing the floor.

I can't take him to the hospital like this; he'll probably get arrested once they confirm he was driving while drunk. Mom should be able to fix him up when she gets in. "Help me get his shirt off," I ask Luc. "I need to check his ribs."

Devin sucks in a sharp breath as we strip his shirt and T-shirt off as gently as we can.

"Fuck's sake," Lucas hisses, his eyes raking over the bruising along Dev's left-hand side.

I shake my head, and sudden fury jumps up and bites me. "I can't believe you drove your truck while you were so hammered! What the hell were you thinking! You could've killed yourself or someone else."

"Don't be mad, baby doll," he slurs. "I'll be okay."

I extract a couple of pain pills and walk to the sink to fill a glass with water. I deliberately bite my tongue because now isn't the time to rip him a new one. He's still totally wasted, and I'd rather save it for morning. "Open your mouth." I curl his hand around the glass and pop the pills in his mouth. Lifting the glass to his lips, I tip the water in. "Swallow, and do not attempt to make some sleazy remark," I warn. The corners of Luc's mouth curve up. "Drink the rest of the water," I instruct, keeping the glass to Devin's mouth as I tap out a quick text to Mom.

"Ange, would it be okay if we both stayed here?" Lucas asks with a worried frown. "Dad blew a gasket, and I'd rather not go home."

"Sure. I know Mom won't mind."

He squeezes my shoulder. "Thanks."

"Don't touch her," Devin slurs. "No touching my girl."

My cheeks turn pink. "Help me with him?" I ask, deliberately ignoring Dev's statement.

Luc helps me bring him upstairs, undress him to his boxer briefs, and roll him onto the bed. I pull the covers up under his chin, turn off the main light, and switch my beside lamp on instead. I read Mom's reply before putting my cell aside. "Sleep it off. I'll stay here. Mom says to wake you every few hours in case you have a concussion. She'll check on you when she gets home."

He mumbles something incoherent and proceeds to instantly conk, light snores ripping from his mouth pretty much straightaway.

Lucas sits on the edge of the bed, while I slide under the covers beside Dev, opening my book. "Thanks for looking after him."

"I couldn't not do anything. Not when he's hurt."

"I'm really worried about him. He's worse since he stopped hanging with you and Ayden. It's a miracle he didn't crash his truck before now."

"He does this a lot?"

Lucas hangs his head. "All the time. He's always drunk, high, or hungover."

"I'm sorry."

"Couldn't you guys make up? Maybe he'll listen to you. All he does is tell me to mind my own business when I try to talk to him."

"It's not that simple."

"I understand," he says, looking like the weight of the world is on his shoulders, and a pang of sadness hits me square in the chest.

I get out of bed, and hug him. "It'll be okay, and I'll talk to him in the morning. I don't know if it'll do any good, but I'll try."

I do my best to stay awake, but when my eyelids start drooping, I set the alarm on my phone and curl up under the covers. Devin hasn't even budged position, and except for the rise and fall of his chest, and the intermittent snores, I would worry he wasn't breathing. I place my hand softly on his back, noticing the faded bruising mingling with fresher ones. Tears prick my eyes as I watch the boy sleeping beside me, hating how much I still love him, but at the same time happy I do, because Devin needs someone to love him, and I'd rather it be me. Even if it's from afar.

The irritating buzzing of my cell wakes me a few hours later. I reach my hand out, turning it off as I brush strands of my messy hair out of my face. My body's like a furnace, and my pajama top is plastered to my back. Devin is wrapped around me like a baby koala, and my chest tightens painfully.

A light cough captures my attention, and I lift my eyes, locking on Mom's razor-sharp gaze. She's sitting in a chair by Devin's side, still in her hospital uniform. "You need to wake him."

"Dev," I whisper, placing my hand on his arm. "Wake up."

He grumbles in his sleep, snuggling closer to me. The arm swathed across my stomach moves a little higher, brushing the underside of my breasts. My cheeks turn hot. I shake him a little more firmly this time. "Dev. Can you hear me?" He presses fully against me, and my skin flares up at the tell-tale hardness pushing against my leg. Lordy, could this get any more humiliating. "Dev!" I hiss, more urgently. "Wake up!"

His eyes flutter open, and he smiles when he sees me. "I thought I was dreaming," he mumbles, his fingers tracing over my face. "Man, you're so beautiful, Ange. Like that chick whose face launched a thousand ships, only more gorgeous." He nuzzles my neck. "And you smell fucking divine too." He inhales loudly, and two red spots darken my cheeks.

Mom struggles to contain her grin.

"Eh, Dev. We have company. You might want to tone it down a notch or ten."

Mom clears her throat, getting up and leaning over the bed. "I need to check you over."

Lazily, he turns over onto his back, smiling at my mom. "Hey, Nat. You're beautiful too, and I can totally see where Ange gets it from."

Mom laughs lightly, lifting his arm and wrapping a blood pressure monitor around it. "Why thank you, Devin. That's the nicest compliment anyone's paid me in a long time."

"Well, that's a darn shame. Beautiful girls should be told they're beautiful a million times a day."

"Oh, dear God," I exclaim, slapping a hand to my forehead. "Are you still drunk?"

"Sober as a judge," he proclaims, flashing me one of his trademark shit-eating grins. Tears spill from my eyes, and an anguished sob escapes my mouth before I can stop it. His grin fades. "Hey. What's wrong?"

Mom pretends not to listen while she takes his temperature and carefully probes the cut on his forehead and his tender ribs.

"You could've killed yourself last night." My tears instantly give way to rage. "You fucking idiot! What the hell are you doing with your life?!"

"Sweetheart," Mom cautions. "I know you're upset, but shouting isn't going to help anyone."

Devin pulls himself into an upright position, remembering to shield his erection with the comforter in time. His expression is grim. "You're right, and I don't know." He scrubs a hand over the thick stubble on his chin. "I know I'm messing up, but I don't know how to fix it."

CHAPTER TWENTY-ONE

Devin's words, and his helpless expression, are still on my mind Monday morning as I drive with Ayden to school. I was on edge all weekend, trying to figure out a way to explain Friday night to my boyfriend. No matter what way I spin it, I shared a bed with Devin, and I know Ayden is not going to be pleased about that. He was already in a foul mood when he arrived home late Saturday evening, so I chickened out, and I haven't told him yet. I'll tell him when he's calmer, I promise myself.

The school morning passes by uneventfully. I haven't seen Devin around, and I'm guessing he didn't show up today, understanding there is no excuse he can offer which would adequately explain the state of his face except the truth. The less people who know about that, the better. Since he left our house Saturday morning, I've texted him a bunch of times to ensure he's taking his pain meds, getting enough sleep, and drinking plenty of fluids. Luc has been taking care of him, and he texted me from Dev's phone telling me not to worry.

I'm walking through the cafeteria, tray in hand, when Becky steps in front of me, blocking my path. Planting her hands on her slim hips, she glowers at me. Nothing new there. My gaze roams over her minuscule hot pink top and short leather mini in disgust. I wear more clothes going to bed, and while I know the weather is getting milder, I can't fathom how she can walk around half-dressed. The more I think about it, the more Luc's words ring true: she's lording something over Devin to keep him by her side. I'd put money on it. "You're in my way. Please move." I keep my tone neutral, not wanting to get into this here.

She prods me in the chest with her finger. "I told you to stay away from him! He's mine." Her face contorts as she growls, and her lips pull into a menacing sneer.

"That's really not a good look on you," I say, watching Ayden getting out of his seat.

Her hands clench into fists at her side. "I know he spent the night with you on Friday, so don't even try to deny it."

My face pales as Ayden stares at me in shock. "It's not what you think," I say over Becky's head, but she assumes my comment is directed at her.

"I know exactly what it is. You fucking skank." She shoves me, hard, and I lose my balance, falling back onto my butt, the contents of my tray upending all over me.

Rage like I've never encountered before splutters to the surface as the crowd in the cafeteria joins Becky in laughing at my expense. Ayden is practically frozen in place, staring at me as if he doesn't know me. Out of the corner of my eye, I spy Mariah approaching, but I thrust the tray away and hop up before she can stop me. My brain switches off as I lunge at Becky, and I smirk at the startled expression on her face before we tumble to the ground. She reacts fast, grabbing fistfuls of my hair and yanking firmly. Ignoring the stinging pain in my scalp, I launch my fist in her face, laughing as she screams. Then we're rolling on the floor, surrounded by classmates who are chanting and calling our names as we throw punches and claw at each other. I shriek when she digs her long fingernails in my cheek and draws blood. Fury darkens my eyes, and I grab hold of her shoulders, squeezing hard. I'm ripped off her in a flash when a muscular arm wraps around my waist, pulling me upright. I hit out, thrashing about, screaming and shouting obscenities, as she does the same while Josh attempts to restrain her.

"Lina," Ayden commands in a stern voice. "Enough."

"What the hell is going on here?" Principal Wells demands to know, appearing in our line of sight. The crowd parts, instantly muting.

"She attacked me!" Becky screeches. "It's all her fault."

"You pushed her to the floor first, Becky," Ayden confirms. "You started this."

"In my office. Right. Now." The principal's tone brokers no argument, and she isn't doing anything to conceal her frustration or her anger.

Ayden removes his arm from around my waist, taking my hand in his as he steers me out of the cafeteria after Principal Wells. Sheepishly, I look up at him. "I can explain."

"Not now." A muscle clenches in his jaw, and I gulp. I've never seen him looking so hurt or so angry.

The principal is holding her office door open, and Ayden lets go of my hand, stepping away without a word. I walk inside, preparing myself to face the consequences of my action.

The principal doesn't hold back, refusing to accept any explanations or apologies. After she's torn a few strips off us, she instructs us to wait outside her office until our parents arrive, and we both drop dutifully into seats. Becky and I stare straight ahead, not looking at one another. When the principal leaves to go to the bathroom, Becky casts a surreptitious glance over her shoulder at the secretary. She has headphones on, and she's tapping away on the computer, not paying any attention to us. "You're going to pay for this, bitch. You are going to regret the day you crossed me."

I ignore her, and judging by the way she grips the arms of her chair, I can tell it pisses her off. If I thought Becky was my enemy before, it'll pale into insignificance in comparison to the war she's going to wage on me now. I've seen how vicious she can be, and now I know I'm going to feel the full extent of her wrath, I'm actually worried. She is going to make the last few months of senior class sheer hell.

Mom sends me a worried look when she rushes into the room twenty minutes later, quickly followed by Becky's parents.

"Mrs. Ward." Becky's dad greets Mom formally, before sending a disgusted look my way.

"Dr. Carmichael." Mom gulps nervously, and I send her a puzzled expression.

The next half hour is torturous as we are both forced to explain what happened in front of all the oldies. Dr. Carmichael sends a sharp, disappointed look at his daughter as he listens to her trying to downplay the part she played.

"I will be taking statements from some of the other students," the principal explains after we have finished talking, "considering you are both giving me different accounts. In the meantime, you are both suspended until further notice."

I hang my head, disgusted that I let that malicious bitch get to me. Now, I'm suspended for the first time in my life, and I hate that I've tarnished my reputation with the principal, dented my exemplary record, and, most of all, disappointed Mom.

Ayden is nowhere to be seen when we exit the principal's office, and that only enhances my shame and my anxiety. I need to find him and explain before he receives some embellished account of what happened with Devin and breaks up with me.

Mom escorts me to the car without saying a word. "I'm sorry, Mom," I admit, once we have driven out of the school gates. "I shouldn't have let her get to me, but she's been on my case for months now, and something inside me just snapped."

"There is no excuse that'll ever be acceptable for resorting to violence." Her voice is low, and now I feel like utter shit. "None."

Shame shrouds me in a veil of regret. "I know. I wish I could take it back."

"If Becky has been bullying you, you should've told me, and I would've come to the school with you."

"That wouldn't have helped, Mom. Girls like her are a law unto themselves."

She sadly shakes her head. "And for it to be Dr. Carmichael's daughter of all people." She sighs.

"He works with you?" I wasn't aware of that fact until now. I thought Becky's dad ran his own practice in town. I never realized he worked out of the hospital too.

"He's the director of the hospital. Essentially, he's my boss."

Double shit. "I didn't know. I'm sorry. Will you get in trouble at work?"

"No. He's a difficult man, but he's a professional through and through. He wouldn't allow anything that happened outside of the work environment to impact my position, but I'd still rather it wasn't his daughter involved."

"It's not my fault she's a class-A bitch."

"It's still no excuse for violence," Mom reminds me.

Ayden shows up after school, knocking on the front door with more vigor than usual. Mom sends me a knowing look. "I know I'm grounded, but I need to explain things to him. He's pissed at me."

"Fine, and you can see him for one hour per day, but that's it. You know I don't like punishing you, but this is a serious matter, and I need to know you understand that resorting to violence is never the answer. No matter what."

"I get it, Mom, and I'll take whatever punishment is coming my way."

I wipe my sweaty palms down the front of my jeans before opening the door to my boyfriend. Mom has made herself scarce so I walk into the living room with Ayden silently following me. "I was going to tell you."

He folds his arms over his chest. "Excuse me if I find that hard to believe. You had all weekend to tell me and you didn't."

"Because you were in a bad mood when you returned, and I didn't want to add to it."

"I'm calling bullshit on that."

"It's the truth. Well, part of the truth," I admit, averting my eyes. I draw a long breath before I prepare to spill my guts.

"Did you fuck him?"

My eyes pop wide. "What? No! Of course not!" Against my better judgment, I step into him, placing my hands cautiously on his chest as I peer into his face. "I would never do that to you."

He stares back at me, and I wonder what he sees. "You're still into him, aren't you?" He shakes his head, refusing to make eye contact. "Even after everything we've shared."

"Ayd." He removes my hands, and there's no disguising the hurt on his face. "Nothing happened between Devin and me. I woke up in the middle of the night to discover him injured and bleeding in his backyard. He was wasted, and he'd crashed his truck. Lucas was there, and he asked me if they could stay here 'cause his dad was furious. We fixed Dev up and put him to bed. Mom said to wake him every few hours to ensure he didn't have a concussion, and I tried to stay awake, but I fell asleep beside him, but it was all innocent. I swear."

He shoots me a disbelieving look, and I hate that he thinks I'm lying. "Ask Mom if you doubt me. She was there when we woke up, and she'll tell you I was fully clothed."

His eyes drill into me, and I hold my gaze steady. I've nothing to hide, and my conscience is clear. All I'm guilty of is helping an old friend out in his time of need and being stupid enough not to come clean with the boyfriend the minute he showed up. It's not like I've murdered someone.

His face relaxes, and air expels from his lungs. "It's okay. I believe you."

A layer of stress lifts off my shoulders. "Are we okay?"

"Do you want us to be okay?"

I frown. "What does that mean?"

"Am I still who you want, Lina?"

"Of course, you are." I snake my arms around him. "I'm sorry I've made you doubt yourself, doubt us, but I couldn't leave him out there, Ayd. He was in really bad shape. Go over and see for yourself."

Slowly, his arms encircle my lower back, and I offer up silent thanks. "It's okay. I know we're not friends anymore, but helping him was the right thing to do. I just wish I hadn't found out the way I had. Now everyone is talking about the three of us again, and I'm sick of all this shit."

"I'm sorry." I look up at him. "I promise it won't happen again."

As he lowers his mouth to mine, I ignore the conflict brewing to epic proportions inside me and open my mouth to welcome him.

Becky and I are suspended for a week, and when we return to school, we are both cautioned to stay away from one another, but I know it's only a matter of time before open hostilities resume. Becky's a smart bully, and she won't do anything while there's a spotlight on our heads, but I know I only have a small window of reprieve.

Devin is also back at school, and most of his injuries appear healed, but he's also back to blatantly ignoring me, and it's like I've regressed in time. I don't know why I thought it'd be any different, but those few hours in his company has reignited old feelings and scars, and I'm sinking back into a bad place.

February turns to March, and it's a couple weeks before spring break. I can't believe I'm close to entering my last semester of high school. It still seems surreal to think I'll be in college in six months' time. Remarkably, Becky hasn't come near me, and things have settled down again.

While Ayd said he forgave me, things aren't quite the same between us, and there's a wall in place that wasn't there before. Not only that, but he's acting strange. Usually, he collects me from the diner after my shift ends most Friday nights, but the last couple of Fridays he has gone out partying, staggering home in the early hours, smashed and rambling incoherently. He falls into bed beside me, smelling like beer and cigarette smoke, snoring loud enough to wake every household in the area. I've also been present for the many rip-roaring arguments with his dad and the disappointed looks from Coach when he saunters into practice late.

I've asked him continuously what's wrong, but he keeps telling me nothing, and I hate that he won't open up to me, but I don't push him, because I'm fearful it's me, and I'm terrified that I'm on the verge of losing my other best friend, so I seal my lips and try to pretend like my boyfriend isn't transforming before my eyes.

CHAPTER TWENTY-TWO

It's the first Friday of the month, and I'm walking to my locker with Mariah after the last class of the day when a commotion up ahead claims our attention. People are huddled around their lockers, pretending they're not listening to the massive argument between Becky and Devin.

"I said we're done, and I meant it," Devin says, glaring at her. "So get the fuck out of my face."

Mariah and I trade surprised expressions.

"Baby, come on," Becky pleads, pouting her lips and fawning at him. "I said I'm sorry and there's no need for anything to change. We're so good together."

Devin slams his locker shut, and she jumps a little. His mouth is curled into a sneer as he puts his face in hers. "We were never good together, and I hated every second of it. Every fucking second was torture for me."

Becky stiffens her spine, glancing subtly at the devout crowd. She tosses her hair over one shoulder, fixing Devin with a fierce look. "There's no need to lie."

He harrumphs. "Are you for fucking real?" He glares at her, and I swear every person close by rears back from the look of pure hatred in his eyes. I'm captivated by the scene unfolding. Although, it's nothing to do with me, and I can't see how anything will change in our situation, I'm thrilled Devin has finally woken up. Thrilled that the bitch is finally getting her comeuppance.

"The only liar, the only cheat, around here is you." He stabs a finger in front of her face. "You're a despicable, pathetic excuse for a human being, and I wish I could lobotomize myself to wipe all memory of you from my mind. I have never met anyone with such a poisoned mind, and, one day, hopefully soon, you'll get what's coming to you. Until then," he says, slinging his bag over one shoulder, "stay the hell away from me." His eyes lock on mine momentarily. "And if you ever so much as look funny at Ange, I will take that personally and come after you with everything I've got. I've never hit a woman before, but, by God, I think I'd make an exception for you."

Shocked gasps greet his words, but my heart is galloping around my chest throwing cartwheels.

"Screw you, Dev. You were a fucking lousy boyfriend anyway." She slams into his shoulder as she moves away, narrowing her eyes at me. "You're welcome to my sloppy seconds. Good luck slumming it." Her expression turns to disgust as she rakes her gaze over me. "Not that you'll have to lower your standards much."

Ayden reaches my side before I can respond. "Fuck off, Becky. Everyone knows Lina is worth a million of you." He loyally laces his fingers in mine. She flips him the middle finger before flouncing off, her minions scurrying after her like the pathetic idiots they are. The crowd disperses, until there's only a handful of people left.

Devin is rooted to the spot, staring at Ayden and me. A muscle ticks in Ayd's jaw. "Get your stuff," he tells me, never taking his eyes off his former best friend.

I scramble to my locker, pulling out the books I need and stuffing them into my bag. Mariah is quiet at my side as I close my locker and turn back around. The guys are still in a silent standoff. I shuffle anxiously on my feet. Ayd reaches out, tucking me into his side. Devin's chest rises and falls, but he still says nothing. I trade looks with Mariah, and Ayd tightens his hold on me. "This changes nothing," he finally says, breaking the tense faceoff. "I'm glad you ditched the bitch, but Lina and I are still dead to you."

I open my mouth to interject, but Ayd cuts me off with a penetrating stare.

Dev's jaw tenses, pulsing in and out, his gaze bouncing between us. Slowly, he nods. Gripping the straps of his bag, he takes off, his long strides echoing through the eerily quiet hallway. Mariah chews anxiously on the corner of her lip. "You go ahead," I tell her. "I'm going to ride with Ayd."

She gives me a quick one-armed hug. "Okay. Call me later."

We walk in silence to Ayd's Jeep, and my emotions are ricocheting all over the place. Ayden thrusts the engine into gear and the car glides smoothly out onto the road. "I think you were a little harsh," I admit, breaking the silence first.

"Was I?" he hisses.

"Yes."

He snorts. "Is this the part where you waltz into his arms now he's a free agent again?"

My spine stiffens. "Excuse me?" I turn the full strength of my glare on him. "That is not what I meant and you know it. I'm with you, and I've no plans to change that. I just think we could all try to be friends again now."

"Grow up, Lina."

His tone and his words piss me off. "Me grow up? How about you give yourself that little pep talk."

"Have you forgotten what he did to you?" I fold my arms across my chest and stare out the window. "Well, have you?" he demands again.

"Of course, I haven't," I retort.

"Good. Because you'd do well to remember that Devin is on a one-way path to nothing, and I'm not letting him take you down with him."

"How can you talk about him like that?" I swivel in my seat, drilling a hole in the side of his face as I speak. "And you don't get to make decisions for me. You're my boyfriend, not my freaking father."

"You're fucking unbelievable, do you know that?" He turns his head, ensuring I see the full extent of his disappointment. "I actually thought you loved me, but I've only ever been the backup plan."

"That's not fair," I cry out. "I do love you, and you weren't some consolation prize, so stop making out like you are."

"If that's true, then why has anything changed just because he tossed Becky aside?"

My protest withers up and dies. Ayden's right. This doesn't change the past or eradicate how much Devin has hurt me.

Devin breaking up with her changes absolutely nothing.

∞ ∞ ∞

Another week passes by, and another wall has gone up between Ayden and me. Devin is like the invisible obstacle in our path. That and whatever Ayden is keeping from me. For the first time in forever, he fails to turn up Saturday night after work to pick me up, and his cell is switched off when I try to call him. Mariah shows up ten minutes later, and I jump in her car. "Thanks for coming to get me."

"No problem. I can't believe he stood you up."

"I know. It's not like him, but he hasn't been himself lately. I don't know what's up with him."

She wets her lips, looking at me anxiously. I lean forward in my seat. "If you know something, spit it out."

"I wasn't sure whether to say anything or not, but Cody says he's getting into trouble with the coach and he's skipped a couple of practice sessions and turned up half-drunk at a few others."

"What?" I can't believe my ears.

"The guys have noticed something's up too, but he hasn't breathed a word to them either."

"Do you know where he is?"

She reluctantly nods. "When you texted me, I called Cody. He's at the party at Zach's house."

"Can you drive me there?"

"You sure you want to do this?"

"I need to know what's going on with him. He won't talk when he's sober. Maybe he'll fess up when he's drunk."

The party is in full swing when we arrive, and I cough as we fight our way through the stuffy, congested hallway, past the crowded living room, and into the kitchen. I hear him before I see him, his loud laugh reaching me from across the room. Cody, Josh, Zach, and Ayden are surrounded by cheerleaders, and he's laughing at something they said. My blood instantly boils. *He stood me up to flirt with Becky's minions?*

I stalk toward him, tugging on his elbow. He looks down at me, blinking, his forehead puckering. "What are you doing here?" he slurs.

I cross my arms over my chest, ignoring the gaggle of girls waiting with baited breath for a new showdown. "I could ask you the same thing. Forget about something?"

His brows knit together, and he squints at his watch, swaying a little on his feet. Considering he's so wasted, I'm actually glad he forgot to pick me up. There's no way I want him driving in that condition. "Shit, Lina. I'm sorry. I didn't realize it was so late."

"Can we please go?"

He batters his forearms. "Don't feel like going home yet."

"Well, tough." I hold out my hand. "Keys. Hand 'em over."

"Chill, babe." He smacks a loud kiss off my cheek. "Stay and have a drink."

"I don't want to stay. I've been on my feet all night and I'm tired. I want to go home."

He shrugs. "Well, go home. There's nothing stopping you."

"I'm not leaving you here."

"You're not my fucking mother, so quit acting like it."

A few of the cheerleaders titter, and I grind my teeth. "You are not driving home when you're fucking smashed, so give me your keys, and let's get out of here."

"No."

"*No?*"

"No," he repeats, sending me a challenging look.

I close my eyes in exasperation. A hand reaches out, patting my elbow. "I'm sober, Ange. I'll drive him home, and he can come get his Jeep in the morning," Josh offers.

My throat constricts as I nod, turning to leave. I've said all I'm prepared to say in front of the others. Before I go, Ayden hauls me to him, smashing his lips against mine. He smells like he drank the brewery dry. Annoyed, I wrestle out of his grip. "I'll talk to you tomorrow."

"See ya, babe." He swats my ass as I walk away, oblivious to the tears welling in my eyes.

"I'll drive you home," Mariah says, looping her arm in mine.

I shake my head. "No, stay with Cody. I want to walk anyway. That's why I didn't offer to drive Ayden's Jeep home." It's only a twenty-minute walk, and I need the time to process my thoughts.

"I don't mind, and Ayden wouldn't want you walking home alone."

I send her an incredulous look as we step outside the house onto the lawn. "Yeah, right," I harrumph. "Were you not just there when he patted me on the ass and sent me on my merry way so he could stay and get drunker and flirt with those sluts?"

"He won't cheat on you."

"He can go and fuck the whole cheerleading square for all I care," I spit out, and the worrying thing is how little that statement genuinely affects me. I should care that my boyfriend would rather stay with those skanks than see me home safely, but I think I'm immune to rejection at this stage.

Mariah tries to steer me to her car, but I shake her off. "I love you, M, but you need to let me walk, because if I don't, I'm going to go into my house and trash the fucking place. I need to walk off my anger. I have my phone, and I'll text you the minute I get home."

She nods sadly. "He's being an ass, but that's not who he is. You know he worships the ground you walk on."

"He has a funny way of showing it lately."

"Maybe he'll talk to you now. Tell you what's wrong."

I hug my friend. "Perhaps. Go back to your boyfriend, and I'll talk to you tomorrow."

She watches me until I disappear out of sight around the bend. I pull my hoodie up over my head, shoving my hands in the pockets of my jeans as I walk home, my head cluttered with grave thoughts and my heart aching.

I've been walking for ten minutes when a truck pulls up alongside me. "Ange?" Devin calls out, and I look up. "What are you doing walking by yourself?" I shrug, unwilling to discuss it with him. He kills the engine and hops out. "Get in, I'll drive you home."

"I want to walk." I keep walking, refusing to look at him.

He jogs after me, gently taking my elbow. "Just stop for a minute."

"Why? It's not your job to take care of me. I want to walk so keep driving." I shuck his arm off and take a step forward, but he plants himself in my path.

"Where is Ayden?"

"At Zach's."

Devin frowns. "And he let you walk by yourself?"

"Yes," I say through gritted teeth.

"Did something happen?" I shrug again. "I'll kick his fucking ass."

"Forget it, Dev. It doesn't matter, and it's nothing to do with you anyway."

"The hell it isn't! He can't let you walk off by yourself close to midnight. It's not fucking safe. Get in the truck now, or I'll put you over my shoulder and drag you myself."

I glower at him. "You wouldn't dare." He sends me a cheeky smirk, and my lady parts swoon. God, I have missed him so much.

"Try me. Go on," he challenges.

I sigh in exasperation, shaking my head. "Fine. I'll get in the truck with you."

We walk side by side in silence. Devin opens the passenger door for me, and I climb into the seat. "You fixed your truck," I say once he is inside.

"Patched it up as best I could. I still need a few parts, but I'll have to save up for them." I pull my knees into my chest and look out the window. "I can't believe Saint Ayden blew you off for a party. What the hell is wrong with him?"

"I don't know. He won't talk to me, but something is up with him."

He's reflective for a minute. "I can try talking to him if you like."

I pin him with a dubious look. "And you think he'd talk to you over me? Hardly likely."

"Probably not, but I can try."

"I know what you're trying to do, and it's too late. He was adamant that nothing's changed. That you don't belong in our lives anymore."

"What about you?" he asks, glancing quickly at me. "What do you think?"

I'm quiet for a bit before replying. "I agree. You breaking up with Becky is great because you deserve better than her, but it doesn't change what happened between us and it won't magically repair the damage. I can't be your friend."

Not when I still want more.

The thought lands in my mind unbidden, and I'm instantly guilty. Although Ayden's acted like a jackass tonight, he's the one who has stuck by me through thick and thin, and he's my boyfriend. I shouldn't be having thoughts of any other guy when I'm with him.

Devin slows the truck down as we turn onto our street. "I wasn't with Becky by choice," he admits, confirming my suspicions. "She lied to me. She said—"

I cut him off dead. "I don't want to hear it. It changes nothing." Devin still doesn't see me as girlfriend material, and I can't just be his friend. It hurts too much to be close to him and not touch him.

"But you don't understand—"

My eyes narrow to slits as I peer out the windshield. An incredulous laugh busts out of my lips. "You're right, I don't. Because if what you say is true, why is Becky standing in your driveway glaring at us right this second?"

CHAPTER TWENTY-THREE

Dev cusses under his breath. "I didn't invite her here, and I don't want anything to do with her."

"Tell it to someone who cares." My hand is curled around the door handle when he reaches across me, holding my wrist.

"Please, Ange. I need to speak to you. I'll explain everything."

"It's too late, Devin, and I'm sick of all this crap. I just want to finish high school without any more drama. I'm tired of it."

Becky storms to my door, yanking it open, almost wrenching my arm out of its socket. "Screw off," she fumes. "I need to speak to my boyfriend."

"For the last time, Becky," Devin sighs exasperatedly, "I am not your boyfriend nor will I ever be again. I've nothing more to say to you, and I'd like you to leave."

"I'm done with this," I say, sliding out of the truck, and rounding the front.

Becky grabs a hold of my hair from behind, catching me off guard as she slams my face into the hood of the truck. Pain rips across my skin, bringing tears to my eyes. Devin roars, shoving Becky off and helping me to straighten up. Warm liquid leaks out of my nose and my vision is blurry.

"Get the fuck out of here now, Becky, or I will not be responsible for my actions." Devin's voice is laden with intent, and his fists are clenching and unclenching at his side.

"What the hell is going on out here?" a gruff voice shouts out as the sounds of approaching footfall tickle my eardrums.

Devin cusses again. "Ange," he whispers urgently in my ear. "I need you to go into your house right this second. I don't want my dad anywhere near you. Can you manage by yourself?"

Instantly picking up on the alarm in his voice, I don't question his request. I nod, and with my vision still blurry, I stumble away, pressing my fingers to my nose to quell the blood flow.

Before I reach the top end of the fence I'm yanked sideways, and I scream at the unexpected contact. "Hey, pretty lady, where'd you think you're going?" Devin's dad asks, his alcohol-laden breath coasting across my face. I'm glad my vision is distorted because I don't want to see the look on his face.

"Get your fucking hands off her," Devin yells, yanking me out of his father's hold and standing protectively in front of me. "She is not yours to touch."

His father barks out a laugh.

"And she's not yours to touch either," Becky hisses, inching up beside Devin.

"Well, who do we have here?" Mr. Morgan asks.

"Go, Ange," Devin whispers in my ear. "Lock all the windows and doors, and don't come out, no matter what."

I don't need to be told twice. I run toward my house on wobbly legs, almost tumbling to the ground as I pull myself over the fence, but I keep going, not looking back. I fumble with the keys, but once the door is open, I fall inside my house, slumping to the floor in the hall. Hot tears course down my cheeks, but I quickly swipe them away. Screw the both of them. And Ayden. Hauling myself to my feet, I trudge up the stairs. As I strip off my clothes in my bedroom, sounds of arguing from outside filter in through the open window. Wrapping my robe around me, I pull the window closed, muffling the sounds of Becky, Devin, and his dad screaming at one another. I pad to the bathroom to clean up the mess that is my face. My nose is bloody and swollen, and a large bruise is already forming on my left cheek. After running a hot bath, I soak in the tub until my limbs have relaxed and the water turns cold. My skin is wrinkled like a prune as I dry and dress myself.

I'm running a comb through my hair as I peer out the window. All appears to be quiet on the home front now. Devin's truck is missing, and Becky and Mr. Morgan are nowhere to be seen. Lights are on in the downstairs of the Morgan house, and I frown as I notice the cracked, broken pane of glass at the side of the house.

Popping a couple of pain pills, I retreat to bed, pulling the covers up over me to ward off the intense bout of shivering that has overtaken my body. It feels like I've lived a hundred lifetimes today, and, as my eyes flicker closed, I say a prayer that tomorrow is a better day.

I lounge around the house feeling sorry for myself the next morning. Mom is in bed, and Ayden is obviously still sleeping off his hangover, so I'm grateful when Mariah calls, inviting me over to her house.

Betsy chugs and splutters when I turn on the engine, but mercifully she behaves the duration of the short journey.

I have my hand raised to knock on the door when it swings open. Mariah gawps at me with her mouth hanging open. "What the hell happened to your face?"

"Becky happened to my face," I reply, stepping inside. Her parents and her little sister are away for the weekend, and Cody is staying over with her, but he's doing stocktaking in his Dad's hardware store today, so we're on our lonesome. "Devin pulled up when I was walking home last night, and he insisted on driving me the rest of the way. Becky was waiting in his driveway when we arrived, and she didn't take too kindly to me being there."

"This has got to stop." Mariah shakes her head. "You have to report her this time."

"It didn't happen on school grounds. They won't care."

"The hell they won't." She nudges me into a chair, handing me a mug of tea.

"Well then, we need a plan to take her down ourselves. I'm not going to stand by and allow this any longer. I can call Madisyn and Gabi right now and get them to come over."

I shake my head. "Not tonight. I'm not in the mood for a group session. I just want to lick my wounds in private."

She tilts her head to the side as she drops down on the couch beside me. "Yesterday was a bitch, huh?"

"Yep. Speaking of, did Ayd get home okay?"

Her brows lift. "You haven't seen him today?"

"Nope. Either he's still dealing with his hangover or he's hiding from me."

"Josh drove him home a couple of hours after you left. He was totally hammered and swaying all over the place, talking absolute gibberish, but he didn't so much as look at any other girls," she says, patting my hand, "so you can rest assured your boy is loyal."

"I wasn't really worried about that."

"Devin showed up and he was disgusted with Ayden which is funny considering it's usually him in that condition."

"Was Becky with him?"

"No. He was alone. He was sprawled across the couch, snoring his head off when we left."

"Did he … was he with anyone?"

She shakes her head, pausing momentarily before speaking. "You still have feelings for him, don't you?"

I nod. "I feel so guilty over that, but I can't help how I feel."

"What about Ayd?"

"I have feelings for him too, but I don't think he's really into this. I'm not sure he ever really was."

"What are you going to do?"

That's the million-dollar question. "I honestly don't know."

∞ ∞ ∞

Ayden finally surfaces Sunday night, groveling and promising faithfully that he won't let me down again. He showed up with three bunches of lilies, and my room smells like a florist shop now. I know he's pissed that Dev ended up making sure I got home safely, but he's not stupid enough to criticize me for accepting the ride. He's still insisting nothing's wrong, just that he feels like blowing off some steam, and I let it drop because it's not like I can coerce him to be honest if he doesn't want to.

I endure a sleepless night, my thoughts consumed with how much things have changed between me, Ayden, and Devin.

The whole school is buzzing with the news on Monday, and I scan the hallways looking for Devin but he's nowhere to be found. The more stuff I hear, the more concerned I become.

"I've heard that Becky's minions are pointing the finger of blame at Devin," Gabi is telling the others as I drop into my seat in the cafeteria at lunchtime.

"He wasn't involved," Mariah pipes up. "He was at Zach's when it's alleged to have happened, and he crashed there all night. Those bitches just want to cause trouble for him."

"What exactly are they saying happened?" I ask, picking at my chicken salad. "All I've heard are unsubstantiated rumors."

"Well," Madisyn leans across the table, lowering her voice. "According to my uncle, it was Lucas Morgan who called it in." Madisyn's uncle is a cop in the local station. "Apparently, he was at a friend's house overnight, and he found Becky unconscious at the side of the road yesterday morning, not far from his house."

All the blood drains from my face as I recall the arguing in Devin's driveway the night before and the broken kitchen window.

"Do you know what exactly happened to Becky?"

Madisyn glances around to make sure no one is listening. "You can't repeat this, or my uncle'll get in trouble." We all nod, leaning toward her expectantly. "She was beat up pretty bad, like she has bruises everywhere, and the sick fuck stubbed ciggies out on her arm and her tits, and it looked like someone had tried to strangle her."

Mariah eyeballs me over the table as nausea swims up my throat. I push my uneaten salad away.

"And that's not all." Madisyn's eyes flash to mine. "When she came to, Becky was hysterical and really frightened, and she's refusing to say who did this to her or why."

I stand up. "I have to go." I turn to Mariah. "Any chance of a ride?" I rode with Ayden today, but I don't want to ask him to drive me, because I know he won't approve of my plan to ditch school and hunt Devin down.

She nods in silent agreement, grabbing the apple and bottle of water from her tray and walking out with me.

"Devin's place?" she asks, correctly guessing where my head is at.

I bite down on my lip as she maneuvers the car out of the parking space. "Yeah. Thanks."

"You're thinking he's involved?"

"He didn't do this." I shake my head resolutely. I know Devin has publicly threatened Becky but he wouldn't do this to anyone; however, I know something went down at his house Saturday night and I need to find out what.

"But Becky was at his house that night so ..." Her voice trails off.

I lean forward in my seat. "You can't tell anyone that. Half the cops in this town would arrest Devin if they knew purely based on his rep."

"I know, and I haven't mentioned it to anyone nor will I. Devin's a lot of things, but I know he isn't capable of something like this."

I visibly relax. "Thanks, M. I need to talk to him to find out what he knows, but he's innocent of assault. I don't need anyone to tell me that." I tap out a quick text to let him know I'm on my way.

She pulls the car alongside the curb outside my house, killing the engine. "What do you want me to tell Ayden?"

"You don't have to lie," I say, opening the door. "Tell him you took me here if he asks."

"Okay. Call me later."

"I will. Thanks for the ride." I shut the door, and walk around the front, bypassing my house and heading straight for Devin's.

He opens the front door, quietly watching me stride toward him. He's dressed in low-hanging gray sweats and a white tank with his feet bare, and he still manages to look completely drool-worthy. Worry lines crinkle the corners of his bloodshot eyes as I approach. "Can we talk at my house?" I inquire.

"Dad's not here." He steps aside, and I enter his house for the first time in years. It's almost exactly how I remember it, and it's a bit like stepping into a time warp. Although the furniture is the same, the years of wear and tear have taken their toll. The fabric couch is ripped and torn in several places, and the mahogany coffee table is scratched and chipped. The faded hardwood floor creaks as I follow Dev into the kitchen. "Coffee?" he asks, looking over his shoulder.

"Please." I remove my jacket, dropping it and my bag on the floor.

"Does Ayd know you're ditching?" he asks while pouring two cups of steaming-hot coffee.

"What do you think?" I pull out a chair and sit down. I look around the kitchen, noticing the tired cupboards, broken appliances, and the taped material over the broken window. The place might be in need of some TLC, but it's clean and tidy, and it's obvious someone has been taking care of basic needs. I'm guessing that someone is the boy advancing toward me. I take the cup from his hand with a grateful smile.

Dev sinks into the chair across from me, smirking. "I'm thinking right about now Ayd is blowing a gasket, and your cell's gonna ping in about five, four, three, two—"

My cell vibrates, interrupting him.

His smirk morphs into a wide grin, and I smile as I shake my head, removing my phone from my back pocket. Ayden's text pops into my inbox, confirming Dev's inkling. I don't open it up; I already know what it says.

Taking a tiny sip of the hot, pungent coffee, I look up at him. "The news about Becky is all over school."

The grin slips off his mouth. "I figured it would be."

The air is thick with tension. "I know this wasn't you, but I also know something happened that night. What's going on, Dev?"

He puts his coffee down, sitting up straighter. Propping his elbows on top of the table, he angles his body toward me, biting on his lower lip. "I don't know exactly what happened. I took off in my truck and spent the night at Zach's. Lucas was at Riley's house. When I got back here, he told me about finding Becky, and calling nine-one-one. They won't let me in to see her, so I don't know what's going on, only that my dad is gone, and that speaks volumes."

"What do you mean gone?"

"He hasn't been here since that night, and I got a call from the foreman at the plant today asking why he didn't show up for work. I checked his closet and it's cleared out. He's left."

I clear my throat. "You think … do you think he did this to Becky?"

Very slowly, Dev nods, averting his eyes to the floor.

Silence engulfs us for a bit.

"Have the cops been round?"

"I took Lucas down to the station yesterday to make a statement, and they hauled my ass in for questioning, but they let me go after checking my alibi with Zach." He scoffs. "Typical they'd instantly think I had something to do with this."

I eyeball him. "You can't really blame them. She's your ex, she was found near your house, and you're regularly in trouble for fighting."

"I don't fucking assault women!" He slams back in his chair. "Nice to know you hold me in such high regard."

I stretch out my hand, touching his knee. "I know you didn't assault her, but you've got to see it from their perspective. It's not a surprise they'd want to question you is all I meant."

He rests his head in his hands. "I could just do without this shit."

I knot my hands in my lap. "Is she badly hurt?"

His pained eyes meet mine. "I believe so."

I clamp a hand over my mouth. "Did he … did he …" I can't even form the words. The thought of that man's hands anywhere near me makes me want to puke. If he did this to her, I can't imagine what's she going through right now.

Dev shakes his head. "That's not his MO. He's all about control. He likes beating on people so they know he's the boss."

I jerk my head up, as certain things slot into place in my head. "Did he—"

He goes rigidly still, and his face shuts down. "I don't want to talk about him anymore," he snaps.

"Why do you keep shutting me out?"

His jaw stretches taut. "You can't fix this. You can't fix me."

"You're my best friend. I want to help."

He harrumphs. "Am I really your best friend? The two of you just cut me off with no trouble."

I swallow the bile in my mouth. "There's been nothing easy about the last few months, believe me."

He cocks a brow. "Tell me, how does superiority feel? I wouldn't know, because my entire life has been spent at the bottom of the food chain."

"Don't be like that. Ayden and I have never treated you like you were any less than us."

He snorts. "You fucking pushed me aside without any thought to how that'd make me feel!"

"You screwed that slut and then went exclusive with her! How the hell do you think that made *me* feel?"

His nostrils flare. "Why would you care? You're fucking him now."

I cradle my head in my hands, groaning as I draw a deep breath. A sharp ache prods me straight through the heart. Lifting my head up, I pierce him with an earnest stare. "I didn't want for any of this to happen. And I miss you. So Goddamned much."

He looks away, saying nothing, and a tense silence perforates the air again. "Say something," I plead.

His face is impassive when he looks at me, completely devoid of any and all emotion. "You should go. There's nothing left to be said, and your mom wouldn't be happy you're here."

And just like that I'm dismissed. I could argue, but what's the point. Devin's hot and cold attitude is nothing new, and I'm getting sick of his mood swings. Whoever said teenage girls are the most dramatic has a lot to answer for. Lately, the boys in my life are definitely giving me a run for my money in the drama stakes.

And, for whatever reason, both Devin and Ayden seem determined to keep me in the dark. Not for the first time, I wonder where those two cute, adorable boys I used to know have disappeared to.

CHAPTER TWENTY-FOUR

When we go back to school after spring break, Becky still hasn't returned to school. Devin shows up sporadically, but he's back to blanking me, and I don't have the energy to fight for him anymore. Ayden is still acting weird, and we're spending less time together than we ever have. My life as I knew it has fallen apart, before I even realized it was happening.

I'm driving myself home after my shift in the diner Thursday night when I spot a familiar figure sauntering up the road. I slow down alongside him, rolling the window down. "Howdy, stranger. Need a ride?"

Cameron Morgan leans his elbows on the lowered window, grinning at me. His dark hair is cropped close to his head, showcasing his beautiful face. Where Devin and Lucas share the same sea-green eyes, Cameron's are more of a gray-green but no less spectacular. "Hey there, pretty lady. You going my way?"

"You betcha, marine. Hop in."

Tossing his duffel bag into the back, he climbs into the passenger seat, adjusting it so it can accommodate his longer legs.

"I didn't know you were coming home," I admit as the car moves forward.

"Me either." He scratches the back of his head. "I've taken a leave of absence for a while. My brothers need me."

"This is because of your dad?" I guess.

"Mainly, yeah. I couldn't leave Lucas and Devin to fend for themselves, especially with Dev talking about quitting school and working full-time at the gas station."

I almost crash the car. "What?"

He sits forward in the chair, pinning me with a strange look. "He didn't tell you?"

I haven't seen much of Devin since our conversation in his kitchen—he's been keeping a low profile. Mom and Ayden's mom have been checking in on them, but it's good that Cameron is back. They need him. "No. We're not really speaking anymore."

Cam's eyes pop wide, and he just stares at me for a couple seconds. "What the hell?"

Crunching pain rattles through my chest. "It's a long story. No doubt he'll fill you in."

He purses his lips, shaking his head sadly. "He fucked up, didn't he?"

I almost laugh at that. "Yeah, he messed things up pretty bad." That image of Becky riding Devon at the party swims to the forefront of my mind again. Tears well in my eyes and I hate that it still upsets me months later.

Cam squeezes my shoulder. "I'm sorry, Ange."

"Yeah, me too."

We're both quiet for a little bit. "Any word on your dad's whereabouts?"

"Nope. Good riddance I say." He grinds his teeth.

"You think he's ever coming back?"

He barks out an embittered laugh. "He won't show his face around here again."

"Maybe it's for the best."

He nods. "No maybe about it. I'm glad he's gone, and I hope he stays the fuck away."

∞ ∞ ∞

March turns into April, and I welcome the warmer weather and longer nights. Mr. Morgan hasn't reappeared, and Becky didn't return to school either. Apparently, she's left town with her mom for her aunt's house, and she's going to finish senior class there. While it seems wrong to feel relieved given what she's gone through, I'm not going to lie and pretend I'm upset over it. Becky being gone is one less thing for me to worry about.

It's Saturday night, and we're at Mona's celebrating Josh's eighteenth birthday. Ayden's happy, which is a rare occurrence these days, laughing and joking with his buddies while keeping me tucked protectively in to his side.

"Sorry I'm late," Gabi informs us, scooting over in the other side of the booth alongside me. "Mom's car broke down, and she was late getting home. I couldn't leave the two nightmares by themselves." Gabi's mom remarried a few years ago, and her twin brothers are only two. She places her order quickly and then turns to me with a sympathetic smile. "How are you feeling?"

My forehead creases in confusion. "I'm fine. Why wouldn't I be?"

"Ow!" Gabi bends down, sweeping a hand over her shin. "What the eff?" She glares at Mariah, and Mariah sends daggers across the table.

All the tiny hairs on the back of my neck lift. "What's going on?" My eyes jump between Gabi and Mariah, and by the way Madisyn is staring at her feet in fascination I'm guessing she's in on the secret too.

"Nothing." Gabi gulps, gratefully accepting her soda from the waitress and sucking noisily on the straw.

I eyeball Mariah. "Just tell me." Her eyes flit to Ayden, and I look up. He's scowling at her, shaking his head, and mouthing something. My eyes narrow to slits. "What is it? What are you hiding?"

"Nothing, babe." He presses a kiss to my temple. "Chill."

The waitress arrives, distributing our food, and all conversation is temporarily halted. The guys start eating, but over on our side of the table it's still deathly quiet. Easing out from under Ayden's arm, I cross my arms, glaring at my friends. "Unless you're planning on never speaking to me again, I'd suggest someone tells me what the hell is going on right now."

Mariah drills a look at Ayden, lifting her shoulders, and tossing her hair back defiantly. "She deserves to know." Her expression softens as she faces me. "Devin's gone."

A messy ball of emotion lodges in my throat. "What? What do you mean *gone*?"

Ayden curses, throwing down his napkin. "For God's sake, Mariah, I told you I'd tell her later."

I elbow him in the ribs. "Let me out."

"Babe."

"Don't babe me," I yell. "Let me out. I'm going home."

Josh and Cody slide out of the booth, leaving room for Ayden and me to get out. They shoot him concerned looks. I stomp out of the diner without looking back. Ayden chases after me. "Lina, wait."

"Screw you, Ayden." I wrestle my arm out of his clutches, rounding on him. "You knew about this and you deliberately weren't telling me?"

"He didn't want me to tell you."

My face drops. "What? You spoke to him?" He nods, and my heart throbs painfully in my chest. "Where'd he go? And for how long?" I whisper.

"I don't know the answer to either of those questions. All he told me was he was leaving for a while and he wasn't going to finish senior class here."

"Does this have anything to do with that Merc that was parked in his driveway the other day?" I'd noticed a flashy black Merc of some type at Devin's house all afternoon, and it wasn't the first time either. Shortly after it had arrived, Devin had gone storming off in his truck, but I hadn't really thought anything of it. Devin *not* storming off in his truck would raise more suspicion these days.

He shrugs, and that incenses me. "Drive me home."

He sighs. "Come back inside, Lina. There's nothing you can do about it now. He's gone already."

Tears prick my eyes. "And it's your fault I didn't get to say goodbye!"

His eyes burn with indignation as he stalks to his Jeep, yanking the door open. "Fine. I'll drive you back, but I'm not staying."

"I don't want you to." I sulk the entire ride, and we don't say another word to each other.

I slam the Jeep door shut with more force than necessary, running toward Devin's house. I thump on the door, and Lucas opens it a few minutes later. "Come in. We've been expecting you."

I trail him into the kitchen, and Cameron looks up, nodding solemnly at me. He's dressed in grubby overalls and he has a paintbrush in hand. The walls are now a fresh, buttery cream color, and the difference it makes to the room is unreal. He's currently painting the rickety kitchen cupboards a soft blue color that works well against the yellowy-cream.

But I'm not here to discuss interior décor. "Where is he?"

Cameron nods at Lucas and he quietly leaves the room. Carefully placing the brush on top of the open can of paint, Cameron removes his gloves and washes his hands in the sink. "Would you like something to drink?" he asks over his shoulder.

"This isn't a social visit," I spit out.

"Take a seat." He pulls a chair out for me, blatantly ignoring my little outburst. "And I'll explain as best I can."

I huff, dropping into the chair and scowling as I cross my arms over my chest. His lips twitch at the corners, and that only infuriates me even more. "I'm glad you think this's funny because you're the only one." My voice wobbles at the end as tears prick my eyes. God, I'm such a girl. I hate how much I've been crying lately. Before these last six months, I can count the amount of times I've cried in the last ten years on one hand. But lately, all I seem to do is burst into tears at the drop of a hat, and I hate how weak I've become.

"Hey, I'm sorry. I know you're upset and it's understandable, but this is the last thing Devin would want. He needs to get his head together, Ange, and he can't do that here, so he's gone to stay with family for a while."

"What family?" My brows knit together. Dev's mom was an only child and both her parents died when the boys were small, and their dad's sole living relative is a brother whom he lost contact with years ago. There is no one.

"Our uncle's resurfaced, and Dev's gone to stay with him."

I'm guessing that's who the fancy pants car belonged to. "For how long?"

"As long as he needs."

I don't like the sound of that. "I can't believe he left without saying goodbye."

"Ange, that would've killed him. You mean more to him than anyone."

"Here," Lucas says, reappearing in the kitchen with a large brown box. He plonks it unceremoniously on the table. "He left this for you."

I stand up, inspecting the contents. It's all the stuff I threw at him that night months ago when I was in a fit of rage. I pull his well-worn T-shirt from the pile, bringing it to my nose and inhaling deeply. His brothers share a knowing look, but I don't care how much of a sap they think I am. "If you're talking to him will you tell him … never mind." I pick up the box, but Lucas takes it from me.

"I'll carry it."

"Thanks."

After Lucas has deposited it in my bedroom, he leaves, and I quietly start unpacking the items and putting them back in their rightful place. I take off my clothes, and pull on Dev's shirt. His scent swirls around me, painfully reminding me of all I'm missing. I place the newly-reframed drawing of me on my bedside table, committing Dev's words to memory. There's a silver-wrapped package at the bottom of the box that's new. Ignoring the nervous fluttering in my chest, I open it with shaky fingers. My eyes well up again at the delicate silver locket. The front of it is etched with the same infinity drawing that's on my wrist. On the back are two simple words: *Never forget.* Tears leak out of my eyes as I clasp it around my neck. Grabbing the framed picture, I crawl into bed, pulling the comforter up over me as I curl into a fetal position, clutching the drawing to my chest.

Why did I forget when he asked me to remember?

Why did I abandon him when he clearly needed my friendship the most?

Why did I let my feelings rob me of one of my best friends?

Why weren't my eyes open? Why didn't I see what was in front of me?

So many questions. So few answers.

Devin tried to explain, to apologize, so many times, but I just kept pushing him away.

I allowed hurt and envy to consume me. Allowed Ayden to keep him from me.

And now I'm paying the ultimate price.

Because Devin is gone.

And I don't know if he's ever coming back.

And the pain in my heart is worse than anything I've ever felt in my whole entire life.

I may just have lost the love of my life.

And the only person to blame is myself.

CHAPTER TWENTY-FIVE

The night Devin left, I sent him my first text.

I hate that you left without saying goodbye, but I understand. Take whatever time you need, but come back. Please come back. I love you. I'll never forget.

When it didn't bounce back undelivered, I started texting him every day. I don't know if he's reading them, but every day, the first thing I do when I wake in the morning is reach for my cell, closing my eyes and silently praying he's replied.

He never does.

But I still send them, hoping that he's reading them and he knows he's in my thoughts. Ayden refuses to speak to me about him, and it seems I'm not the only one spiraling into a pit of depression. I wear the locket every day, but I always conceal it under my clothes. I know Ayd wouldn't appreciate the gesture, so I never mentioned it. The fact I'm wearing Devin's chain while I'm going out with Ayden doesn't sit well with me, but I carry the guilt rather than not wear it.

Not sure what that says about me.

Ayden grows more and more dejected by the day, and I can't remember a time we were ever this distant from one another.

Prom comes and goes, and I leave early, sobbing into my pillow instead of spending the night with Ayden in the hotel room he reserved. I don't think he was surprised or overly upset when I asked him to take me home instead. All week, I'd been hoping and praying Dev would make an appearance, but he was a no-show.

Tucked up in bed, crying that night, I'd sent him another text. I know he's trying to get his life back on track, and I don't want to upset him, so I deliberately shielded the full extent of my heartache.

I missed you tonight. Prom wasn't the same without you, and I was thinking of you, like I always am. I love you. I'll never forget.

My eighteenth birthday arrives, and still there's no word from him.

I send him a birthday text on the day of his eighteenth, and still nada, zip, zilch. Not a squeak from him. It's as if he's disappeared off the face of the planet.

We graduate, and school ends, and the start of a long summer commences. Ayden takes over Devin's job at the gas station, and I've taken on more shifts at the diner. While the college fund that was set up at the time of my parents' divorce provides adequately for me, I want to save as much money as possible so Mom doesn't ever feel like she needs to supplement my income.

I'm still sending texts to Devin, although they're less regular. It's hard to hold onto hope when I'm getting nothing in return. I pester Cameron weekly for updates, but it's always the same: he won't tell me where he is or when he's planning on coming back, if at all. All he's said is that Devin is feeling better and the move has been good for him. Once a month, a chauffeur-driven car arrives to collect Cam and Lucas, and they disappear for the weekend. I've thought of begging to go with, but, thankfully, I still have some self-respect, and I've managed to stop myself from sinking so low.

The weeks go by, and finally we're into August and the thick of college preparations. We're leaving in ten days, and I've gotten the day off work to spend with Mariah. A letter recently arrived, confirming we're sharing a dorm room together, so we're shopping for our impending move. Honestly, it's the first thing that's excited me in months.

"Do you think Cody and Ayden would like this for their room?" She holds up a black and gold patterned rug in the colors of the Iowa Hawkeyes. It's even emblazoned with a gaudy tiger-hawk emblem.

I snatch it out of her hands, putting it back on the shelf. "That's hideous. They'd hate it."

She pouts, and I playfully nudge her in the ribs. "Stop that. You know I'm right. You'd only be wasting your money. Besides, they could've come with if they wanted."

She snorts, running her fingers over a pretty pink and purple floral-patterned set of bed covers. "They're typical boys. Too lazy to bother. No doubt they'll rope their moms into getting what they need."

"No doubt." I dump a couple of items into my basket. "Ayden has shown zero interest in college. I don't understand it. I can't wait."

We pay for our items and drop the bags off in the car before crossing the road to the little coffee place on the corner.

We order muffins and lattes and take a seat in the far corner. "How are things with you and him? You both seemed quiet the other night." We'd gone for dinner and a movie with Cody and Mariah, and they carried the conversation the entire night.

I chew on the inside of my mouth. "Honestly, I think we were better just as friends. Now, it's like we're barely friends who sometimes kiss and very occasionally have sex. He's so closed off, and he won't tell me why." The waitress places plates and mugs on the table, and I wait until she's left to resume talking. "I think it must be me. That's he's uncomfortable in our relationship too."

She shakes her head. "You can't jump to conclusions. I'm betting it's not you. Cody has mentioned Ayden is very distracted these last few months. I've wondered if it's tied up with Devin. You three were so close for years. You're not the only one to lose a best friend, and I bet you're not the only one who's missing him either."

"He never wants to talk about him."

She props her chin in her hands. "I think that's your answer. Things will be better when you get to college. It's a new environment, and neither of you will be surrounded by things that remind you of him."

"Except that our plan was always for the three of us to attend UI together."

"You can't let him hold you back anymore, Ange. Devin is gone, and it's looking like he's not coming back. He's moved on, and you need to too. I've said nothing, because I know how you feel about him, but you've kinda moped around all summer, and you've got to put it behind you. You have a life to lead. You have a mom who loves you, a boyfriend who loves you, and I love you. I want to see my friend with a big, happy smile on her face again."

I reach across the table the same time she does, and we clasp hands. "I have been a big Debbie Downer again, haven't I?"

"Pretty much, so what are you going to do about it?" she challenges.

"College is a fresh start, and I'm going to make the most of it. I am really looking forward to it except"—air whooshes out of my mouth, and a caustic pain lances my heart in two—"I think I'm going to have to break up with Ayden, but I'm terrified I'm going to lose him as a friend. I couldn't bear that. I couldn't bear to lose him too."

"Do you want my advice?"

I smile. "Always."

"I wouldn't be too hasty. Why not wait until you get to college? That could be what you both need to get back on the right track. Ayden loves you, Ange. I see it every time he looks at you."

"I know that, M. And I love him too, but I'm not sure it's the right kind of love. Besides, it doesn't feel right that I'm still pining for Dev when I'm with Ayden. It feels like a betrayal, and he deserves better than that."

"You don't have to make any hard and fast decisions now."

"No, I suppose I don't."

∞ ∞ ∞

"Need any help?" Mom asks, propping her hip against the doorframe.

"Nope." I zip my case. "I'm all packed." I scan my shell of a room, and it looks cold and impersonal without all my possessions in place.

Mom rushes me, sweeping me into a mammoth hug. "I'm so proud and so excited for you. You've always wanted to be a psychologist, and now your journey is starting." She squeezes me. "But I'm going to miss you so much, kiddo."

"I'm going to miss you too, Mom. But I'm not that far away, and I'll come home every second weekend like I promised."

She sniffs, and her eyes are red-rimmed and glossy when she pulls back. "You make sure you do, missy." She tweaks my nose. "Did you talk to Ayden last night?" she delicately asks.

I frown, shaking my head. "He didn't answer any of my calls, and I was too afraid to drop over." I don't know what went down at the Carters last night, but we heard raised voices, shouting, and doors slamming. Prickles of unease dance across my skin, as they have done since I overhead the ruckus at his house.

The thud of approaching footsteps on the stairs captures our attention. Mom's brows lift, and she eases out of my embrace when Ayden appears in the doorway. "Am I interrupting?"

"Not at all." Mom pats his elbow, smiling, as she squeezes past him. "She's all packed and ready." I can tell how difficult it is for her to sound happy about that fact.

Ayden scratches the back of his head, averting his eyes, and pressure settles on my chest. Mom shoots me a concerned look and I shoo her away with my eyes. Taking his hand, I pull him into my bedroom, shutting the door behind me. "We heard all the commotion last night, and I tried calling you, like, a hundred times, to find out if you were all right."

He drops down onto the bed, and I sit down beside him. He rests his elbows on his knees and leans his face on his chin. "I'm sorry I didn't call you back. I was too fucking pissed, and I didn't want to tell you until I was calmer."

My stomach lurches to my toes. "Tell me what?"

He sucks in a long breath, straightening his spine before twisting around to face me. Reaching out, he takes my hands in his. He brings them to his mouth, tenderly kissing the tips of my fingers. "You know I love you, right?" I gulp over the wedge of alarm in my throat, nodding. "You know you mean so much to me, and that I'd do just about anything for you, but the time has come where I need to put myself first."

Oh my God. *He's breaking up with me?* Even though I've thought the same thing several times over the last couple months, now that we're in the moment, I don't want this. I can't lose Ayden.

"It's not what you're thinking," he rushes to reassure me, before frowning. "Or maybe it is." His eyes crinkle with worry. "I—"

"Just say it," I cut in, needing this to be over.

"I know this is going to come as a shock, and I'm sorry it's all so last minute, but I thought it was for the best."

My knee starts tapping up and down, and I think I might throttle him if he doesn't spit the words out.

"I'm not going to UI. I've notified the college, and I've given up the full ride."

My eyes widen. I was *not* expecting that. "What?" I splutter. "Why the hell not? Why would you do that?" We've been planning this virtually our whole lives, and I don't understand. I don't have a freaking clue why he's changed his mind.

He wets his lips. "I don't want to play college ball. I've known for years that my heart wasn't in it. It's my dad's dream, not mine, and he can't live vicariously through me anymore. It's killing me, Lina."

"That's what's been going on with you?" He nods. "Why wouldn't you talk to me about this? I thought it was me! I thought I was making you miserable and you were too afraid to break up with me."

"I'm sorry I made you feel like that, but I couldn't tell you. It was my burden to bear. My secret to carry."

I hop up, anger rushing to the surface. "That is a fucking cop-out, and you know it. Couples tell each other this stuff! *Friends* tell each other this stuff! Does anyone know? Did you talk to anyone about this?"

He stands up, placing his hands on my shoulders. "I know you're mad, and you've every right to be. I didn't tell anyone until that letter came from the college about the dorms, and then I told Cody, because he needed advance notice to secure a new roomie."

I throw my hands into the air. "Great, so Cody and Mariah knew? And they were keeping it from me too?"

He shakes his head. "Mariah doesn't know. I made Cody swear because I knew there was no way in hell she'd keep that to herself."

I cross my arms over my chest, my head spinning. "If you're not going to UI, then where are you going? What are you planning to do?"

"I've joined the marines."

My jaw slackens. "You did what?" If he told me he joined the Bolshoi Ballet I wouldn't have been any more surprised.

"Cam pulled some strings, and he got me in. After training, I'm being deployed overseas for an initial stint."

I drop to the ground on my butt, barely feeling the sharp pain skittering up my spine. Tears prick my eyes. "You're leaving me too?"

And, yes, the prize for most selfish goes to me.

He winces. "Never. I'll always be with you even if I'm not physically present."

"You promised you'd always be there for me," I whisper, looking at him as reality gives me a swift kick in the rear. "You promised, and now you're leaving as well." I choke on an anguished sob.

He sinks to his knees in front of me, pulling me into his warm chest. I should resist but I'm numb. "Lina, I'm sorry you're hurt. You're the last person I want to upset, but I need to do this for me. I need to … find who I really am, and I can't do that here under Dad's constant shadow. I have to break free."

The numbness spreads, infecting every part of me. My voice sounds eerily calm as I ask the next question. "When do you leave?"

He cups my face, tilting my head up to him. His lips collide with mine in a fierce, desperate kiss. I can't summon the effort to kiss him back. I'm too distraught. Resting his forehead on mine, he breaths heavily as tears course down his face. "I'm leaving in an hour."

I say nothing, do nothing, and it's like we're frozen in time. Emotions churn inside me, panic mixing with pain and fear and a huge bucket load of disappointment. Then rage does a number on me, and the blank, empty feeling is replaced by soul-deep anger. I don't know the boy cradling me in his arms. The boy I've known since I was two years old has lied to me for months. *Am I such a lousy confidante that he couldn't unburden his secret to me?* I know I'm not. If he'd told me, I would've been shocked, but I would have listened and understood. There is no way I want Ayden to pursue something he has no interest in. If the marines are his true calling, then I would've supported him with that.

But he never gave me the chance.

I push him away, and he tumbles back onto his heels. "Get out." I scramble away from him until my back hits the edge of my bed. "Go. Leave now."

"Lina." He starts to crawl toward me, but I stall him with a death glare. "You wanted to leave, so leave."

"Not like this, baby. Please. I don't want to leave it like this. I love you."

"I don't care what you want. You've had months to talk to me. To tell me how you were feeling." I glare at him. "God, how many times did I ask you what was wrong? I knew you were hurting, but you continually pushed me away. Maybe, if you'd explained, I'd understand, but you've just sprung all this on me." I pin venom-filled eyes on him, and, in this moment, I hate him with a passion unrivalled. "You say you need to put yourself first, well, I need to do that too. You've broken my heart, Ayden," I sob, losing control of my tenuous emotions. "You and Devin. The two people I entrusted it to without any fear have shattered me beyond recognition, and I'm the one who's left alone to pick up the pieces. So, if I ask you to leave, I expect you to do that one last thing for me. I need you to leave now before I say or do something I'll come to regret."

Bending over, he presses a lingering kiss to my forehead, before standing up. I can't even look at him. He pauses in the doorway, turning back around, but I continue to stare straight ahead.

"I love you, Lina, and this isn't goodbye. Just goodbye for now."

He walks out the door, leaving me broken beyond repair, sobbing on the floor of my bedroom.

PART II

Freshman Year of College

CHAPTER TWENTY-SIX

My squeal of delight filters down the phone line. "Have a fab time, Mom, and, remember, no putting out on the first date!" I hang up with her laughter ringing in my ears.

Mariah pushes her face in mine, excitement lighting up her eyes. "Your mom's going on a *date*?"

I lie back on my bed, grinning. "Yep. Provided she still remembers what that entails. She hasn't gone on a date in almost twenty years."

"I'm happy for her." She returns to the mirror to apply another layer of lip gloss.

"Me, too." I prop up on my elbows. "Me leaving for college has given her a fresh start, and from the way she's talking about Dr. Williams, I think she's already half in love with him. I really hope it works out for her. I don't like the thought of her being alone in the house on her own all the time."

"You go home every other weekend."

"I know, but it's not the same."

"Any word from Ayden?" She twists around to face me.

I shake my head. "Not since that letter last month. You know communication channels are abysmal in Afghanistan, and he doesn't have much opportunity to keep in touch."

"I still can't believe he's overseas and not here with us."

Nearly three months later, I still can't believe it myself, but life goes on, and I refuse to dwell on it, even if the status of our relationship is completely up in the air. I miss him a hell of a lot, and while I always knew I relied on him, the last few months have been a real eye opener. I leaned on Ayd *a lot*. Learning to be more independent has been good for me though. "I know. Me either."

She looks at her watch. "We need to leave soon, so you should get ready."

I glance down at my jeans and Hollister sweater. "Why can't I go like this?"

She casts her eyes to the ceiling. "Because it's a frat party and you need to look hot." She drags me up by the elbow, gently shoving me into the bathroom. "Chop, chop. Get a move on."

I emerge with a full face of makeup and my hair curled twenty minutes later. She claps her hands gleefully. "That's much better." She thrusts a little black dress at me. "Put that on, and I've left your shoes by your bed."

I inspect the tiny garment in my hands. "You can't even call that a dress," I grumble.

"Stop bitching and moaning, and just put it on." She plants her hands on her hips, slanting me her "I mean business" look. She's wearing a cute black and silver dress and her hair is pinned messily on top of her head. "You look gorgeous. Cody won't be able to keep his hands off you."

She winks. "That's the plan."

"Yuck!" I make a face. "You two are so nauseating these days."

"Because we're finally free to have as much sex as we like, and it's freaking awesome," she gloats. Now it's my turn to roll my eyes. "You'd know if you got back on the saddle."

I shuck out of my jeans and sweater and shimmy the dress up over my hips. "Ayden is still my boyfriend, M," I tell her for like the umpteenth time. I whirl around, holding my hair up, and she helps me close the zipper.

"In name only. He's not here. You are, and you're wasting your college experience. Besides, I'm sure he doesn't expect you to be a nun."

Maybe he doesn't, but it's not just about what he thinks. I'm not ready. Sinking onto the edge of the bed, I squeeze my feet into the stilettos. "We didn't discuss our relationship that day, and neither one of us broke up with the other. You know I don't want to have that conversation in a letter or over a rushed phone call where we can barely hear one another. I owe it to him to wait until he's home, and then I'll end things officially."

"Then will you date?"

"Maybe." I send her a defiant look. "Why are you so invested in my love life anyway?"

"Because I want you to be happy."

"I am happy." And I am, most of the time. I made a promise to myself as I drove with Cody and Mariah to campus that fateful day in August— that I was done wallowing in the past, and all the what ifs, and I was going to embrace college life—and I've stuck by it. It's only in the middle of the night, when I can't sleep, when the pain in my heart cripples me, that I allow myself to indulge my grief. To remember my loss. To miss the two boys who mean the world to me.

I've still heard nothing from Devin, and I've given up texting him. I can't promise myself I'll move on and continue to cling to feeble hope. When I'm back home, I don't even visit Cam for an update any more. Wherever Devin is, I hope he's well and that he's happy.

She sits down beside me, taking my hand. "I'm proud of you, you know." I arch a brow, and she graces me with a smile. "For putting it aside and throwing yourself into college life, and, I guess I'm just so in love with my man and all sexed up, and I want that for you too. You're gorgeous, Ange, and you have no shortage of admirers on campus."

I stand up, smoothing a hand down the front of the minute dress. "I'm really happy you're still so in love with Cody and he's such a good guy, but you don't need to worry about me. I'm happy with where my life is at, and I'm not ready to date. There is still too much unresolved emotion surrounding both of them, and I'd much rather focus on my studies and enjoy my ballet and art classes."

"The odd steamy make-out sesh would be good though," she persists. "You don't want your lady parts to shrivel up and die."

I roll my eyes again. "You're relentless. Give it up. I'm not going there until I've properly ended things with Ayd, so you're wasting your breath."

She gets up, grabbing her purse and jacket, before looping her arm through mine. "Aw, look, it's cool, I understand. You're loyal to Ayden and I'm sure he'll appreciate that. Don't mind me."

The party is kicking by the time we arrive, the bottom level of the frat house crammed with sweaty bodies. Music blares out from two large speakers in the main room, and a lively crowd dances energetically to the rhythmic beats. Mariah leads me out through the kitchen to a side room. The vibe is more chilled in here. Guys are huddled around two pool tables, drinking and chatting as they play. An energetic game of beer pong is taking place in the top corner of the room. Guys and girls sit cross-legged on the floor and clustered across the three massive leather couches propped against the walls. Music is on low in the background. Cody shoots up his arm, waving us over. He's seated in one of the three leather recliners, game controller in hand. His buddy Jack hands us a couple of red cups. "Looking hot as fuck, ladies," he proclaims with a wink.

"My girl always looks hot," Cody says, without taking his eyes off the game.

Mariah leans in, kissing his cheek. "And my man's sexy as fuck."

A few of our friends arrive then, and we move over to the corner to chat. "Tyler Cooper is totally eye-fucking you right now," Mariah exclaims at the top of her voice, a little while later, nudging me in the shoulder.

"Oh my God, tell the whole room, why don't you."

She sniggers, waggling her brows. "He's hardly disguising it. Look."

She starts pointing her finger in his direction, but I slap it back down. "Stop it," I hiss. "I told you I'm not interested."

"Okay, you need to chill out. Come on." She yanks on my elbow. "Let's hit the dance floor." The rest of our group follows, and we make our way to the middle of the dancing crowd. My heart pounds in tune with the sultry beat as I let loose, swaying my hips and letting the music take control.

Prickles of awareness ghost over my skin, and I look around, scanning the room. Tyler is with a couple of his buddies, lounging against the side wall, his eyes fixated on me. His lips curve up when he spots me watching, and he blows me a kiss. How cheesy. I feel like gagging. A firm prod in my back almost sends me flying. "What the heck?" I turn and glare at the girls, wondering which one of them thinks she's being helpful.

Mariah looks over my shoulder and grins. "He's coming over."

My head whips around, and I groan, slamming a hand to my forehead.

Mariah looks sideways and gasps, her eyes popping wide. "Holy shit!" she cusses. "I don't believe it." Before I can question her or see what's captured her attention, Tyler lands in front of me, blocking my view. "You're Angelina, right?" He blasts me with a devastating smile.

"Yes, and you're Tyler."

His grin expands. "You've heard of me."

Hard not to notice when his eyes seem to follow me everywhere these days. He's watched me from a distance the last few times we've been at the frat, but this is the first time he's plucked up the courage to approach me. I've noticed him leaving every other party with a different girl on his arm, and even without the Ayden complication, I've no desire to be another notch on his bedpost.

"Would you like to dance or get a drink or even get out of here?" He turns his hand palm up in invitation, his eyes glinting suggestively.

I tuck my hair behind my ears, preparing to put Tyler firmly back in his box. "Actually, I—"

"She's spoken for." The deep masculine voice is low, the tone suffused with warning. Everything goes on high alert inside me. A warm hand lands on my arm, sending delicious tingles over my skin, and my knees buckle underneath me. His arm encircles my waist from behind, helping steady me. My lower lip is wobbling, and my heart is thudding wildly in my chest. Butterflies swarm my stomach, and every limb in my body is shaking uncontrollably.

"Who the fuck are you?" Tyler demands to know, his cocky, confident swagger replaced by a look of displeasure.

"Someone you don't want to cross" is the reply.

I'm almost afraid to turn around, but that sentiment clashes with the surge of exhilaration replacing the blood flowing through my veins. I twist around, looking up, and our eyes meet. The room fades away as I stare into his crystal-clear sea-green eyes. He rakes his gaze over me from head to toe, and his eyes shine with a myriad of different emotions. I gasp, tears pumping out of my eyes as he gently cups my cheek. "I've missed you, baby doll," Devin admits, his voice choked. "I've missed you so fucking much."

CHAPTER TWENTY-SEVEN

"Dev," I whisper, clinging to his shirt, leaning into him to make sure he's real. His arms wrap firmly around my lower back, and his hold is the only thing keeping me upright in the moment. Mariah has her hand over her mouth, and her eyes are bugging out of her head. My hands creep around Devin's neck, and I press desperately against him. I'm afraid if I let go, that I'll wake up. That it'll all have been a dream. "You're here," I stupidly say.

He nods, drilling into my eyes in that intense way of his, and I get lost in the hypnotic lull of his gaze. He looks so good. His hair is shorn really tight at the sides and the back but still longer on top. Strands fall forward into his gorgeous eyes, framed by the ever-present thick jet-black lashes. His skin is smooth and flawless, his lips full and pink, and he radiates health. "How are you here?" I ask, trailing my fingers across the hair at the back of his neck.

He strengthens his grip on my back. "It's a long story." Glancing up, he notices the curious faces surrounding us. Tyler and his crew have disappeared, thank God. "Can we get out of here? Go somewhere to talk privately?" he asks, taking my hand.

"Sure." I smile, and his answering smile melts my heart. He squeezes my hand, and my heart is fit to burst.

"Devin, dude. Is that you?" Cody asks, materializing in front of us with shock splayed across his face.

"Hey, man. Good to see ya." They touch knuckles. "Ange and I are gonna split, but let's catch up this weekend," he suggests.

"Cool." Cody reels Mariah in to his side.

"Hey, Mariah." Dev greets my friend for the first time. "You look good."

"Holy shit, Devin. Way to make an entrance." She grins, leaning in to give him a quick hug. "And you look good, too."

"Thanks. We're out of here, but we'll see you guys later."

He places his hand on my lower back as he guides me out of the frat house. I shiver in the cold night air, remembering I left my stuff in the house. I spin around, prepared to go back inside, but he holds out my purse and jacket, a smirk twisting the corners of his mouth. "How did you ..." I shake my head. "Never mind."

He takes my hand in his again. "Text Mariah and tell her to stay at Cody's place tonight. I've a lot to tell you, and I don't want to be interrupted."

I tap out a quick text as Devin leads me to a nearby parking bay. Opening the passenger side of a sleek, brand new black SUV, he helps me inside before jogging around to the driver side. "Is this yours?"

He nods, switching the engine on. "I've tons to catch you up on. You hungry?"

"I could eat."

His grin is out in full force as he eases the car out onto the road. "I've never known any girl to share your appetite and banging curves."

"Thank you, I think."

His grin magnifies. "And look at you, all graceful in the face of a compliment."

I shove him playfully. "Maybe I've changed."

His expression turns reflective. "I think we all have."

When he joins the line at the drive through, he engages the hand-brake, and turns to face me. There's an anxious look on his face, and he swallows hard. "Be honest. Are you mad at me?"

"I don't know yet," I admit truthfully. "I should be, but I'm too freaking happy to summon anger."

He places his hand atop mine. "I'm so happy to be here with you. It's all that's kept me going for months."

I want to quiz him instantly, but I hold my tongue. He places our order and shortly after we're on our way with a piping hot bag of greasy goodness nestled in my lap.

My brows knit together as he pulls up in front of the residence hall Mariah and I call home. "How did you know I lived here?" I ask, because I hadn't given him directions.

He drags his lower lip between his teeth, and my eyes latch onto the movement greedily. I blink my eyes, forcing myself to focus. Devin's ability to turn my brain to goo hasn't dissipated in the slightest.

"Promise you won't freak."

I pin him with a stern look. "You know me better than that."

He sighs, dragging a hand through his silky hair. "I go to school here too and … I looked you up the minute I arrived. I know where you live, and I probably know your schedule better than you know it yourself."

My mouth falls open, and my heart rate speeds up. That sounds more than a little stalkerish. "Since when?"

"Since the start of the semester."

My spine stiffens. "What? You've been here this whole time and you waited almost three months before approaching me?"

"I had good reason."

"Like what?" I bark. Anger is simmering in my veins.

"I wanted you to settle in without my interference. I didn't want to hold you back."

Steam practically billows out of my ears. "What a stinking pile of crap! How dare you presume to know what I did or didn't need." I slam my hand against his chest, disgusted when tears sting my eyes. "I've been to hell and back worrying about you!" I scream. "I've texted you hundreds, hell, probably thousands of times, and you didn't even once text me back." My chest heaves up and down. "I haven't seen you for over seven months. Seven fucking months, Dev! And for some of that time you've been here? Screw you! Fucking asshole!" My blood boils as months of pent-up frustration and longing find an outlet. I'm out of the car before he's had time to blink. I'm mad as all hell as I race toward the building. A *bleep, bleep* sound echoes behind me, but I don't look back as I yank the door open and run inside.

I'm breathless by the time I reach our apartment. Slamming the door behind me, I sag on the floor, absolutely fuming. I can't believe he's been here this whole time and I'm only now finding out about it. Funny thing is, for ages I felt like I was being watched, but I convinced myself I was paranoid. Now, I'm wondering if I was right all along—has Devin been watching me all this time?

He raps loudly on the door. "Ange, please. Let me in and I'll explain everything."

"Go away!" I roar. "I'm too fucking mad right now."

"I'm not leaving."

"Then I hope you like the cold floor."

I stomp to our shared bedroom, viciously slamming the door shut behind me. Peeling the dress off my body, I replace it with sleep shorts and a tank top. I lie on my side on the bed, clutching the framed picture to my chest while all manner of conflicting emotions skitters around my brain.

After a while, my anger has faded, and I've calmed down. I'm still pissed at him for making decisions that concern me without consulting me, but I don't want to lose sight of what's important—he's here, and he has answers to questions that have long since puzzled me.

I get up and pad to the door. Opening it, I peer into the quiet hallway. Dev is sitting on the ground with his knees tucked in close to his chest, his back flat against the wall. He knows my temper tantrums are usually short-lived, and I was banking on him still being here. He looks up, his gaze scrutinizing mine. "You can come in now," I confirm in a meek voice.

He climbs to his feet, following me in to the apartment. Handing me the brown paper bag, he looks sheepish. "It's probably stone cold by now."

"It wouldn't be the first time we've chowed down on cold burgers," I say, reminding him of the time we left our takeout bag on the sidewalk outside the diner where I worked. Dev only realized it when he'd pulled into his driveway. Despite Ayden's protests, he'd turned the truck around and driven back for it. Starving, the three of us had happily munched on the cold food on the drive back home.

He chuckles. "I remember."

I retrieve some plates and napkins, and we sit on the couch eating our burgers in silence. After I've cleared up, I snatch two cans of soda from the small refrigerator and flop onto the couch. I pass one to him. "I'm sorry for overreacting before you had a chance to properly explain."

He kicks off his sneakers, pulling his feet up onto the couch. Twisting around, he leans back against the arm rest so he's facing me. I mirror his position at the other end of the couch. "I don't blame you for being angry, and, for what it's worth, I'm sorry for leaving without saying goodbye, for cutting off all contact, and for hiding my presence here for so long, but I had good reasons for doing what I've done."

"I'm listening."

He blows air out of his mouth. "I've planned this conversation so many times, but I'm still not sure where to start."

I take pity on him. "Why did you leave?"

He wets his lips. "You know I wasn't in a good place, hadn't been for quite some time. After all that shit went down with Becky, and Da ... Dad took off, I could barely keep everything together. I'd reached a point where I didn't think I could go on. You and Ayden weren't speaking to me, Cam was gone, Lucas was relying on me to hold our family together, and I just felt like crap inside. Then my uncle showed up and flipped my world upside down and I lost it."

My brow puckers. "What does your uncle have to do with anything? I didn't think you even knew him?"

"I didn't. We didn't. That's the way Dad wanted it. The last time I'd seen him was when I was a little kid. He'd just set up his medical supplies business, and he used to drop by the house most every weekend. Lucas was only a baby the last time we saw him, so he doesn't remember him, and it was a shock when he turned up one day a couple weeks before Dad left begging for our help. His youngest daughter was ill with leukemia, and he was desperate. She needed a bone marrow transplant, and none of them were a match. It was a long shot, but he wanted Dad, Luc, and me to be tested too."

He closes his eyes momentarily. "I was a match, but the tests also revealed my uncle was actually my biological father."

I jerk forward. "What the hell?" The disbelief carries in my tone.

He nods. "I'd no idea. Neither did he, but that asshole who raised me knew." His eyes darken with anger. "It explained a few things. Dad had flown into a massive rage after my uncle showed up and he was worse than usual those couple weeks. That night when I picked you up after the party, when we got back to the house and Becky was waiting there, I knew he was ready to flip. I sent you home because I was afraid he'd hurt you."

Our eyes meet. "But he hurt Becky instead."

Dev nods. "Becky is a bitch, but she didn't deserve that."

I knot my hands in my lap. "Why did you go out with her, Dev? I still don't understand it."

He scoots forward, taking my hands in his. "She blackmailed me." I tilt my chin up. "That Saturday when I showed up at your house, the day I gave you the drawing, I meant everything I said, but she turned up at the gas station that night while I was working my shift. She told me she was pregnant and that it was mine." I gasp, withdrawing one of my hands and planting it over my mouth. "I didn't believe her at first, but she had the pregnancy test, and it clearly showed a blue line. I was in complete shock, and I had no one to talk to about it. I knew there was a chance it was someone else's, but she was adamant it was mine, and I couldn't walk away. If that was my kid, I was going to be there for it."

He doesn't need to elaborate. I understand why he'd felt like that.

"She told me if I didn't make things official between us that she'd abort the baby." Torment saturates his eyes. "She also insisted I cut all ties with you. I discovered she planted one of the cheerleaders in the closet the night of the party, and she had explicit photos of me, of us together, and she was threatening to send them to you."

A resurgence of hurt and jealousy batters me on all sides.

He looks suitably embarrassed. "I had already hurt you so much, and I couldn't let her do that."

I shake my head in disgust, speaking over the rancid taste in my mouth. "She's far nastier than I ever gave her credit for."

"You've no idea." He gulps. "She also threatened your mom's job."

"She what?" I shriek.

"Her dad manages the hospital where your mom works. She told me she'd have her fired if I had any more involvement with you."

"That stupid fucking bitch." I'm seething. "You should have told me this." Based on what Mom has said in the past about Dr. Carmichael, there's no way that would've happened. Becky manipulated him perfectly, knowing exactly which buttons to push.

"I couldn't take the risk. Besides, you pretty much hated my guts, and with due cause."

The usual pang prods my chest, like it always does whenever I think of the night I found Dev screwing Becky. As long as I live, I don't think the hurt will ever go away. He leans in, caressing my cheek. "I wish I hadn't gone to that party Thanksgiving night. If I wasn't so wasted, I would never have slept with her, and none of this would've happened."

My smile is sad. "We can't change the past."

He rests his hands on my shoulders. "No, but that doesn't mean I can't try to repair the damage, because I want to. I need you in my life, Ange. I can't breathe without you."

I'm not ready to confront that shit. Not until I have all the answers. "What happened to the baby?"

A muscle ticks in his jaw. "There was no baby. The bitch played me." An embittered look is etched across his face. "Turns out, it was her older sister who was pregnant. Becky found the test in the trash, and she concocted the whole plan. We were in her room one night, and I noticed blood on the comforter. I freaked out, thinking something was wrong with the baby."

"But it was only her period," I surmise.

"Yeah. She couldn't hide it from me any longer. She came clean, professing to love me. I actually think the crazy bitch thought I was in love with her and that I'd still want to be by her side even after her deception came to light."

"She always was delusional." I shake my head. "And crazy, especially when it came to you, but the whole thing is hard to believe."

"I know." He sighs. "The relief I felt is indescribable. I can't tell you how fucking relieved I was to be free of her."

"And you tried to tell me, but I wouldn't listen."

"I don't blame you. You were only trying to protect yourself. I've hurt you a lot, Ange, and I have so many regrets. So many things I wish I could do differently."

"We all do," I whisper.

He cups my face. "But I'm here now, and I'm good, and I'm not going anywhere. And, if you'll let me, I want to make it up to you. I want to prove that I'm worthy of a place in your life."

CHAPTER TWENTY-EIGHT

"You've always been worthy of a place in my life, Dev. I've never felt like you haven't."

"I know, baby. That was all on me. I've never felt good enough for you, and, when things were spiraling out of control, the last thing I wanted was to take you down with me. But things are better now. Much better, and I want you back in my life if you'll give me another chance."

I decide to park that for the moment. "You still haven't explained where you went or why you didn't contact me."

"Jim—that's my real dad's name—he wanted me and Luc to live with him. Luc's actually his son too."

My jaw slackens, and he chuckles. "Your face is a picture. We were shocked too. According to Jim, he and my mother had an affair for four years while she was married to my dad. Jim is Dad's younger brother, but he's nothing like him. He's a very successful businessman and a real gentleman. They're like night and day. Jim says he begged Mom to leave Dad for him, but she refused. He went on to marry someone else, and they had two daughters, but the marriage didn't last. He doesn't know how Dad found out about the affair or how he knew we weren't his sons, but he said Mom called him one day, after years of no contact, crying and upset and saying she couldn't stay with him any longer. Jim again offered to help, and she was going to take us with her to live with him in Ohio, but she failed to show up at the rendezvous point, and he presumed she'd changed her mind."

Dropping his hands from my face, he looks away, breathing heavily. I reach out, entwining our fingers. "That was when she left?" I guess. He nods, still not looking at me. "Why didn't she take you all with her?" He shrugs, finally lifting his head to look at me. The pain of her departure is still written all over his face. "I don't know, and I guess we'll never find out. When Jim found out she'd left without us, he was worried, so he started searching for her. He's hired tons of different PIs over the years, but every lead is a dead end. I guess she doesn't want to be found."

"Did Cam know all this?"

He shakes his head. "He had no idea either, until Jim contacted him. By this time, Jim could see I needed help, so he fixed things with Cam. Luc didn't want to leave school and his friends, and he was angry and frightened. He didn't want to move to Ohio. I didn't either, not at first. Even though you and Ayd weren't speaking to me, I didn't want to leave you behind. But Jim spent hours and hours talking to me. He listened to me, really listened to me, and I just got a good vibe off him, you know? Like I knew he was a decent guy. So, we talked some more and came up with some options. He made it immediately clear that he would look after us. He's a very wealthy man, and he insisted that Luc and I would be treated equally. He'd set up college funds for his daughters and he straightaway set the same up for us."

"Wow."

"I know. We've gone from having nothing to having everything. It's still a lot to take in."

"That's where the new car came from? And how you're here?"

"Yeah. He also paid for my rehab." I peer into his eyes, beseeching him to continue. "He got me into a private facility in Detroit. That's why I left. That's where I was up to summer break. I was able to complete my last few credits, and I graduated with my diploma. Then he tapped a few contacts and managed to get me in here. I owe him so much."

"Oh my God, Devin, he sounds incredible, and I'm really happy you've turned things around."

"He is, and I can't wait for you to meet him. I've told him all about you."

I pull at my lip, a shy blush creeping across my cheeks. "You have?"

He grins, leaning forward to kiss my forehead. "He wanted to know about my life. You and Ayd have been the biggest parts of it. Of course, I was going to tell him about you."

"Oh." It's all I can think to say.

Moisture gleams in his eyes as he stares at me. He's so close, and the urge to touch him hasn't gone away. With Devin, I don't think it ever will. His soul calls to mine in a way I can't explain.

"You've no idea how much your texts meant to me during that time, Ange." He grips my hand tighter. "I wanted to text you back, so badly, but I was only allowed my phone for one hour a week, and my counselor wanted me to cut all contact with the outside world to aid my recovery. I didn't even speak to Jim, not until the end, when he came in for a few sessions."

He presses his forehead to mine. "They had this really nice sunroom at the rear of the facility, and every Sunday when I was given my cell, I'd curl up on one of the couches and read through all your texts. To know you hadn't forgotten me, that you were still thinking of me"—he lowers his voice—"that you loved me"—his voice cracks, and he reels me into his arms—"it meant everything to me, Ange. Everything."

I wrap my arms around him, closing my eyes, and his musky, woodsy scent swirls around me, bringing so many happy memories to the forefront of my mind.

"I honestly don't think I'd have gotten through it without that. Your words kept me going. They buffered me on dark days when I wanted to give up, but I wouldn't. Not when I knew you were thinking of me. When I had hope you'd be here for me to come back to. I know I don't deserve it, but I'm glad you're here. That we're both here. Right where we should be."

I have so much I want to say, but the words are stuck in my throat. I'm overcome with emotion. I still can't believe he's here, and I'm not sure what exactly the future holds, but, for now, I want him to know he's important to me. I pull the locket out from under my top, running my fingers over it. "I never take it off." His eyes brim with emotion. "And I could never forget you, Devin. No matter what, you'll always be a part of me."

∞ ∞ ∞

Devin left shortly after that. I think he was as emotionally drained as me. There's still so much we need to talk about, but as I drift off to sleep, I can't keep the gleeful smile off my face. One of my best friends is back in my life, and I'm unbelievably happy.

Mariah jumps on my bed bright and early the next morning. "Ugh, go away, you're far too exuberant for this time of the morning." I bury my head under the pillow, hoping she'll take the hint.

A breeze wafts over my head as she whips the pillow off me. Guess that'd be a no.

"No can do. I've been bouncing around Cody's apartment all night dying to know what's going on with Devin. My boyfriend actually threw me out. Can you believe that?" I hear the mock pout in her tone. "He said I was giving him ear ache." She laughs, bending down to hug me. "Come on, *baby doll*, sharing is caring."

I brush knotty strands of hair off my face, yawning as I pull myself upright in the bed. She sits beside me, leaning her head on my shoulder as I tell her everything. She oohs and aahs in all the right places, emitting a string of expletives when I get to the Becky part of the story. "I knew it!" she shrieks. "I flippin' knew that slut had something on him."

I cover my ears. "Too. Loud."

She titters. "So how did you leave things?"

I yawn again. "We're going to catch up later, I think." I slip back under the covers. "Now you know everything, and I need more sleep. Shoo."

She kisses the top of my head. "I'm really glad he's here, Ange, but if he hurts you again…"

"We're friends, M, that's all, and I believe him when he says he's changed. I could see the difference in him."

My phone beeps and I slide it off my bedside table, squinting as I open my inbox. I can't curtail my smile as Devin's name pops up. Mariah is grinning from ear to ear as she slips out of the bedroom.

Hey, beautiful. Want 2 meet 4 a l8 lunch? Jim's dropping by. He'd love 2 meet u. No pressure if it's 2 soon.

What time?

4?

C u then.

Dev knocks on my door on the dot of four, and the fluttering in my chest builds to epic proportions. Grabbing my jacket, purse, and keys, I walk to the door and fling it open. My heart stutters at the sight of him. He's wearing dark jeans, sturdy brown boots, and a thick gray jacket with a UI scarf around his neck. He graces me with his trademark grin, and his eyes sparkle with joy as he looks me over. "Look at you," he says, pulling me into his arms. "You're even more beautiful than I remember."

I send him an incredulous look. "Since last night?" I quirk a brow.

He tweaks my nose. "Yep. Every hour you grow more beautiful." He takes my hand, pulling the door shut behind me.

"You're ridiculous."

"Just telling it like I see it." He weaves his hands through my hair. "You are gorgeous, Ange, and I haven't told you that enough. And I'm not just referencing what's on the outside, even if I have missed your beautiful face so much."

My heart is spinning a hundred miles an hour, and while I'm loving his words, and I can tell he means every bit of it, it's a little overwhelming, and not what I'm used to. I'm a little out of my comfort zone with this version of Dev.

"Hey." He tips my chin up with his finger. "Is this too much?"

"No, yes, maybe." I worry my lip in my teeth. "You do know I'm still going out with Ayden?"

If he's surprised or disappointed, he hides it well. "I wasn't aware of that. I guess I just presumed because he's overseas that you two had called it quits."

He steps back, creating a little distance between us.

"You heard about the marines?"

He nods. "Cam filled me in."

Of course. "Well, he sprung it on me an hour before he left. I was way too mad to start any conversation about our relationship, so I'm not really sure where we stand, and I won't know until he's back."

"And when is that?"

"Not until Easter."

He purses his lips. "I understand." An awkward silence pervades the air, and I'm confused at the turnaround in this conversation. *I mean, did Devin think in coming here that we were going to be together?* Because he's never really given me any indication that that's how he sees me, and now isn't the time to explore it. He plasters a smile on his face, closing the gap between us. "That's not stopping us from resuming our friendship though, right?"

"Of course not. You've been my best friend since forever."

"Cool." He offers me his arm. "We'd better make tracks. Jim's probably already there, and he's a stickler for good timekeeping."

"Let's not keep the man waiting so."

I'm fiddling with the scarf around my neck as we walk toward the restaurant to meet Jim. "You should've told me we were going someplace snazzy, and I would've made more of an effort."

He chuckles. "It's not like you to worry over what you're wearing."

"Yeah, well, Mariah's made me her new pet project, and it's kinda rubbing off on me. Usually, she won't let me leave the apartment until she's given me the seal of approval."

"So, I guess I have her to thank for that hot little number you were wearing last night?"

My cheeks flare up, and he laughs, opening the door and beckoning me inside. "You liked it?"

His breath is warm on my cheek as he whispers in my ear. "What wasn't to like? You were fucking sensational in it."

I'm all hot and bothered under my coat so it's a welcome relief when the maître d' offers to take it from me, hanging both our jackets up before guiding us through the restaurant. Devin grips my hand and steers me through the packed dining room, heading straight toward a booth at the back.

A distinguished-looking man with a fine head of jet-black hair looks up, smiling as he notices our approach. I can't help gasping as we get closer. "My God," I mutter under my breath. "You look so much like him."

Jim taps his watch, his lips pulling into an affectionate smile. "Only ten minutes late this time, Devin. That's got to be a new record."

Devin offers him an apologetic smile. "Sorry we're late."

"I'm afraid that's my fault," I say. "I kept him talking at the door."

Jim stands up, stepping out of the booth, and taking my hand in his. "It's wonderful to finally meet you, Angelina. My son speaks very highly of you."

I flush. "It's nice to meet you too, sir."

He turns to Devin. "She's every bit as beautiful as you said."

My cheeks flare fire-engine red, and Dev chuckles as I launch myself into the booth, burying my face in the menu to hide my embarrassment.

We place our orders, and the conversation flows naturally around the table. Jim goes out of his way to relax me, and Dev keeps his hand secured in mine until our food arrives. After the meal, we say goodbye to Jim and leave to hook up with Cody and Mariah.

"He's really nice," I remark, once we're tucked up in Dev's SUV with the heat pumping out. "And you two seem to get along very well." Which is heartwarming to see because Devin hasn't had a proper father figure in his life.

"I was a bit of an asshole to him at the start," Dev explains, and I bark out a laugh.

"Why doesn't that surprise me?"

He smirks, before his expression turns more serious. "But he won me over quickly. It's good to have a decent role model in my life. Someone I can look up to and learn from." He glances over at me briefly while he drives. "I used to look at you and Natalie and wish I had that kind of relationship with my dad. Now I do, and it's fucking awesome."

CHAPTER TWENTY-NINE

We meet Mariah and Cody at the movie theater, and, afterward we return to campus to attend another frat party. The guys have disappeared to procure drinks while Mariah and I wait in the crowded living room. We have to practically shout over the music to be heard. "You're right," she hollers in my ear. "Devin is different. He seems to have his shit together."

"I think so." Only time will really tell. As I spy Devin and Cody making their way through the room toward us, I don't miss the admiring looks he's picking up from all quarters. Devin has this magnetic presence that draws every girl in. A sour taste pools in my mouth as a familiar sickening feeling twists my insides into knots. A girl jumps out in front of him, tugging on his arm and stopping his progress. My stomach drops to my toes, and all the feel-good hormones are replaced with a bunch of anxiety-laden ones. I suffered this agony the whole way through high school, and I don't think I can bear to go through it again now we're in college. My heart has taken a battering this last year, and I think I've reached my breaking point.

Grabbing my coat and purse, I hightail it toward the door. My pulse is pounding in my ears, and my heart is a dense block of concrete in my chest. Tears prick my eyes, but I hold them at bay. I can't cry any more over Devin. I just can't go there again.

A hand circles my waist from behind before I reach the front door, and I'm pulled back against a strong, warm body. "Where are you going?"

Dev asks, twirling me around to face him. I look down at my feet while I attempt to plant a poker face on. He tilts my chin up. "What's wrong?"

I open my mouth to lie. To tell him nothing's wrong, but I think better of it. "I've no desire to watch other girls pawing at you, especially not after we've had such a great time today, so I think it's best I call it a night."

He opens his mouth to speak, but I place my finger against his lips, quieting him. "You have nothing to apologize for, and you're free to do whatever you like. I'd just rather not bear witness to it."

He grips my face firmly in his palms. "The only girl I'm interested in spending time with at this party is you. Please, don't leave. I'm not ready to say goodnight to you yet." His eyes glisten with sincerity and longing, and my resolve wavers on the spot. My willpower has always been extremely weak when it comes to Devin. I nod shyly, and he takes my hand, leading me back into the room.

Mariah subtly mouths at me. "You okay?"

I nod, offering her a small smile as Dev hands me a red cup. "Thanks."

He wraps his arm around my shoulder, keeping me close to his side as we chat. I notice he is only drinking a soda, and he ignores every girl who approaches or attempts to catch his eye across the room. When I need to go to the bathroom, he comes with me, checking his cell and refusing eye contact with every girl while he waits outside for me. Conversation is lively, and it's almost like old times. Except that Ayden should be here with us, and he isn't. A wave of sadness sweeps over me, and Dev notices. "Why do you look so bummed out?" he whispers in my ear.

"I was just thinking about Ayd."

"You miss him," he says, and it's not a question. I nod. "Me too."

"Have you heard from him at all?"

He shakes his head.

"He doesn't have many phone privileges," I explain, "but he usually calls every second Sunday. I'm expecting his call tomorrow. You could come over and talk with him, if you like?"

"I'm not sure Ayden will be happy I'm going to college with you."

I touch his arm. "I know it was tense between you two before you left but things are different now. I think he'll be happy to know you're in a good place, and he'll feel less guilty knowing you are here with me. He thinks he let me down by bailing on the college plan."

"Well, he did. You guys had this all figured out years before I knew what I wanted to do. I couldn't believe it when Cam told me he'd ditched his football dream and joined the marines. Still can't wrap my head around it."

A couple get up from the couch, and we pounce, dropping into their seats before anyone can beat us to it. Dev keeps his arm around my shoulder, crossing one knee over the other. "Did he ever talk to you about it?" I ask.

"Nope. He never said a word. I thought he lived and breathed football, and he is so Goddamned talented."

"I'm glad he had courage to follow his heart, even if I did feel like throat punching him at the time." Dev chuckles. "It was just such a huge shock, and I'm still pissed that he didn't confide in me. No wonder our relationship…" I trail off, uncomfortable discussing my relationship in front of Devin. It feels disrespectful to Ayden to do so.

He's quiet for a couple of minutes. "Can I ask you something?"

I look into his eyes and promptly melt on the spot. His gaze ensnares me, holding me in place, sucking all the air out of the room and my lungs. I could drown in Devin's hypnotic gaze and not regret a thing. His lips fight a smile, and I realize he's waiting for a response. All I can manage is a wide-eyed nod.

"Are you planning on waiting for him indefinitely?" A flicker of hope, of expectation, shimmers in his sea-green eyes, and my heart can't help reacting. I don't know if he realizes it, but his fingers are drifting in and out of my hair, toying with the strands, and it feels comfortable between us but different. I'm sensing things Devin hasn't said, and though I shouldn't get my hopes up, I think he wants more from me.

But I can't indulge that now. Perhaps, when Ayden and I have drawn a line under our romantic relationship, Devin and I might have a chance at something, but I can't entertain those thoughts now. I spent years pining for him, and I can't get sucked back into that space. It's not healthy for me. "I can't answer that question until I've spoken to Ayden, Dev. It wouldn't be fair for me to tell you how I'm feeling before I've had the chance to tell him."

Slowly, he nods. "That's fair, Ange. I hope he appreciates your loyalty."

I'm not sure that he does, but that's neither here nor there now.

Ayden calls later than usual the next night, and Devin and I have just spent a pleasant afternoon in my place watching old movies and stuffing our faces with a host of our favorite junk food. The relaxed, happy mood becomes tense as I pick up my cell to answer my boyfriend. "Hey, baby," Ayden greets me. "Can you hear me okay?"

"Hey, yourself, and yes, the line is clear."

"I've missed you."

"I've missed you, too. How are things over there?"

"Pretty shitty, to be honest. It's not what I thought it'd be."

His mood sounds low, and I wish I could project myself through the phone to cheer him up with a hug. "Is there no way you can get home for Thanksgiving?"

"Not a chance in hell, unfortunately. Are you going home?"

"Yeah. It won't be the same without you."

"I'll be there in spirit."

Dev is watching me closely as I clear my throat. "I have someone here who wants to speak to you." I hold the phone out to Dev.

"Hey, man," Dev says. I can't hear the response on the other side. "I go to school here too." There's a brief pause. "That's not it. She hasn't been hiding it from you." His eyes lock on mine, and there's a fierce intensity in his gaze. "She didn't know I was here until recently." A muscle clenches in Devin's jaw. "It's not like that, and I've gotten my act together. I'm clean, and sober, and I'm just trying to pick up the pieces of my life." He grabs fistfuls of his hair. "You know how much our friendship has always meant to me." Devin starts pacing the room. "Don't put this shit on me, again. You know, now that I look back on that time, there are plenty of things that don't make any sense." His eyes burn angrily, and he harrumphs. "Yeah, why doesn't that surprise me? Sure. I'll put Ange back on the phone. See ya, *buddy*." His voice is like ice as he spits out the last word, thrusting phone at me.

"What was that all about?" I ask Ayden.

"Nothing for you to worry about."

I grind my teeth to the molars, although I shouldn't be shocked. Shutting me out has always been Ayden's forte. "I'm not sure why you're pissed, but Devin's my friend, *our* friend, and I'm thrilled he's here. When you get home, we're all going to sit down and thrash things out. I don't care whether you agree or not, it's happening. We're putting our friendship back on track, and there's nothing you can say that'll make me change my mind. We need each other. We've always had one another's backs, and it's time to emphasize that."

"I've got to go, Lina."

His voice is curt, and now I wish I could reach through the line and strangle him. But I refuse to end our call on a sour note. Not when he's out there, dealing with God knows what. "Okay." I sigh. "I love you. Stay safe."

"Love you too. Bye." Then he hangs up. Devin is sitting on the couch with his head in his hands. I toss my cell on the table, and sit down beside him, gently placing my hand on his knee. "What did he say?"

"Just more of the usual bullshit." He looks up, and I recognize the strain in his eyes. "I don't think he'll ever be able to look beyond the crap of the last year."

I squeeze his knee. "He will. You've got to give him time. And he's over there dealing with so much shit. His reaction is probably more to do with that than you."

$$\infty \infty \infty$$

The next couple of weeks fly by, and Devin is a permanent daily fixture in my life. The more time we spend together, the less I remember our separation.

It's as if we were never apart.

I'm glad when Wednesday rolls around and we're making the trip home for Thanksgiving. Mariah is traveling with Cody, and I'm going with Devin in his SUV.

The closer we get to Mason City, the happier I feel.

Mr. Carter is still fuming with Devin, blaming him for what he perceives to be Ayden's litany of bad decisions, so the Morgans are banned from the usual Thanksgiving dinner at the Carters. Mom and I decided to host our own Thanksgiving this year, and she's invited Dr. Williams along with Devin and his brothers. Jim is also coming. He shares the various annual celebrations with his ex-wife, and it's her turn to have their daughters for Thanksgiving this year, so he's delighted to be able to spend it with his new family for the first time.

Mom and I are up half the night prepping the food for the next day. We chat while sipping wine and catching up. She's deliriously happy, and completely head over heels in love, and I'm thrilled for her. I've only met Dr. Williams—Jon—a couple of times, but I can tell he's a decent guy.

"Thank you for such a gorgeous dinner," Jim says the next evening after we've all stuffed ourselves silly.

"I don't think I'll be able to eat for a week," Luc acknowledges with a groan, massaging his swollen belly.

"You'd swear I never feed you," Cam jokes, messing his hair as he stands up, starting to clear away the empty plates.

"He's a growing boy, and I still remember how much food Devin used to put away at that age," Mom remarks with a grin, leaning into Jon as he circles his arm around her shoulder.

"That was everything to do with the delicious food you cooked and the stunning company. I was always trying to delay the time when I had to leave," Devin replies with a cheeky wink, staring in my direction as he stacks plates atop one another.

Mom smiles warmly at me. "I'm glad to see you doing so well, Devin. Angelina tells me you're majoring in criminology, law, and justice, and taking art classes, and that you've stopped drinking. Your mom would be so proud."

"That she would," Jim adds, smiling sadly.

Devin clears his throat. "I've never had a chance to thank you, Natalie. For everything you did for me and Luc." He bends down, hugging her. Tears well in my eyes. He whispers something in her ear, and Mom stands up, hugging him properly. She returns his whisper, tears pricking her own eyes.

I look away, not wishing to intrude on their intimate moment, happy that Dev seems so content and secure in himself.

"Want to stargaze with me?" he asks a few hours later, his eyes twinkling in expectation. A yawn slips out of my mouth as the movie credits roll on the screen. Jim is busy chatting to Mom and Jon, Luc has gone out with his buddies, and Cam has left to meet up with the girl he's currently dating, leaving Dev and me to our own devices.

I take his offered hand, allowing him to pull me to my feet. "We're going out on the balcony," I tell Mom.

"Grab a couple of blankets," she calls out. "The temperature's due to drop significantly tonight."

We're out on the balcony, sitting on bean bags, wrapped up warmly as we stare up at the inky-black canvas in the sky. A light smattering of stars streak across the dark skyline. I'm sipping on my glass of red wine, and Dev's drinking a soda. "This is the first Thanksgiving night in years that I haven't been wasted," he admits, taking my free hand in his.

"Do you miss it?" I look at our conjoined hands, savoring the warmth passing from his body to mine.

He pauses considerably before replying. "Sometimes I could literally kill for a drink, but I don't want to fall down a slippery slope. I don't like the person I am when I drink, and maintaining my progress is more important than any temporary high. I was sick of partying and ..."

He doesn't need to say it. We both know what he means. Talk of partying and drinking and screwing only serves to remind me of this time last year. My heart aches in remembrance, and I look away, not wanting him to see the pain etched on my face.

He repositions his bean bag, wrapping his arms around me from behind and pulling me into his chest. "I hate that I hurt you," he whispers, pressing a kiss to my temple. "Please tell me you know all that shit I said last year was just drunken talk."

I shrug, still not looking at him. "Some people say the truth comes out when you're drunk."

He twists me around in his arms, forcing my face to his. "Maybe that's true for some people, but not in this case. I didn't mean any of those horrible things I said to you last year. Nothing could be further from the truth." He cups my face. "I've messed up pretty bad with you, but our time hasn't started yet." He presses a feather-soft kiss to my forehead, and an embarrassing little whimper flies out of my mouth. Just that one touch has my body thrumming with need. Devin has always had this unerring power over my body. Whether it's a subtle touch or one of his intense looks, he turns me into a mass of quivering cells any time he turns his attention on me. No one has ever affected me so potently.

He drags in a gulp of air. "I wanted you," he whispers over my mouth. "I wanted to make love to you. I wanted to be your first, and I've kicked myself so many times for walking away, yet I can't regret it either, because you deserved better than that version of me."

I peer deep into his eyes, seeing so much emotion there. My heart is doing a funny little jump in my chest. "I wanted it to be you, but I can't have any regrets either because that's as good as implying I regret sharing the experience with Ayd."

A pained expression darts across his face. "If it couldn't be me, I'm glad it was him, even if thinking of it makes me want to swing for him, but I can't fault him for being there for you when I wasn't. I'm so sorry I let you down."

I caress his cheek, talking softly. "We've got to stop doing this. Stop focusing on the past. We can't change it and it only makes both of us sad. I want to focus on the here and now."

"Not the future?" He arches an inquisitive brow, amusement flickering in his eyes.

"No. I live in the present now. The future is too unpredictable."

His hands meander through my hair, and he cups the back of my neck in a firm grip. My hands land lightly on his waist. "I like the here and now," he rasps. "There is nowhere in the entire galaxy I'd rather be in this moment than here with you."

"Ditto. You'll always be one of my all-time favorite people, Dev."

He leans in, his lips brushing my cheek as his mouth makes a round trip to my ear. "What if I told you I want to be your most favorite person? The one you adore above everyone else?" His warm breath is doing strange things to my insides. My entire body is tingling, and my limbs feel like they've turned to rubber. He moves his hand up and down my spine, and a soothing warmth seeps bone deep. I clutch his waist harder, subconsciously moving closer until there's barely a sliver of space between us. Every cell in my body screams for him, and I should pull back, withdraw from temptation, but I'm already under his spell.

He kisses my cheek again, and I melt into him. "What if I wanted that, Ange?" he prompts. "What would you say?"

I should refuse to answer. Throw out a lie and put a halt to this. But I can't. "That you already are." My heart is thumping wildly in my chest, and I can scarcely hear for the blood rushing through my ears. "That you always have been."

He cups my face firmly, and fierce emotion blazes in his eyes. "I've wanted you to say that to me for a long time. I suspected, but I needed to know, because I'm a selfish, greedy bastard when it comes to you."

"Dev, I—"

"Ssh," he interrupts, sweeping his thumb along my lower lip, and the look in his eyes almost melts my panties off. My body sways forward, my craving for him reaching an unparalleled high. "This is the most supremely selfish act of all, but I can't resist."

"Resist what?" I croak out, my voice hoarse, raw with need. I'm holding my breath in anticipation. Every nerve ending in my body is on heightened alert.

He licks his lips, dropping his hungry eyes to my mouth. My body pulses with need, and I squirm a little, keeping my eyes locked on his, knowing the desire I see is mirrored on my own face.

"This," he confirms, closing the gap between us and slanting his mouth over mine.

CHAPTER THIRTY

He kisses me softly and sweetly, bundling me in his arms and holding me close, like I'm precious cargo. I angle my head, kissing him back with more urgency, and his tongue runs over the seam of my lips, asking permission. I open for him, moaning as his tongue tangles with mine.

I'm on fire: every cell, every tissue, and every fiber of my being is sizzling. The innermost chambers of my heart and the deepest, darkest corners of my soul are bursting with joy, and I'm blissfully drowning in a sea of contentment. His touch awakens every part of me, reaching hidden depths, and, without a shadow of a doubt, I know that Devin has been created especially for me. He's got to be, because he ignites sparks inside me, invokes feelings I've never felt before, and our bodies blend together perfectly. More than that, he's been my best friend for years, and he knows me inside and out. We've always been in sync, and now I know it's in every conceivable way.

He eases me down onto my back, covering my body with his. I lift my knee, opening my legs, and he settles between them. We both groan, gently grinding against one another as the kiss turns frenzied. Devin's devouring my mouth, and I moan loudly as he nips and bites at my lower lip. His hand skims over my body, caressing my curves, and I'm lost to sensation. The more he kisses me, the more I want to consume him. I claw at him, my hands exploring everywhere, wanting more, needing more, craving more, feeling so much, and yet not enough at the same time.

His hand slips under my top, and I gasp at the skin on skin contact. His mouth moves off mine, and he starts tracing a line of kisses down my neck, onto my collarbone and lower.

An image flashes in my mind, and it's like cold water sluicing over my skin. I push his shoulders, and he lifts his chin up. His mouth is swollen, his pupils dark with lust. "Ayden," I whisper, my voice choked with pain. "We can't do this to Ayden." I slide out from under him, scurrying over to the far side of the balcony, not trusting myself to be strong enough to do the right thing.

My breath is heaving in and out in exaggerated spurts, and my emotions are veering all over the place. Pulling my knees up to my chest, I draw measured breaths in an attempt to gain control of myself. Devin sits up, watching me carefully. We stare wordlessly at one another for several minutes until I feel composed enough to speak. "We shouldn't have done that."

"I can't bring myself to regret it. Not when I've spent months, hell, years, wanting to kiss you like that."

My eyes pop wide at his admission, and I wish I could push the agenda, but I can't. Things are complicated enough between the three of us without making things worse. "We can't do it again."

He peers intensely into my eyes. "I'm going to fight him for you this time. He knows how I feel about you, and he didn't hold back in taking what was mine." He climbs to his feet. "I know you want to talk to him properly, and I can respect that. If you don't want me to kiss you again, I won't. But when he's back, when it's an even playing field, I'm going to fight with everything I've got. You belong with me. You always have, and I'm not giving up this time."

∞ ∞ ∞

Devin was true to his word. The rest of the time we were at home, we hung out, but there were no more kisses, no more touches, and he made an effort to keep a reasonable distance from me. I respect him for honoring the boundaries I've erected.

I'm the one who's struggling to maintain them.

When we return to campus, life settles into a comfortable routine. I throw myself into my studies and spend a huge amount of my free time with Devin. We hang out with Mariah and Cody a lot, and it reminds me of old times. Good times. I switched art classes, and now Devin and I are in the same one. It's only a hobby, for both of us, but I can't help wishing he was pursing an art major instead of criminal justice. He's so gifted, and it seems like such a waste of God-given talent.

We attend another frat party, and Devin scarcely leaves my side. He has no shortage of offers from willing girls, but he never once indulges. He is still abstaining from drink and drugs and anything that would jumpstart his hyper-addictive personality into play.

Ayden called again, but he refused to speak to Devin, and there's a new layer to the underlying tension in existence during every call. As the days pass, the more assured I become of the decision I've made.

I miss Ayden. I really, really do.

But I don't miss his arms or his lips or the feel of his body as it moves against mine.

My body doesn't hum at the mere thought of him.

Not like it does every second I'm thinking about Devin, and don't even get me started on how difficult it is not to jump his bones whenever we're together. Some days, I physically sit on my hands to stop myself touching him.

I was never like that with Ayden.

It's not a competition between them, but, the time apart has given me new insight into my relationship. Ayden and I have never really worked as a couple. Sure, there were moments at the start, but they were fleeting, and I wonder now if we were both hankering after something that just didn't exist. Perhaps the divide with Devin forced both of us down a path we should never have taken.

I don't want to disparage what we shared, and I won't regret giving Ayden my virginity, but I wish we had stayed purely platonic.

Devin has said he's prepared to fight for me, but I'm not quite sure exactly what that means. I hope it means we are finally on the same page, but he hasn't come outright and said it. Nonetheless, I need to end my romance with Ayden before I can consider starting anything with Devin.

If he still wants me by then.

It's three days until Christmas break and I'm walking through campus alone when I notice the flyer pinned to the lamp post. My mouth pulls into a wide smile as I scan the announcement. The college is holding an ice skating event at a nearby rink tomorrow, and I want to attend.

When we were younger, we used to go skating every winter on the little lake on the west end of Clear Lake with my grandpa Joe. Devin and I were naturals on the ice, and as the daredevils of our group, we liked to push the boundaries, trying various turns, spins, and jumps until we perfected some skills. Ayden, with his nervous disposition and inelegant gait, always stuck to simple maneuvers. He was constantly picking us up off the ice while my grandpa doubled over with laughter from the sidelines. I lost count of the amount of times I came home covered in bruises.

It's been years since I've ice skated, but now that I've got my partner in crime back again, I can't wait to relive my love affair with the ice. Tucking my hands into the pockets of my coat, I turn around, leaving campus and making my way toward Devin's apartment. It's only a ten-minute walk from the college, so it won't take me long to get there. I've never actually been at his place. Devin's a bit weird about it, although I met his roomie Danny at the last party, and he doesn't seem like a freak or anything.

Danny and Devin. I chuckle to myself. With matching names, and their scorching-hot good looks, they belong in a boy band or modeling on the front cover of magazines.

I enter their building, bounding up the stairs to the third floor, bubbling with excitement. As I approach the right apartment door, Danny emerges, all wrapped up snuggly for the cold weather in a parka and thick woolen scarf. "Hey, Ange. What's up? You looking for Dev?"

"Yeah. Is he here?"

"He's just stepped out. We needed a few things at the store, but he should be back shortly. I'm running late to meet my tutor, but you can wait, if you like." He opens the door, gesturing me inside.

"You're sure he won't mind?" I've gotten the distinct impression that Devin doesn't want me visiting him here. We *always* hang out at my place.

Danny's eyes widen as if he's just realized something. "Nah. Course he won't. Make yourself at home. *Explore.*" He enunciates the word, his eyes dancing with merriment, and a tinge of apprehension creeps up my spine as I step foot over the threshold.

The door shuts behind me, and I stand awkwardly in the middle of their living space. It's a large, bright, airy room and a total mancave. A ginormous three-seater black leather couch rests in front of the bay window. The small coffee table houses a multitude of men's magazines. Two black leather recliners face a large TV, and there's a game console and a myriad of gaming equipment on the floor underneath the TV. Posters of topless girls hang on the walls, and I roll my eyes. How cliché. The small kitchen and dining area is neat and tidy, and I know that's pure Devin.

A corridor leads to two bedrooms and a bathroom. I poke my head into the rooms—Danny said I could nose around so I don't feel too guilty. I know I've found Devin's bedroom the instant I open the door. I stand rooted to the hardwood floor in shock as the door swings fully open, exposing what Devin clearly didn't want me to see.

Danny knows it too. The little sneak.

I walk into the room slowly, my eyes bugging out of my head. Every spare inch of wall is covered.

With pictures and photos of me.

It's like a shrine, and I don't know what to make of it. My fingers trace over Devin's drawings. There are so many of them! He's signed and dated them all and they span years. He's captured me in all manner of poses and activities. Playing baseball with Ayden in my backyard. Swinging off the trees in the woods near our hideout. Sunbathing on the wooden deck out by the lake. Throwing snowballs with Mom on the road outside our house one Christmas. He's even drawn my ballet recitals, capturing me mid-flow during school plays, and racing around the running track at school, trailing my classmates like the slowpoke I am.

Devin always had a pad in hand when we were younger. He was *always* drawing, but he rarely showed us his work, and after a while Ayden and I gave up asking.

Now I know what he was doing.

He was immortalizing me on canvas, and I. Had. No. Idea.

Tears cascade down my cheeks as I walk around the room, my fingers tracing the drawings, my eyes struggling to take it all in. An errant sob slips out of my mouth as I zone in on the photos of me at prom. These ones aren't drawings. They are actual photographs, clearly taken at the event. Either someone took them and sent them to him or … he was actually there.

I drop to the ground on my butt, surrounded by evidence of Devin's love. Some might call it obsession.

I'm calling it a miracle.

How many nights did I cry myself to sleep begging God to make him love me? Wishing it was me he was kissing and taking to his bed and not some skank he picked up at a party.

More nights than I care to admit.

Now I'm in the midst of the confirmation my heart has sought.

And I'm confused.

Or scared.

Probably a bit of both.

I don't know what to do with this knowledge, and he was keeping it from me for a reason.

Do I let him know I know or keep quiet about it?

One part of me wants to fling myself into his arms and never let go.

Another part of me wants to flee. Afraid to confront the magnitude of both our feelings and what it might mean.

This room is the physical manifestation of all my dreams come true.

But I'm terrified.

And the fleeing part wins out.

Racing out of Devin's apartment, I run all the way home, not stopping until I'm safely tucked up in bed, curled into a fetal position, wondering what the hell to do now.

CHAPTER THIRTY-ONE

Have you ever wished for something so badly, and then, when your wish has been granted, been absolutely terrified to embrace it? Like, it was okay when it was an abstract desire. When you were free to imagine it panning out the way you wanted it to in your own head, because there was no way in hell it would ever come true. But when it's right there in front of you for the taking, all your bravado, and all your longing, transforms to anxiety. Because it was imaginary up to this point, and the reality is scary, even if it's still something you want so badly.

I'm rambling, talking to myself, acting like a crazy person. Gah! I don't know what I'm saying or what I want. I'm even confusing myself.

Mariah has a late-night study session at the library, and she won't be home for hours, and I'm going out of my freaking mind. I could use her advice right now. I throw off the covers and pad to the living room, switching on the TV, in the hope it might distract me. When a knock sounds on the door five minutes later, I sit frozen in place, my heart banging against my ribcage in blatant panic. I don't need to open the door to know it's Devin.

I've been expecting him.

"Ange, it's me. Open up. Please."

I'm still rooted to the spot. Terrified to open the door and confront everything I've ever wanted.

I'm scared of what I might do.

And equally scared I'm incapable of doing anything.

"Baby, please open up. I need to talk to you."

Pulling my bravery cap on, I walk over and open the door, standing back to let him step inside.

I close the door, flattening my back to it, staring at the ground. I'm acutely conscious of him standing in front of me, watching, waiting. The silence is charged with the usual electrical spark that always crackles between us.

"On a scale of one to ten, how freaked out are you right now?" he asks in a husky voice.

"About a hundred," I whisper.

"Look at me. Please." I drag my gaze up, startled at the anguished look in his eyes. "I didn't want you to find out like that. It's why I deliberately didn't have you over to my place."

I clear my throat. "Every time you were drawing, you were drawing me?"

He nods slowly. "In case it hasn't been obvious, I've never been able to take my eyes off you."

"Were you … were you there at prom?"

His face lights up. "I was. God, Ange, you looked so beautiful."

Tears leak out of my eyes. "I couldn't enjoy it, because you weren't there."

He takes a step closer. "I wanted to go to you. To hold you in my arms and dance with you like I'd always imagined we'd dance at prom, but I couldn't. I didn't want to show up and butt into your life without warning. Besides, Ayden was your date, and I wouldn't do that to him. And I had to get back to the facility before dark. They had made special allowances to release me for a few hours so I could see you."

"Why, Dev? Why hide your feelings from me? Didn't you know how I felt about you?"

"Did you know how I felt about you?" He takes another step closer.

"No. Never. But it wouldn't have made sense … you were with all those other girls. You didn't see me."

He closes the gap between us, standing in front of me, peering into my eyes. "You are all I've ever seen." He lightly touches my cheek. "Trust me. And I wanted to tell you when we were younger, but I was too much of a pussy. Then stuff turned to crap after Mom left, and I was broken, too broken to drag you into my mess, but I never stopped loving you. Not once. I've loved you forever, Ange. It's always been you. Only you." He smooths my tears away with the back of his thumb. "And I didn't realize you felt the same way until it was too late."

I wind my fingers around his wrist. "You love me? You really love *me*?"

"I love you, I love you, I love you. I love you so much it hurts." He presses his forehead to mine.

My heart almost skyrockets out of my chest. More tears fall, and I can't stop them. "You don't know how much I've yearned to hear you say those words."

"I'm sorry it's taken me so long, but now they're out there, and I'm never taking them back." He kisses my cheek. "I love you, Ange. I fucking love you so much."

Without pausing to think about it, I grab his face and fuse our mouths together. There's nothing soft or tender about the marriage of our lips. Years of unrequited love and pent-up desire have meshed together in one explosive mix. His mouth is working fiercely against mine, his tongue plundering my mouth, and I'm lapping it up, matching his searing-hot kisses, one for one. My hands tangle in his hair as we ravish one another. He grabs me to him, thrusting his erection into my pelvis, leaving me in no doubt as to how much he wants me.

I need zero convincing.

I'm tugging on his coat, pulling at his shirt, ripping the material in my haste to feel his bare skin. We break apart for a second so he can remove my tank top and bra. Then our mouths are fused again, and we're kissing like we've never kissed before. I jump up, wrapping my legs around his waist, and he holds me tight to his naked chest. Releasing my mouth, he rolls my nipple between his teeth, and my core throbs with need. He walks us toward the bedroom, kicking the door open with his foot. I point to my bed, and he throws me down on the comforter before crawling over my body, resuming his assault on my mouth.

I fumble with the button on his jeans, my fingers trembling, and he chuckles. Standing up, he shucks them off along with his boxers. Before I can admire him in all his naked glory, he's back on the bed, tugging my sleep shorts down with his teeth. When we're both fully naked, he climbs back up my body, capturing my mouth in yet another searing-hot kiss. I grab fistfuls of his hair, yanking his body down on top of me, and we both groan as our bodies strategically align in all the right places. My hands explore every dip and curve of his torso, roaming freely over his toned abs and butt as he continues worshiping my mouth and my neck, sucking on that sensitive spot just under my ear.

I'm writhing and panting like a woman possessed, and I need to feel him inside me now. I've never wanted anyone as much as I want Devin. Pushing rationale aside, I refuse to feel anything but the heavenly sensations coursing through my body. Devin works my body like a skilled violinist plucking strings—knowing when to alternate between precise, measured gentle touches and determined, intense, hard strokes, tweaking my body until I'm primed to explode.

Spreading my legs, I buck my hips up, gripping his butt and pulling him closer to me. Ripping his mouth from mine, he props up on his elbows, staring at me with dark, sultry, lust-drenched eyes. Our chests rise and fall at the same time while we hold a silent conversation.

He asks a question. I give permission.

Removing a condom from the pocket of his jeans, he rolls it on, his eyes never leaving mine. Bringing my wrist to his mouth, he plants a delicate kiss on my skin, in the exact place where my infinity tattoo resides. I shiver, feeling his touch all the way to my toes. Then he shimmies down a bit, positioning himself at my entrance, and he slides inside me in one powerful, confident thrust.

I cry out as he fills me, submerged in the most incredible, other-worldly sensations. Every part of my body absorbs his touch while he holds himself still inside me. His fingers sweep reverentially over my body, caressing every curve, every ounce of bare flesh, and I'm putty in his hands. He leans down into my face. "I love you. I love you. I love you."

"I love you too. I love you so completely. You're my everything, Dev."

He plants the softest, most delicate kiss on my lips. "I feel the same. You'll always be my whole world." Then he starts moving, slowly and carefully, like he plans to savor each millisecond of our joining. His hands and his lips worship every part of my body as he moves inside me with infinite tenderness. I've never experienced anything like it, and I could stay locked around him for eternity and never get enough.

Our first time is slow, and soft, and an unspoken eternal declaration of our love. The next two times are frantic, wild, and we devour one another, pushing our bodies to the max, screaming our releases in unison. Devin throws me over his shoulder, our sweat-slicked bodies slapping against one another as he pulls me into the shower with him. We take turns washing each other, and then he backs me into the wall, pushing my knee up high as he enters me hard and fast. "Harder. Oh my God," I yell, lost in the throes of desire. Lifting myself up a smidge, I wrap both legs around him. He pounds into me like a porn star, and the sounds and naughty words coming out of my mouth are like they're coming from someone else. Devin brings the inner sex kitten out in me, and I'm thrashing and moaning with wild abandon.

We go back to bed and sleep for a couple of hours. I wake up in the early hours of the morning when Devin slides inside me again, my limbs all sore and sleepy, and I'm aroused in an instant. When we finally collapse in a heap of sweat-glistened skin, he spoons me from behind, and I'm more content than I've ever been in my life. "Love you, baby doll," he whispers in my ear, and I pull his arms more tightly around my waist. "You're mine. Now and forever, Ange. All mine."

Angling my head back, I kiss him passionately, pouring everything I'm feeling into the kiss. "I'm yours. I've only ever been yours." His answering smile is ecstatic, and I'm so happy I could burst.

I know we shouldn't have done it like this, but I refuse to regret it. And I'm not looking back.

He's mine. I'm his. Now we've finally found our way to one another, I'm not letting him go. He's mine for eternity.

∞ ∞ ∞

I wake a few hours later, confused as a gust of cold air slithers over my skin. Rubbing my sleep-deprived eyes, I glance over at Mariah's unmade bed, grateful she obviously stayed at Cody's last night. Neither of us had given any consideration to my roomie when we were ravishing one another. I stretch my torso, and my limbs are deliciously sore and achy. I look over at Devin, lying on his stomach, snoring softly. His hair is all messed up, sticking out in all directions, but he looks adorably gorgeous. I press a feather-soft kiss on his shoulder, only narrowly avoiding the urge to kiss him awake and start round six.

A throat clearing at the door turns the blood in my veins to ice. All the tiny hairs rise on my arms, and bile swims in my mouth. In slow motion, I lift my head up, blinking profusely, praying my eyes are deceiving me. A little shriek rips from my mouth, and I yank the covers up, covering my bare chest.

Ayden is dressed in military-green pants with a khaki long-sleeved button up shirt and matching tie. He's wearing a cap, and there's a duffel bag at his feet.

He looks so handsome.

So grown up.

So angry.

"How could you?" he asks, slanting a hurt look my way. "How could you do this to me?"

CHAPTER THIRTY-TWO

I shake Devin's shoulders, beseeching him to wake up. He starts stirring, and I redirect my attention to Ayden. "I'm sorry. I'm so sorry." He purses his lips, and the anguished look in his eyes almost kills me. "How are you here?" I whisper.

"I was granted leave to come home early for Christmas. I thought I'd surprise you on my way from the airport. Guess the surprise is on me though." His lips curve into an ugly sneer.

"How did you get in?" I ask, shaking Devin again, more firmly this time. He grunts, finally lifting his head up off the pillow.

"I bumped into Mariah and Cody in the lobby. She gave me her key. She thought we'd need privacy for our reunion." He snorts out a harsh laugh. "What a fucking joke."

"Ayd," Devin says in a throaty voice, realizing we have company. "It's not exactly what you're thinking." We share a look, and he's letting me know he'll do the talking. "Last night was the first night we've spent together."

A muscle ticks in Ayden's jaw. "Don't treat me like I'm an idiot."

Devin pulls me into his side, sliding his arm protectively around me. "I'm not. I'm telling you the truth. We kissed at Thanksgiving, but Ange pushed me away. She didn't want to start this until she had spoken to you."

Ayden folds his arms across his broad chest, his eyes skimming over us in disgust. "Yeah, it sure looks like she tried real hard."

I know he's hurt, and he's every right to be. This shouldn't have happened like this, but I can't rewind the last few hours, and I don't want to. Last night was magical. But I hate that we've hurt Ayden. He doesn't deserve that. I need to try and make him see it from my perspective. To salvage our friendship before we collapse under the carnage. "I did try, but we can't deny our feelings any longer. Neither one of us meant to hurt you, and I hate that you've found out like this, but you're the one who walked away without giving me any warning, without any discussion of whether we were still together or not. I know it doesn't excuse what we've done, but I haven't been with anyone while you've been gone, not until last night. And let's not pretend like we had this great love affair. You barely touched me half the time."

He stalks into the room, putting his furious face right up in mine. "So, this is about sex? If you wanted to be fucked like a worthless whore, all you had to do was ask." Color blooms in my cheeks. "Excuse me for wanting to treat you with more respect than that."

"Don't you dare speak to Ange like that," Devin hisses.

"Screw you, asshole. You're in no position to interfere." He prods his finger in Devin's face. "That's *my* girlfriend you're in bed with." He sends me a contemptuous look. "Did he fuck you good? Did he fuck your brains out until you screamed the place down? I hope you got your fill, because you know he'll toss you to the curb now. You're nothing but another easy lay. Another whore to fuck while he tries to plug that ugly hole in his chest."

"Ayden." My gasp is laced with shock. I know this is hurt speaking, but he can't talk to either one of us like that. We're in the wrong, and we'll totally own that, but it doesn't give him the right to abuse both of us like this.

Devin jumps up, rounding the bed, butt naked, shoving Ayden back. "You know that's not the truth!" he yells. "You fucking know how I feel about her! How I've always felt about her!" He jabs his finger in Ayden's chest, but Ayden roughly pushes him aside. Devin stumbles a bit, and I get out of bed, wrapping the sheet firmly around my naked body. Lining up behind Devin, I thread my fingers in his. His entire body is shaking; every muscle and sinew locked in a heady rage, and he's primed to rip through Ayden. He's beyond furious, spitting his words out as if they're laced with airborne venom. "You purposely stole her from me! I know you planned this whole thing. Don't try and pretend otherwise."

Ayden glowers at Devin. "You know shit."

Devin straightens up, and the tone of his voice is scarily menacing when he speaks. "I know you convinced me I had to stay away from her. That it was the best way to protect her."

"And knowing what you know, are you still denying that?"

Devin's jaw is taut. "It might have been for the best, but you used it to your advantage."

"Like I said, you know shit."

I finally find my voice. "Look, let's get dressed, and then go out for breakfast and talk about this when we're all calmer."

Ayden snorts. "Yeah, I don't think so, Lina. There's nothing to talk about." He glances at the wrinkled sheets on the bed. "You've already made your bed. Now you can lie in it." He stalks to the door, bending down and swiping his bag. "Have a nice life together," he tosses out over his shoulder, storming toward the front door.

I run after him, almost tripping in the knotted-up sheet. "Ayden, please," I beg. "Don't go like this. Please. Even if we're not together, you're still one of my best friends, and I don't want to lose you."

He turns around, one hand on the door handle. "You should've thought of that before you jumped into bed with him." A look of intense pain spreads across his face as he stares at Devin. Devin wraps his arm around me from behind, pulling me into the protection of his body.

"I came back determined to let you in. To tell you what's been going on with me, but this … this fucks everything up." He presses his forehead to the door, and his breathing becomes erratic. "I've lost everyone. Nothing's changed, and everything's changed."

Devin and I trade concerned looks. "Ayden." His name is a whisper on my tongue.

He lifts his head up, and the look on his face as he turns to us one final time sends chills down my spine. "There's nothing you can say that will make this better. I want you to leave me alone. Both of you."

∞ ∞ ∞

It's early evening, and we're in a corner booth of the diner, silently picking at the cold, untouched food on our plates. My eyes are still sore and bloodshot from crying. "He'll come around," Dev says. "He's just hurt now. He didn't mean what he said."

"What if he doesn't?"

"We just need to give him time. I know what it's like to lose you, and he's in hell right now."

I push my uneaten plate away, scowling. "If that's supposed to make me feel better, you suck at it."

Reaching across the table, he takes my hands in his. "Babe, we'll work through this. We'll fix it. I promise. Once you and me are okay."

I worry my lip between my teeth. "I feel so guilty."

He sighs. "I know, me too. It was a shitty way for him to find out."

"This is all my fault. I'm the one who lunged at you."

A familiar cocky grin appears on his face. "If you think I wasn't primed to pounce, then you're sorely mistaken. You just beat me to it." He runs his thumb over the back of my hand. "I want to touch some part of you every second I'm in your presence. The last few weeks have been absolute torture, and I've had the worst case of blue balls known to man."

"We should've been stronger."

The smile slips off his mouth. "Do you regret it?"

I lean across the table and peck his lips. "No. I wish we had gone about this the right way, but how can I regret last night. Last night was …" Heat spreads up my neck and onto my cheeks.

"Incredible. Mind blowing. The abso-fucking-lutely best night of my life, hands down," Dev says, finishing my sentence.

My cheeks are on fire as I shyly meet his eyes. "You mean that?" I'm a lot less experienced than most of the girls Dev's been with, and while it was amazing for me, I'm sure he's had better.

He smiles softly, caressing my face. "You're too fucking cute when you blush. And, of course, I'm sure. No one has ever made me feel like that, Ange, because I've never loved any other girl. Last night was the best experience of my life."

"I didn't think it was possible to feel closer to you, but I do," I quietly admit.

He gets up, moving over to sit beside me. He holds my face in his hands, staring intently into my face. "I'm feeling that too." He presses a kiss to my forehead. "And I've got to warn you, I don't think I can let you out of my arms." As if to prove his point, he wraps his arms around me, reeling me into the warmth of his body. "I have an indescribable addiction to you, Ange. I can't bear to be parted from you. I think you'll have to switch majors," he jokes. "Sign up for all the same classes. And move in with me. I'll even join your ballet class. Anything to not spend a single second apart."

I look up at him, smiling. In a heartbeat, Devin has elevated my mood and has my soul singing. "I think you'd get sick of me pretty quickly in that scenario."

"Never." He kisses me sweetly. "Never in a million years would that happen."

I place my hands on his chest. "So, we're doing this?"

His answering smile is bright. "Yes. We're doing it. There's no going back now." He winks, and my heart surges with joy. "And I meant what I said." He brushes the pad of his thumb across my mouth. "Move in with me, baby. Share my life."

His phone pings before I can form any coherent response. Wanting me to move in with him shouldn't surprise me—Devin lives his life in the fast lane, and he's not one to hold back once he's decided on something.

"Hold that thought, beautiful," he says, frowning at his phone as he puts it to his ear. A look of alarm appears on his face as he listens to whomever is on the other end. "Yes, she's with me." His eyes dart to mine.

"Who is it?" I mouth, but he shakes his head, tucking me in to his side.

He turns a deathly shade of pale the longer the conversation continues. The arm around my body falls slack as tears spill out of his eyes. The cell clatters to the ground, shattering into pieces. Several heads turn in our direction. Devin is trembling. Like his whole body is convulsing, as if he's on the verge of a fit.

"Devin, what is it? What's wrong?" Imaginary sirens are blaring in my ears.

He stands up, bending over at the waist, clutching his stomach, and the most tormented howl rips from his mouth, filtering through the air, capturing the attention of every person in the diner. A solemn hush descends over the room, and his frantic breathing is the only sound in the place. He runs toward the exit, and I scramble out of the booth after him. Stumbling out the door, he almost trips over his feet. My heart is thudding painfully against my ribcage as I follow him. A dreadful sense of foreboding has settled over me, compressing my chest, and constricting the oxygen flowing to my brain.

Whatever it is, it's bad.

I push through the door, scanning left and right. Devin is slouched against the wall, hugging himself, sobbing uncontrollably. I'm way beyond alarm at this point. I reach for him, but it's as if I'm invisible. He doesn't move a muscle as I try to wrap my arms around him. Agony has transformed his features. Tears continue to course down his face. "Baby, please. You're scaring the shit out of me. Please tell me what's wrong."

He opens his mouth, but all that comes out is a raw choked sound. He's panting, his breathing heavy and quick, and he claws at his chest, as if he's struggling to breathe.

I don't know what to do. How to help him.

"Is he okay?" a timid voice asks, and I whip my head around. A blonde-haired girl holds out my purse and our jackets. "You left these inside." Her worried gaze bounces between us. "If you need any help..."

"Thank you, but we're okay." My voice sounds remarkably composed considering I'm so freaking panicked on the inside.

Devin leans into me, dropping his head on my shoulder and clinging to my body like he'll fall over if unsupported. I almost buckle under his weight. My cell rings in the back pocket of my jeans, and I pull it out, cradling it between my head and my shoulder as I continue to prop him up.

"Ange." Mom's voice is wispy soft, barely there, and laced with obvious pain.

Butterflies go crazy in my stomach, soaring to my chest and back down again. Bile travels up my throat. "Mom," I croak out. "What's going on? Devin's falling apart, and I can't get a word out of him. What's happened?"

There's a sinking feeling in the pit of my stomach as a horrific thought crosses my mind.

Please, God, no!

"Honey, I'm so sorry. There's no easy way to say this." She breaks down, crying down the line, and I'm already crying even though she hasn't spoken the words.

"No, Mom, no. Please, no." My vision turns blurry with tears.

"Ayden's gone, baby. He's passed away. You need to come home."

CHAPTER THIRTY-THREE

"No! No!" I wail. "He can't be dead!" Sobs burst free of my soul, and an anguished scream rips from my throat. I'm crying hysterically but the tormented cries sound far away, like someone else's entire world has just been flipped upside down. My nose runs, and my eyes bleed tears. Chills rip up and down my spine, and I'm so cold. I'm shivering all over, and my knees buckle, but Devin holds me to him, keeping me upright. My fingers grip my cell fiercely, and I can vaguely hear Mom calling out to me, but it's in the distance. Like everything surrounding me. My world's gone hazy, and this hollowed-out sensation in my chest is my new reality.

The phone is plucked from my hand, and Devin speaks to Mom. I look up at him, seeing him yet not seeing him. His mouth moves, but I can't hear the words. He straightens up, pulling himself together. He draws me in to his chest, holding me super close, but I barely feel his touch, can scarcely register anything over the silent splintering of my heart. Bit by bit, it rips apart, until that life-sustaining organ in my chest is a bloody, messy pulp barely beating behind my ribcage.

Devin lifts me up, cradling me to his chest, and walks us to his SUV. He places me in the passenger seat, buckling my seat belt. I stare straight ahead, still crying, still trying to make sense of the words replaying in my mind. Devin gets in his side, and I feel his eyes on me. "Ange, look at me." His voice is shaky, lacking its usual confidence.

I can't summon the strength to turn my head. Gently, he does it for me, turning my head and tilting my chin up so I'm looking at him. "I need you to hold it together, baby doll. I can't concentrate on the road if I'm worried about you. Can you do that for me?"

I gulp, and it's painful. I clasp Devin's face, needing his touch to ground me. Tears leak out of his eyes again, and his chest heaves. His pain is a replica of my own. We cling to one another, both crying, and I'm still so cold. I bury my head in his chest, grabbing fistfuls of his shirt, needing his closeness, his warmth, his strength. He trails his hands up and down my arms, kissing the top of my head. "I've got you."

"How?" My voice is strangled as the word forces its way up my throat. "How did he die?"

He lifts my head up, keeping his hands on me, and I don't miss the traumatized, conflicted look on his face. He doesn't want to tell me this, but he knows he has no choice. He sucks in a deep breath. "He killed himself, Ange. His mom found him hanging in his room."

My eyes pop wide in horror, and my whole body starts shaking. Immense pain consumes me. The knot in my stomach, the agony in my head, and the ache in my heart all intensify until I can bear it no more. Wrenching myself free of Devin's arms, I stumble out of the car in the nick of time. Bending over, I empty the contents of my stomach all over the side of the road. Tears slide down my face as I retch until there's nothing left to expel.

If only I could purge the guilt as easily.

Devin is crouched over me, rubbing my back. Wordlessly, he hands me a tissue, helping me to my feet. He moves to hug me, but I push him away. "Don't," I warn. "Don't offer me sympathy. I did this. This is my fault!"

Ignoring my wishes, he draws me into his arms. "This is *not* your fault."

I pummel his chest with my fists. "It is! This is our fault!" I beat on his chest harder. "We destroyed him!"

"You don't know that, and we need to get home to find out what happened."

I start crying again, and I collapse against him, all fight leaving me. He hugs me to him, but I'm too numb to even feel his body pressed against mine. Helping me back into the car, he hands me a bottle of water and a blanket. "Drink this, and try to sleep. I'll wake you when we arrive."

I don't sleep. Even the suggestion that I could, at a time like this, is preposterous. I can't switch my brain off, even though I wish I could because the crap in my head is making it difficult to breathe. Eventually, my tears subside, giving way to a strangely comatose state. I'm here, but not here. Alive, but not alive. Breathing, but only barely.

We don't talk about it anymore.

We don't talk at all.

Devin drives, and I stare out the window, inwardly remarking how the silence of my environment mirrors the silence in my heart. As if my soul has died along with Ayden.

Flashing lights greet us as we turn onto our road. Two cop cars, a fire truck, an ambulance, and a van bearing the logo of the medical examiner's office is parked outside Ayden's house.

Mom is waiting at the end of our drive when we arrive. Running around to the passenger door, she pulls me out and into her arms. I fall apart again, sobbing and shaking and clinging to her like I did when I was a little kid. She and Devin converse in quiet voices over my head, but I hear none of it.

"I want to see him," I blurt. Swiping the tears from under my eyes, I straighten up, looking her in the face. I sniffle, placing a hand over the sore spot in my chest. "I want to see Ayden. I need to tell him I'm sorry. Tell him I still love him." Sobs rip me apart, slaying me on the inside and outside, and I bury my face in Mom's shoulder as my entire body convulses. Pain wracks me on all sides.

"You don't have to do this now, Ange," Devin says in a hushed tone.

I sniffle, looking over my shoulder at him. "I do. I need to see him. I need to touch him. I …" I double over, winded by intense pain the like of which I've never felt before. My tears return in earnest.

"Sweetheart. I think you should rest, and when you feel up to it, you can see him," Mom softly suggests.

I reach out, clutching Devin's arm, using him to straighten up again. "No. I want to go now." I cling to Devin's arm. "Take me to see him? And can you do this with me? I can't do it alone."

He hugs me. So tightly, I almost can't breathe. "I'm not leaving your side," he confirms.

"The police have cordoned off the house, for the moment, so everyone is inside our place," she explains. "But you can go straight to your room if you're not up to company."

"I want to see Ayden," I whisper.

"Okay." She nods, shooting a concerned look at Devin. "Come inside and talk to Nancy and Carl," she coaxes. "They've just finished speaking to the police, and they are wrapping things up in the house. You should be able to see Ayden soon."

Devin keeps his arm around my shoulders, and Mom takes my hand as we walk slowly to the front door. It's a wonder I can put one foot in front of the other. Everything is so surreal. Like it's not happening or happening to someone else. Not to us. Not to our Ayden.

Mr. Carter materializes in the doorway. His face is all splotchy, and his eyes are glassy with tears. I fling myself at him, wrapping my arms around his waist. He hugs me back, stifling his cries, while my tears continue to fall freely. "Lina," he whispers, kissing the top of my head. "I'm glad you're here." In a surprising move, he pulls Devin in for a hug next. They don't talk, but words are redundant. Although he seems reluctant to let Devin go, he does, clamping a hand down on his shoulder and squeezing. Devin laces his fingers in mine, and we follow Mom and Carl through the kitchen and into the living room.

At least twenty people are crowding the space, talking quietly and drinking coffee. Most are family. Ayden's aunts and uncles. His sisters and his mom are not here. Mr. and Mrs. Belso, the Carters' other neighbors, say a quiet hello, smiling sadly in our direction.

"I'll get you some coffee," Mr. Carter says, heading back into the kitchen while Mom pats the arm of the couch.

"Sit," she commands, all but pushing me down. Devin stands behind me, wrapping his arms around my chest and resting his chin on my head. I cling to his arms, his touch being the only thing keeping me sane right now.

Nancy Carter walks into the room. Mom goes to her. "Are the girls okay?"

She sighs, and the heartbroken look on her face is evident for all to see. "They're resting now. Thank you for this, Natalie."

Mom hugs her. Nancy's eyes lock on mine over Mom's shoulder. She frowns, raking her gaze over Devin and me. I stand up, moving to go to her, but Devin holds me back, locking his arms around my waist and keeping me in front of him.

Nancy shucks off Mom's embrace, walking slowly toward me. A multitude of different emotions flicker in her eyes. "What did you do to my son?" Her voice cracks and tears pool in her eyes.

A deathly hush settles over the room as all conversation mutes.

"Please don't do this," Devin asks quietly before I've had time to speak. "Ange loved Ayden. We both did."

"I'm not asking you," she says, keeping her gaze focused on me. "Lina? I need to know what happened. The last time I spoke to my son was when he landed at the airport and he was en route to campus to surprise you. Then I come home and I find him … I find him …" Pain-filled anguished cries rip through the still air as she breaks down, dropping to her knees and sobbing.

I sink to my knees in front of her, crying too. The tension in my chest increases. "I loved Ayden, I really did, and I'm sorry. I'm so sorry."

She composes herself a little, sniffling as she gestures at Devin with a sharp flick of her head. "What did you do? I need to know what happened. I need to know why my son did this." Her damp, red-rimmed eyes plead with me, and she's searching for answers we may never find.

My heart is rupturing in my chest again. My lower lip wobbles when I open my mouth to admit the truth. "I didn't mean for him to find out like this," I sob. "But he knew how much I loved Devin. We were going to fix this … it was going to be okay …"

A stinging pain zips across my cheekbone where her hand impacts my face. "You dirty little slut! I knew this was your fault! This is both your faults!" she shrieks, glaring at Devin as he lifts me up, moving me away from her.

"I'm not going to let you blame Ange," Devin protests. "Ayden did this. Not Ange or me."

Nancy lets out an inhuman roar as she lunges at Devin. Mr. Carter pulls her back before she can reach him. She writhes and wrestles in his arms, thrashing, screaming, and crying, and I shudder against Devin, clinging to him as if my life depends on it. Mom looks torn, her concerned gaze shifting from me to Nancy and back again.

"Let me go, Carl!" Nancy yells. "You know this is their fault. Her fault! You know it."

Ayden's three sisters appear in the doorway, sporting red, bloodshot eyes and staring at the scene in front of them. Kayla is in her pajamas, clutching her raggedy teddy bear and leaning in to her older sister, Mia. Mia looks from me to Devin, and her eyes narrow suspiciously.

Mom steps forward, planting herself in front of Ayden's mom. "I'm dreadfully sorry for your loss, Nancy. More so than I can describe. Ayden was like a son to me, and I'm devastated, so I can't begin to imagine the pain you are in. But, I cannot allow you to speak to my daughter like that, and you most certainly can't assault her. I'm very sorry, but I have to ask you to leave." Mom glances at the Belsos, and they stand up, nodding their heads in a knowing fashion.

"I will never forgive you for this! Never!" Mrs. Carter screams at me before Mr. Carter removes her from the house. Everyone else leaves with them.

I adhere myself to Devin, fisting his shirt, feeling like a shell of a person. I'm trembling all over, and my limbs are quivering and shaking. Mom pulls me down on the empty sofa, circling her arms around me. "Devin, can you make some hot, sweet tea for Ange and bring in a few of those sandwiches. She needs to eat."

Dev nods, kissing my cheek before walking into the kitchen. Mom rocks me back and forth in her arms. My tears have dried up, and now I'm back to feeling numb and hollow on the inside. "Sweetheart, Nancy is grieving, and she needs to find someone to blame. She doesn't mean it."

"She's right," I say as if on autopilot. "This *is* my fault."

She brushes damp strands of hair off my forehead. "It's no one's fault, honey. Least of all yours. I've come across this so many times in my line of work, and it never gets any easier to understand. No one knows exactly what triggers cause a person to take their own life."

"I. Know." I look up at her. "He found me and Devin in bed together, and it broke his heart. I'm the trigger. I'm the reason Ayden snapped. I'm the reason he's dead."

CHAPTER THIRTY-FOUR

Ayden's mom refuses to let me or Devin into the house to see him, and my depression reaches new lows. An autopsy is performed, and then his body is taken to the local funeral home. She blocks me from there too, and though I want to fight her on it, I can't summon the strength to do it. Besides, Ayden would hate that, and though he's not here to chastise me, I don't want to do anything he would be unhappy about. I've done enough to dishonor his memory as it is.

So, the first time I see him is at the funeral. I'm glad she didn't try to ban me from attending because I would have screamed bloody murder. As it is, she refuses to let Devin speak at the ceremony, and that sticks in my throat. We were Ayden's best friends, and it's not right that we're being shut out, even if I understand the reasons for it. Devin read me the speech he prepared on both our behalf last night and it was perfect. As perfect as anything could be in such difficult circumstances.

Devin holds me close as we approach the casket to say goodbye. I wanted to do this, to see Ayden one final time, but now I'm here, I have to force myself to look. The only other time I've seen a dead body was when my grandpa died. He looked weird too—like a warped version of himself.

Ayden is the same.

It looks like him, but at the same time he's different. I hate the horrible makeup they have on his face and how stretched and papery his skin looks. His beautiful blond hair is styled severely, brushed back off his face in a way he would never have worn it. He's wearing the suit he wore to prom, and he looks stiff and uncomfortable in it. I'd rather he was wearing jeans and his favorite shirt, with no makeup, and his hair gelled and spiky like he wore it when he was alive. Yes, he would look pale and lifeless, and it would be harder to see, but he'd look more like himself. Like a person who used to live, and breathe, and laugh, and tease, and frown, and act all serious when he should have been carefree. Tentatively, I reach out, touching his cheek. It's rubbery, and cold, and I snatch my hand away, not wanting to remember him like this. Tears roll down my face as hundreds of happy memories float through my mind. "Why?" I whisper, leaning over him. "Why did you do this? How could you do this?" My heart aches so badly, and I don't know how I'm going to deal with the continuous pain. "I loved you so much. We both did. That would never have changed."

Devin grips my waist more firmly. "Don't torture yourself," he whispers.

"He promised he'd never leave me," I cry. "He promised he'd always be there for me. He promised, Devin. He *promised*." I bury my head in his chest, sobbing profusely. Mom gently takes me in her arms, and we step aside while Devin says his goodbyes.

The wake back at his house passes me by in a blur. I sit in an arm chair, just staring off into space, not hearing any of the murmured condolences, not feeling any of the handshakes, barely sensing the weight of Nancy's disdain. Tears have dried on my face, leaving watery, mascara-laden streaks across my skin. Devin only leaves my side to get food and drink. When he returns, he holds the cup to my mouth, forcing me to take a few sips. He insists I need to eat, but I push his hand away after a few mouthfuls of food that taste like sandpaper in my mouth.

The next eight days seem to blend together, until I've lost track of what day it even is. I can't get up out of bed. Mom begs me. Mariah begs me. Devin refuses to leave my side. He seems to be handling this far better than me, although that could be a front. He lies beside me, holding me, kissing me, and whispering how much he loves me.

But nothing works.

Nothing eases the sharp ache in my chest. My eyes well up every time I look at the framed photo of the three of us by my bed.

We were thirteen, and Grandpa had taken us out fishing on the lake. Between us, we'd caught a thirty-three-pound walleye. We're holding the scaly, dead fish across our bodies, grinning wildly, as if we'd just taken gold at the Olympics. Our wide smiles are matching, meeting our eyes, and the moment captured our joy perfectly.

I can't look at that photo now without tormenting myself.

Without asking how I let this happen.

How we went from best friends forever to three people who hurt and disappointed one another.

Ayden left no note, so no one really knows why he did it.

And no matter how many times Mom and Devin tell me it's not my fault, I can't agree.

I look back over the last year in particular, and all I see are the many ways I failed him.

I knew something was troubling him, but I didn't push enough.

When he landed the marine bombshell on my lap, I wore a "woe is me" hat, never fully thinking about how difficult that decision must've been for him.

While our phone calls were short, I didn't probe enough. I didn't ask him why—Why did he give up his football dream? Why the marines? Why did he leave me when he promised he wouldn't? Why didn't he want to repair things with Devin? When he told me things were tough in Afghanistan, and that the marines weren't what he expected, I didn't ask him to explain.

Because I was too Goddamned selfish to think of anyone but myself.

∞ ∞ ∞

It's been ten days since Ayden's funeral, and I wish I died too. It's Christmas Eve but you won't find much holiday cheer around here. Devin knocks on my door before stepping inside. His eyes pop wide at the sight of me. I'm freshly showered and wearing clothes—instead of grubby pajamas—for the first time in a week. My bed is made, and my room is tidy. I can see the relief on his face, but it's short-lived.

I stand up, wanting to get this out before he draws me into his arms, making it harder. "We can't be together anymore. We're done, and you have to stop coming over here."

"I'm not going anywhere, Ange." He folds his arms, standing his ground. "I know you're hurting, and I know you blame yourself, but pushing me away won't change those feelings." He steps into me, tilting my chin up. "I love you, and I'm going to be here for you whether you want me or not."

"He's dead because of *us*, Devin, and any notion of 'us' died with him. I can't do this. It's only adding to the pain."

He tries to hug me, but I sidestep his arms, crossing to the wall and wrapping my arms around myself. "Don't make this worse. I can't be with you. I can't love you. It's all ruined now."

He walks toward me with determination in his eyes. "It's not. It only feels like that now because it feels like everything died with Ayden that night." He plants a hand over his chest, and tears prick his eyes. "I'm feeling all those things too, but I'm trying to be strong for you, so if you think I'm not hurting, you're wrong. I'm in pain, and I miss him so fucking much it's hard to breathe some days, but he's gone, and we're still here, and I'm not going to let you sacrifice what we have out of guilt."

"You can't tell me how to feel," I yell. "Or compel me to do things I don't want to do. I want to break up with you, not that we were ever really together. I can't even look at you without guilt crippling me. While we were professing our love in the diner, he was back here killing himself!" I scrub a hand over my face. I'm so tired of this. I just want to retreat into my shell and be left alone. I don't even have the strength to fight Devin about this, so I play my trump card now. "If you love me, really love me, you'll do this for me. You'll leave me because it's what I want."

"That's bullshit, Ange, and I'm not letting you blackmail me into this." A glint of anger flashes in his green eyes before he controls it. His features soften as he takes a few steps forward, stopping a couple feet in front of me. "You need some space, and I can give you that. But don't ask me to walk away indefinitely, because I can't agree to that. And if you try to push me permanently away, I'll just keep coming back. There is nothing you can say or do that will keep me away from you." He touches my face before I can stop him. "Loving you means I stick by your side even when we've both hit our lowest points. Loving you means I understand that you need time to come to terms with this and being selfless enough to give it to you." He kisses me softly. "I'm leaving now, but it's not goodbye. This is me giving you your space."

He stops in the doorway. "Take as much time as you need. I'm going nowhere."

The next month rolls by in an agonizing slow fashion, and I hardly step foot outside the front door. I should be back at college by now, Devin too, but I can't summon the strength to even care. Devin texts me every single day to tell me he loves me and he's thinking of me, but he doesn't come over, and the tightness in my chest eases a little.

Now, I only have to pretend for Mom.

She's worried sick about me. She's begged me to meet with a therapist, but I'm steadfastly refusing. I know what she wants. What Devin wants. To have someone *neutral* tell me the things they are repeating like a mantra: that it's not my fault, that Ayden wouldn't want me to throw my life away like this, and that it's a tragedy no one could've predicted.

But I don't want to hear those things anymore.

All I know is he's dead, and it's my fault, and I'm still here.

And I'm beginning to really hate myself and my shallowness. Maybe if I hadn't been so obsessed with Devin, I'd have seen Ayden. Like *really* seen him. If I was any use as a friend, as a girlfriend, I would have seen the extent of his despair. But I was too wrapped up in myself to notice.

Why can't they see what a horrible person I am?

Why can't Devin see that I'm the rotten apple in our pack? So many times, we pointed the finger at him, when I was the damaged one all along. I'm doing him a favor by pushing him away. He can do so much better than me. And who knows, if he stays with me, I may end up driving him to take his own life too.

I can't hurt anyone else I love, which is why I made the plan. Now I just need to execute it.

∞ ∞ ∞

Mom's used up all her vacation time, so she has to return to work. I know she doesn't want to leave me alone, so it's no surprise when I come downstairs and discover Devin sprawled across the couch watching the TV on low.

"I don't need a babysitter," I huff, yanking the refrigerator open. I pour a glass of juice, before slamming the refrigerator closed again.

He gets up, sauntering into the kitchen, his eyes roaming my body in alarm. I'm in dirty yoga pants and Ayden's old football sweater. The bird's nest in my hair is matted and greasy, and I know I've got massive bags under my eyes. He looks as perfect as ever. Clearly, I'm the only one struggling to deal with this.

"Jesus, Ange." He sucks in a gasp. "You're skin and bone. You need to eat."

"I repeat. I. Do. Not. Need. A. Babysitter. I don't want you here. Go home." I feel a tinge of guilt at the hurt look in his eyes but not enough to stop. "Better yet, go back to college where you belong."

"I'll return when you do."

"Then I guess you'll be waiting a while." At this point, I've zero intention of ever returning.

"I guess so."

"How long are you going to keep this up?"

"For as long as I need to."

"That's going to be a very long time indeed."

He shrugs. "I can wait."

His stubborn determination jars something loose inside me. I freak out, screaming from the pit of my lungs as I throw my half-empty glass at the wall. It shatters upon impact, spraying shards of glass and sticky liquid all over me and the floor.

"Fuck." Devin carefully lifts me up and onto a stool, inspecting my arms. Tiny streaks of blood pool in all the places where bits of glass have embedded in my arms. "Stay here." He bounds up the stairs, three at a time, returning a minute later with the first aid kit. I'm like a mute statue as he tends to my cuts, sweeps up the glass, and mops the floor. He comes to stand in front of me. "Ange, you need to speak to someone. Please, I'm begging you."

I wet my dry lips, staring off into space as an idea comes to me. I keep my gaze averted, not wanting to lie to his face. "Actually, I think I want to return to college."

"You do?" I detect the skepticism in his tone.

"Yes. Routine will be good for me, and there are less memories of him there."

He holds my head in his hands, forcing my eyes to lock on his. He carefully scrutinizes my face, probing for the truth. I keep my face impassive. I've spent years shielding my true emotions from him, so it's a cakewalk. "That's good, but you still need to speak to someone."

"I will. They've got counselors on campus, right?" I hop down off the stool. "I'll make an appointment as soon as we get back." He frowns and his eyes narrow. He knows something's up, but he can't figure out why. "I'm going to pack."

"You want to leave *now*?"

I look over my shoulder. "First thing in the morning. I need to say goodbye to Mom first."

We are both dressed, with our bags packed, and waiting in the kitchen when Mom arrives home from her shift very early the next morning. I've showered, styled my hair, put on some makeup, and I'm wearing clean clothes. I look together, and that's all that counts. She's uneasy when I tell her the plan, refusing at first, clearly uncomfortable with the speed at which I'm moving, but Devin assures her he'll take care of me, and I promise faithfully that I'll make a therapist appointment as soon as I can.

I hug her for much longer than usual, squeezing her tight, closing my eyes against the stab of tears, committing her smell to memory, silently begging her forgiveness.

I wave to her from Devin's SUV, forcing the messy ball of emotion in my throat to back the hell down. I'm lost in thought the whole trip. Devin tries to engage me in conversation, but he gives up after a while— it's hard to have a conversation all by yourself. Every few minutes, I feel his eyes on me, and he almost gives himself whiplash alternating his gaze between me and the road.

"Are you sure you're ready to do this?" he asks, once we're parked outside the residence hall. "I can turn around and take you back if it's too much."

I send him an incredulous look. "You want me to go home and hide in my room like a recluse again?"

His gaze dips for a fraction of a second. "Of course not. I want the girl I love back, but I don't want you to feel pushed into doing this if you aren't ready yet."

"I'm taking it one day at time," I reply, jumping out of the car. Devin carries my bag up to my room.

"Thanks," I say, dumping it on the floor. "I'm going to go through my emails and try to get a handle on the stuff I missed."

"I can stay here with you."

I shake my head. "I need to be by myself." He doesn't trust me; I see it in his eyes—I need to do better. For the first time in weeks, I wrap my arms around his neck and nuzzle into him, trying to ignore how good it feels to be back in his safe embrace. He relaxes against me. "I'm sorry I've been so hard on you," I whisper. "Thank you for being so patient."

He tips my chin up. "I love you so much, Ange. Seeing you like this has been killing me." His Adam's apple jumps in his throat, and he's on the verge of tears.

Oh, God, I hate myself. I hate myself so much.

I lean up on tiptoes and plant my lips on his. He kisses me softly at first, but then need takes over, for both of us. He carries me to the bedroom, and we silently undress one another. I whimper when he enters me, peppering his face with kisses, remembering how incredible it felt to love him with no restraints. Burying my head in his shoulder, I cling to him while soft, silent tears stream down my face as he makes tender love to me.

He shoots a lazy, satisfied grin my way as he gets redressed. I'm in the bed, with the covers under my arms, drinking in the sight of him. As long as I live, I'll never forget how utterly magnificent Devin Morgan is. There is no finer male specimen on the planet. He sits on the edge of the bed while he pulls his boots on. Leaning in, he kisses me passionately. "We're going to be okay, Ange."

I thread my hands through his hair. "I love you, Devin. I'll love you my whole life."

He leans his forehead on mine. "I love you too, baby doll. You're my everything."

I try not to lose it as he's leaving, keeping a fake smile plastered across my face. He frowns a little. "You okay? I don't have to go to class. I can—"

I cut him off with a passionate kiss. "I'm good," I whisper in a breathless tone against his mouth. "Now get your delectable ass to class, and I'll see you tonight."

He steps out into the corridor, blowing me a kiss, and I mentally record the moment, capturing his happy smile, the love glistening in his eyes, his gorgeous dark hair heading in all directions—totally messed up from my fingers—and his firm ass in the low-hanging jeans as he walks away. I memorize the way his shirt stretches across his chest and biceps as he spins around, blowing me another kiss and shouting out "I love you."

The horrid pain in my chest worsens the farther away he moves, until it feels like I'm suffocating. I slam my door shut before I run after him, sagging to the floor amid a flurry of tears.

I wish I didn't have to do this, but it's the only way.

I wait a half hour, to ensure he's gone, and then I pull on my coat, take my bag, and hightail it across campus to the bus stop.

I get off in the center of the city, in the heart of the prestigious banking district, and walk to an office building I swore I'd never enter.

The name over the door sours my stomach as I walk underneath it, stepping foot onto the glossy porcelain floor of the lobby. The glamorous redhead at reception eyes me curiously as she calls upstairs, the surprise playing across her face as she's told to let me up.

My nerves are hanging by a thread as the elevator shoots to the top floor, bringing me to a man I never, ever intended to meet.

But needs must.

He doesn't get up from behind the desk as I'm shown into his office, but he can't disguise his shock. We have the same hair, and now I know where I got the dimple in my left cheek from. My eyes flit to the framed wedding photo on his desk. His pretty, young wife smiles up at him, little realizing she's peering adoringly into the eyes of a monster.

It's hard to reconcile the good-looking, polished, professional businessman in the expensive suit, sitting across from me, with the image I've always had of him in my head. He may look calm and in control, but the catalog of physical abuse my mother suffered at her young husband's hand tells a different story. And I don't need to hear his version of events. There is no scenario he can paint that will ever excuse his behavior or cause me to doubt my mother. Mom has never lied to me, about anything, and especially not when I finally plucked up the courage to ask her why my father wasn't in the picture.

One part of me wants to lash out at him. To inflict pain. To make him feel even a sliver of what Mom felt living with an abusive spouse, but I'm not here for that. I have a purpose, and that purpose overrides everything else. So, as much as it frustrates me to push those sentiments aside, I do what I need to.

I'm quietly confident as I tell him why I'm there. He's reluctant to agree, until I threaten to go to the press. To divulge all the secrets he's hiding. He doesn't ask why I want to change the terms of my trust fund. Why I want access to all the cash that has been earmarked for college or why I need him to put me in touch with someone who can change my identity.

He doesn't question it; he just makes it happen, because I'm one of his dirty little secrets, and my father just wants to make me go away.

∞ ∞ ∞

A week later, I open the front door to my new life. I'm halfway across the country. I've cut and dyed my hair, and I'm traveling under a new name.

Angelina Ward no longer exists. She died the same day Ayden Carter did.

I enter the small one-bedroomed second-floor apartment I now call home, hoping that the rigidity in my chest will someday loosen. As I look out the large window onto the bustling street below, I promise myself that today is the last day I'll think about them: Devin, Mom, and Mariah. My cell is chock-full of texts, missed calls, and messages. All heartfelt, teary pleas, no doubt—I can't confirm it because I refuse to read or listen.

Doing this was harder than I thought. On more than one occasion in the last week, I've almost turned around.

But that's only my selfishness talking.

I was the very one who preached the message to Devin. "If you love me enough, you'll leave me," I'd told him.

He wasn't strong enough to do what needed to be done.

But I am.

Or at least I'm pretending I am.

Dropping my cell on the floor, I smash it with the heel of my shoe until it's crushed to pieces. Walking to the kitchen counter, I remove the bottle of vodka from my bag, unscrewing the cap as I flip off my shoes and collapse on the couch.

I tilt my head back and take a long swig from the bottle, grimacing at the burning taste in my throat.

I love them too much to drag them down with me.

I swallow another glug, welcoming the sting.
One day, they'll thank me for doing the right thing.
I guzzle from the bottle, relishing the acrid taste.
Because if I stayed, I'd only have ruined them too.

PART III

(Almost) Five Years Later

CHAPTER THIRTY-FIVE

Devin

"I'm not available," I tell the good-looking woman sidling up alongside me at the bar. I've noticed her attentive gaze for the best part of the last hour, and I know from experience that it's best to knock it on the head rather than let her waste any more of her time on me. Her mouth droops, and her eyes narrow with disappointment.

She doesn't realize I've just done her a favor.

If she did, she'd be thanking me.

Over the years, I've had no shortage of offers from hot chicks, but the one woman I crave is still elusive.

Ange exists now only in my memory, but those memories are enough to keep me moving forward. To bolster my spirit, even on days where I lose it, when I think I can't do this anymore.

I nod at the bartender, and he slides another Coke and three beers my way. I toss two twenties on the counter, telling him to look after the lady and keep the change. I make my way back to our table in the corner of the crowded club, handing Danny, Trev, and Matt their beers while I sip my soda.

"Ruined another woman's night I see," Danny teases, gesturing at the blonde I've just rejected.

"Don't start. This night is stretching my patience thin as it is." I'm getting sick of this scene. A sure sign I'm getting old. If we weren't away for the weekend on Rick's bachelor party, I'd have bailed an hour ago. The persistent, loud, up-tempo beat of the music has already given me a headache.

"Are you ever these days?" he asks with a knowing look.

Danny and I met in college, and we both entered the police academy a little under three years ago after graduating UI early with honors degrees in criminology, law, and justice. After Ayden died and Ange left, I threw myself into my studies taking a full course load and additional classes at night and during the summer to graduate in half the usual time. At one time, I'd had notions of joining the Bureau, but I relinquished that ambition when I realized how much I loved my job as a cop and how much of a natural I was. I had the most arrests of any patrol officer in our unit, and I was pivotal in helping ATF capture a known arms trafficker. Thanks to that joint force operation, I was given an award and promoted six months ago, and now I'm assigned to the homicide division which is perfect because it gives me access to resources which enable me to continue my search.

Considering I spent a large part of my teenage years in and out of trouble with the local cops, I think it's fucking hilarious I've ended up one. Ange would get a massive kick out of that.

Danny is looking at me pensively.

"You know why. It's getting close, and this year will be the hardest one yet," I tell him.

His look turns sympathetic. "I know, man. I'm sorry."

"Forget it." I empty the soda into my mouth. "We're here for Rick. I don't want to think about that shit tonight." God knows, it's occupied enough of my headspace since it happened. It's hard to believe the five-year anniversary of Ayden's death is only a few short months from now—that it's been almost *five* years since he last walked the planet; almost *five* years since I last set eyes on the love of my life.

The usual ache punches a hole in my heart. *How the fuck can one girl drop off the radar so completely?* I still can't fathom it. Outside of work, I spend hours trawling the net, scouring the streets, hitting my contacts up, and putting out feelers—using every means at my disposal to search for Ange—but she may as well have been abducted by aliens. I can't find any trace of her. She's vanished, and I've no clue where she is. Or if she's even still alive. She was in a dark place when she fled, and I haven't stopped worrying about her since or chastising myself for not trusting my gut that last day. I knew something was up with her, but I allowed her to play me perfectly. By the time I realized what was happening, it was too late.

She was already gone.

I need to find out what happened to her. I'll find no peace until I do.

Danny's smile is sad as he sits twiddling the wedding band on his finger. All the guys are starting to settle down, and this is the third bachelor party I've attended, so far, this year, while I'm still searching for the girl who ran away with my heart.

"I know you don't want to hear it, but maybe it's time you moved on, man. She's gone, and you can't put your life on hold anymore."

I sigh. This shit is starting to sound real old. "I'll never give up on her. You know that, so stop wasting your breath."

He gestures toward the blonde, still staring in my direction with a wistful look on her face. "What harm would it do to try with another woman? You haven't had a relationship since the Dark Ages."

It's so damned ironic that the only relationship I've ever had was with Becky Carmichael. If you could call that epic fuck-up a relationship. "I just can't go there."

"You barely even hook up any more."

Fact. Because the pain of waking up beside another woman, knowing it isn't Ange, isn't something I can handle anymore. Sex is a necessary release, and I only indulge when I'm primed to explode. It's either that or turn to booze, and that's not so easy to recover from, whereas sex with a random stranger is forgotten the instant I come.

"It's not easy for me."

"Sure it is." He smirks, grabbing his crotch. "You just take that nice broad back to your hotel room, strip the clothes off her smoking hot body, and jam your rod into her pussy. Then it's rock and roll, dude." He rolls his hips forward, drilling his point home.

I poke him in the ribs. "Cut that shit out, you're making me ill. How you ever managed to convince Juanita to marry you is a fucking miracle. Does she know her husband still uses words like rod? Rod? Seriously, dude?"

A loud roar erupts from our table, and a chorus of wolf whistles rings out, drawing the attention of the nearby crowd. Danny looks over my shoulder, rubbing his hands in glee. "Showtime, baby."

The bartender appears with a chair and a smug smile, setting it down in the center of the floor. Matt shoves Rick into it, not that he needs much persuasion. The music changes, and a sexy, sultry beat reverberates off the walls. The stripper enters the far side of the room, and the crowd hollers their approval. I squint in the dim lights, focusing on her rocking body as she struts confidently toward the groom to be. She's dressed in a hot pink open-necked shirt, displaying a magnificent cleavage and the edge of a lacy black bra. Long, slender legs poke out from under an ass-skimming black mini skirt. Sheathed in fishnet stockings, her legs are the stuff of dreams. Dainty feet are encased in killer sky-high heels as she struts toward Rick. Wavy red hair tumbles out the back of her cap, reaching beyond her shoulder blades, and she's twirling a baton, so I guess she got the memo we're cops. She's, arguably, the hottest, sexiest, classiest stripper I've ever seen.

"Hot damn," Danny shouts in my ear. "Why the hell didn't you hire her for *my* bachelor party?"

I turn to him, struggling to contain my laughter. "Your bachelor party was fourteen hundred miles away, and I doubt she'd have traveled that far." I can't fight my smile any longer. "Besides, you loved the fat stripper. Especially the part where she buried your head in her tits." I bark out a laugh as a familiar look of horror washes over his face.

Catcalls ring out around us, and we return our attention to the action on the floor. The stripper has her back to us as she leans over Rick, showcasing a peach of an ass, barely covered in a lacy black thong. She flicks her palm back and forth across his crotch, and Rick spreads his legs, locking his hands behind his head, grinning as he eye-fucks the girl without shame.

"Oh, fuck," Danny exclaims, articulating what I'm thinking. Rick's inability to keep his dick in his pants has already led to two failed attempts up the aisle. I have a feeling we could be looking at number three in the works. Thing is, Rick's a stand-up guy—when he's not drinking. He's one of the few guys I know I can always rely on to have my back. But put a beer or ten in his path, and he turns into the biggest dick of all time.

The girl whips off her shirt to the delight of the mostly male crowd. The muscles in her slim back move as she straddles Rick, grinding against him in tune to the music. She thrusts her chest in his face, in and out, in a teasing fashion, never quite letting him make contact. Rick is practically foaming at the mouth.

He grabs her ass, and she playfully swats his chest, removing his hands and putting them back on the arms of the chair. She leans in, whispering something in his ear. He smirks, and she tosses her hair with a flick of her wrist.

"Holy shit. I'm as a hard as rock just watching," Danny announces. I don't confirm I'm the same, because my vocal cords have stopped working. Along with my heart. The lighting is shit in here, so I can't see the exact pattern of the ink on her wrist, but even the thought of it is enough to send me into coronary-inducing territory.

Get a grip, I caution myself. Plenty of girls have tattoos on their wrists.

She writhes on top of him, simulating sex, and my buddies all groan. Usually, this kind of thing is seedy, cheesy, and the last thing to get me hard, but this girl is different. Although I haven't seen her face, I can tell by her body and the way she carries herself that she's confident in her looks. And she knows how to move in a sexy non-cringing way. Rick looks in pain when she wraps her legs around the back of the chair, bringing her body tantalizingly close to his. I chuckle at the expression on his face. The man is panting like a dog in heat.

Then, slowly, ever so slowly, she starts leaning back, using her legs to anchor her to the chair and arching her body in a way that thrusts her tits up. Every man in the room has his gaze locked on her sexy body, myself included. Her tits are almost falling out of the black lacy bra, but my eyes are fixated on the expanse of smooth, creamy skin on display. A small, silver locket rests in the dip of her collarbone as she tilts her head back farther. Her hair fans out around her on the floor, and her features are lit up under the glare of the overhead spotlight, offering a perfect view of her stunning face.

I sway on my feet, almost losing my balance. Gripping the edge of the table to steady myself, I can scarcely breathe. My heart is beating ferociously in my chest. Out of the corner of my eye, I notice Danny looking at me funny, but I ignore him. I can't take my eyes off her. She's oblivious, continuing to put on the show of all shows for my buddies. I skim slowly over her features, needing to be one hundred percent sure before I make a move. I immediately locate the dimple in her left cheek and the tiny scar over her right eyebrow. The one she got the day she was racing me and Ayden to our treehouse hideout in the woods and she tripped over a log, splitting her head open on the jagged corner. Natalie had applied paper stitches the minute we brought her home, but it still left a faint scar. Only noticeable if you were looking for it.

The table rattles as my legs almost go out from under me. "What the hell?" Danny arches a brow. "Shit, man, are you okay? You're not looking so hot."

Sweat beads on my brow, and I'm having trouble breathing. I can't even summon any embarrassment when my tear ducts start working overtime. "Dev?"

He stands in front of me, and I shove him aside, terrified if I take my eyes off her for even a second she'll disappear. He opens his mouth to protest, but I grip his arm. "Ange," I croak.

"What?"

Grabbing his shoulders, I twist him back around and point at the stripper. "It's Ange, Danny. *She's* Ange. I've finally found her."

CHAPTER THIRTY-SIX
Angelina

I ease myself up off the floor, my abs contracting with the movement. Situating myself back in the client's lap, I do my best to ignore the hard length prodding my ass. This guy is, maybe, three or four years older than me, and pretty hot, but he's got a bad dose of grabby-hands and grabby-ass disease. Still, I can't complain. The guy I performed for last night was well over fifty with a beer gut spilling over the band of his pants and a bad combover. He almost shot his load the instant I straddled him. Ugh. I shiver at the memory. When the set was finished, he propositioned me, and when I politely declined, he withdrew his sizeable tip.

Asshole.

At least Diana pays well, and she runs a professional company. Strictly stripping, no extras, and that suits me fine. I'm many things, but I'm not into offering sex for money.

I give it away for free enough of the time.

Most times, I end up fucking some dude from the bachelor party by the end of the night. Not the groom—I still have *some* standards, and I have enough reasons to hate myself as it is. Not that it deters most of them from trying. It sickens me, and I pity the poor girls they're marrying, but still I can't turn the work down. If it wasn't for these couple of gigs every week, I'd never be able to survive on my miserable waitressing income. I still mentally kick myself in the ass every time I think of how quickly I blew through my sizeable trust fund.

I shriek as the client nips at my bra with his teeth, attempting to pull it off. Before I can slap the douche and crawl out of his lap, I'm lifted and hauled against a warm, hard chest. "Quit that fucking shit, Rick," a deep voice from my past says, sending shivers ricocheting all over me. Tears immediately prick my eyes, and I'm suddenly transported back in time. My knees buckle, and a mewl escapes my mouth. I'd know his husky voice anywhere. And there isn't any part of my body that doesn't want to respond to him right now. I'm struggling to fight the almost overpowering need to turn around and fling myself into his arms. Dev has always had that effect on me. Alarm bells are wailing in my ears, and I can't concentrate over the rush of blood to my head. My legs turn to Jell-O, and I'd fall if he wasn't holding me up.

Shit. Shit. Shit. This can't be happening.

I scramble for a way out of this, my mind desperately craving an escape plan. For years, I've pined for these arms. Cried myself to sleep with a suffocating pain in my heart because I missed him so much. I need to get out of here, and pronto, because I'm scared I'm not strong enough to resist temptation.

Sensing my panic, in that innate way Devin always had around me, he strengthens his arm around my waist. I look down, still avoiding eye contact, my gaze latching on the tattoo on his wrist.

My God. It's really him.

He's found me.

"Don't run," he whispers in my ear. "You can't run from me again." My internal panic meter cranks to the max

The client frowns. "What's it to you?"

"I know her, and the show's over."

"The hell it is," I exclaim, attempting to wriggle out of his arms. "I don't get paid if I don't finish the gig."

"You'll be paid," Dev coolly replies, and the muscles in his arms bulge as he maintains a firm hold of my waist.

I keep my eyes pinned straight ahead, too afraid to look at him. His arm is broad and tanned with defined muscles and thick black hair, and if it's any indication, Devin's all man now. If I couldn't resist him before,

I sure as hell won't be able to now. But I can't let this happen. I haven't suffered through the last few years to cave now. "Let me go."

In a super quick move, he spins me around, sliding a white T-shirt down over my head. Then he pulls me into an organ-crushing hug. Like he can scarcely believe it's me either. I inhale sharply, the mix of musk and pine filling my nostrils with nostalgia. He still smells the same, and he still feels like home, and that thought drives the first knife deep in my heart.

Might as well just kill me now.

It would be effortless to give in to this; to melt into his loving arms and never leave. His body is warm and solid against me, and images of him naked unhelpfully flood my mind. No guy has ever stacked up to Devin. Not even close. He feels good, he smells good, and he feels like home and safety and a host of beautiful things I've missed so much. I close my eyes, fighting tears and the urge to grab him and never let him go. We hold each other tighter, and my chest heaves with pent-up emotion. His muscles quiver underneath me, and I can tell he's all twisted up on the inside too.

How did this happen? After all this time, how the hell did he find me?

Because this can't be coincidence. I don't believe in such things anymore.

"Morgan, what the hell is going on here?" the client asks, his black mood evident in his challenging tone.

I try to pull away, but Dev keeps me locked in place, fastening a hand to my back and pressing me into his chest, as if he's afraid to let go of me. "Devin, please. I can hardly breathe," I muffle into his shirt.

Reluctantly, he loosens his hold. "Look at me," he whispers, blatantly ignoring his friend. "Please, baby doll, let me look at you."

The tears spill softly over my cheeks as I raise my head slowly to lock eyes with the man I still love after all these years. I suck in a gasp. We stare at one another, and even though the music is blaring in the background, and the drone of many voices surrounds us, all I hear is silence. All I see is him. Nothing and no one else exists in this moment except Devin Robert Morgan.

Jesus. Devin's always been drop dead gorgeous, but the man standing in front of me is a knockout. His good looks have matured, and he seems to fit his skin more comfortably. He's even more gorgeous than he was growing up. His hair is shorter in the front now but still clipped at the sides, and it's still glossy and jet-black. Those long, thick lashes I used to love blink in fast succession as he rakes his gaze over me. His sea-green eyes glisten with raw emotion as he peers deep into my eyes. A coating of dark hair covers his jawline, giving him a rugged, purely masculine look. His skin is smooth and unblemished, and he looks so damn good. I can't help it. I reach up, running my fingers along the soft stubble on his cheeks, cupping his face.

"Morgan," the client growls, slicing through our moment.

Devin glares at him, and I almost laugh at the all-too-familiar menacing scowl on his face. "Do me a favor, Rick, and just fuck off."

Rick does *not* take too kindly to that. "This is my bachelor party, asshole, and I have every right to know why the fuck you stopped my fun."

A muscle pops in Devin's jaw. "How long have we known each other, Rick?" He gestures toward me. "Use your brain."

Rick frowns, trading looks with the tall, dark-haired guy standing beside him. I catch his eye, and he winks.

"Danny?" I splutter.

He grins. "Hey, Ange. Long time no see."

Rick startles. "Wait up? *You're* Ange." His eyes almost bug out of his head. "As in Angelina?"

A flash of red on the outskirts of our little group captures my attention. Cara is looking at me with a puzzled expression on her face.

Great. This is just what I need.

Rick cracks up laughing. "Oh my God. This is priceless." He grins at Devin. "You've put your whole life on hold to find your childhood sweetheart, and she's whoring herself out for a cheap buck?!" He slaps his leg, as if this is the funniest thing ever. He's doubled over, almost pissing himself he's laughing so much. If I gave a crap, I might feel offended. Predictably, Devin erupts, launching himself at the guy with his fists swinging.

A few other guys jump in, Danny included, and chaos ensues. I seize my opportunity, not stopping to talk myself out of it.

I race toward Cara—not easy to do in towering seven-inch stilettos—grabbing her urgently by the arm. "We need to get out of here."

Cara is sharp as a tack, and we always pair up at gigs, so she trusts me, and vice versa. We flee into the night without any explanation asked for or given. I fling my bag in the back seat of my car and dive into the driver's seat, yanking the killer shoes off my feet and slipping on my flats before cranking the engine. Cara has barely closed the door before I take off.

An hour later, we're in a dingy club over on the other side of town, knocking back shots, and I'm counting the cost of my near disastrous encounter. The quarter bottle of vodka I knocked back before the gig has helped, and I'm already more than nicely buzzed, but my hands are still shaking like crazy, and my heart is beating way too fast. We've ditched the nasty stripper outfits for tight black dresses, and we're occupying our usual corner booth, watching the idiots attempting to dance on the scuffed hardwood dance floor.

"So," Cara says, dragging the word out. "You gonna explain what that was about back there."

I throw back another shot, but I'm still not nearly drunk enough for this conversation. "Nope."

She pouts, but I know my friend. She's not giving up that easy. "Who was the hottie?"

"No one."

She purses her lips, draining her shot. "Is that so." She sends me a wicked grin. "So, you won't mind if I take an Uber back to the club and drag him home to my bed." I growl, like a legit deep-throated growl not heard since caveman times. She laughs. "Yeah, thought as much."

"He's off limits. Permanently."

Her expression turns more serious. "Tell me what's going on, Ro." She cocks her head to the side. "If that's even your real name."

I bury my head in my hands, groaning. I've managed to keep my cover for almost five years, and, in one night, Devin is unraveling everything.

She leans across the table. "I'm your friend. You can tell me, and I promise I won't breathe a word." I lift my head, mortified when tears pool in my eyes. "Hey, you, don't get upset." Her expression softens as she reaches over, lacing her fingers through mine. "Who is that guy?"

I sniffle, removing my wallet from my purse and extracting the dog-eared photo. I slide it to her. "His name is Devin Morgan, and I've been in love with him forever." I spend the next hour telling her everything, and she listens attentively, never interrupting.

"Holy fuck, Ro, or do I call you Ange now?" she asks, after I've finished speaking and I'm hunched over the table, physically and mentally drained from reliving the sordid details of my past.

"Ro. I'm still Roberta. Angelina Ward died years ago."

"Does Scott know all this?"

"Fuck no, and you can't tell him." I pierce her with pleading eyes.

"Chill. I already told you I'll keep your confidence."

I crick my neck from side to side, trying to loosen some of the tension. "I know. Sorry, I'm just really on edge right now."

"Why'd you keep Scott around anyway? It's not like either of you are faithful." She lights up a cigarette, blowing smoke circles into the air.

I shrug. "Better the devil you know, I suppose. Besides, he pays half the rent, and he's a worse alcoholic than me so he doesn't care if I stumble in the door barely knowing my name," I half-joke. Her pitiful look sours the vodka sloshing around in my stomach. "He's low maintenance," I add, feeling a need to justify myself, "and it's better than living alone." Not that it really makes much of a difference.

You can be surrounded by people and still be the loneliest creature in existence.

She props her elbows on the table, blowing smoke out her mouth with a pensive look on her face. "I think you should talk to him," she says after a bit. "You didn't see the look on his face when he first noticed you. I did. That Devin guy has missed you like crazy. Loves you like crazy. I'd bet any money on it." She stubs out her ciggy, and her expression softens. "I get why you ran away, but maybe it's time to put it behind you. You can't still feel responsible."

"I do," I rush to confirm. "I *am* still responsible. I made bad choices and those choices led to someone I loved taking his own life. He doesn't get a do-over, so why should I?"

She takes my hand in hers again. "For a smart girl, you sure are fucking dumb sometimes."

I yank my hand away, irritated at her cutting remark. "I didn't tell you so you could sit in judgment or lecture me."

"Sometimes the truth hurts, chica. You're purposely hiding away in this shithole with a shit for brains lowlife as a boyfriend and a dead-end job instead of facing facts. And you have options, girl. Options I would kill for. You don't have to live this life. You choose to. Why the hell can't you see you're just making more bad choices?"

I toss the last shot down my throat, slamming the glass so hard on the table, it splits and cracks up one side. "And you wonder why I didn't tell you the truth before."

She grabs her wallet and slides out of the booth. "I love you, you idiot, but sometimes you are your own worst enemy."

A couple hours later, I'm three sheets to the wind, blissfully plastered, and being towed out to the corridor leading to the bathrooms. The guy's hand is warm but callused, dwarfing mine. He's older but still hot with dirty blond hair, gray-blue eyes, and he wears his jeans well. Haven't a clue what his name is. Didn't stop to ask before I launched myself at him out on the dance floor. He didn't complain, instantly shoving his tongue into my mouth and grinding his obvious arousal against me. After fifteen minutes of sweaty dry humping on the dance floor, I didn't object when he suggested we take this someplace a little more private.

"Fuck, you're sexy," he exclaims, slamming my back against the wall as he kneads my tits through the thin material of my dress.

"And you're not moving fast enough," I taunt, flicking the button on his jeans.

"In a hurry to get off, sweetheart?"

"Stop talking," I hiss, irritated by the rough cadence of his voice. He was much more attractive when he wasn't speaking. Shoving my hand down the front of his boxers, I grab his erection, happy it's long and thick in my hand.

He moans. "Fuck, yeah, baby. That feels good." His hand creeps up my thigh, finding my lace thong, and he shoves it aside, plunging two fingers inside me. "Nice, baby. Real nice. Do you want Daddy's cock now?"

Rolling my eyes, I ignore his pitiful attempt at dirty talk, tugging his jeans and boxers to the floor.

He rolls a condom on and then lifts my leg up and out to the side, ramming into me in one swift thrust. I ignore the brief sting of pain, wrapping my leg around his waist while steadying my other foot on the floor and flattening my back against the wall. My hands dig into his shoulders as he starts thrusting in and out. He doesn't hold back, grunting and groaning as he fucks me hard, just how I like it. My head falls back, my eyes close, and I lose myself to the carnal act, ignoring the way my head is spinning and my empty stomach is slopping copious liters of vodka around.

Tiny tendrils of awareness seep into my semi-comatose state, and my eyes flick open. The corridor is dark and camera-less on purpose. You can bet we're not the only fornicating couple to have hidden in the shadows for sex tonight. A form moves at the far end of the corridor, nearest the exit to the club, and, even in the dark, I can detect Devin's shape. He's not moving, he's simply watching, his body strung tight.

Our eyes meet, and he stares at me with dark intensity. His jaw clenches but he's in control. Watching. Waiting. Biding his time.

Well then.

I guess he didn't get the memo earlier.

Time to make sure I drill the message home.

I shove the guy off me, clamping his mouth shut before he can protest. Wrapping my hand around his slippery cock, I stroke it in deliberate, hard, long caresses. "No speaking," I command, aware my voice is slurring a little. Still keeping my hand over his mouth, I deliberately raise my voice, making sure I'm heard. "I'm going to turn around and I want you to fuck me hard from behind. I want you to fuck me so hard that I scream the place down and people rush in thinking you're fucking killing me. I want you to fuck me until I'm so sore I can barely walk. I want you to fuck me like you wish you were able to fuck your wife." Yeah, asshole, I saw the indent on your ring finger. "Put your hands, your fingers, where you want. It's your lucky night, *Daddy*."

I turn around, placing my palms flat on the wall as he yanks my dress up to my waist. Ripping my flimsy thong off, he scatters the torn strands on the filthy floor. I spread my legs, angling my head in Devin's direction. "Do your worst, *Daddy*," I say, staring only at Devin. "You can't make me bleed any more than I already do."

CHAPTER THIRTY-SEVEN

Devin

I know what she's attempting to do. But if she thinks this'll scare me off, she's clearly forgotten how stubborn I can be. Forgotten how much I fucking love her. This isn't my Ange. The sweet girl I grew up with would never have fucked some cheating sleazebag in the public corridor of a nasty joint like this. *What the hell has happened to her? And is there any of the girl I knew still left?*

Her defiant stare bores a hole in my skull as she watches me, her body jolting back and forth as the asshole thrusts into her over and over. My hands clench at my sides, and the urge to knock the shit out of that douche is strong, but I've learned to rein in my anger over the years. Ange isn't the only one who's changed. Still doesn't mean I'm going to stand here and accept this crap.

I've seen enough.

Stalking forward, I keep my focus on her as I approach. Her eyes narrow, and a flash of panic sweeps across her face until she controls it. Now, her expression is orchestrated fury. I smirk as I grab the slime ball by the shoulders, yanking him back and away from her. Caught unaware, he stumbles, landing flat on his butt, his dick poking upright, stoking my anger a level higher. Before she can swing for me, I position myself in front of her, reaching behind to grip her waist. "Get dressed," I snap over my shoulder. "You're leaving."

"Screw off, Devin. You can't come in here and do this." Her speech is garbled, and she reeks of booze.

The perv climbs to his feet, holding his pants up with one hand. "You heard the lady. Get lost, asshole. This is nothing to do with you."

I prod my finger in his chest, silently cautioning myself to keep it together. Pulling my badge out of my pocket, I flip it open, flashing it at him briefly. "That's where you're wrong. Unless you want me to arrest you for indecent exposure, public lewdness, and adultery, I'd suggest you get your cheating ass out of here in the next five seconds."

I've never seen a dude move so fast in my life. He doesn't even cast a glance in Ange's direction before abandoning her to her fate.

"You're a cop?" I hear the incredulity in her voice, and if it was any other time, I'd find humor in this situation. Thank fuck, I'm a cop, or else I'd never have found her after she fled the bachelor party. When I realized she'd run, I hightailed it to the local station and got the CCTV footage pulled. I was able to trace her movements and follow her here.

I turn around, my heart pounding in expectation. This woman still has the ability to rattle me to my core. She's always had this indescribable hold over me, and that hasn't changed. She's fixed her dress and smoothed her hair behind her ears, but she still has that flushed just-got-fucked look on her face, and I'm pissed. I want to race after the douche and beat the shit out of him, but I resist the temptation. I'm not jeopardizing my career because of a guy like that. "Yes, and you're lucky I'm not arresting you right now."

She glares at me, folding her arms across her chest in a move that pushes her tits up higher. It takes colossal willpower to keep my eyes trained on her face. "I'd like to see you try."

"Don't test me. You haven't seen me in a long time. You've no idea who I am today."

She shimmies sideways along the wall, swaying a little, but I reach for her elbow, holding on before she runs away again. "And there was a reason for that," she spits out, glaring at my hand on her arm. "Let me go, Devin."

"No."

"What?"

"No. I'm not letting you go. Not until we sit down and talk like civilized adults."

"In case you hadn't noticed, I'm not all that civilized these days," she retorts, laughing, as if she's proud of her behavior.

Rage simmers in my veins. I lean in close to her face, almost passing out from the strong smell of vodka on her breath, struggling to keep a leash on my anger. I've spent years searching for this woman, and if she thinks she's getting away from me without at least talking to me, she has another thing coming. "In case you hadn't realized, I'm so fucking mad at you right now, I'm about two seconds away from hauling your ass into a cell. You *will* talk to me, or you're getting booked. Your choice."

A layer of armor drops to the floor. Her lower lip quivers as she faces me, and that one tiny gesture infuses me with hope. She's still in there somewhere. All isn't lost.

"Why?" she whispers. "Why are you doing this? What do you want from me?"

Everything. "Answers."

She shakes her head sadly. "Then you'll be disappointed."

Keeping a hold on her arm, I steer her down the corridor. "I just want to talk, Ange. You owe me that much."

All the fight leaves her as we maneuver a path out of the skeezy club. Danny has the engine running when we reach the parking lot. I open the back door, gesturing for her to get in first. Then I haul myself up beside her, nodding at my buddy.

"Where to?" he asks, easing the car slowly out onto the road.

"Stop at the nearest diner you can find."

He looks at me curiously, but I just stare out the window. My emotions are shot to pieces. I've spent what feels like eternity searching for her, but I never stopped to actually plan what I'd say when I found her. There is so much to be said, and I don't know where to start.

Her foot taps nervously off the floor, and she chews on the corner of her lip. The familiar gesture tears me up inside. This is the woman I love, but she's almost a virtual stranger. I know nothing of her life these past years. Nothing of the woman she is today. Or the hardships she's endured. "How did you find me?" she asks without looking at me. "How did you know I lived here?"

"I didn't know you lived here. We're in town for the weekend for Rick's bachelor party. Never in a million years did I expect to find you here." I move a little closer, dismayed when she discernibly flinches. "I've searched all over for you, Ange. I never stopped looking. And the irony that I'd bump into you so coincidentally isn't lost on me, trust me." My laugh is sharp.

Finally, she tilts her face up to look at me, and I'm falling all over again. I sit on my hands to stop myself touching her. I want to bundle her into my arms and never let her out of my sight again, but I can't come on too heavy. I won't scare her off. "You're still so unbelievably beautiful, Ange," I admit, my voice sounding all choked up.

"You know what they say—beauty is only skin deep. I'm completely ugly on the inside." She speaks without a trace of reticence, without any feeling. This isn't self-deprecation, because she's detached from any and all emotion; she's merely stating a fact.

"I can't agree."

A flash of anger shimmers in her eyes. "You know nothing of the person I am now. Nothing." This time I detect the bitter note in her tone. And she's wrong, because I still remember the person I used to be, and, unless I'm sorely mistaken, Ange uses alcohol as a crutch. She's clearly hammered, her eyes watering and bloodshot, slurring her words, and unsteady on her feet, but she's functioning, and still capable of firing back retorts, and you only have that sliver of awareness with repeated abuse. I should know. I've walked in her shoes.

"Maybe I know you more than you realize."

She barks out a laugh, her look lethal as she glares at me. "You know jack shit, Devin, and that's the way I like it. I left you for a reason, and it wasn't so you could chase halfway around the country looking for me. This is a waste of your time; I don't want you here."

"I think I'll be the judge of that." It's a miracle I sound so in control when it feels like I'm breaking apart inside.

Danny sends me a sympathetic look through the mirror as he pulls up in front of The Roadhouse Diner and kills the engine. I get out, rounding the back of the car and opening the door for Ange. She glowers at me but slides out, shucking my hand away and trotting into the diner by herself.

"Good luck, man," Danny says through the half-open window. "I have a feeling you'll need it."

We're seated across from one another, and Ange is being petulant, refusing to give me any more than one-word clipped answers.

"Goddamn it, Ange." I slam my hand down on the table. "Just fucking talk to me. How difficult can that be?"

"I told you already," she hisses. "I'm not interested in talking to you. Period. I said everything that needed to be said before I left. You shouldn't have come here. Whatever we had is in the past. A stupid childhood crush. We're adults now, and it's time you accept the truth."

"And what exactly is that?" I sneer. "What crap are you spouting as truth these days?"

She strains across the table, her eyes narrowing in fury. "That you and I are in the past. That there's absolutely no reason why you should still be searching for me after all this time. That I have a life, and it's time you got one too. That I've moved on." She gulps, digging her fingers into the edge of the Formica table. "You mean nothing to me anymore, Devin. Nothing." She sits back in the seat, staring blankly at me. "Like I said, you're wasting your time. I don't want to have anything to do with you. In fact, I pretty much despise you and everything you stand for now."

Her words have the desired effect, slamming into me like a savage blow to the chest. I'm reeling from the impact, but I also recognize bluster when I see it. She wants to believe that's the truth, but it's not. I see behind the façade. She's doing everything in her power to push me away, but the signs are there.

The waitress sets two plates down in front of us, and I thank her. Ange starts wolfing her pancakes down, and it's like someone's taken a sledgehammer to my heart. Even though she's whippet thin, and clearly not looking after herself properly, my girl still has one hell of an appetite, and I'm glad to see it. I need these little things to remind me why I'm here, why I'm doing this, when she's trying everything in her power to turn me away.

I wait until I'm completely calm before responding to her. "If you don't want anything to do with me, why do you still wear my tattoo on your wrist, my locket around your neck, and why did you take my name?" Her fork clangs to the table, and surprise is splayed across her face. My mouth curls into a smug smile. Can't help it. "I'm a detective, Ange. Did you really think I wouldn't have looked up everything I could about you the minute you reappeared in my life?" I push my uneaten plate away, leaning my arm along the top of the booth. "I've got to hand it to you, baby doll. That was clever. Real clever. I did think about it, you know. I've run numerous nationwide searches for Angelina Morgan and Angelina Carter, but I'd never have thought to search for my own name."

I can't describe my feelings in the moment I realized she'd assumed my name. "Roberta Devina Morgan." I roll the name she goes by now over my tongue, loving how it sounds. "Or Ro to your friends, I believe. I like it. I like it a lot."

"It wasn't for your benefit," she says, pouting, "and there's no need to act so smug. I was a fucking mess back then, and it was the only name that sprung to mind, so you can quit acting all sentimental over it. It means nothing. Just like you." She stands up. "I've had enough of this. I'm leaving. My boyfriend will be wondering where I am." That's news to me, and I don't hide my disappointment in time. She leans across the table, putting her face right in mine. Noxious fumes waft through the air, and I close my nostrils off for a few seconds. "And I still need to get off, seeing as someone"—she pokes a slender finger in my chest—"ruined my fun tonight."

"Does your boyfriend know you fuck random douchebags in public?"

She straightens up, tilting her head to the side, wobbling unsteadily on her feet. Clutching the edge of the table, she smirks at me. "That's for me to know and you to find out, *de-tec-tive*."

She enunciates the word, her voice dripping with sarcasm, and I'm done. It's almost three a.m. and I can't do this anymore tonight. Disappointment, hurt, and regret wage a vicious war inside me. "Have it your way," I say, fishing out my wallet and slapping some cash on the table. "But we're not done talking. I'll drop you home and then you and I are making plans to meet tomorrow."

A laugh bursts out of her. "Eh, yeah, don't think so."

"I can still arrest you."

She holds out her wrists. "Arrest me then."

She's calling my bluff, and I'm tempted to follow through, if only to ensure I know exactly where she is, but I'm not walking her into a police station and booking her for indecent exposure. She doesn't need that on her record. Shocked me that she had one. Two counts of drunk and disorderly in the last three years. She's lucky her lawyer knew what he was doing, and managed to get her off with a fine. If she's not careful, she could end up doing time.

"Don't. Push. Me." I try to take her arm, but she shoves me away, almost falling on her butt in the process. I wrap my arm around her shoulders. "You will let me escort you out of here or I will throw your butt in jail. I'm warning you, Ange, you've tested me enough for one night."

"Asshole," she mumbles under her breath, but she gives up trying to wriggle out of my hold. The instant we step foot outside, she slams to a halt. "You're not driving me home. I'll call a cab."

"Get in the car, Ange."

"I don't want you knowing where I live."

I roll my eyes. "I already know where you live. Detective, remember?"

She scowls as she clambers into the car, muttering more obscenities under her breath. Danny quirks a brow, and I just shake my head.

The journey is undertaken in complete silence. My eyes are closed as I rest my head back. My chest is tight with pain.

When we reach the building where Ange lives, she can't get out of the car quick enough. The heel of her shoe catches in the rim of the door in her haste to get away from me, and she falls headfirst onto the sidewalk.

I hop out of the car the same time Danny does, and we both race around to her side. She's groaning, clutching her head, and trying to sit up. "Let me see." I push her hair back, inspecting the nasty gash in her forehead. "Shit. You might need stitches."

"I'm fine."

She swats my hand away, attempting to stand up. Danny helps her to her feet, and she doesn't mount any protest at his touch, which fucking messes with my head. She leaves her shoes on the sidewalk as she stumbles toward the door in her bare feet, staggering all over the place. Blood drips down her face, and I reach my limit, storming after her. "You need to go to the hospital."

"The fuck I do."

I start dragging her back to the car. "You could have a concussion."

"Get the hell away from me," she screams, trying to pry my hand off her arm.

I strengthen my grip, hauling her to the car. She's remarkably strong for a drunk, fighting me the entire time. When her nails dig into my flesh, piercing skin, and drawing blood, I roar out in pain, but I don't let go. We're at the car now, and she's struggling as I'm trying to get her in the back seat. "Ange, stop. Please. Just let me take you to the emergency room to get checked out."

She leans back, making a grating sound at the back of her throat, and then she lets a loogie loose from her mouth. Her saliva hits me square in the face, and I jump back, disgusted, staring at the woman I love with abject horror.

She laughs hysterically, doubling over and clutching her stomach. Blood is still oozing out of the cut on her forehead, trickling into her eyes. Pain slices across my chest. My heart actually fucking hurts. I don't know what to do there. How to help her.

Danny steps forward, subtly shaking his head in my direction. "Let me try," he mouths, and I nod. Then I rest my head on the hood of the car, all out of ammo. Tonight has drained me in more ways than one.

"Ange," I hear Danny say. "Will you let me take you inside and clean your cuts?"

Her manic laughter trails off. She sniffs. "Yeah, once *he* stays out here."

I don't even look at her as I walk around the front of the car and get in the passenger seat. With mechanical movements, I open the glove box and remove a pack of tissues, wiping the spittle off my face. Balling the tissue in my hand, I slam my palms down hard on the dash, repeatedly, roaring as frustration gets the better of me. "Fuck, fuck, fuck." I rock my head in my hands as despair blankets me.

It feels like I'm losing her all over again.

And I have to wonder if she was ever mine to begin with.

CHAPTER THIRTY-EIGHT

Angelina

My head is thumping like a million bongo players are testing a new rhythm out in my skull. My mouth is dry and icky, and my chest burns with a combo of acid reflux and heartache. After Danny patched me up last night, I collapsed in a heap on the couch, passing out almost instantly. I woke a couple hours after that, in bed beside a snoring Scott. Pushing his leg off mine, I managed to race to the bathroom before I spewed up my guts. Vodka seeped out my nose and my mouth, mixing with course tears as they slid down my face. When I had nothing left to expel, I lay on the cold tile floor, sobbing.

Devin's reappearance in my life has brought everything to the surface again, and I'm no more equipped to deal with the maelstrom of emotions than I was back then.

I roll over in the bed, wondering how I got here a second time because I'm pretty sure I cried myself to sleep on the floor in the bathroom. I move my hand across the bed, but the sheets are cold and empty. Scott must have decided to go into the dealership today. His dad owns the place, and he reluctantly gave him a position a couple years ago when he'd been fired from his job again. Only family can put up with his shit.

I shuffle out of bed, dragging my achy body to the kitchen. Rummaging in the cupboards near the sink, I find a couple of pain pills and swallow them with a mouthful of vodka, ignoring the ache in my throat as the liquid goes down. I open the other cupboards, hoping there's even a dry cracker or some breakfast cereal, but the cupboards are bare. I take another swig from the vodka bottle, grateful I still have my priorities in order. *Who needs food when you've got booze, right?* Bending down to open our small refrigerator, I wince as a dart of pain shoots up my spine. Lifting my shirt, I prod at the blossoming bruise that stretches from my left hipbone around my back. Shit. I strip off my shirt, standing in my undies in the kitchen as I inspect every inch of my body.

More bruising is evident on my shins, and I saunter into the bathroom to examine my reflection in the mirror. Christ, I look like shit. Mascara has clumped my lashes together, and smeared makeup across my cheeks makes me look like a scary extra from a horror movie. I scrub my face clean, washing carefully around the Band-Aid on my forehead. A large purplish bruise covers my chin and my left cheek, and I sigh. At least I can cover it with makeup and avoid having to cancel any gigs. I desperately need the cash.

I walk back into the kitchen and slam to a halt. Devin is standing in the middle of the space, scanning the room with a look of absolute horror on his face.

"What the hell are you doing here, and how did you get in?"

He lifts his head in my direction. "Another resident let me into the building, and your door was unlocked."

"Fucking idiot, Scott," I murmur.

"Jesus Christ, Ange. You're covered in cuts and bruises." His eyes roam my undie-clad body, and then he quickly looks away.

"See something you like, Devin," I taunt in a singsong voice, tossing my tangled hair over one shoulder.

"Stop, Ange. Please." He bends down, picking up my shirt and throwing it to me. "Put some clothes on."

I take the shirt, sauntering toward him holding it in my hands. "What if I don't want to?"

He places his hands on the dirty kitchen counter, leaning his head forward as he draws a sharp breath. Then he seems to think better of it, yanking his hands away and crossing to the sink to wash them.

"Still a clean freak," I tease.

"Wouldn't be hard in a place like this." He dries his hands on the front of his jeans, scowling as he spots the open vodka bottle. I snatch it before he picks it up, hugging it to my chest possessively. He swallows hard, and I detest the look of pity in his eyes. "I can't believe you're living like this. Your mother would be so upset if she knew."

All teasing evaporates at the mention of her name. The vodka bottle drops, smashing into smithereens, but I barely notice. Stepping around the broken glass, as if on auto-pilot, I walk to his side, and grab his arm, attempting to pull him toward the door. "Get out. Get out and stay out. I mean it."

"No." He holds me by the shoulders. "I'm not leaving until this place is clean and you've eaten something."

My eyes narrow as I spot the three grocery bags on the far counter. "What the heck is this? You don't get to barge in here unannounced and buy me groceries and mention my mother and ..." A rush of pain so extreme jumps up and waylays me. I try not to think of my mother, because it hurts too much. "Oh God." I drop my head, hiding my face so he can't see the tears brimming in my eyes.

"Ange, babe." He sweeps hair back off my face, and I flinch.

"Don't touch me! I'm not yours to touch."

He takes a couple of steps back. "I'm sorry. I'm just trying to help."

"I don't need your help," I spit out, latching on to my anger, using it to dry my tears. "I've survived without you this far. I'm sure I'll manage to get through the rest of the day." I'm acting like a bitch, but I have no choice. I can't let him get to me. I can't let him back in. As it is, looking up at his sad, sorrowful face is doing a number on my fragile, vulnerable heart. I need some distance. "I'm going to take a shower, and you better be gone by the time I get out."

Of course, he's still here when I reappear in the kitchen a half hour later. If I'm being honest with myself, I knew he would be. Devin's always been a stubborn motherfucker, and he's never liked anyone telling him what to do. My hair is damp, falling in loose waves down my back. I've put some makeup on, managing to conceal the hideous bruising on my face. I'd like to say I feel more human, but I still feel like death warmed up. I'm wearing skinny jeans and a baggy T-shirt belonging to Scott. It was the only clean top I could find, but, watching the scowl deepen on Devin's face as he notices the shirt, I'm glad I had no other options.

My stomach rumbles at the delicious smells filtering through the air. "Sit and eat," he demands in a gruff voice, setting a plate of bacon, eggs, and toast down on the clean kitchen table. My brows climb up to my hairline as I scan the kitchen. Every surface is clean and tidy, the glass debris has been swept up, and two bags of trash are knotted and resting by the front door. I'm reluctantly impressed, not that you'd know it by my face.

My mouth waters as I debate throwing the plate in his face. Hunger wins out, and I tuck in, shoveling the food in my mouth like I haven't eaten in a year.

"Take it easy, baby doll. You don't want to make yourself sick."

I slam my knife and fork down, chewing ferociously until my mouth is empty. "You don't like people telling you what to do and neither do I, so quit it with the motherly routine. And don't call me that."

"Why not, baby doll?" His trademark smug grin makes an appearance, and I want to ram my fist in his mouth.

"Because I never liked being counted as one of your whores."

He leans forward, his eyes blazing with fire. "Firstly, I never slept with whores. I hooked up with some girls in high school, but my rap sheet is a lot less full than most gave me credit for. And, secondly, the only person I have ever called baby doll is you."

"Well, good for you Mr. Squeaky Clean Detective."

He plops into the seat beside me, crossing one delectable leg over his knee as he silently fumes. I shovel food in my mouth, smirking. He watches me eat, making me hugely uncomfortable. His presence seems to crowd my tiny kitchen, and I'm acutely conscious of his broad chest and the way his jeans hug his body in all the right places. His scent swirls around me, bringing me back in time, making me wish things were different. Wish I was different. That I'd been strong enough at the time to do the right thing. That we were in a different place right now.

But we're not.

And I can't lose sight of the facts.

I'm a noose around Devin's neck. I thought by leaving I was setting him free. The knowledge he hasn't given up on me has muddled my brain so bad. I wish it was enough.

Love.

But it's not. Love can't undo my past. Can't wash me free of sin. The only thing I can do is make him hate me. And hope that this time he will finally be free of me to live his life.

Because I don't want him fixated on the past.

I do enough of that for the both of us.

He should have a ring on his finger like Danny. He should have a happy smile on his face instead of a look full of regret.

And he can't stay here much longer, because I've never been able to deny him anything, and if he continues to look at me with so much longing and so much love, I'm terrified I'll cave.

And that just can't happen.

I push my half-eaten plate away, appetite vanquished. "There. I've eaten. Now you can go."

He props his elbows on the table, and rests his chin in his hands, probing my face with a familiar deep, intense, penetrating lens. A few strands of his hair fall over his forehead into his eyes, and my fingers twitch as the craving to touch him starts building momentum inside me. I sit on my hands, and he notices, his eyes crinkling as he smiles.

"If you don't leave, I'm calling the police," I blurt, desperate to get rid of him.

"I am the police." He grins, extracting his cell from his pocket. "Call them, and then I'll page them and let them know I'm already here." His smile widens until he's gracing me with that annoying cocky grin of his again.

"You have no jurisdiction around here," I hiss, taking his cell and making a point of stabbing the buttons.

"I do now," he replies smugly.

"What?" I'm sure my face has turned a sickly green color, and it's not from my hangover.

"I've transferred to the local station on temporary loan."

My mouth hangs open. "For how long?"

"For as long as it takes you to come to your senses."

I jump up, biting on the corner of a nail. "That's a long ass time, Dev, because hell will freeze before I'll do whatever it is you're waiting for me to do." I refuse to confirm the "come to my senses" statement. This is a fucking nightmare.

"I've waited a long time to find you, and I have infinite patience."

"You can't do this," I shriek. "I'll leave town!"

"And I'll follow you." He crosses his arms over his chest, pinning me with a solemn look. He damned well means it too.

"I'll have you arrested for stalking!"

"You can try, but I doubt they'd take your word over one of the youngest decorated homicide detectives, but feel free to give it your best shot."

I launch myself at him, pounding my fists against his chest. "You can't do this to me! I won't let you!"

He restrains me effortlessly, holding my wrists up. His expression softens, and his voice is quietly determined as he speaks. "I've lost you a couple of times already, Ange. I've learned how to live broken, but I refuse to do that anymore. I'm not making the same mistakes again. This time I'm not letting you out of my sight. I'm back in your life, baby doll. The sooner you surrender, the easier it will be."

"I'm not your baby or your baby doll or your anything! I have a life here. I have a job and a boyfriend, and you don't get to stroll in here and try to take over!"

"If I had shown up here, and you were happy and healthy and in a good place, I would've left you alone if you told me that's what you genuinely wanted. But that is not the fucking case." He clenches his jaw. "You're a drunk, working tables by day and stripping at night, and that loser you call a boyfriend is an alcoholic junkie who can in no way take care of you. How am I doing so far?"

I try to wrest my wrists away, so I can hit him, but his hold is too strong. Using the only other weapon at my disposal, I scream—purely to distract him—and raise my knee, burying it in his groin. He goes down like a lead balloon, his eyes watering as he cups his junk. He struggles to breathe, curling into a fetal position on the floor, cradling his manhood with his hands.

"How dare you show up here and cast judgment on my life. I've told you several times that I don't want you back in my life and I mean it. That alcoholic junkie also happens to be pretty skillful with his hands, and he's got a nasty temper, so you really don't want me setting him on you, but I'll do it—I'll tell him if you don't … Leave. Me. The. Fuck. Alone." I scream those last few words, hammering my point home.

Awkwardly, he pulls himself to his feet, still holding his groin. His face contorts in anguish, and I want to look away because I know I'm responsible for putting it there. An extra layer of hatred washes over me. "Why do you hate me so much, Ange? What did I do to you to make you hate me like this?"

"You loved me, and I hate you for that."

He shakes his head. "You know who I hate?" he asks, but he doesn't wait for me to respond. "I hate Ayden. This is all his fucking fault."

I take a step back, reeling. "You can't say that! You can't hate *him*. You need to hate *me*!"

He starts hobbling toward the door. "I could never hate you, Ange." Stopping in the doorway, he straightens up a little, grimacing as he removes his hands from his groin. "Never. You can hurl your hateful words at me. You can threaten me. You can scream and shout and push me all you like, but it won't make the slightest bit of difference. I love you. I've always loved you, and I always will. And I'm going nowhere, baby doll." His eyes glisten with resolve. "The only possible way you'll get rid of me is if you kill me."

And with those parting words, he walks out, slamming the door shut behind him as I sink to the floor in a flurry of tears. I wish I did hate Devin, because it would make this so much easier. But I love him to bits. As much as I always have. Maybe more so thanks to that declaration.

He can stay here and try to fight for me.

But he's missed sight of the most important thing.

This isn't about him winning back my heart. You can't win something you already own, and my heart has always belonged to him.

But if he realized how blackened my heart is, how corrupt and mangled and twisted it's become, he'd give it back. He'd throw it in my face and run a million miles away from here.

He'd stop fighting for the dead girl with the dead heart.

He'd finally realize what I've known these last five years: that I'm not worth fighting for. I never have been.

CHAPTER THIRTY-NINE

Devin

I don't attempt to talk to her again, but I'm not taking any chances either—I can't lose her again. Now, my days consist of following her around town. Parked outside the diner where she works, I watch as she moves between tables, chatting and flirting with customers, scowling every time she looks out the window and notices me. I salute her, and she flips me the bird. It's almost comical at this stage. I follow her a few nights to a couple of sleazy joints where she performs her routines for guys older than my dad. Hiding in the shadows, it takes every scrap of willpower I possess not to drag her ass out of there. I didn't quite lie when I told her I was working for local law enforcement—I just bent the truth a little. I've taken an extended leave of absence from my unit, and I'm consulting on a couple of cases for the local guys, but, essentially, I'm a free agent.

I've taken minimal vacation time since joining the force, so the captain knew he had little grounds for declining my request. He knows I'm a damn fine detective and that I'm independently wealthy thanks to the share allocation in my dad's business. I don't have to work, but I do because I love it. However, there's no competition between work and the love of my life.

In any such battle, Ange wins, hands down.

So, now I've ample time to trail her around town. She may have no regard for her own welfare, but I sure as shit do. She's trying her best to ignore me, but she's close to blowing a gasket.

I'm getting to her, and that can only be a good thing. I just need to remind her of the things she left behind.

The things she has to return home to.

There is nothing holding her here. The thin file my PI Nate produced confirmed everything I've surmised about her. She's lived here since she fled, only once briefly leaving the state of Oregon. She didn't work for the first few years, existing on her trust fund and limitless supplies of vodka, according to her financial records. Then she got her job at the diner, and she started stripping on the side last year. That asshole she's shacked up with is a good for nothing loser who's clearly sponging off her. Apart from a few brushes with the law, she's done a very good job of keeping on the down low.

She has a few friends in town, and she owns the piece-of-shit apartment she's living in.

But those are the only ties.

Nothing that can't be cut.

But I can't push her on this. She won't even speak to me, for fuck's sake. So, I've got to play smart and ease my way back into her life nice and slow.

For now, I'll bide my time, and channel inner patience. Something which is becoming increasingly challenging because it's so hard being this close to her and not being an active part of her life. I still don't understand why she left. I know she blames herself for Ayden's suicide, but why she felt she needed to change her identity and hide from everyone she knew still perplexes me.

I want to sit her down and ply her with questions until I understand it.

But that wouldn't go down well, and my priority at this time is keeping her safe. The answers I desperately seek will have to wait.

It's my third Friday in town, and I'm parked outside Ange's place in the dark, drinking copious amounts of coffee and listening to the radio to try to stave off boredom. Usually, she goes out with that asshole she calls her boyfriend on a Friday night. It's basically the only time in the week when they spend time together. I'm questioning if he's even her boyfriend at all. If he isn't some friend she's just roped in to fuck with my head.

Twenty minutes later, I have the answer to at least one of my questions.

Light blooms to life in Ange's second floor apartment as the living room curtains are opened. The wide window offers an excellent view into her small apartment as I bring the binoculars to my eyes. Her head is angled in the direction of my car, and she's staring right at me. I don't make any secret of my presence so there's nothing surprising about that. What *is* surprising is the fact she doesn't appear to have told the knucklehead about me. And he hasn't noticed me hanging around outside his place these last few weeks either, which doesn't instill any confidence in his ability to protect her.

He appears in the room, and she says something to him over her shoulder. He takes off his jacket and tie, approaching her with a smug expression. When she stands up, all the blood in my body rushes south. She's topless, standing in black lace panties with a garter belt holding her fishnet stockings in place. Her legs are long and slender in the black high heels, invoking old memories which aren't helping with the growing bulge in my pants. Grabbing him, she spins him around so his back is flattened against the window, and I sense where she's going with this.

I should put the binoculars down and get the fuck out of here, but I can't bring myself to do it.

She strips his pants and boxers down and turns him to the side a little, making sure I can see. Then she takes his cock in her mouth, proceeding to suck him off. She makes a meal of it, dragging it out for my benefit, no doubt. I'm caught between arousal and anger and envy—wanting to whip my cock out of my jeans and stroke myself to release *and* wanting to charge up the stairs, rip her away from him, and pummel his face into next week.

When she's done, she stands up, staring out the window, licking her lips, and teasing her nipples between her thumb and her forefinger. Jerk face grabs her tits from behind, slipping his hand in the front of her panties in full view of the street below. A couple walking their dog along the sidewalk stare up at them, open-mouthed, struggling to believe their eyes.

Bile floods my mouth, and I've reached my limit. I put the binoculars down and send a text to Nate, asking him to take over for me. Nate is the PI who's worked for me for years. As soon as I found Ange here, I called him up, offered double his fee, and he got on a plane straightaway. He usually takes the night shift while I follow Ange during the day.

He pulls up twenty minutes later, and I take off, stopping outside the next liquor store I come across, frantically trying to talk myself off the ledge. I haven't touched a drop of alcohol since high school, but there've been plenty of occasions where I've been tempted. Most all of them were Ange-related, but this is the worst episode yet. If I close my eyes, I can still smell it, still taste the pungent sharpness of JD swirling on my tongue and sliding down my throat. Images of Ange sucking that asshole off refuse to empty from my mind, and I get out of the car. Staring at the store, I grab fistfuls of my hair, kicking the tires on my SUV. I start pacing, praying for strength that's in limited supply. She fucking pushed my buttons tonight, and if she keeps this up, I know I'm going to crack and do something I'll regret.

Right now, I'm so fucking tempted to just kidnap her cranky ass, tie her up, and not let her go until she expunges the guilt and the grief from her soul. While I don't have all the answers I seek, I know this is related to Ayden's death. I can't believe she's still blaming herself for it.

And I meant what I said to her.

I fucking hate my former best friend.

His suicide was the most fucking selfish thing he ever did. He may as well have taken us with him. It wasn't just one life, one family, that was ruined that day.

His death was the catalyst that destroyed the girl we both loved.

And she still hasn't recovered from it.

Has she done this deliberately as some form of self-punishment? It's really the only thing that makes sense, but how long does she intend to keep this up? Was she ever planning on coming back home? Natalie's heart is broken. There isn't a day goes by when she doesn't miss her daughter. I hate that I'm keeping my newfound knowledge from Ange's mom, especially when I promised her she'd be the first to know, but she can't see Ange like this.

Drunk, lost, and out of control.

It would destroy her all over again.

It's up to me to get through to Ange. To help her clean up, and then I can take her home. Reunite her with the mother I know she still loves.

That reinforcement is all I need to pull myself together.

Caving to the demon drink would be so easy, but I can't do that to myself or the people depending on me.

I get back in my car, power up the engine, and floor it out of there before I capitulate.

Whether she wants to face it or not, Ange needs me.

The last time she needed me, I let her down.

I'm not going to fail her again.

∞ ∞ ∞

I'm watching TV on low in my bedroom, nursing a lukewarm coffee when Nate calls. "Devin, I think you need to get here."

Hearing his urgent tone, I grab my jeans off the floor, shucking them on as adrenaline courses through my veins. "Talk to me."

"I followed Angelina and her boyfriend to a club. They've both been heavily drinking, and now they're arguing, and it looks like it's about to turn nasty."

"I'm on my way," I say, shoving my feet into my sneakers.

When I pull up a little while later, Ange is in the middle of the parking lot outside the club shouting at the douche. She's wearing a strapless black minidress and high heels. It's freezing outside, and I can see her shivering from here. She's also stumbling a lot, struggling to maintain her balance.

"They got thrown out of the club a few minutes ago," Nate explains when I reach him. He's standing in front of his car, about three hundred feet away from the warring couple, with his arms folded, watching them bicker. We're not close enough to make out exactly what's being said. "He appears to be blaming her for that."

At that second, Ange pushes the douche, beating her fists against his chest as she screams obscenities at him. I watch in horror as he raises his hand, slapping her across the face. My feet move, and I'm racing toward her as she falls on the asphalt, clutching her cheek. "Call the station," I shout over my shoulder at Nate.

The asshole lifts his booted foot and kicks her in the ribs. She cries out, instinctively curling into a ball and trying to shield her body as he continues to kick her. I lunge at him, knocking us both to the ground. Grabbing the collar of my shirt, he pulls my face close and head butts me. Blinding pain explodes in my skull, and warm blood starts pumping out of my nose. "Fuck." I'm scrambling to my feet, dizzy and swaying, when he yanks me back down. My head slams off the hard ground, and stars blur my vision. Pain ricochets through my body, and I groan. A dense weight presses down on me, and then the guy is swinging, raining blows on my face and my chest. He's strong, and his aim isn't bad, but he's still inebriated, and he lacks the skill and training I have. Ange is screaming and crying in the background, begging him to stop. I blink until my vision clears, attempting to buck him off me. When that doesn't work, I lob a blow at his neck, striking him precisely at the point of his carotid artery. It's a move I've perfected over the years, and it never fails me.

His eyes roll back in his head, and his body goes limp as he slumps to the side. I sit up and something sharp pierces my back, sending an intense burst of stabbing pain shooting through me. Ange screams. I roar, shoving the guy off me, as I reach around, probing the sore spot on my upper back, my fingers coming away bloody.

What the fuck just happened?

I turn, lightheaded, and plummet to the ground, moaning. The pain in my back intensifies, but I push myself up off my hands, staggering to my feet.

"Oh my God, Dev," Ange shrieks, landing in front of me in her bare feet. Tears are pumping out of her eyes. "Are you okay?" I sway, almost blacking out as I feel blood gushing out of the wound in my back. I reach out, holding on to her, vaguely hearing the sirens in the distance.

A strong arm winds around my back, and Nate is there, helping to prop me up. "I called an ambulance. It's on its way."

Ange drops to her knees crying. She looks up at me, and my heart breaks. "I'm so sorry," she slurs, in between sobs. "I thought he was going to kill you and I didn't think." Big, fat tears roll down her face. "I threw my shoe at him, and I don't know what happened. It wasn't supposed to hit you!" she sobs. "It was meant for him." She lashes out at the unconscious guy lying on the ground, pummeling his stomach with her tiny fists.

"Fuck." I suck in a breath as my vision blurs in and out.

"You're losing some blood, but I don't think it's serious," Nate supplies, peering at my back. "I'm no expert, but if I had to hazard a guess, I'd say the stiletto missed penetrating any vital organs."

Ange rocks on the ground, wailing and crying, and I hate that I can't go to her. "Help her," I tell Nate, as the sirens grow closer. "It's okay, baby," I croon, as Nate leans me against the nearest car before going to Ange. He lifts her up in his arms. She's crying so much, I don't think she's even realized. He brings her over beside me, placing her on top of the hood. I reach out, touching her hand. "Don't cry, baby. It's going to be okay."

She sniffles, fixing forlorn eyes on me. "No, it's not. I'm not okay."

"I know, baby, but you will be. You will be."

CHAPTER FORTY

Angelina

They take Devin and Scott away in separate ambulances, and I'm arrested. I can't stop crying. I thought Scott was going to kill Devin, and all I could think was he was going to die believing I hated him. Cara is right. All I'm doing is making more bad choices. And I'm so tired. Of all of it. Of thinking. Of hurting. Of life.

After they booked me, they put me in this cell to sober up. I'm lying on the floor, with only a thin blanket covering me, shivering, nauseated, and terrified that I've just killed my other best friend. Tears leak out of my eyes, and I think I may have permanently broken my tear ducts.

"Stop your fucking sniveling, woman," the hooker with the mad eyes and the frizzy red hair says for the umpteenth time. Just my luck to be locked up with a crazy bitch.

"Screw off," I mumble, in between sobs.

I barely even flinch when she yanks me up by the hair, ramming her fist in my face. Blood spurts from my nose, but I still don't stop crying. That only incenses her further. She rains blows on my face as I wonder where the fucking officer in charge is.

My head spins back as she hits me, darts of pain crashing around my face.

I'm crying harder now, and a wall of shame descends upon me.

How did my life come to this?
How have I ended up here?
Why did my life go so off track?

Pain lances me on all sides, but the pain in my heart is the worst pain of all. And it's all my own doing.

I just want it to end.

To not think. Not feel. Not hurt anymore.

Mom would be bitterly disappointed in me. I'm glad she's not here to witness my lowest moment.

The crazy bitch yells at me to stop crying, and I cry louder. When she slams my face down on the bench, stars explode behind my eyes and rattling pain bursts through my skull. The last thought I have before I pass out is that I hope I don't ever wake up.

$$\infty \; \infty \; \infty$$

When I come to, sounds of hushed voices talking are the first thing I hear. I blink my eyes open, squinting at the harsh glare of the overhead lights. The room is white and sterile, and the little beeping of the machine by my bed confirms I'm in the hospital. My tongue is stuck to the top of my mouth, and it tastes like mothballs have taken up permanent residence there. I cough, and the sound is coarse and croaky.

"Hey, baby," Devin says. "How are you feeling?"

I turn toward the sound of his voice, wincing as pain shuttles through my skull. The door snicks shut as the nurse leaves the room. "Sore," I rasp, struggling to focus my vision. As my eyesight clears, I whimper at the sight of him. He's slouched in a chair by my bed, with a blue blanket loosely covering his lower half. His face is covered in a medley of bruises, and his left eye is swollen and a horrible blue-black color. "Are you okay?"

"I'm fine." He lifts his shirt, showcasing the white bandage strapped firmly around his upper torso, concealing the bulk of a tattoo on his right side. "A little stiff and sore but no permanent damage."

"I thought I killed you too."

Compassion fills his eyes. He leans forward in slow motion, lacing his fingers in mine. Warmth spreads up my arm. "It was an accident, and you were only trying to help."

"You still got hurt. I hurt you."

He sighs. "I think you probably hurt yourself more."

I know what he's inferring, and he's right. "I tried to tell you this. That no good will come from associating with me, but you're so damn stubborn. I hope you understand now. I ruin everything I touch—everything and everyone I come into contact with. I hope you're getting ready to leave."

"Come on, Ange. You know me better than that. I'm not leaving you ever again."

"I almost killed you!" I hiss, ignoring the stabbing pain in my head. "Where's your sense of self-preservation?"

"Where's yours?" he snaps back. "Why are you still punishing yourself?"

I go into lockdown mode. I'm not getting into this with him. "I'm not talking about this with you. Not now. Not ever."

"Where you're going you won't have much choice."

Tendrils of ice creep up my spine. Alarm bells scream in my head. "What do you mean?" I whisper.

"The cops arrested you for aggravated assault, Ange."

The world goes deathly quiet. Bile floods my mouth. "I'm going to jail?" I hate how my lower lip wobbles when I speak.

He pulls his chair in closer, his mouth contorting in a painful grimace as he moves. He leans into me, threading his fingers fully through mine. "I managed to make a deal on your behalf. You'll do a ninety-day stint in rehab instead of jailtime."

"I don't want to go to rehab." I don't want to dry out. I won't be able to blank it all out if I'm sober.

"It's jail or rehab. Those are your only options."

Neither option is appealing, and both mean going cold turkey. "I can't be sober, Devin. Don't ask that of me, please. I just can't do it."

He brushes his fingers across my uninjured cheek. "You can't keep running, Ange. You've got to stop and face up to this."

Tears stream out of my eyes. "I'd rather die."

He closes his eyes briefly, and when he reopens them, raw anger coats his retinas. "Don't you fucking ever say that."

"It's the truth. I don't want to live."

He grips my head between his hands. "I want you to live. I need you to live. To not give up."

"Why are you doing this?"

His eyes glisten with determination. "You may have forgotten how to love yourself, but I haven't. I love you, Ange, and there isn't anything I won't do to save you, including this. You're going to rehab, and you're going to get better, and I'll be right there with you, every step of the way."

I start sobbing again, and my eyes sting. My chest constricts. My heart aches. "You shouldn't care. I'm not worthy of you."

"And I wasn't worthy of you once," he tells me softly. "But you never gave up on me. And I'm not giving up either." He presses his wrist to mine, aligning our tattoos. "Infinity, Ange. Our bond may be broken, our awesome-threesome connection may be gone, but we're still here, and while there is air in my lungs, I will continue fighting for the both of us."

∞ ∞ ∞

Rehab sucks. At least it does at first. After I was checked in, I had to undergo a full series of health checks and a thorough evaluation. Detoxing over a few weeks was determined to be the best approach rather than going cold turkey, because my body has been drip fed a continuous daily injection of alcohol for years. It's still hell on earth, as my body struggles to survive without its usual coping mechanism.

I think I spent the best part of the first week with my head over the toilet bowl, vomiting until there was nothing left in my stomach to expel. I've grown used to the constant headaches, although the pain is dulled through medication. Nighttime is difficult. Between prolonged bouts of insomnia, profuse sweating, and suffocating bouts of self-loathing, I don't get much rest. But, the anxiety is the worst, and it attacks most frequently at night when I'm lying in bed. My heart starts beating too fast, and an intense fluttery feeling builds in my chest, until it feels like there's a ticking time bomb behind my rib cage. Every night it happens, it's like I'm on the verge of a coronary. It's the scariest feeling of all.

The doctor gave me anti-anxiety medication, but I had to come off it because it didn't agree with me. It only enhanced the panic attacks and intensified my insomnia. Now I'm on plain old-fashioned sleeping pills, but even they don't work sometimes.

With nothing to do all day but think and talk about myself, I'm having huge trouble shutting off my brain. My mood swings ricochet all over the place, and I'm not pleasant company right now.

Devin drops by every day, but I refuse to see him. Initially, it's because I was so angry with him. Those early days were particularly difficult, dealing with sweats and shakes and the craving for a drink. Like I expected, everything I've worked so hard to push aside occupies front and center stage now I'm sober, and I can't avoid thinking about things I don't want to. I was furious with him for forcing me into this. For forcing me to confront my painful past. But I was only deflecting the anger.

It's really me I'm mad at.

And I'm still struggling to deal with that.

I've been the orchestrator of my own destruction, and I always thought I was smarter than that.

"How are you feeling today, Angelina?" Dr. Bennett asks as I settle on the couch in her office. Daily psychology sessions are an essential part of my treatment along with bi-weekly group therapy sessions. Drawing the myriad of conflicting emotions to the surface chips away at my soul; it's a slow, excruciating extraction process that prods and probes and tugs and ultimately leaves me shattered and vulnerable and exposed.

I still balk at her use of my real name, but she's insistent I need to reclaim my identity to effectively deal with the demons from my past. "Much the same."

"And what about our discussion yesterday. Have you given that any more thought?"

Horrific pain presses down on my chest. "It's all I've thought about in the intervening period."

"And have you reached any decisions?"

"It's too soon. I can't talk to him about it yet."

"Let's put it aside for a little while and work on your feelings of low self-worth."

The weeks come and go, and life settles into a strangely comforting pattern. While I'm still battling insomnia and anxiety, most of my other symptoms have faded. My mood shifts, stabilizing somewhat, and the unerring vacillations of the early days sharpen in focus. I don't have all the answers, far from it, but certain things are becoming clearer. My soul is being cleansed, a little bit at a time.

I keep to myself most of the time, but there are a couple of people I chat with on occasion. Some evenings, I watch TV with them in the communal room. My favorite pastime, though, is sitting outside on one of the wicker chairs, reading, drawing, and looking over the side of the mountain at the stunning views below.

I know now that Devin found this place. And I'm pretty sure he's paying for it too. It's in a secluded spot, on top of a mountain, occupying over one hundred acres. There are walking trails and bicycle paths as well as an outbuilding with a large pool. I take a swim every morning before breakfast, and I'm learning to appreciate the little things again. Like the cool mountain air on my cheeks and the smell of fresh cut grass or the delicious ache in my arms after a swim reminding me my body's still alive. The scent of fresh baked bread as I walk past the restaurant or the zingy citrusy smell in my room after the cleaning staff have departed. I've still a long way to go, and I'm nowhere near ready to deal with my guilt, but I'm making progress. For the first time in a very long time, I'm starting to want things from life again. Starting to feel a smidgeon of hope.

But I'm still no clearer to understanding where I go from here, and as the weeks become months and my date of departure nears, my anxiety rises. So much of what I feel is tied to Devin and Dr. Bennett has started pushing harder these last couple of weeks. She wants Devin to attend a session, but I can't even bring myself to risk a casual conversation with him, so how can I expose my bleeding heart to him?

He still shows up every day at the same time, without fail.

And every day I turn him away, without fail.

I don't know what I'd say to him. I'm embarrassed and ashamed, and the longer it goes on, the harder it gets. I know I'm being unfair, but it's all tied up with this crap in my head, and I'm so scared of opening all that up.

It's Friday, a day I've been dreading for months, and I'm heading back to the compound after a long, solitary walk when I come across Devin shouting angrily as he's being escorted off the premises. Benny, my favorite of all the security guards, is dragging him along the path. I start toward them with an extra ache in my heart.

I can't ignore him. Not today.

I slam to a halt a few feet away when I notice Devin is crying. And he's not putting up a fight anymore. He's letting Benny lead him away. Slowly, I walk toward them, fighting tears myself. There's something so emotive about seeing a man cry. Especially someone like Devin, who has never been the overly emotional type. A pang of guilt hits me. I've been so selfish. Turning him away because I couldn't face my feelings. Never once stopping to think about how hard this must be for him.

Especially today.

"Devin." I land in front of him, and the tormented look in his eyes almost kills me. He doesn't hide his tears from me, from Benny, and my heart aches in empathy. "I'm sorry," I whisper, wondering if they'll write that on my tombstone. They ought to. It seems to be the mantra I live my life by now.

"Why won't you see me?" he cries. "I can't fucking take it anymore, Ange. This is killing me. I need you today of all days."

"Can he come back inside?" I ask Benny, beseeching him with my eyes.

His nose wrinkles. "I don't think so, Ms. Ward. He made quite the scene. My instructions were to let him go home and cool off. He can come back tomorrow."

Devin is uncharacteristically quiet.

"Please, Benny. I need to speak to him now."

He rubs his chin, frowning a little. "How about you take a seat on that bench over there and talk for a few minutes? That's the best I can offer."

I lean in and kiss his cheek. "Thank you."

I take Devin's hand and lead him to the bench, gently pushing him down. He seems to have zoned out a little. I sit down beside him, clasping both his hands in mine. "I'm sorry for pushing you away, Devin. I've been scared to confront my feelings and to tell you some things I should've told you already, but it doesn't mean I haven't been thinking of you every day because I have."

He twists around, and the vulnerability and fear in his eyes takes me back to a younger Devin. One who was unsure of the world and his place in it. I haven't seen any evidence of that boy in grown-up Devin, and I hate that I'm the one to have sent him back there. "I've tried to be patient, and I understand what you're going through. I went through the same, and I didn't even tell you where I had gone, so I know it's really hypocritical of me, and I don't want to set back your recovery or pressure you in anyway but it's just today …"

"I know. I remember which day it is too."

"One part of me can't believe it's been five years since that day, because in some ways it feels like it was much shorter than that. Another part of me feels like I've lived a hundred years since Ayden died."

"I know. I feel the same. As I have done every year on the anniversary." I look down, almost choking on the burning lump in my throat.

"I've lived five years without both of you Ange, and I can't do it anymore. I miss you so much. I just want things to go back to the way they were." He leans his head on my shoulder, and I wrap my arms around his waist, savoring the feel of him against me.

"I want that too," I whisper, my heart thumping wildly in my chest with the admission.

He lifts his head, a spark of hope glimmering in his eyes. "You do?"

"I think so. I mean, I'm getting there, but it's scary. I haven't been that person, lived that life for a long time, and I've hurt so many people…"

"The people who love you will forgive you. I already have."

Tears soak my eyes. "I always seem to be crying around you."

He presses a soft kiss to my head. "One of these days they will be happy tears."

"Can I ask you something?"

"You know you can."

"Would you attend a therapy session with me? My counselor has been suggesting it for weeks, and I didn't feel up to it. Until now." Ignoring the dreaded fluttering in my chest, I take a deep breath, padding my lungs with bravery as I push the words out of my mouth. "I want to move forward in my life, and I can't do that until we get everything out on the table."

He leans in swiftly, planting a kiss on my cheek. "I'm there. Just tell me when and where, and I'll be there."

CHAPTER FORTY-ONE

Devin

I park my car, climb out, and start walking toward the facility. Tension coils in my gut as I head for my therapy session with Ange. A lot hinges on today. I think we both understand that. I know she has stuff to get off her chest, but so do I. I want a fresh start, a clean slate, and neither of us can do that without exorcising our demons.

She looked so good yesterday. With the exception of the dark circles under her eyes, she looks better than I've seen her looking in months. Her eyes are clear, her skin luminous, and she's starting to fill her curves again. I know they put considerable emphasis on overall health here, and following a nutritional diet and exercise plan is part of the program. Dr. Bennett is also a leading expert in the field of cognitive behavioral therapy, which is the main reason I chose this facility for Ange.

I tap my foot nervously off the floor as I wait outside Dr. Bennett's office. Then the door is opened, and I'm welcomed by the woman herself. After we've made introductions, she ushers me inside. Dressed in a pretty green dress, Ange is sitting on the comfortable soft gray couch. The red dye has almost fully disappeared from her hair, and she's nearly back to her normal hair color. She looks so much like the Ange I remember, and it's hard to avoid the urge to sweep her into my arms.

"Hi." I smile, dropping onto the couch alongside her, conscious to leave a gap between us. I don't want her to feel overwhelmed, and I'm just ecstatic to be in her presence after months of being shut out.

She tucks her hair behind her ears, answering me with a shy smile. "Hi yourself."

Dr. Bennett settles into a seat across from us with a pad and pen in hand. "Thank you for joining us today, Mr. Morgan. Before we commence, I'd just like to mention a few things. Anything that is discussed in this room shall remain confidential between all parties. This is a neutral environment with no judgment. You can speak freely, although, I may intervene should Angelina become distressed as my patient's welfare is my primary concern. Does that sound reasonable?"

"Absolutely, and I want to help. I'm here for Ange."

She smiles, before turning her focus on Ange. "How would you like to start? What would you like to say to Devin today?"

She knots her hands in her lap, biting on her lip, and little lines furrow her brow. Her entire body is shaking. Reaching out, I lace my fingers in hers. "Don't be afraid. I meant what I said. I'm here for you, no matter what."

She nods, gulping before she speaks, and then the words gush forth. "I'm sorry I ran off in the way I did, and I'm sorry I hurt you. I know that was a horrible thing to do to you and Mom, but I convinced myself you were all better off without me, but, really, I ran away to punish myself. I don't believe I deserve a future, not when I've taken Ayden's from him."

I open my mouth to protest, but she holds up a hand. "I need to get this out, Devin. All this stuff has been fermenting in my head for years, and I need to release it. Consequences be damned." She stops to draw a shaky breath. "I know you'll want to respond, but let me say my piece first."

I lift our conjoined hands to my mouth, planting a kiss on the back of her hand. "I understand. I won't interrupt."

She gulps nervously again, and I can tell how difficult this is for her. "I feel guilty every time I think of that day—the day Ayden died—because I can still recall how blissfully happy I was that morning after spending the night with you. How euphoric I felt because we were finally in the same place. That we were going to be together, as a couple, in the way I'd always dreamed of. You made me so unbelievably happy that day." She stares at me, and the truth radiates in her eyes. A second later, the dreamy look fades. "I also remember the phone call and the expression on your face as you heard the news." Her chest heaves up and down. "I don't think I'll ever forget that look or the deep sense of foreboding that swept over me or the incredible, indescribable pain I felt when Mom told me he was dead." She breaks down then, sobbing, and I pull her to me, my own tears mingling with hers. We hold one another, quietly crying for several minutes. "I don't know if I can ever forgive myself for that," she says, sniffling. "I cheated on him, and I broke his heart, and he went home and killed himself. How can I ever defend myself?"

It's so hard not to respond, but I promised I wouldn't interrupt.

She wipes her tears away. "Everything good in my life seemed tarnished. And it wasn't getting any better. I was in agony, and I hated myself so much. If I hadn't been so weak, if I'd just stuck to my guns and stayed away from you until he returned, and I'd talked to him, then none of this would've happened. But there was no point dwelling on that. I couldn't change the past, but I could alter the future."

She grips my hands tighter. "I didn't believe I deserved a chance at happiness. Why should I get a do-over when Ayden doesn't get one? I believed if I stayed my guilt and my anger would have doomed our relationship anyway, and I knew I couldn't handle it if I hurt you too. So, it seemed easier to take myself out of the equation, so I couldn't hurt you or my mom or Mariah anymore. It seemed like a winning plan at the time."

She half-laughs, bitterness slicing through her tone. She shakes her head sadly. "I knew how much it would hurt me to leave you all behind, and I wanted to hurt. I wanted to feel physical pain. But it was more than just that. Ayden and you always protected me. I felt it was my turn, so I left to protect *you*."

Dr. Bennett interjects, looking at Ange. "I'd like to ask Devin how he feels about that."

She nods, and I roll my shoulders, trying to loosen the tension in my muscles as I peer into her beautiful blue eyes. "I hate hearing you blame yourself for someone else's actions," I start off saying. "Even though a part of me can relate, because I felt horrific guilt for years too. I continued to see my therapist, and he helped me work through my feelings. The reality is Ayden is the only one responsible. We don't know why he took his life, and we never will, but he's the one who made that decision. Not you. Not me. I'm not saying that I don't understand why you felt like that, but I don't understand how you didn't blame me? We slept together. There was a pair of us in it, but you only blamed yourself."

"Because you weren't his girlfriend. I was."

I moisten my parched lips with my tongue. "I seem to remember that being a bit unclear. Besides, I was his best friend, and I shouldn't have slept with his girl, but there were things you didn't know back then. Things he knew, and I've often wondered if I'd told you would you have felt differently?"

"What things?" She looks confused. "I knew you both hid stuff from me out of some misguided sense of protection, but I don't see what that's got to do with this?"

I draw a deep breath. "I need to tell you some stuff, and I need to start at the beginning for it to make sense, but I need to know you're up for this." I glance over at Dr. Bennett, and she deflects to Ange.

Slowly, she nods. "That's why we're here today. I want to hear it."

I exhale deeply before speaking. "The man who raised me, who I thought at the time was my father, used to beat me." Her beautiful face pales. "It only started after my mother left. Before that, he used to beat her."

She gasps, but I keep going. "As you know, I found out years later that his brother, Jim, was actually my father. It seems apparent the asshole discovered the truth around the time my mother left. I don't understand why he didn't tell Jim that Lucas and I were his kids. If he hated us that much, he could've offloaded us pretty easily. Jim thinks he kept quiet to spite him."

Before I wander off topic, I redirect the conversation where it needs to go. "Anyway, those bruises you saw on me weren't always from the boxing ring. Most were from his fists. The first few years, he took the brunt of his anger out on Cam and me. As Cam got older, he protected me, stood up to the ol' man, and the beatings died down, until Cam left. When he joined the marines, he worried about what would become of us, but I assured him we'd be fine. I didn't want him giving up his dream for us. But as soon as Cam was out of the picture, the beatings resumed. I was old enough, and skilled enough, to fight back, and I did, but it didn't stop him from going after me when he was wasted. We fought viciously. Beat the crap out of each other time and time again. I started drinking heavily in an effort to block it out, and then I'd feel so guilty, because I worried I was exposing

Lucas, and I'd done everything up to that point to shield Luc from him."
I stare into her eyes. "Ayden knew. As did your mom."

"What?" Shock is etched across her gorgeous face.

"It was your mom who called social services those couple of times.
She was worried about us. But Cam and I went to her and begged her
not to do it again. We were terrified they were going to split us up, put
us into foster care. I didn't want to be separated from my brothers. That's
when it was agreed that we'd eat dinner at your house, and your mom
made it clear we could sleep over any time we needed to. She couldn't
promise she wouldn't involve the authorities if she saw evidence of further
abuse, so, after Cam left, when the beatings restarted in earnest, I had no
choice but to deliberately put some distance between me and you. If you
knew, you'd tell her, and I couldn't take that risk. Even though I know
you would've kept the secret if I'd asked you to, I didn't want to put that
kind of pressure on you."

"Oh my God." She clamps a hand over her mouth. "I had my suspicions during our final year of high school, but I'd no idea it'd been going
on for years."

"I didn't want you to know for a couple reasons. I was ashamed, and
I didn't want you thinking less of me. It made me feel like less of a man."
It sounds so stupid now, but it's how I felt at the time. "But mostly it was
because I was protecting you from him."

She goes deathly quiet. "In what way?" she whispers a minute later.

"Cam and I always believed Dad had a hand in Mom's disappear-
ance. That was proven three years ago. You probably don't know this, but
he died the year after you left. He was stabbed to death in a bar brawl
in Cincinnati. Lucas was living with Jim, I was in college, and Cam was
abroad with the marines, so the house lay idle. We eventually sold it, and
when the new owners were renovating, my mom's remains were found
in the backyard."

"Oh my God, Devin. I'm so sorry."

I nod over the football-sized lump in my throat, the usual torment
ambushing me. The thought that my mom was buried in our backyard
the whole time kills me. Especially when I think of all the nights I cursed
her for leaving. Wished ill of her. Not knowing she was dead all along
and right under my nose. I don't think I'll ever overcome the clusterfuck

of emotions surrounding her death and my upbringing. But now isn't the time to get into it.

This is about Ange. Not me.

"The point is, we always knew he had issues with women. We suspected foul play in relation to Mom, and then he tried to attack Cam's girlfriend, Lori, one night when he was drunk. Cam protected her and convinced her not to press charges, but we knew then we were living with a monster. I didn't want him knowing I had feelings for you, so I tried to stay away, and I slept around, in part, to throw him off the scent."

A familiar wounded look sweeps across her features, reminding me how much I hurt her back then.

"As graduation neared, my resolve was weakening. You were always beautiful, Ange, but my God, that year you really blossomed." I cup her cheek. "And there were cracks in your veneer too. I couldn't be sure, but I thought you shared my feelings, and I didn't know how much longer I could stay away from you."

She places her hand over mine, her chest visibly shuddering.

"I confided in Ayden the summer before senior class. I told him about my father and about my feelings for you. Ayden wanted me to report him, but he backed down when I told him I couldn't put Lucas into foster care. He understood, but he made me promise to stay away from you, and I agreed, because I knew it was the only way to keep you properly safe, but I kept relapsing. I struggled to stay away from you."

"That's why you were both fighting all the time?" she asks.

"Yeah. He was furious every time I got close with you. I believed at first that it was because he wanted to protect you, but, later on, I felt like he pushed me away on purpose. He wanted that separation between us so he could have you himself."

She shakes her head. "Ayden wouldn't have done that. That's not who he was."

"He wasn't a saint, Ange. He had flaws like the rest of us. He just didn't wear his as visibly as I did."

CHAPTER FORTY-TWO
Angelina

"You can't say that about him. You can't cast doubt on his character retro-spectively," I protest, feeling so many conflicting emotions.

"Why? Because he's dead?" I suck in a shocked gasp at the venom in Devin's tone. He removes his hand from my face, pinning me with a stern look. "His death and your leaving changed me. My outlook on life is differ-ent now. I don't care about petty bullshit, and I won't hold back on saying things that need to be said. Life's too fucking short. I learned that lesson early. I've held back up to this point, but, fuck it, this shit needs to be said."

"I don't see how you bad-mouthing Ayden after he's dead achieves anything," I shout. "It's not going to help either one of us move forward."

He drags a hand through his hair. "How can you say that when you're still sitting here wallowing in guilt for something he did? You've thrown away your whole Goddamned life because of his selfishness, and you expect me to sit here and keep my mouth shut?"

He gets up, pacing the room, shaking his head, and muttering under his breath. Then he's on his knees in front of me, taking my hands in his. "He knew, Ange. Ayden knew I loved you and that you loved me. He knew it when we were kids, and he sure as fuck knew it when he took you as his girlfriend. Why do you think he didn't want to speak to me on the phone those times he called during college?" He arches a brow.

"Because he was pissed."

He nods. "He suspected you and I were together or, at the very least, he anticipated it. Him catching us in bed that day wasn't that big of a shock. Think back, Ange. Think to his reaction."

"How can you say that?" I cry out, snatching my hands back and leaning away from him. "He was upset. He said he wanted us to leave him alone."

"He also said he'd come home to tell you the truth. Haven't you ever thought about what he meant?"

"I … in all honesty, no. I haven't dwelled on that."

He sits back up on the couch, sighing deeply, and his tone is resigned when he speaks. "No, of course, you wouldn't have thought of that. You were already convinced of your guilt. You'd already meted out our punishment."

Bile swells in my throat as his words offer a hint at his true emotions. He's far angrier at me than he's letting on. Not that I begrudge him or resent him his anger. He is perfectly entitled to it. I took matters into my own hands five years ago, and I cut him out of the decision-making process. I know I'd be angry if our positions were reversed. Before I can say anything, he turns anguished eyes on me.

"Look, I didn't come here to argue with you. That's not going to help either one of us. But I need you to at least try to look at it differently; otherwise, you'll never be able to move past it."

"I don't know why we're analyzing what he said that last day, because we're never going to know what he meant. He took it to his grave."

He throws his hands in the air, frustrated again. "That's my exact point!" he yells, anger rearing its head again. He draws several quick breaths, forcing himself to regain control. His voice is quieter when he resumes speaking. "You're right—we don't know what he was thinking. You're assuming he was upset about us and that's why he did it. But I've spent years thinking about this as objectively as I can, and it just doesn't add up. You said yourself once you became a couple he didn't seem into it, and I know he knew we were in love, so why exactly would him catching us in the act propel him to kill himself? I think there was more we didn't know."

I'm quiet as I ponder his words. "Like him giving up football and joining the marines," I say, voicing concerns I've had over the years.

He nods, and a hopeful light flickers at the back of his eyes. "I think we have to face facts, Ange. He didn't confide in us about that, and I think there was other stuff he was hiding too. We didn't really know him at the end, so how can we say we knew what was in his mind in that moment when he decided to take his own life?"

There's a pregnant pause.

"How can we say he did that because of us?" His voice sounds choked as he takes my hands again. "We can't say that, because we just don't know. And you can't continue to blame yourself for something that may have had very little or even nothing to do with you. With us."

If ever there was a profound moment of clarity in my life, this is it. Perhaps, if I hadn't fled all those years ago, I would have reached this eureka moment a lot sooner. "It might not have been my fault?"

He presses his forehead to mine. "It wasn't your fault, babe. You're not responsible."

Dr. Bennett ended the session there. She felt we'd covered enough ground for one day. Devin agrees to come back tomorrow to continue the session. I walk him out to his car, and we're both initially quiet, locked in our own thoughts. He toys with the keys in his hands as we walk side by side to the parking lot. "Are you okay after that?"

I pause briefly before responding. "Yeah, I think I'm more than okay." I offer him a tentative smile. "That wasn't as scary as I was expecting it to be." Then again, I still haven't divulged everything.

He stops, pulling me into his arms unexpectedly. I like it. I like it a lot. "I'm proud of you, you know."

I rear back, shooting him an incredulous look. "I don't see how. I haven't done anything even remotely worthy of your praise or your pride."

His answering smile almost blinds me. "Sure you have. You're moving forward. I know from personal experience that it's not easy to carve your heart and soul open and face your ugliest truths and your worst fears, but you're doing it, and I'm proud of you for that."

"Thank you," I whisper, still not entirely sure I'm deserving of the compliment.

He holds me firmly at the waist as his eyes probe mine. Fear and uncertainty stare back at me. "Do you think you're up to hearing one more confession?"

I frown a little. "There's more?"

He nods. "I didn't want to tell you this in there. I've never admitted this to another living soul and I wasn't about to do it in front of her, but I need to get this off my chest before I lose my nerve."

I shuck out of his embrace and take his hand. "Come on. We can talk on our bench."

"Our bench?" he teases with a smile as we stroll across the lawn.

"Yeah. I've claimed it for us. It's our new place."

His face takes on a faraway expression. "I rebuilt the treehouse," he blurts, startling me.

I slam to a halt. "Get out. You did not?!"

He grins, tugging me forward. "I did. When I'd go home, all the memories were so hard to deal with, but when I walked in the woods, I kept being drawn to that spot. Those were good times, Ange. Back then before everything turned to shit."

I squeeze his hand. "They were the best times, and those memories have carried me through my darkest days. At times, they were the only things tethering me to this life." He opens his mouth to speak, but I shut him down. I don't want to think about those times now. Not when today feels like a new beginning. "Tell me about this new treehouse."

He eyes me quietly for a minute, and then he smiles. And it's like the sun emerging from behind the clouds, casting glorious warmth and light over everything it touches. That's how I feel in this moment, bathed under the glow from Devin's smile. "The two trees were still there, and withered planks of wood from our treehouse littered the debris on the ground. That's when the idea came to me, and I spent a couple of months, coming down on weekends when I had spare time, building it. Danny helped a bit. We built it completely from scratch, and it's an awesome job, if I do say so myself." He puffs his chest out, and I laugh.

An awestruck expression flickers across his beautiful face. "You've no idea how amazing it is to hear you laugh." We stop in front of the bench, looking at one another. He rests his hands on my lower back, pulling me in close to his body. "I was fearful I'd never hear that sound again," he whispers.

"I didn't think I could," I whisper back, blown away by how far I've come in recent months. For years, I believed I was a lost cause, but Devin's presence in my life again has reawakened my interest in living. Given me renewed hope. With his support, I think I can find the strength to finally move on. Tears stab my eyes as a surge of emotion hits me square in the chest. "I haven't thanked you for everything you've done for me. I couldn't do this without you."

"You don't need to. Getting you back is all the thanks I need."

Butterflies swarm my chest, and my mouth feels dry, but I open up, speaking my mind. "What is it you want from me, Dev?"

He presses his lips to my forehead. "You. I just want you back in my life."

"I can't give you any big commitments. I've still a lot to work through, and I can't even think about that until my head is firmly screwed back on."

"That's totally fine by me. I'm here in whatever capacity you need me. Just don't cut me out. I can't lose you a third time. I couldn't survive it again."

I push his head back, palming his cheek. "I promise I won't leave. I can't promise that I won't get melancholy or low or retreat into a shell or become untalkative because that's how I've coped these last few years, but I'm here to stay. And I'm truly happy you're back in my life, Devin. I really missed you, and I'm so grateful you didn't give up on me even if I'd given up on myself." My voice quakes, and tears stream down my face.

He brushes his lips against mine, soft and fleeting, but my skin turns tingly from the brief touch, reminding me our connection is still very much alive. "I would go to the ends of the earth for you, Ange. There is no one more important to me than you."

With his arm wrapped around me, he pulls me down onto the bench. We lean into one another, like magnets who can't resist the natural pull. "There's one more thing I need to explain. This isn't going to help my cause, but you need to know everything."

I nuzzle his shoulder. "There is nothing you can say that will turn me away. I promise."

His chest swells, and his voice is terse when he speaks. "You remember the night Becky got attacked?"

I nod, and a sour taste pervades my mouth. "The night your father attacked her."

He nods, his jaw rigid with strain. He doesn't avert his eyes as he stares at me and admits, "I left her in the house with him knowing he was going to attack her."

I draw upon every ounce of acting ability to keep the shocked horror from my face. "What? Why would you do that?"

"I'd done everything to hide my feelings for you, including pushing you into your house that night before he could read anything on my face. I told Becky to go home, and I stormed inside, dragging my father with me. He threw a punch, and I fell on my ass in the hallway. The front door was still open, and I knew Becky was watching." He smooths a hand over his chest, and I snake my arm around his waist, squeezing tight.

"I had a lock on the outside of my bedroom door because I didn't want that asshole in my room. Didn't want him seeing all the drawings of you on my walls. He never seemed to care, but that night, he broke into my room. He'd seen it all. He knew. As I lay on my ass on the floor, he kicked me repeatedly while taunting me about you, telling me he knew you were alone in your house and he was going to pay you a little visit. I went crazy, jumped up and hit him, and we really got into it, lancing blows at one another. Then Becky appeared, screaming, trying to pull him off me. I saw it. The look in his eye when he swung his gaze around on her. He asked who she was, and she told him she was my girlfriend, little realizing what she was doing. I saw the gleam in his eyes, the need to exert control, to inflict pain."

He looks away, pulling out of my embrace, and resting his head in his hands. I smooth a hand up and down his spine. I don't speak, letting him do this his way, in his own time.

After a bit, he lifts his head up, torment brewing in his eyes. "I told him to take her. I said I wouldn't tell if he agreed to leave you alone."

I can't keep the shocked look off my face this time. I open my mouth to speak but close it again. I have no words.

"He nodded his agreement, and I walked out of the house, ignoring Becky's cries and pleas as he dragged her inside."

His breath flies out in anguished spurts, while I clamp a hand over my mouth in horror. "I drove around to the back road to keep watch on your house. I wanted to make sure he didn't renege on his deal. I saw him haul Becky out an hour later. She was flung over his shoulder, limp, and beaten to a pulp. He had two bags with him and I knew he was leaving." A muscle clenches in his jaw. "I should've followed him. Gotten help for Becky, but I didn't. I stayed outside your house until I was confident he wasn't coming back. Then I went to the party and got wasted. Crashed there so I had an alibi."

He disturbs the earth underfoot with the toe of his boot. "Now you know how truly black my soul is." He gives me a wry smile. "And you think you're not worthy of me." He shakes his head.

I'm in complete shock, and I need time to process, but I can't let that statement go unanswered. "Maybe that's why we found each other again. We've both done things we're not proud of. Things we would do differently if we could. What's important is that we feel remorse, and I can tell you do."

"I am remorseful," he says, twisting around a little. "But I wouldn't do it differently. Protecting you will always come first."

"I'm not going to criticize you for that." What he did was wrong. So very wrong, even if he believed he was doing it for the right reason, but it's over and done with now, and he'll be dealing with the guilt for the rest of his life. Besides, he did it to protect me, and I'm not going to start yelling at him for that. Who knows what might've happened if he hadn't intervened. The thought makes me uncomfortable—that Becky suffered in my place—but I'm not going to pretend I'm ungrateful either. "And you can't tell me not to blame myself for Ayden's actions if you're going to blame yourself for that night. You didn't beat Becky up; that monster did."

His eyes penetrate mine, and I see the conflict there. He wants to argue against my rationale, but he knows it's an argument he can't win. Instead, he says, "I thought you'd run screaming for sure after hearing this."

"I see you, Devin Morgan. I've always seen you. I promised I'm going nowhere this time, and I meant it."

"Thank God." He hugs me to him, and we don't talk for several minutes. My mind goes into overdrive, thinking of the secret I'm still keeping hidden.

"I went to see her a couple years ago," he admits. "She's married now with two kids. She went crazy when I appeared at the door. Threw a few things at me. Said if I darkened her door again she'd have me arrested. I never even got one word out."

"That sounds like Becky, although I can't fault her in any way for reacting like that."

"Me either. And it was selfish of me to go there. I wanted to apologize and thank her for keeping it secret—the fact she had spoke volumes. He clearly terrorized her into keeping her mouth shut, and that only added to my grief. But I shouldn't have gone near her, it wasn't fair, and I was only thinking of appeasing my guilty conscience. I wasn't thinking how my presence would affect her."

I nod distractedly, the secret ready to burst free. "Dev?" I ask quietly.

He detects something in my tone. "Yeah?" His voice is cautious.

"I have something I need to tell you too. Do you think you can handle more of the heavy because this is going to be the heaviest of all?" My heart is jackhammering in my chest, about to take flight, and I think I'm going to be sick, but I need to purge the secret. He needs to finally know.

His face pales, and the intensity in his eyes sucks all the oxygen from the surrounding air. "Why do I get the sense this is going to destroy me?"

My hands shake. "Because it most likely will."

He stares at me, as if he can delve into my mind and extract the words before I speak them. Our chests rise and sync in tandem, and you could cut the tension with a knife. "I want to hear it, because we can't move forward until all the secrets are laid bare. Like you said to me, nothing you tell me at this point will scare me away." He intertwines our hands. "We're in this together. We always have been."

A tear trickles out of my eye, and my voice is trembling as I rip the Band-Aid off. "I discovered I was pregnant four months after I left."

Shock splays across his handsome face, and his skin looks leeched of all color. His eyes pop wide, and his gaze slams into me. "What?" he chokes out.

"I was pregnant with your child. He died," I whisper. Caustic pain rips through my chest, and the sobs start in earnest. Devin is shell-shocked, frozen stiff, and staring off into space. "I stopped drinking straightaway, the minute I found out, I swear, but it was too late." Tears cascade down my face, and the shock on his face mixes with horror and confusion. "Our son was stillborn at birth," I explain, openly sobbing now. "He looked so perfect, so beautiful, but I killed him. I killed him too, and as long as I live, I'll never forgive myself for that."

CHAPTER FORTY-THREE

Devin

I can't move. I'm frozen in horror, sitting there in absolute shock as her words filter in and out of my ears. A pang of sorrow and grief consumes me. I'm feeling all manner of things as Ange softly sobs beside me. I want to pull her into my side, to crush my arms around her and ease her pain, but I can't.

Today has been exhaustive, and I'm drained. I worked hard to rein in my anger during the session, but I'm not strong enough to keep a leash on it now. My God. No wonder she was in such a bad place when I found her. She's spent the best part of the last five years believing she killed two people she loved. While I'm upset she had to go through that alone, she had no right to cut me out.

It was my baby too.

"Did the doctors say it was connected to your drinking?" I inquire, not bothering to soften my gruff tone.

She shakes her head, sniffling. "They said he had a congenital heart defect, but I've always believed they said that to relieve my guilt. It's like I'm cursed, or maybe that was God's way of punishing me for Ayden."

"Why didn't you call me? I had a right to know."

Wrapping her arms around her waist, she hugs herself, rocking gently back and forth on the bench. It hurts to see her like this, but I can't comfort her. My own pain won't allow it. A mounting sense of futility is growing inside me. "I picked up the phone to call you so many times," she tearfully admits. "When I first discovered I was pregnant, my initial thought was to hop on a plane and jump into your arms, but I couldn't make myself do it." I close my eyes as she speaks, struggling to get a grip on my emotions. "I cried after every prenatal appointment. It always felt so wrong that you weren't there with me. I promised myself I'd tell you after he was born. That I wouldn't keep your child from you."

She breaks down, crying so pitifully it almost tears me apart, but I still don't reach out to touch her. "When he was stillborn, I cried nonstop for a whole day. I wouldn't let the doctors take him. I kept him close to my chest, and I hugged him all night until I had to let him go. I couldn't call you then. I couldn't tell you I'd failed you again. When they lowered his little coffin into the ground, I wanted to throw myself in after him. Another part of me died with Devin Junior that day."

I don't realize I'm crying until I turn to look at her, and I can barely see her through my tears. "You named him after me?" I croak.

She nods. "I had to name him so they could issue a birth and death certificate. Of course, I was going to name him after his daddy."

Something shatters inside me. I jump up on shaky legs. My entire body is suffused with stress. "I can't believe you shut me out of that. You had no right!" I yell, drawing fearful looks from a couple of girls passing by. "How could you not tell me? How could you think it would be okay to deny me all that? I should've been there with you! I should've been by your side for every appointment and holding your hand as you gave birth. I deserved to hold him too! I never even got that chance. You stole that from me too!"

Pounding footsteps approach. Ange is sitting rigidly still, silent tears coursing down her cheeks.

"You fucking left me! You tricked me and then you left. You didn't just punish yourself that day. You fucking punished me too, and I've been in this hell with you all these years. I may look more together on the outside, but you aren't the only one who's been hurting. And now this!" I fling my hands in the air, as Dr. Bennett cautiously approaches with two security guards. "I can't believe you kept your pregnancy from me. I can't believe you went through it alone." The level of despair and heartache I feel is incomparable to any other time in my life, and that's saying a lot. The security guard takes my arm. "I need to escort you off the premises, Mr. Morgan."

I shuck his arm away. "No need. I'm going."

"Devin, please. I'm sorry!" Ange calls after me, but I don't stop, don't look back, sprinting toward my car. I get in, thrust the stick into gear, and floor it out of there, my heart torn asunder as I make the trip home.

I stare at the bottle of JD on my kitchen counter for a solid half hour, battling an internal enemy. The devil on my shoulder urges me to take a sip. *Just one sip. One sip won't hurt. One sip doesn't count. You deserve it. She lied to you again.*

I drop to the floor, pulling my knees into my chest, and sob like I haven't sobbed since I was a little kid. When my tears dry, I call Michael. He's a retired cop and an alcoholic like me. He's been my sponsor since I started going to AA meetings, and I need him to help talk me off the ledge.

After our call, I empty the whiskey down the sink and toss the bottle in the trash. I need answers, and I won't find them at the bottom of a bottle. I pick up my cell, punching in the familiar number. Nate answers on the first ring. "I need your help," I tell him, and I start explaining.

∞ ∞ ∞

A week goes by, and the craving for booze hasn't dissipated, but I have managed to maintain control.

I didn't attend the second session with Ange, and Dr. Bennett has been blowing up my phone. I'm still so fucking angry with her, but my heart hurts for her too—for enduring that all alone, for believing she had to suffer on her own.

I can't wrap my head around the fact I was a father, and I didn't even know it. I wonder what he looked like. Whether he had my eyes or her cute dimple. I'll never know. I can't ever get that time back, and I honestly don't know if I can look at her the same for depriving me of the opportunity to hold my own child.

We're such different people now, and I wonder if too much has happened for us to ever be happy.

Anger at Ayden has resurrected too, and I can't help blaming him. His suicide set all this in motion. If he was here, I'd boot his selfish ass all over town. But he's not, and I need to make some decisions. And fast. Ange is due to be released tomorrow, and I'm supposed to be picking her up.

I'm still undecided the next day, pacing the floor restlessly, warring with myself. "Fuck it!" I grab my keys, glancing at the clock and racing out of my rented apartment. I'm thirty minutes late pulling up to the front entrance, and Ange is just about to set foot in a taxi. I call out to her, and she whips her chin up. Leaving the engine running, I run to the taxi, thrusting a fifty at the driver. "Thanks, but I've got it."

Her expression is impressively calm as she walks to the trunk and removes her case. I take it from her without a word, lingering as she wraps Dr. Bennett in a big hug. The doctor shoots me a cautionary look, and I get it. I'm supposed to be supporting her recovery, not making things worse, but I can't shut my feelings off. This is a bolt out of the blue, and it's totally shattered me.

We don't speak as we drive to her old apartment. I follow her up the stairs and into her place. "Where's Scott?" she asks, running her fingers along the thick layer of dust on top of the table.

"In prison," I confirm. She stares at me, willing me to elaborate. "He assaulted a police officer, and he was physically abusive to you in public. Nate wasn't the only witness. He's gone away for twenty months."

She purses her lips. "I guess I should feel something hearing that, but I don't feel anything." Leaning back against the table, she folds her arms, scrutinizing my face. "It's okay if you hate me. I understand why, and you don't need to hang around. I've made my decision. I'm going home to see Mom, and I'm going to get my life back on track. You've done more than enough, and I won't ask you for anything else. I can take it from here."

"I don't hate you. Maybe it'd be easier if I did." I press my knuckles against my brow. "But I'm still pissed at you, and I'm still processing."

She nods before walking off. I hear her rummaging around in her room, and then she returns with a battered, faded blue box. She drops down on the couch, patting the space beside her. "Sit with me?"

My heart is thrashing around in my chest as I walk to her side and cautiously sit down.

"Before I show you this, I need you to understand something. I was wrong to keep my pregnancy from you, to keep our son from you. I wish I had made better decisions, but I was in agony, Devin, and not thinking straight. I thought the pain I felt after Ayden's death was the worst pain I'd ever felt, but I was wrong, because it paled in comparison to the pain and grief I felt after the loss of our son. After DJ died, I pretty much gave up on life. Not a single day passed where I wasn't consumed with thoughts of him. His beautiful little face was the first image I saw in my mind's eye when I woke every morning and the last vision before I fell asleep at night. It got to the point where I feared going to bed and I hated waking up because the pain was too much. I couldn't bear it." She runs a hand over her chest. "His loss accelerated my downward spiral, and I sunk into a deep depression. I started drinking again, and drink was the only thing getting me through each day."

An errant sob flies out of her mouth, and she looks away, her eyes burning with years of self-loathing and pain. Tentatively, I place my arm around her shoulder, and when she looks up at me with so much vulnerability and pain, more of my anger fades, helping to put things in a different perspective. "I'm sorry for the way I reacted last week. It was such a shock, and it was hurt speaking. I hate that you went through all that alone, that I wasn't there to support you with it, and I know you would never consciously exclude me. And it's not like I haven't made plenty of mistakes. That I don't have my own dark secrets. I had no right to judge you as I did, and I'm sorry."

She smiles, but it's sad. "It's okay. I totally get it, and I don't blame you for your reaction." She leans in, kissing my cheek, and I hold her to me for a couple seconds. She pulls back. "I have something to show you." Drawing a deep breath, she opens the box carefully, and my heart starts pounding anxiously. She removes a small bunch of photos and hands them to me. Tears are streaming down her face. "I got the nurse to take some pictures because I didn't want to forget what he looked like."

With shaking hands, I look through the pictures. "My God," I exclaim, running my finger over the image. He looks so small, but so perfectly formed. His dark hair is thick. I don't know much about newborns but I didn't think they had that much hair. His eyes are closed, and he's resting in Ange's arms, as if he's asleep. The devastation on her face is plain to see, and walls come crashing down around me.

"What color were his eyes?" I whisper, flipping to another photo. This one is of my son on his own, swaddled in a pristine white blanket, tucked neatly in a crib.

"Green," she rasps, snuffling. "He was all you, Devin. I didn't recognize a bit of myself in him."

Intense pain explodes in my stomach, and I can scarcely speak. "Where is he buried?"

"In the local cemetery. I can take you, if you want."

I find myself nodding, and we leave her apartment, making the short fifteen-minute journey to his graveside in silence. When I see his name in big letters on the tombstone, I fall apart, collapsing on my knees in front of my son's grave as shuddering sobs wrack my entire body. Ange is crying beside me too, and I reach for her, pulling her into my arms. We cling to one another, on our knees, crying rivers.

I don't know how long we stay there, but it's getting dark by the time we've both stopped crying. I stand up, pulling her with me. I brush the dirt off the knees of her jeans. "It's not your fault he's dead, and I don't want you to blame yourself. I spoke to the doctors this week."

"You did?"

I nod. "Nate didn't find anything on our son when he conducted his initial investigation, but I'm guessing you know that." She nods her head curtly. "You paid someone to bury the records, didn't you?" Again, another terse nod. "It's okay. I know you did that to protect me."

"I did," she says in a meek voice. "I knew there was a chance you'd find me one day, and I didn't want you finding out about DJ from anyone but me."

"I appreciate that. I'd hate to have found out in such a brutal way." Air whooshes out of my mouth, and my chest feels tight. "Anyway, I've done a lot of soul searching this past week, and Nate dug deeper, and we found the hospital records, so I paid a visit."

She looks petrified, and I pull her into my arms, pressing a kiss to the top of her head. "It's okay, baby. They said no one knows definitively why these things happen, and that it wasn't anything you did. He did have a heart defect, but it was as a result of a chromosomal abnormality that could not have been prevented, and that's what killed him. You are *not* responsible for his death."

She breaks down again in my arms, and I hold her close, tears sting-ing the backs of my eyes. No one should have to endure the suffering she's endured.

When her crying subsides, I take her hand and lead her back to the car. Once she's settled in, I buckle myself into my seat, but I don't start the engine. I look over at her, at the woman I've loved virtually my whole life, and I'm so tired of all the hurting and the pain. I hate the mistakes she's made, but I know she was trying to do what she thought was right, and I also know she wasn't in the right frame of mind to make good decisions. I've known her since she was a little kid, and she's inherently good. She's just lost her way. We both have, but I want to make it right. There will be time to work through all our issues, and I believe we can do it, because I love her enough to find a way to get through it. I take her hands in mine. "I forgive you. For everything."

She eyes me warily. "How can you?"

"Because I love you."

"It's not that simple."

"No, it's not. Nothing about us has ever been simple, but I love you enough to keep fighting, if you can promise to do the same."

"This here," she whispers, fighting tears again. "This is what I mean. I'm not worthy of you."

"You've made some shitty decisions, Ange, but you're still you. You're still the same sweet girl I fell in love with all those years ago."

She swipes at her tears, and a look of defiance crosses her face. "Devin, I don't know what I did to deserve you, but you are the only man I've ever loved like this. The only one I ever will. I'll love you until my dying breath."

I pull her over into my lap, wrapping my arms around her, and some of the stress releases. We've a huge way to go, but I have faith in us.

Faith that love will be enough this time.

CHAPTER FORTY-FOUR

Angelina

I pack up the rest of my stuff over the next couple days and stop by the diner to say goodbye to Cara and the girls. Devin has already made arrangements for my apartment and my car to be sold, so there's little left for me here now. I don't like leaving our son behind, but Devin assures me he'll find a way to bring him closer.

The walls between us are dropping, and his unflinching support is comforting. I've slept at his place the last two nights, in his bed, in his arms. Nothing sexual happened. We didn't even kiss. Neither of us are ready for that yet, but I slept in his embrace, and it's been the best sleep I've had in years.

When we step off the plane in Iowa, his father and Lucas are waiting to greet us. I almost keel over as Luc runs toward me. When I left, he was only a kid, but he's all grown up now, and so much like his older brother. He draws me into his arms without hesitation, swinging me around, and I laugh. When he places my feet on the ground, he continues to hug me, and it's kinda getting embarrassing.

"I didn't just find her for you to squeeze the life out of her," Devin quips, unwrapping his brother's arms from around my waist and hauling me back into his chest.

"Good to see you're still a possessive, jealous freak around Ange," he replies with a wink.

Jim steps forward then, patting my shoulder and cupping my face. "I'm far too afraid of him to chance a hug," he teases, his eyes shining happily as he looks over my shoulder at his other son. "But it's fantastic to see you again, Angelina. Your mother is going to be so happy."

My smile cracks. I want to see Mom so badly, but I'm terrified too. I abandoned her, and I'm so ashamed. She did nothing to deserve that kind of treatment from me. Jim changes his mind, pulling me into his arms. "She won't judge you, sweet girl. She'll just be happy to have you back."

"You didn't say anything, right?" Devin asks.

Jim relinquishes his hold on me, shaking his head. "No. I was in too much shock this morning when you called to even consider it anyway."

"This morning?" I look back at Devin.

"I couldn't tell anyone about you yet. If I'd told them when I first found you, they would've been on top of you straightaway, and ... well—"

"You didn't want them to see me like that," I supply for him.

"Are you mad?"

"Are you kidding me?" I twist around, placing my hands on his chest. "I didn't want them to see me like that either. You made the right call." I kiss his cheek. "Thank you."

Lucas wraps his arm around my shoulder, bombarding me with questions as we walk to the waiting Mercedes. Devin gets in the back beside me, and Lucas hops in the other side. Jim drives us to a massive three-story house in a secluded area of a plush, quiet neighborhood on the outskirts of Minneapolis. "Welcome home," Devin whispers in my ear, holding my hand and pulling me up the front steps. Jim and Lucas retrieve our luggage from the trunk and join us inside.

Devin gives me a whistle-stop tour of his lavish mansion, while Jim orders takeout. We sit at the long dining table, which overlooks the stunning landscaped lawn outside, while we eat and chat.

After they've gone, Devin runs me a bath, and I soak in the tub for an hour. When I emerge, swaddled in a comfy bathrobe with red cheeks and wrinkled skin, he's waiting for me, an anxious look on his face. "I'm wondering where you want me to put your stuff?" He gestures with his arm. "I have plenty of guest bedrooms. You can have your pick, or you can stay with me." He shrugs, attempting to make the gesture casual, but I know him too well.

"I like sleeping with you," I admit truthfully, "and I want to share your room, but I don't want to complicate things. We're making progress, but I don't think we should rush it."

He's not happy, but he doesn't push me. I choose a soothing green room just down the hall from the master suite, and Devin leaves while I unpack. An hour later, I join him downstairs in the living room. The TV is on mute in the background, and he's dressed in sweats and a plain T-shirt, lounging on the couch with a laptop in his lap. He puts it aside when I enter the room, smiling warmly at me. He jumps up, kissing the tip of my nose. "I like having you here."

"I like being here."

"Would you like some hot chocolate?"

"That sounds great."

We drink our yummy chocolaty drinks in his homey kitchen, chatting about my mom and talking through my ideas to return to college. Devin wholeheartedly supports my plan, and he's quick to offer to fund it, but I won't hear of it. He can't swoop in and fix everything. Not when I need to learn to stand on my own two feet, without any crutches.

We go to our separate bedrooms, and I lie awake for a couple hours worried and nervous about the next few days. In three days, we'll travel to Mason City for Christmas. I'm so excited to see my mom, but I'm petrified too. She doesn't know I'm coming yet. She thinks she's hosting Christmas dinner for Devin and his family. Jim is going to call her Christmas morning and tell her the good news. It seems they've become close friends during my absence, and he fed me some tidbits over dinner earlier. I was pleased to hear she's still with Jon—Dr. Williams. Knowing she wasn't alone goes some way toward assuaging my guilt.

As the clock chimes three, I get out of bed and tread softly to Devin's room. He's snoring softly as I peel back the covers and slip underneath. He stirs when the bed dips, his arms opening automatically for me. "Come here, baby," he muffles in a sleep-laden tone. I curl up against him and fall instantly asleep.

Devin works overtime to fill the hours and my headspace over the next few days, and I love him for instinctually knowing that I desperately need distracting. He takes me shopping, insisting on buying me a whole new closet despite my protests to the contrary. We go out for dinner, go biking and walking in Lyndale Park Gardens, catch a show at the Guthrie Theater, and stay up talking into the early hours of the morning. I fall into bed each night exhausted but happy. The more time I spend in his company, the more I relax, and, in a lot of ways, it's as if we were never apart.

∞ ∞ ∞

My leg jerks up and down as I stare out the window at the fields whizzing by. Devin plants a hand on my knee as he drives. "Try to relax. It's going to be okay."

"And Mom knows I'm coming now? Because I don't want to spring this on her and give her a coronary."

"She knows. Jim said she screamed and cried down the phone for a half hour. She can't wait to see you, and she told him to tell you not to worry because all she cares about is seeing you again."

"I don't how she can be so understanding," I mumble.

"Because she's your mother, and she loves you unconditionally."

The closer we get to the street where we grew up, the more nauseated I become. By the time Devin pulls into the drive, behind a shiny new SUV, I've broken out in a cold sweat and my entire body is convulsing in fear, which is ridiculous, because it's my mother and she's already told me not to worry.

The front door opens, and my heart stutters. Then my mother is racing toward us, tears streaming down her face. I'm out of the car and on my feet before I've even registered the movement, running to meet her halfway. We collide in a blend of arms and sobs, desperately hugging one another. The familiar scent of vanilla and strawberries, from her shampoo, surrounds me, and I bury my head in her shoulder, my body shaking as I cling to her.

"Honey," she whispers in my ear, her voice catching. "I can't believe you're here. I've prayed so hard for this moment."

"I'm sorry, Mom. I'm so sorry."

She smooths a hand over the back of my head, emitting soothing sounds as I sob. We continue clinging to one another, both of us afraid to let go, until Devin clears his throat. "It's freezing, and you're both shivering. Let's take this inside."

"Give me a minute, Devin. Let me look at my baby girl." She leans back, keeping me at arm's length as she scans me from head to toe. Fresh tears creep into her eyes. "My God. Look at you. You're so beautiful." The skin around her eyes creases as she frowns. "A little too thin but we'll rectify that."

Keeping a grip on my hand, she moves aside, leaning up to kiss Devin on the cheek. "Thank you for bringing my little girl home to me. This is the best Christmas present ever."

"I told you I would, and I was determined to keep my promise."

"I'm still pissed at you though," she adds, narrowing her eyes. "You lied to me."

He scratches the back of his head. "I'm sorry, Natalie, but I promise I took care of her."

"Don't be mad at Dev, Mom. You would not have wanted to find me the way he did. I'm glad he waited until now to tell you, because it would've only hurt you more."

Her keen eyes probe mine. "I wouldn't have cared. Getting you back is all that matters."

"Honey, come inside," Jon says, pressing his hand to Mom's arm. "Your skin is like ice." I hadn't really had time to get to know Dr. Williams before I left, so he's a virtual stranger to me. But he's still here, and I haven't missed the massive diamond on Mom's ring finger. He's clearly supported her through my absence, and that's good enough for me. When he leans in, I willingly accept his embrace. "It's fantastic to see you again, Angelina. We're glad you're home."

Mom doesn't let go of my hand as we stroll toward the house. I discreetly check her out as we walk. Her blonde hair is cut in a stylish bob, and she owns the lilac fitted dress she's wearing. She's still sporting an amazing figure and a great sense of style. She has a few tiny lines around her eyes and her mouth, but apart from that, she hasn't changed much. On the outside at least. God knows what my leaving did to her mental state.

My eyes wander to the house next door. Devin has already confirmed the Carters still live there, and part of my anxiety over this visit was tied up with them. Nancy blames me for Ayden's death, and while the thought of facing her again almost brings me out in hives, I know I can't avoid it.

But one step at a time.

Jim, Lucas, and a pretty redhead are waiting in the kitchen. Lucas introduces me to Lucy, his girlfriend, with a proud smile, and we chat casually for a few minutes as if it hasn't been years since I last stepped foot in my home.

The interior of the house is vastly transformed. Sleek, white gloss cupboards have replaced the old pine ones in the kitchen. A snazzy marble island unit and a mammoth refrigerator are new additions. Dark hardwood floors and cream-painted walls contrast with vibrant furnishings. In the living room, the old open fireplace is gone, replaced with a fitted gas fireplace. A wall-mounted TV is affixed above it, and deep shelving has been built into the fireplace on both sides. "Wow. I love what you've done with the place."

"Thank you. Jon and Devin completed a lot of the work themselves."

I arch a brow, turning around to look at Devin. "You always were good with your hands."

His answering smirk pulls a laugh from me as I realize how my words could be construed. When Mom bursts out crying, I falter, my smile fading at her obvious distress.

"I'm sorry, honey." She reels me into her arms again. "I just can't believe you're here. I'm overcome. I've missed you so much."

The others quietly disappear.

Mom pulls me down on the couch, and we hug it out for ages. Another layer of stress filters away. After a little while, she eases back, brushing strands of my hair behind my ears. "I know we have lots to talk about, but I don't want to put a dampener on today. Today is a cause for celebration because my baby's home." Tears invade her eyes again, and I'm reminded of my selfishness. "But you have to promise you won't do anything like that again. I won't survive if you leave again."

I hold her hands firmly in mine. "I'm home, Mom, and I promise I'll never leave you again. I was in such a dark place after Ayden died, and it seemed like the only choice, but I know I was wrong to leave as I did. I'm an adult now, and I know running away was not the solution. Leaving you was the hardest thing ever, and you were in my thoughts every day.

I must've picked up the phone a million times to call you, but I always chickened out. I convinced myself you hated me because I abandoned you, and you didn't deserve that."

"I could never hate you, sweet girl. You're the love of my life, and that will never change, but I'd be lying if I said I wasn't furious with you too, because I was, because I still am."

"I understand, and you have every right to your anger."

She takes a deep breath, and then she's smiling at me again. "Not today, though. Today is a happy day, and there will be plenty of time to work through the rest."

We eat dinner in the new sunroom at the rear of the house, surrounded by memories. Although the backyard is totally remodeled, and not at all how I remember it, every time I look out at Old Man Willow, I'm reminded of so many childhood memories. Photos adorn space on almost every wall in every room of the house, cataloguing my life from infancy. Being back here again has my emotions in a tizzy, in both a good and a bad way.

Jon moves to pour wine in my glass, but I place my hand over it. "I'm a recovering alcoholic," I admit. "And I don't drink anymore." Devin covers my hand with his, squeezing in understanding. Mom looks upset. "I'm sorry," I say softly.

She shakes her head. "Don't be. I don't want you hiding your past from me. I just hate that you had to go through all that alone."

I look around the table at familiar faces, and I'm choked with emotion. Devin links his fingers through mine, and I cling to his touch. "I'm not alone anymore, and it feels so good to be back home."

"It's good to have you home," Jon says, wrapping his arm around Mom. "The place has felt empty without you." I smile warmly at him. He turns to Mom, and there's a hopeful glint in his eye. "Maybe now your mother will finally agree to set a date." I arch a brow. "When she accepted my proposal of marriage, it was on condition that the wedding would only take place once you were home to give her away."

My heart aches again, but I smile expansively, determined I'm shedding no more tears. "Well, I'm back for good, so I think it's time you honored your promise, Mom, and I would be so proud to give you away."

After dinner, Dev and I take a stroll out in the woods. I've been dying to see the treehouse he built with Danny. "Is it hard being back?" he asks, swinging our conjoined hands between us as we walk.

"Yes and no. On one level, it's comforting, and I'm so happy to see Mom happy, but all the changes remind me of how much I missed, and the memories aren't always good ones."

"I know what you mean," he says.

I've never doubted the connection between Devin and me, but we're in sync on so many different levels now. "But I can't dwell on the what-ifs anymore or allow the guilt to waylay me. Every step I take is a step forward, and I have to let go of the past. I made bad choices, choices which hurt me and those I love, but I can't change that. I can just ensure I make better choices, the right choices, moving forward."

He lifts our conjoined hands to his mouth, pressing a soft kiss on the back of my cold skin. "There she is," he whispers, moisture building in his eyes. "There's the girl I fell in love with as a kid."

I pull him to a stop. "I'm still me. I might have lost my way for a while, and I'm undoubtedly changed, but underneath it all, I'm still the same girl who has adored you for most of her life."

He draws me into his arms, and I willingly go there. Everything has always felt right with the world when I'm wrapped up in Devin's embrace, never more so than now. Everything is going to work out. I say it in my head, and, for the first time, I really, truly believe it.

"Oh my God, Devin. You built that?" I ask, looking up at the beautiful glass and cherry pine wooden structure nestled between two trees. Calling it a treehouse seems like an insult. It has a proper roof and windows and a sturdy ladder.

"Come on," he pulls me forward excitedly. "Let's go up."

We have to dip our heads when we reach the top even though the space is taller, wider, and longer than the treehouse we used to play in as kids. Comfy bean bags litter the floor, and we drop down onto them. Devin pulls a blanket out of a box in the corner of the space, covering us fully.

My eyes drink in my surroundings, tearing up as I note all the personal touches. The wall is covered in drawings and photos of us as kids. The framed photo that used to sit on my bedside table, the one of the three of us holding the walleye fish, is tacked to the wall. A small fish tank sits on the sturdy shelf alongside books and games. Two goldfish swim lazily through the hazy water, and emotion clogs the back of my throat. "Best to keep me away from those," I laugh, remembering the time I overfed the fish and came back the next day to find all three of them bloated and floating at the top of the tank. I'd cried my eyes out for three days solid.

"You were only nine, and you didn't know both me and Ayd had already fed them. I think they're safe in your hands now."

"Are those our actual old games?" I ask, kneeling up to inspect the faded boxes on the shelf beside the tank.

He nods. "Your mom had them all in the attic."

Of course, she did. She's a hoarder, especially when it was anything to do with me. I knew she kept a big trunk in the attic crammed full of my old school reports, drawings, ballet certificates, and other childhood memorabilia.

My eyes latch on the other framed item on the wall, and I stop breathing. The memory regurgitates in my mind as if it was only yesterday. I scoot closer, reaching out to skim my fingers across the glass, examining our childish signatures, and the faded blood. "You found it," I whisper.

He kneels up beside me. "I kept it all these years. Guess, somewhere deep down inside, I still believed in our pact."

"I always believed in it. Up until Ayden died."

We are both silent, lost in our own thoughts as we stare at it.

"So, do you like it?" he asks, a few minutes later, breaking the silence.

I grin at him. "I love it. It's perfect."

His answering smile almost knocks the air out of my lungs. "I came up here every time I visited your mom. It helped me feel closer to you. To both of you."

My heart aches in a familiar way. Ayden should be here with us, and I hate that he isn't, but thoughts of our lost friend doesn't dredge up the same conflicted feelings. Letting go of my anger and guilt is allowing me to properly mourn him for the first time. And to fully appreciate my other friend—this man at my side, the one who has stuck by me through thick and thin, who pulled me back from the brink when I was ready to throw in the towel. I peer into his eyes. "I love you, Devin. I love you so much."

"I love you too."

We stare at one another, and a customary, electrical current charges the tiny space between us. We lean toward one another at the same time. When our lips meet, I feel a sense of deep contentment that has eluded me for years. He pulls me in to his arms, and the kiss deepens, strengthens, infused with years of longing. It's not frantic, or wild, or the result of pent-up sexual frustration—which I'm sure he feels as much as I do—but tender and loving and full of unspoken promise. When we finally break the kiss, we stay wrapped around one another, silently holding onto each other without the need to say anything.

We're walking back to the house, hand in hand, when someone steps out in front of us on the path. "Lina." Nancy Carter's eyes well up. "Your mom told me you were home. I'm glad. She's missed you terribly." Shoving her hands in her coat pocket, she shuffles nervously on her feet. "I was hoping you might have a few minutes to talk."

Dev subtly squeezes my hand, letting me know he's here for me. "I'd like that," I say softly, even though every instinct in my body screams at me to run in the other direction. We follow in silence as she leads us to her house, my heart pounding in my chest the entire time. When she opens the back door to let us inside, I falter, unsure if I can follow through with this.

Her gaze is kind when it lands on mine. "It's okay, sweetheart. They're looking forward to seeing you."

Putting a lid on my fear, I step into Ayden's house for the first time in five years. They've redecorated, changing the color on the walls in most of the rooms, and dark wooden floors have replaced the carpet in the living room, but, apart from that, everything looks exactly how I remember it. Pictures of Ayden and the girls are everywhere.

"Lina." Carl—Ayden's dad—steps forward, pulling me into his embrace without hesitation. "It's good to see you, girl." He hugs me close, and tears prick my eyes.

"You too," I whisper, easing myself out of his arms. "Where are the girls?"

"Mia and Ellie are at a friend's house, but Kayla is upstairs. She's dying to see you, but we asked her to give us privacy for a few minutes. There are some things I need to say," Nancy explains.

Mr. Carter hugs Devin, whispering something in his ear.

"Me too," I reply.

"Have a seat, please." She sits down on the long couch, patting the space beside her.

I sit down, and Devin sits on my other side, taking my hand in his again. Mrs. Carter notices, and I squirm uncomfortably, but I don't remove my hand from his. I need his touch to steady my nerves.

"I owe you an apology, Lina," she says, looking me straight in the eye. "I never should have blamed you or Devin for Ayden's death. I was devastated, naturally, and looking for answers. I needed something or someone to blame, but it wasn't fair or right of me to put that responsibility on your shoulders, and I know my son would be upset that I hurt you, that I pushed you away. Your mother lost a daughter the day I lost my son, and I hate that I might have contributed to your decision to run away."

Tears roll down my face unbidden, and she takes my free hand in hers. Before I can respond to her statement, she continues. "I'm sorry you felt you had no other choice, and I'm sorry if my words added to your guilt." Tears trickle out of her eyes. "The fact is, none of us really know why Ayden did it. Why he felt he had no other choice but to take his own life. And there are so many things his father and I wish we had done differently. I can't throw blame in your direction without casting the same doubt over my own actions."

"Nancy." Mr. Carter sits down on the arm of the chair, wrapping his arms around his wife's shoulder. "We've been over this. No one is to blame, and no good comes from reflecting on all the what-ifs."

"If it's any consolation," I say. "I blamed myself for years, and I still would have, whether you said that to me or not. And you didn't force me to run away. I made that decision by myself because I was hurt, and confused, and grieving, and suffocating under the weight of guilt I felt. I don't know that I'll ever fully forgive myself for failing Ayden, because there was clearly something going on with him, and I should have made him tell me, but I ignored the signs because I was so wrapped up in myself and I didn't want to lose my other best friend."

"Stop, Lina." Mr. Carter leans over his wife to touch my face. "Ayden loved you, and you were a great friend to him. If he didn't confide in you, it was for his own reasons."

"It's never ending, isn't it?" Nancy says, sniffling. "The questions that we'll never get answers to." She shakes her head sadly. "We work hard to put it aside, because we have three daughters who need us, but, God, it's so difficult at times. Not a day goes by where I don't miss my boy."

Devin wraps his arm around my shoulder. "We miss him too. So much."

We chat for a while, and Kayla joins us, and I can't believe how big she's grown. She was only eight when I left, and now she's a teenager. She has the same blonde hair and blue eyes as Ayden, and it looks like she's going to be nearly as tall as him as well.

When Nancy hugs me at the door as we are leaving, another crack mends in my heart, and it feels as if everything is slotting into place as its meant to.

Devin stays with me that night, holding me close as we sleep in my childhood bed. We stay another day and night, but then it's time to return to the city. Devin needs to get back to work, and now I know about my inheritance, I have college applications to complete.

Mom told me last night that my father passed away a couple years ago after a short battle with cancer. He left half his vast estate to me, which surprised me enormously. I'm guessing it's guilt money, but I'm not going to refuse it. Why should I? He was my father, and he gave me very little in life. This money sets me up for the future. I don't have to work ever again if I don't want to, but that's not my intent. I need a purpose, and I want to go back to college. To get my psychology degree and eventually set up my own practice like I always planned to. My life experiences have made me even more determined than I was back then. This money will help, and it means I don't have to rely on Devin financially, something which I'm uncomfortable with anyway.

Mom hugs me desperately, clinging to me as she makes me promise to call every day and to visit as soon as I can. I reassure her, and tease her about setting a date, and then we're on our way.

Looking out the window, as we drive past familiar landscape, I reach across the console, laying my hand over Devin's, smiling the first, real, genuine smile in years.

I'm home, and it feels unbelievably good to be back.

CHAPTER FORTY-FIVE

Devin

I hang up the phone, tossing my cell on the table and walk to Ange, wrapping my arms around her from behind. She's chopping vegetables for dinner, and mouthwatering smells waft around the kitchen. I've only recently grown to like this house. I'd been on the verge of selling it before she reappeared in my life. Now, I wouldn't dream of disposing of it. It finally feels like my home, now that the woman of my dreams is sharing it with me. While there are no labels, and we haven't progressed beyond kissing and innocent touching, we turned a corner last weekend. She's happier in herself, and that makes me happy in turn. I'm content to let her set the pace, once she understands where this is heading, and I'm confident she does.

"Who was that?" she asks, leaning back into me.

I kiss the top of her head. "Your mom. She forgot to give us some letters that came for us. She was calling to let me know she's popped them in the mail."

"What letters?"

I shrug. "Don't have a clue." I nestle my chin on her shoulder. "What are you making? It smells divine."

She twists her head around, pecking me all too briefly on the lips. "Lasagna. Your favorite."

"I think you're spoiling me." I wink.

"I think you deserve it." She kisses me again.

After we've eaten, we curl up on the sofa watching TV, and I can't recall the last time I felt so happy. She belongs with me, and I belong with her, and I'm going to make sure this time is for forever.

The next couple of months settle into a comfortable pattern. I return to work, and Ange spends her days redecorating the house, attending college interviews, and helping her mom with her wedding planning.

In our spare time, we do everything together, and it's the first time in my life when I've properly dated, when I've fully shared my life with a woman, and I love it. I love coming home to a warm house and a home-cooked meal. I love snuggling up with her on the couch, messing with her hair, and dotting her face with sly kisses, as we watch a movie. I love going to sleep beside her and waking up with her curled around me, murmuring contentedly in her sleep. I love taking her to a show and seeing her eyes light up in wonder. I love spoon-feeding her dinner over the table of a restaurant, watching in amusement as she giggles in nervous embarrassment. I love holding her hand, going for walks in the moonlight, and glancing over my shoulder in the gym to see her checking me out while she works out.

There isn't a single thing I don't love about having her back in my life, and I make a point of telling her every day. In the first few weeks, I showered her with flowers and gifts until she made me promise to stop. When she told me she didn't need grand gestures—she only needed me—my heart melted, and I couldn't mount any argument.

While she's moved her stuff permanently into my room, *our* room, and we share a bed every night, our intimacy hasn't moved beyond kissing and hugging. I want to take it further, to bury myself in the woman I love, but I'm letting her lead this. Even if I have the worst case of blue balls in history.

We talk about our son, and though it's painful to hear some of her stories, it's cathartic at the same time. I'll always hate that I wasn't there to support her, but I've forgiven her for concealing it from me. Besides, I plan on giving her plenty more babies, and there'll be time to make some new precious memories. For now, I want to honor the memory of the child I never knew, and I've made inquiries into relocating his grave. We want him close so we can visit often.

It's Friday night, and I'm at a local bar with some of my colleagues waiting for Ange, when slender arms curl around me from behind. The smile on my face is instant as I spin around, leaning down to press my lips to hers. Her returning kiss is exuberant and demanding, and blood rushes straight to my dick. I'm instantly hard. "Hey, baby," I say, grinning and breathless as I break the kiss before I decide to ravage her right here in front of my buddies. "You look happy."

"I am!" Her grin is so wide it threatens to split her face, and she's practically bouncing on the ground. "I got in, Devin! I got accepted to North Central University!"

I kiss her again. "Congrats, baby. I'm so proud of you."

"I'm so excited. Everything is falling into place."

Her stunning blue eyes are twinkling with excitement, and her face is radiant, glowing with happiness. I've never seen her look more beautiful or more content, and it fills me with so much emotion. "This calls for a celebration," I say, taking her hand. I wave at my buddies, steering her out of the bar. I take her to Les Miserables, an expensive, popular French restaurant, and we gorge ourselves on fine dining and non-alcoholic champagne.

Snuggled into my side, she's singing along to the radio in the car as I drive us home, and I know I won't be able to wait much longer. I've been patient, but that patience is running low. I need her to know she's my forever girl. I need to ensure she's fully mine.

Proving how deep our connection runs, she takes my hand the minute we step inside the house, pulling me silently up the stairs, as if she's read my mind.

She pushes me down on the bed and straddles me. Leaning down, she kisses me passionately, running her tongue around the seam of my lips. When her tongue slides into my mouth, my dick surges to life, greedily taking whatever she's offering. She rubs herself against me, and we both groan. Ripping her mouth from mine, she starts unbuttoning her blouse. When she tosses it to the floor, I reach for her, but she shakes her head. Her eyes glisten and her features soften as she stares at me. "There are so many things I love about you, Devin, but more than anything, I love how patient you've been with me. I want you. I've wanted you from the minute you reappeared in my life, but I kept my distance because I needed to be sure I could give you what you need." She leans down, planting a scorching hot kiss on my mouth. "Sleeping in this bed every night and not touching you has almost killed me, but I needed to ensure I was ready to take the next step, and I am."

Her chest inflates and deflates as she stands up and unclips her bra. Saliva pools in my mouth, and my dick is straining against my zipper. She shimmies out of her skirt, panties, and stockings and kicks her shoes off. Then she crawls back over me, naked and utterly magnificent. "I'm ready, Devin. I love you so much it feels like my heart could burst out of my chest. I've known since I was a little girl that you're the only man for me. I'm all yours." She starts unbuttoning my shirt. "Make love to me, Devin. Make me yours."

I need no further encouragement. She helps me strip completely bare, emitting a little shocked gasp as she finally sees the tattoo with her name just over my heart.

"This is why you always sleep with a top on?" she asks.

I nod. "I didn't want to scare you."

She tilts her head to the side, looking at me as if I'm crazy. "When did you get it?"

"The week after you left." I take her hand, placing it against my bare skin. "I told you, you were in here, and this tattoo let everyone else know it too. No one else has ever owned a piece of my heart. It's always been yours."

Her eyes are drenched with lust as she flings herself at me, ravishing my mouth and letting me know everything she's feeling. Then we're feasting on one another as if we've never eaten. Her lips brand my skin in every place they touch, and my hands are greedy as they roam the curves of her body. I flip her onto her back, devouring her mouth as my hand wanders lower. She arches off the bed when I slip one finger inside her, pumping slowly through her wet warmth. I add another finger and she moans into my mouth, almost making me come on the spot. I move down her body, kissing, nipping, and licking as I go, paying lavish attention to her breasts as my fingers continue moving inside her. Placing my head in between her legs, I lick up and down her folds, and she goes wild, bucking and thrashing, and I can't keep the smug grin off my face.

My fingers move inside her again, and I pick up the pace as my lips suction on that little bundle of nerves. I suck her hard, my fingers pumping manically inside her and she explodes, screaming my name with her release.

I stroke my straining cock, positioning myself at her entrance. Her face is flushed, her lips swollen, and her eyes look drunk as she stares at me. Her fingers tickle the bristle on my chin, and she smiles. "I'm on the pill, and I'm clean. I got tested in rehab."

"I'm good too," I confirm, easing the tip of my cock inside her. Her eyes roll back in her head, and she produces the horniest sound ever. "Fuck, you're so sexy."

"Then show me, big boy," she demands, sending me a naughty grin. "Show me how sexy I am."

I slam into her, all semblance of patience gone. She wraps her legs around my waist, flexing her hips upward to meet me, and I pound into her, thrusting over and over, lost to sensation and emotion and the joy of finally being inside her again. She moans and screams without shame, and it's hot as fuck. I sit upright, pulling her with me until she's riding me in my lap. Placing one hand on the headboard, I thrust up into her in sharp, precise movements as she continues grinding against me, tightening her pussy around my cock. My teeth pull at her nipples, and I continue thrusting, slamming into her with years of repressed sexual frustration. She slips a hand down between us, rubbing herself, and I almost spill my load. Grabbing the back of her head, I pull her mouth to mine, and I kiss the shit out of her as I hammer us both to oblivion. She screams as her orgasm hits, and I roar as release detonates through me at the same time.

We're both panting as I wrap my arms around her sweat-slicked skin, holding her close to me. I can feel the vibration of her heart beating against my chest. I pepper her face with soft kisses, whispering how much I love her.

"Devin," she rasps, her voice heavy with desire and awe. "No one else has ever made me feel this way. I don't have words to properly describe it. And it's more than that—you have saved me in every way it's possible to save a person."

I lean back a little, still buried inside her, not willing to forgo the connection yet. Peering deep into her eyes, I brush damp hair back off her face. "I do. We fit together in every conceivable way. We always have. We just get one another. We were meant to be together. There's never been any doubt in my mind about that."

She smiles broadly. "Nor mine. When I looked at my future, it was always you."

Gently, I pull out of her sweet body, kissing her lips softly. Then I reach over, removing the black velvet-covered box from my bedside table. I kneel up in front of her, watching her eyes go wide. "I wanted to do this smoother. I had a huge romantic proposal all planned out, but I can't wait any longer. I love you, Ange. I love you so, so much. You're my forever girl. Marry me, baby doll. Be my wife." I flick the box open, and the large diamond sparkles in the dim lighting of the room. "Make me the happiest man on the planet."

She grabs my face, tears coursing down her cheeks. "Yes, Devin. Yes, I'll marry you. I want to be your wife. Nothing would make me happier or prouder."

Then we're both crying and hugging one another, kissing and laughing, and it's the best fucking moment of my life. "Here," I say, removing the ring from the box. "Let me put it on you."

"Wait," she says, squinting to inspect the ring. "What does the inscription say?"

I hold it up for her, until she can read the etching on the inside of the band.

"Always remember," she whispers.

I nod as I reach out to touch the small locket she still wears around her neck. "I asked you once before to never forget what you meant to me." I gulp, choked with emotion as I slide the ring on her finger. It's a perfect fit, as I knew it would be. "Now I'm asking you to always remember. I need you to remember what we've been through to get to this point." I look into her eyes, rapidly filling up again. "Because we've been through a lot, but it's shaped us as individuals, defined our relationship, strengthened our bond, and made us who we are today." I trace one finger over the tattoo on her wrist. "While some of those memories aren't pleasant, it's part of our story, and we should always remember how hard we both fought to find our way back to one another. How much we've sacrificed for our love."

"Devin," she whispers, touching my face as tears blur her vision. "No proposal could ever be more romantic. No man more perfect. I will love you till my dying day."

CHAPTER FORTY-SIX
Angelina

I'm floating on a cloud the next morning, ecstatic over Devin's proposal, and still reeling from the most magical night of my life. For a reformed bad boy, Devin sure has turned out all sweet. Mom screamed down the phone when we called her to tell her our good news. Just when I thought I couldn't possibly love Devin anymore, she explained how he looked after her in my absence and how he attended dinner religiously ever Sunday for years. I cried when she told him she'd always considered him a son, but she was looking forward to making it official now.

I leave them chatting when the doorbell chimes, moving to open the front door. A stunning brunette stands on the top step, frowning a little as she regards me. She recovers quickly, offering me a smile. "Oh, hello. I was looking for Devin. Does he still live here?"

I nod cautiously. "He's on a call. Can I help? I'm his fiancée." It gives me enormous pleasure to say the word.

Her frown disappears, and a huge smile lights up her face. "I wasn't aware he'd gotten engaged. That's fantastic news. Congratulations."

Any anxiety I was feeling washes away at her genuine expression. "Thank you. I'm over the moon."

"He's a great guy."

"I know. I'm very lucky."

She hands me two white envelopes. "I'm sure he's very lucky too. These were delivered to my house in error." She glances over her shoulder, pointing at the house across the way. "Myself and my husband live there. I'm Gwyneth, by the way." She offers me her hand, and I shake it. "I probably should've opened with that!" She laughs, a soft tinkling sound. "Anyway, my husband travels a lot for business, and I usually go with him. We've been away for the last two months which is why I'm only giving you these now. Hope they weren't important."

"No problem. Thank you, and I'm Angelina."

"Nice to meet you," she says, before backing up. "We'll have you over to dinner one night. Get to know each other properly." She waves. "Tell Devin I said hi and congratulations."

I turn the envelopes over as I pad back to the living room, frowning as I stop the same attorney's stamp on the back of both letters. One is addressed to me, and one is addressed to Devin.

"Who was at the door?" he asks, tugging me into his arms. "And why have they put that frown on your face?"

"It was your neighbor, Gwyneth, and she didn't put the frown on my face. These letters did." I hand him his, and recognition dawns on his face.

"I wondered what had happened to those letters your mom mailed."

"Ah." I remember now.

He takes a letter opener out, slitting both envelopes on top. Taking my hand, he pulls me down onto the couch, and we read side by side. Bile rises in my throat as I scan the correspondence from Ayden's attorney. "What does this mean?" I whisper, clutching the paper in my fist.

Devin pulls a worried face. "I don't know, but I guess there's only one way to find out." He grabs his cell, punching the number in.

"It's Saturday. They're probably closed for the weekend."

"I'll leave a message."

I listen as he proceeds to do that. "Oh, hello," he says, a few seconds later. "I wasn't expecting anyone to pick up on a Saturday." He nods while whoever it is talks on the other end of the line. His shoulder muscles are corded with tension, and his foot taps restlessly off the floor as he listens. "There was a mix-up, and the letters were sent to the wrong house. We've only just received them. Yes, Angelina Ward is here with me." He glances at me, and I arch a brow. He links his fingers in mine. "Yes, we could be there in an hour. Okay. We'll see you then. Thank you."

He hangs up, leaning forward on his knees, expelling air from his mouth in a loud rush.

"Someone is there?"

He nods. "That was Mr. Fuller, the attorney who sent us the letters. He has a couple of appointments this morning, but he can squeeze us in. Ayden instructed him to send those to us on the fifth anniversary of his death." He pins me with a grave look. "He has something for us. Something from Ayden."

I smooth a hand over the sudden ache in my chest. "What do you think it is?"

He presses a kiss to my temple. "I've no idea, but maybe it will give us the answers we've been looking for." Taking my hand, he hauls me to my feet and we go upstairs to get dressed.

∞ ∞ ∞

I'm pacing the carpet in the small waiting room of the attorney's office. My stomach is in knots, has been the entire ride here. Devin stands up, moving behind me. His hands go to my shoulders, and he digs his fingers in as he starts massaging my tense muscles. "Try to relax, baby. Whatever this is, we're in it together." I nod, wanting to reassure him. He kisses my cheek. "Always remember." Circling his arms around my waist, he pulls me in to the comfort and safety of his body. He's right. I can deal with this. Nothing I'm about to hear is going to change who we are or how far we've come.

The door swings open, and a small wiry man with a mop of thick gray hair steps out. He nods curtly, offering us a brief smile. "Mr. Morgan and Ms. Ward, I presume?"

Devin takes my hand, nodding in acknowledgment. I slant a brittle smile his way. "I'm Michael Fuller. Thank you for coming in on a Saturday. If you'll follow me." He gestures us inside.

"I can't wait until you share my surname," Dev whispers in my ear, leading me in to the attorney's office. Although we haven't discussed the specifics of our forthcoming nuptials, there's no way I'm not taking my husband's name. I can't wait to be Mrs. Devin Morgan. Thinking it reminds me of all the times I doodled that name on the back of my school journal, bringing a smile to my face. It's the perfect thing to say, helping to distract me and slay the edge off my nerves.

I grin at my husband-to-be and he winks. The attorney guides us to a circular table at the side of the room. We take seats alongside each other, and Devin automatically links our hands. Mr. Fuller remains standing, powering up a laptop that rests in the center of the table. He clears his throat. "Mr. Carter engaged my services shortly before his death. I thought it was strange for a young man of his age to be so concerned with his last will and testament, but I didn't question it." His expression highlights his regret. "He gave me a few sealed items for safekeeping. A few days after his death, I received a letter in the mail with various instructions. It seems he was well prepared."

Devin and I share shocked expressions. I've always thought Ayden's suicide was a spur of the moment thing, but this hints at premeditation, and that makes me unbelievably sad.

The attorney flicks a button on the laptop, and a video recording displays on the screen. I grip Devin's hand tight. Ayden's face is framed on the paused screen, and tears automatically well in my eyes.

"He wanted you both to watch this together," he confirms.

I gnaw on the inside of my mouth, leaning into Dev, as the attorney presses the play button and quietly leaves the room. Tears stream down my face as I look at my friend. He's exactly as I remember him with the exception of the resigned look on his face.

"Hey, guys." Ayden leans forward, adjusting the webcam, before sitting back on the edge of his bed. The curtains are open, and it's dark outside. "If you're watching this, it means I did it. I finally summoned the courage to go through with it. I imagine you have lots of questions, and it didn't feel right bowing out of this world without letting my two best friends know why I did what I did. I've deliberately instructed my attorney to wait five years before showing this to you, because I want to ensure you're both in a good place when I tell you what I need to tell you. I'm hoping by now, you've come to terms with my death, and this will bring you that final closure."

He says this so bluntly, without any show of emotion, as if he's discussing whether to have raspberry or strawberry jelly on his toast.

"To put this in context," he continues. "It's the night before we're due to leave for UI, and I'm about to break the news to you, Lina. I'm a chicken shit, because I should've told you how I was feeling, but I couldn't bear to watch your heart break again. We've both done it to you now, and you deserve better."

I close my eyes momentarily. Devin brushes his lips across my cheek, renewing me with courage. I open my damp eyes again.

On the screen, Ayden exhales deeply. "You need to forgive Devin," he says. "Because he loves you the way a guy should love a girl. I've gotten in the way of that, and, for what it's worth, I'm sorry." He leans forward, and I see the anguish in his eyes. "I love you, Lina, I always have, and I always will, but I can't love you the way you deserve to be loved. If I was going to love any girl, it'd be you. There is no girl sweeter, kinder, more generous, or more beautiful than you. I wanted to love you properly. I wanted that so badly, and I tried, but I can't force myself to feel things I don't."

He looks away, and Devin and I lock gazes. I'm hearing what I didn't hear back then. When Ayden starts speaking again, we return our attention to the screen. "I'm gay," he admits in a low voice. "But I don't want to be." Tears glisten in his eyes. "I want to be normal. And I tried. I tried with you, Lina, but it wasn't enough, and that's not on you. That's all on me." He buries his face in his hands, and his shoulders heave as he cries. I place a hand over my mouth, and my heart is beating furiously in my chest. Never in a million years did I suspect this.

Ayden lifts his head, focusing on the camera again. "I'm sorry. I told myself I wouldn't do this. I wanted to tell you for so long, but I couldn't. Because admitting it out loud would be like accepting it, and I don't want to accept it. I don't want to be like this. I don't want to have these feelings, and my whole life feels like one giant lie. The football dream was always my dad's dream. It hasn't been mine for years, but I've been too afraid to tell him."

He laughs, and it's bitter sounding. "I told him tonight, and he went apeshit on me. I told him I've joined the marines, and he's threatened to disown me. Very soon, I'll have no one left." He hangs his head, and I want to reach into the past, hug my friend, and tell him it's fine to be himself. That we love him no matter what. That his sexuality makes no difference to our friendship.

Devin is struggling to maintain composure beside me. I stroke his back, fighting the swell of emotion in my chest.

Ayden looks back up at the camera. "I've deliberately interfered in your relationship with Devin, Lina, and I'm truly sorry for that. He's right. I wanted to drive a wedge between you, because if you two are together, then our bond is broken, and I'll be left on the outside. I couldn't deal with that." He gulps, and it looks painful. "But it's more than that." He wets his lips, clasping and unclasping his hands in his lap. "Because I love him too."

Devin goes rigidly still.

"I love you, Devin, in the way a guy shouldn't love another guy." His voice cracks, and he breaks down sobbing. After a minute, he swipes angrily at his tears, speaking up again. "I was fifteen when I first began to understand I had certain inappropriate feelings for you. We were out at the lake. It was our first summer there without Grandpa Joe. We were drying off on the dock when Lina started crying."

I remember it. My grandpa had only died three months previous, and it was still so raw. Being back at the lake had dredged tons of emotions to the surface, and I broke down in front of my friends.

"You went to her straightaway," Ayden continues speaking. "You wrapped your arms around her and pulled her into your lap. You were whispering in her ear, kissing the top of her head, and running your hands up and down her arms." He locks his hands behind his head. "I was so jealous, but then I realized I was jealous of Lina, not you. When I looked at you with your arms around her, I found myself wishing you had your arms around me."

I'm a blubbering mess, tears flowing down my face unrestrained. Devin is deathly quiet beside me.

"From that point on, I was acutely aware of your presence, and it affected me in ways it shouldn't. It didn't take long for me to work out I was in love with you. I know you don't return my feelings. I know you never will," Ayden continues. His laugh is coarse. "There's no doubting you're hetero, and I know you love Lina, but that doesn't seem to make any difference to me."

He swipes at his tears again, brushing them away. "No matter what happened, our friendship was always destined to be ruined, man. We both love you, but I've always known who you'd choose." He composes himself. "And I'm fine with that. I've learned to accept it. You are my two best friends, and I want you to be happy. I'm just getting in the way of that. And I'm so tired of it all. Tired of feeling this way. Why me? Why couldn't I have just been normal?"

He straightens up. "I'm joining the marines because I figure there's no better alpha male environment to be in. Maybe it'll help. Maybe it'll make things worse." He shrugs. "If you're listening to this, it means it didn't work. It didn't fix me. But at least you guys are together, and I'm not there to get in the way anymore. I'll die happy knowing I've at least done something right."

He moves to shut off the camera feed. "I'll miss you guys. Know you've been the very best part of my life. Be happy, and take care of each other."

The feed cuts out, and the screen pauses. My sobs are the only sound in the room, until Devin hops up, knocking his chair to the ground with a loud thud. He storms from the room, and I jump up, running after him.

CHAPTER FORTY-SEVEN

Devin

I race out of the attorney's office, barely thanking the guy, running down the stairs and out onto the sidewalk. Hunching over, I place my hands on my trembling knees, struggling to breathe. Ange is beside me then, wrapping her arm around my back, ushering soothing words. I cling to her, sucking oxygen deep into my lungs as I wait for the anxiety attack to pass.

When I'm more composed, I straighten up and let her guide me to the car. She takes charge, strapping me into the passenger seat and sliding behind the wheel. I lean my head back, closing my eyes, as the cyclone in my head reaches peak pressure. My head is a mess. My thoughts conflicted.

We drive for ages, in silence. She glances at me every few minutes, concern etched across her gorgeous face. I want to reassure her, but the knot in my chest has stolen my ability to speak. She's handling this much better than me. Seeing Ayden's face again was excruciatingly difficult but not as difficult as listening to what he had to say.

The car slows down, and I look out the window at the tall, gray gates of the cemetery. I'm not surprised she's driven us here. I get out, stretching my neck from side to side in an effort to release some of the tension. She locks the car and takes my hand, and we walk quietly toward Ayden's resting place.

We stop in front of his grave, holding hands and staring at the tomb-stone. Someone has been here recently. A low circular vase houses a bunch of vibrant purple and white carnations. Their signature scent wafts through the air. Ange breaks free of our hold, sinking to her knees on the grass. She sits cross-legged, and her voice is strained as she speaks.

"You should have told me. I would have understood. I can't believe you suffered with that all alone. Don't you know we would have loved you regardless? Your sexual orientation didn't change who you were. You were still one of the best men I've ever known, and I'm so sad for you. That you had to deny what was intrinsic. That you felt there was something wrong with it. That you're not here now to know how acceptable it's become. That you didn't get to live a full life. And I'm sorry for failing you. For not noticing what now seems abundantly clear. I love you, Ayden. You will always have a place in my heart."

Her words are heartfelt, and underscored with compassion, demonstrating how far Ange really has come, how effectively she's dealt with her guilt and her grief.

I wish I could say the same, but I can't. The cyclone erupts in my head, and I lash out at my dead friend. "You're an asshole," I fume, pacing in front of his grave. "You stupid, selfish, cowardly, motherfucking asshole. How dare you keep that from us! How dare you kill yourself rather than admit the truth to the people who loved you unconditionally. How dare you deny yourself truth and acceptance. It's inexcusable, and if you were here, I'd punch your lights out."

My pacing accelerates, rage boiling in my veins. "We were your best friends. I told you everything that last summer. You knew all my secrets, but you were hording yours. I may not have reciprocated your feelings, and, hell, at the time I probably would've freaked the fuck out that you loved me, but you still should've told us."

I drop down beside Ange, leaning my head on her shoulders as my anger gives way to sorrow. We're both quiet for a while. "You know, there were a couple times where I wondered if he might be gay," I tell her. "But I always dismissed it because he dated girls, he had sex with girls, and I thought the vibes I felt were wrong. Maybe if all that shit hadn't been going down at home, I might've paid more attention."

"We all had our own stuff going on, Dev. Ayden should have told us, and I hate that he thought he couldn't."

"My heart aches for you, man. I know what it's like to struggle with the person you are and how tormented that feels at times. I wish you'd confided in me. I wish you hadn't felt like you'd no choice." My chest aches. "I wish you were here, so I could kick your stupid ass."

Ange looks up at the darkening sky. "Wherever you are, Ayd, know how much we love you."

"How much we miss you," I add.

"And that you're forgiven," she says, her voice clogged with emotion. She looks at me, her eyes probing to see if it's true, if I've forgiven him too.

I glance up at the sky. "I should hate you for the pain you've put us through. You deliberately sabotaged my relationship with Ange while you were alive, and in death, you stole her from me too. But I'm done with hate. And I'm done with regret." I kiss Ange on the lips. "I have the woman of my dreams by my side, and all that would make life complete is my best friend at my other side." Sobs burst free of my soul, and I give in to them. "I wish you hadn't taken yourself from my life, but I forgive you, buddy. And I love you. You've given me more than you'll ever realize."

Ange cries, and I wrap my arms around her, holding her close as we both finally unburden ourselves fully. It's pitch-black and freezing cold by the time we get up. "Let's get you home and get you warm," I tell her, bundling her into my side as we walk away.

A man steps out from under the shadow of a nearby tree, startling both of us.

"I apologize," he says, in a rich, sonorous voice. "I didn't mean to frighten you. My name's Tom, and I was a friend of Ayden's."

I regard him warily. We know most of Ayden's friends, and this guy doesn't look familiar. "We were in the marines together," he adds, detecting my suspicion. "I didn't mean to intrude, but I came to pay my respects before I leave town. I was here this morning, and something brought me back here on my way to the airport." He smiles, removing his glove, and extending his hand. "You must be Devin and Angelina. He told me all about you."

I shake his hand and then Ange does. "We are, but I'm afraid he didn't mention you," I tell him, somewhat apologetically.

His sad smile is knowing. "That doesn't surprise me in the least." He looks between us. "I have an hour to spare. Could we go somewhere warm to talk?"

I look to Ange, and her eyes reveal her agreement. "Sure. I know a coffee place off Plymouth Road. Just follow us."

Ten minutes later, we're tucked into a quiet corner of the coffee shop. Ange and I are sipping coffees, while Tom drinks a green tea. He leans his elbows on the table. "Ayden talked about you both all the time. I know how close you all were."

"He was our best friend," Ange supplies. "And his death devastated us."

Tom nods. "Me too. I'd often thought of looking you guys up, but Ayden couldn't admit he was homosexual, so I doubted he had told you." His eyes are earnest as his gaze bounces between us. "I didn't mean to eavesdrop, but I heard the tail end of what you said back in the cemetery, so, you're aware that he was gay?"

"We only just found out. He never told us," I admit.

"What was the nature of your relationship with Ayden?" Ange asks getting straight to the point.

"He was the first man I loved."

"Did he love you back?" Ange asks, and she's not pulling any punches tonight.

"I believe so, although he never said the words. Ayden was still in denial when I met him. He only joined the marines because he thought it would reinforce his masculinity, but he didn't seem to understand they're not mutually exclusive. He was so confused. I tried to help, but I only made things worse."

"How?" I jump in.

He kneads his taut jaw, the overhead light glinting off the silver wedding band on his finger. "I've always been comfortable in my skin, and I've never doubted who I am. I came out when I was thirteen, and while it wasn't all plain sailing, it wasn't overly difficult either. My family was very supportive, and most of my friends stood by me. I tried to relate to Ayden's situation, but I didn't fully understand. I was young and in love and a bit naïve back then, because I can see now how it wasn't black or white for Ayden. I didn't quite grasp that at the time, and I thought he needed a little push to help him along."

A pained expression flits over his face. "I broke our relationship off just before he came home on leave. I loved him, I really loved him, but I couldn't be with someone who was hiding their true self. I knew he had feelings for me, and I thought it'd be enough. I thought he'd come back ready to face who he was. I thought our love would be enough to convince him it was worth revealing who he was." Tears cloud his eyes. "I never thought he'd kill himself, and I almost gave up on life myself when I heard the news. I spent the first couple years drowning in guilt, convinced I drove him to suicide."

Ange reaches across the table, taking his hand. "I did the same, because he returned home and discovered me in bed with Devin, and I thought I broke his heart."

Tom shakes his head, holding onto her hand. "He knew you two were in love, but he was jealous." He looks me directly in the eye. "He never told me outright, but I knew he was in love with you too."

I can only nod over the painful swelling in my throat.

"He wouldn't have wanted any of us to suffer in the aftermath of his death. I may not have known him as long as you did, but I knew enough to see the man he was. The man he was becoming. He would not have wanted that."

"He wouldn't," Ange whispers. "And that's why I know what he did that day was something he couldn't control, because, if he'd been of sound mind, he would've realized that, and I don't think he would've gone through with it, even if he had been thinking of it before. He was just in so much pain, he couldn't see another way out. And I hate that he felt he had no choice, and I miss him every single day, but blaming ourselves won't bring him back."

"No, it won't, and it took me some time to come to the same conclusion. But I'm in a good place in my life. I recently got married to a great man, and we have a good life. Every year, I come back here to visit Ayden and to let him know I've never forgotten him. He left an indelible mark on my heart, and I only wish I'd had the chance to get to know him better."

"I'm glad he met you," Ange says. "I'm glad he got to experience love. To know he wasn't alone in Afghanistan comforts me."

"Thank you for telling us," I say. "We'll never know exactly why he did it, when he did it, but this helps bring some closure."

And as I make love to my fiancée later that night, my heart is freer, my conscience is clear, and the future is looking brighter.

EPILOGUE

Angelina – 5 Years Later

"Ayden," Mom hollers, "get down from that tree!" My stepdad joins my husband and me in laughing as we watch her race across the backyard to drag our precocious three-year-old down from the tree.

"I keep telling her it's pointless," I say, pushing myself up off the chair, groaning as the familiar ache spreads across my lower back. "He's got mine and Devin's genes—he's a born mischief-maker."

"This one better be quieter," Devin says, sliding his arms around me from behind, and caressing my protruding belly. "Or she'll blow a gasket."

"*She* will not blow a gasket," Mom says, stepping back up onto the deck. Ayden is clinging to her back like a little spider monkey. She swats my husband across the back of his head. "I've had plenty of practice with hell-raisers. And you two turned out all right," she teases.

"That we did." Devin lifts Ayden off Mom's shoulders, holding him up horizontally and flying him through the air.

Ayden giggles. "I'm flying, Gramma!" he shrieks, wiggling his hands in the air. "Again, Daddy! I wanna fly again!"

Devin indulges him, running up and down the deck with Ayden elevated above him like a mini Superman in the making. Watching Devin with our son is an absolute joy to behold. There is no more attentive, more devoted dad in the world. He's strict with him on manners and routine, but he knows how to ensure he has fun, how not to clip his wings. Ayden has a lively personality, and there's no doubt he's a handful, but he's the sweetest, smartest, happiest child going.

We've brought Ayden to Devin Junior's grave a couple times since we moved him closer. He doesn't quite understand it yet, but he will in time. All he knows is his older brother is an angel, watching over him from heaven.

I was a hot mess during my pregnancy and delivery with Ayden. Old fears returned to haunt me, and, at every turn, I was convinced something was wrong. I was more closely monitored because of my previous pregnancy, and they conducted a fetal echocardiography during my second trimester—which came back clear—but I still couldn't relax. I was petrified the same thing would happen again. I'm sure the doctor was sick of the sight of me by the time I delivered.

This pregnancy has been different. Because Ayden's delivery was uncomplicated, and he came out all pink and healthy, I've managed to chill out, so this experience has been more enjoyable. I'm not going to lie and say I don't have fears, because I'm still plagued with them, but it's within more normal confines. Every parent worries their baby will be fine, and we're no exception.

But Devin has been amazing—never chastising me for my irrational fears and always listening, always supporting, always reassuring me.

"How's business?" Jon asks Devin from his position in front of the grill.

"Booming," Devin replies, and I smile proudly at him. While it was all totally Devin's idea, I was delighted when he quit his job to set up his own security consultancy company. It's less dangerous, and the hours are better. Besides, we need the flexibility now we have another baby on the way and I'm entering the second year of my PhD. Life is hectic, but I couldn't be any happier.

The doorbell chimes, and Mom scurries off to answer it.

"Lissa!" Ayden squeals. "Lemme down, Daddy!"

Devin places our son's feet on the ground just as the triplets come racing out onto the deck.

"Melissa, Melody, and Mason!" Mariah screams after them. "Stop running!"

Her face is flushed and red as she joins us on the deck. Cody is behind her, weighed down with bags. Devin pulls out two chairs for us. "Ladies, rest your feet."

Mariah waddles to the table, flopping into the chair with a relieved sigh. "Thank you, Devin. I'm like a demon today. The three amigos were awake at the crack of dawn," she says, gesturing toward her triplets who are now playing on the swing and slide set with Ayden. "And the twin minxes in my belly were having an energetic game of football in the middle of the night." She yawns, as if to prove her point.

"I can't believe you're going to have five kids under the age of five," I admit, shuddering at the thought. "And you're not even thirty yet!"

"Oh, God," Cody says. "Please don't remind us. You'll be lucky to see us this time next year. We'll be run ragged."

"You better not be too busy to finish the treehouse, slacker," Devin teases. He concocted the plan with Cody a couple of months back, and I think it's sweet he wants to replicate our childhood treehouse in our own backyard, so the next generation can have as much fun as we had. They've started building it, but it's nowhere near finished.

"Don't worry. I'll pull my weight. The kids wouldn't have it otherwise." He rolls his eyes, before leaning down to kiss his wife's cheek. "Besides, we'll need it with our expanding family; otherwise, we'll take over when we come to visit. Not that I'm complaining," he hurries to add, kissing Mariah briefly on the lips. "I've always wanted a big family, and we're blessed."

"Me too," Devin says, standing behind me and angling his body into mine. "I was disappointed we weren't having twins."

"I wasn't!" I blurt. "One at a time is all I can manage." I touch my friend's arm, smiling, so she knows it's a compliment. "I'm no Mariah."

"Aw, you're too sweet." My friend leans in to hug me. "And feel free to borrow ours anytime your house seems too quiet. Our lot will rectify that in seconds."

Melissa emits a loud shriek right that second, as if perfectly timed. "See what I mean?" Mariah deadpans. We all look out into the yard. Ayden has his arms wrapped around Melissa, and he's trying to kiss her.

"Oh boy," Devin says, smirking. "I think we're in trouble."

"It's Ange and Devin part two," Mom says, her tone nostalgic. "They're so sweet together, just like you two were at that age."

Devin drapes himself around me, sweeping my hair aside to plant a delicate kiss on my neck. I shiver all over. My insane addiction to Devin hasn't lessened in the slightest. Add in pregnancy hormones and I'm relentlessly horny. His touch ignites fireworks inside me, and I can't get enough. The minute Ayden is asleep at night, I pounce on my husband, although the bigger I'm getting, the more creative I have to be.

"I hope Ayden's as lucky," Devin says, "because there's no greater feeling than getting to spend the rest of your life with the girl you've grown up loving."

Mariah slaps Cody's arm. "Why don't you say stuff like that to me?"

"Thanks, man," Cody faux glares at Devin. "You've gone from bad ass to pansy ass in the flick of an eye."

"If loving my woman makes me a pansy ass, then I'll wear that crown with pride," my husband retorts. I yank his head down, smashing my lips against his. He doesn't shy away, kissing me deeply, and if we didn't have guests, I'd straddle his lap and have my wicked way with him. But we do, so I reluctantly break the kiss, pulling away.

"Your mom's right," Mariah says, smiling. "You two are still so sweet together."

I'm not sure the thoughts filling my mind could in any way be considered sweet right now, but I'll accept the compliment.

∞ ∞ ∞

After Mariah, Cody, and the kids left, Mom took Ayden upstairs for his bath and bedtime story while Devin and I left to meet Tom at the cemetery. We've kept in touch since that first meeting, mainly through phone contact, but we make time to catch up with him every year when he comes back to visit Ayden's grave. I love that Tom still does that, even though he lives out of state and he's moved on with his life. It only further highlights what a wonderful man he is. Every time I ponder what the future might have held for them as a couple, it makes me so incredibly sad that Ayden missed out on that.

Ayden has missed out on so much, and it was all so needless. He also left a video recording for his parents, and we've talked with them at length about his revelation. They were shocked, like we were, but accepting of it. It's heartbreaking that Ayden didn't feel like he could tell any of us he was gay. If he had only opened up, if one of us had had the chance to talk it through with him, things could've worked out so differently.

The frustration I feel at the futile waste of a beautiful life will never leave me, but I've learned to move on. We've had to.

Tom is already at the cemetery by the time we arrive. His husband Sean is with him, and we exchange hugs. "I can't believe it's ten years," Tom says, shaking his head sadly. "Where has the time gone?"

"I know. It's flown by."

"How's little Ayden?" he asks.

"Wonderful," Devin replies. "He's an amazing kid." He nods toward the tombstone. "His namesake would be proud."

I hook my arm in Devin's as we survey the new gravestone. We sought Ayden's parents' permission to upgrade the marble marker. Now it proudly displays Devin's infinity design and this line: "The bond of true friendship never dies. Always in our hearts."

I'll always acutely feel Ayden's loss. No day will pass where he isn't present in my thoughts and in my heart, but I've learned to live in the moment. To appreciate how fantastic my life is.

My eyes dart to the tattoo on both our wrists. When we got inked all those years ago, I believed the tattoo symbolized the permanency of our connection, that our friendship would outlast time. When Ayden died, and I left, I viewed the tattoo in a different light. Those tiny, looping fine lines Devin had drawn, the ones I had once felt were intricately interwoven into every facet of our lives, looked delicate and feeble and not strong enough to sustain pressure. Now, I look at the symbol as proof that the lines may bend and shake, may quiver and falter, may even rip and tear, but they grow back, stronger and firmer and more powerful than before. Because the bond of true friendship *does* outlast time.

Leaning up on tiptoes, I kiss my gorgeous husband, confident that we'll be together forever. And as I look up at the sky, sending my love heaven bound, I know the fearless awesome-threesome will be reunited again one day.

The End

If you need to talk to someone regarding suicide, please call the American Foundation for Suicide Prevention in the US at 1-888-333-AFSP (2377) or via email: info@afsp.org

If you need to talk to someone regarding your sexuality, please call the LGBT National Hotline in the US at 1-888-843-4564.

If you need to talk to someone regarding the loss of a child due to stillbirth, please call the National Stillbirth Society in the US at 1-602-216-6600.

If you live outside the United States of America, please contact your local support services.

ACKNOWLEDGMENTS

I give my absolute all to every book I write, but I truly poured my heart and soul into writing *Inseparable*, and I hope that came across as you read Ayden, Devin, and Angelina's story. I've cried writing every book to date, but I was an emotional mess writing this book, especially part three, and I still well up every time I read over it. I really hope you had an emotional connection with it too, and if I've done my job correctly, you will have felt all the feels.

I don't usually draw too much on my own personal experiences when writing my stories, but with this book, I did in two ways. A few months after I got together with my husband (then my boyfriend) someone close to him committed suicide. As long as I live, I will never forget the moment he found out. I was with him, and we were in a very busy pub enjoying a night out. The events are very similar to what happened when Devin got the call from Ange's mom in the diner, and I hope I managed to convey the emotion of that scene, because I still feel a pain in my heart when I think back to that day.

Someone I care about came out as gay in his early twenties, after spending years trying to deny who he was. Over the years, we've spoken about his experiences and his feelings during his teenage years, and I've drawn, somewhat, from that insight to help me create certain aspects of Ayden's character.

It saddens me enormously that suicide rates continue to accelerate and that some people still deal with prejudice because of their sexual preferences. To reach a place in your life where you feel like you have no other option but to remove yourself from this world is truly heartbreaking.

I hope I have dealt with all the difficult topics in this book appropriately. Although I write fiction, and it's often deliberately dramatic and angsty, it's never my intention to gloss over serious subject matter, and I try to present things as authentically as I can within the confines of the story.

I'm very proud of this book, and I genuinely hope you enjoyed reading it.

As always, I have a wonderful group of people who support me that I need to thank. In no particular order: Kelly Hartigan, Lola Verroen, Robin Harper, Tamara Cribley, Jennifer Gibson, Deirdre Reidy, Sinead Davis, Angelina Smith, Dana Lardner, Danielle Smoot (keep those play by plays coming girl!), Karla Carroll, and my wonderful street and ARC teams. I'm very grateful to bloggers and book reviewers the world over who do so much to help spread the word about my books.

Massive thanks to you, dear lovely reader, for reading this book and continuing to support my work. I couldn't do this without you, and I really appreciate each and every reader who has taken a chance on one of my books.

Thank you, Trev, Cian, and Callum. You put up with my mood swings, my unsocial working hours, my conversations with imaginary characters, a messy house, and crappy dinners, without complaining too much! Ha. Love you all.

FINDING KYLER

(The Kennedy Boys Book One)

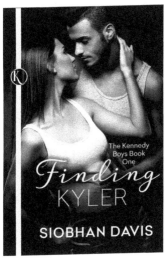

Two fractured hearts and a forbidden love they can't deny.

You shouldn't want what you can't have...

Faye Donovan has lost everything. After her parent's tragic death, she's whisked away from her home in Ireland when an unknown uncle surfaces as her new guardian.

Dropped smack-dab into the All-American dream, Faye should feel grateful. Except living with her wealthy uncle, his fashion-empire-owning wife, and their seven screwed-up sons is quickly turning into a nightmare—especially when certain inappropriate feelings arise.

Kyler Kennedy makes her head hurt and her heart race, but he's her cousin.

He's off limits.

And he's not exactly welcoming—Kyler is ignorant, moody, and downright cruel at times—but Faye sees behind the mask he wears, recognizing a kindred spirit.

Kyler has sworn off girls, yet Faye gets under his skin. The more he pushes her away, the more he's drawn to her, but acting on those feelings risks a crap-ton of prejudice, and any whiff of scandal could damage the precious Kennedy brand.

Concealing their feelings seems like the only choice.

But when everyone has something to hide, a secret is a very dangerous thing.

ABOUT THE AUTHOR

USA Today bestselling author **Siobhan Davis** writes emotionally intense young adult and new adult fiction with swoon-worthy romance, complex characters, and tons of unexpected plot twists and turns that will have you flipping the pages beyond bedtime! She is the author of the international bestselling *True Calling*, *Saven*, and *Kennedy Boys* series.

Siobhan's family will tell you she's a little bit obsessive when it comes to reading and writing, and they aren't wrong. She can rarely be found without her trusty Kindle, a paperback book, or her laptop somewhere close at hand.

Prior to becoming a full-time writer, Siobhan forged a successful corporate career in human resource management.

She resides in the Garden County of Ireland with her husband and two sons.

You can connect with Siobhan in the following ways:

Author Website: www.siobhandavis.com
Author Blog: My YA NA Book Obsession
Facebook: AuthorSiobhanDavis
Twitter: @siobhandavis
Google+: SiobhanDavisAuthor
Email: siobhan@siobhandavis.com

BOOKS BY SIOBHAN DAVIS

TRUE CALLING SERIES
Young Adult Science Fiction/Dystopian Romance

True Calling
Lovestruck
Beyond Reach
Light of a Thousand Stars
Destiny Rising
Short Story Collection
True Calling Series Collection

SAVEN SERIES
Young Adult Science Fiction/Paranormal Romance

Saven Deception
The Logan Collection
Saven Disclosure
Saven Denial
Saven Defiance
The Heir and the Human
Saven Deliverance
Saven: The Complete Series

KENNEDY BOYS SERIES
Upper Young Adult/New Adult Contemporary Romance

Finding Kyler
Losing Kyler
Keeping Kyler
The Irish Getaway
Loving Kalvin
Saving Brad

*Seducing Kaden**
*Forgiving Keven**
*Adoring Keaton^*
*Releasing Keanu^*
*Reforming Kent^*

STANDALONES
New Adult Contemporary Romance

Inseparable
*Incognito**

ALINTHIA SERIES
Upper YA/NA Paranormal Romance/Reverse Harem

The Lost Savior – coming Jan 2018
The Secret Heir – coming Feb/Mar 2018

MORTAL KINGDOM SERIES
Young Adult Urban Fantasy/Paranormal Romance

*Curse of Gods and Angels**
*Infernal Prophecy^*
*Mortal Ascendance^*

SKYEE SIBLINGS SERIES
(TRUE CALLING SPIN-OFF)
New Adult Contemporary Romance

*Lily's Redemption^*
*Deacon's Salvation^*

* Coming 2018
^ Release date to be confirmed.

Visit www.siobhandavis.com for all future release dates.

CPSIA information can be obtained
at www.ICGtesting.com
Printed in the USA
LVHW04s2259010518
575645LV00001B/154/P